# Beyond Shiloh

*A Story of an Arkansas Family*

The Shiloh Saga ...Volume 3

*written by*

PATRICIA CLARK BLAKE

**Published by**
Scotchwood Hill
3101 Scotchwood Drive
Jonesboro, Arkansas 72401
patriciaclarkblake.com

**Cover Design:** *Diane Turpin Design*
**Photograph:** Adobe.com by John Smith
**All Scripture Quoted in the Book:** King James Version c1850, 1611bible.com/KJV-king-james-version-1850


Beyond Shiloh: A Story of an Arkansas Family c2018
**ISBN:** 978-0-9998416-1-7
**ISBN:** 0-9998416-1-0
**Library of Congress Control Number:** 2018909030

**Other titles by Patricia Clark Blake:**

*In Search of Shiloh: A Journey Home Through Arkansas c2017*
**ISBN-10** 1547069228
**ISBN-13** 9781547069224
**Library of Congress Control Number:** 2017909011

*The Dream of Shiloh: An Arkansas Love Story c2018*
**ISBN-13 9780999841600**

# DEDICATION

*For the inspiration to create the Shiloh Saga books...*

- Praise God
- Praise Christ, His Son
- Praise the Holy Spirit, God with us

*For their wisdom and knowledge, their dedication to my project, their friendship, and their belief in me...my editors, beta readers, and proofreading team...*

- Beverly Thompson
- Mary Lee Cunningham
- Martha Rodriguez
- Brenda Thakkar

*For their support, their love, and their encouragement...*

- My family
- My readers
- My daughter and son-in-law, Tara and Kinley Gatewood
- My granddaughter and grandson, Kennedy Sellers and Noah Gatewood

# CHAPTER ONE

*Bear ye one another's burdens, and so fulfill the law of Christ. For when a man think himself to be something when he is nothing, he deceiveth himself.*
*Galatians 6:2-3*

Dressed only in his buckskin pants, Patrick MacLayne leaned against the door jamb, watching his wife Laurel dance across the plank floor of their log home on Crowley's Ridge. The sun kissed the window panes with gold and a tinge of warmth that October morning.

"O for a thousand tongues to sing my great Redeemer's praise." Laurel sang as she picked up the hem of her nightdress and twirled as if in the arms of her beau. "The glories of my God and King, the triumphs of His grace." Laurel took the heavy iron poker from its hook and stirred the glowing embers back to life. She pulled her arms around her shoulders and shivered but not from the chill in the room. A smile broke across her face, and she laughed in the quiet of her Arkansas home. "Jesus, the name that charms our…"

Half a smile touched Mac's lips. *She's happy now. Papa Campbell, I believe I've kept my promise to you.* His smile faded and his brow furrowed until he saw Laurel looking at him. He picked up the old hymn as he walked toward her. "He speaks and listening to his voice, new life the dead receive." Laurel's alto voice joined his. "'Tis music to the sinners' ears ..." Mac's morning kiss silenced the end of the verse.

"Good morning, wife. What a sight I found in my cabin!"

"My cabin...but I should have taken a few minutes to dress."

"Don't know why. Here's an angel dancing, singing praise, and thinking to make me breakfast in a warm cabin. What more could a man want?" *I wish I knew.*

Laurel nuzzled into Mac's arms and rubbed her hand across his bare chest. "Patrick, I'm so happy here at Shiloh with you. Can heaven come on earth? Let's stay here on our land, love each other, have our family, and live our lives right here together always. I'll never ask for anything beyond this. We are so blessed."

"Since we got home from Bolivar, we've lived a blessed life, Laurel. We found each other. We are meant to build a life together. We've tasted paradise, but we have to go back to living with the rest of the world soon."

"I don't see why. We've got everything we need right here, don't we?"

"No, darlin', we don't. The good Lord didn't put us on this earth to live in Eden alone. We both have work to do beyond Shiloh's boundaries." Mac again pulled Laurel into a tight embrace. His tender kiss brought a tear to Laurel's cheek. "Why the tear, Laurel?"

"I'm being selfish, I guess. I'd like to retreat into your arms and back into the beautiful old four-poster we got from Widow Parker when she left for California. I promise, Mac, I will be the helpmate you want to work in the world beyond Shiloh as long you want me by your side. I intend to keep the vows I made to you when we married. Thank you, Patrick, for my home. I love Shiloh. Everything I want is here."

"I love you, Laurel Grace." Mac kissed Laurel one last time. "Now get me some breakfast, woman. The sun's well above the ridge, and we'll be late for church again."

That mid-October Sunday, Mac fidgeted on the wooden pew in Shiloh Church, trying to listen to the message Matthew Campbell spoke from the pulpit. Instead, his eyes focused on the drifting leaves just outside the windows. Gusts of wind pulled them in swirls among the dust and sunbeams along the ridge. *Lord, I am grateful my wife is happy at the homestead, but why do I feel such dread? What is wrong with me?* Mac pulled his hands through his hair and straightened his back as he forced his attention back to the sermon.

Matthew Campbell finished his sermon. "Friends, we'll begin our new school term here at Shiloh school soon. We're lookin' forward to havin' our boys and girls back with us. I hope y'all got your young'uns signed up and got caught up with your tuition so we can pay our teacher, Laurel MacLayne." Matthew went on, but again Mac lost the thread of what the preacher said. Thinking of the days ahead at the homestead without Laurel laid an even deeper shadow over him. He tried to pray, but then like a lightning bolt, the reason struck him. The answer couldn't have been clearer. *Father in Heaven...I haven't built a homestead in all these years because I don't want to be a farmer. Building the homestead was a challenge and purposeful, but now what? How much fenced pasture does it take to care for one cow and two horses?*

Laurel reached over and laid her hand on his. Everyone else already stood up for the hymn of invitation. As he rose, Mac saw a look of concern in Laurel's eyes, and he flashed a quick, if not too convincing smile as he joined in the singing. *I have to find a few minutes to talk with Matthew today.* "Amen."

After sharing dinner with the Campbell family, Mac pulled Matthew Campbell aside to walk in the warm autumn afternoon. The gnawing thoughts all morning allowed him no peace. Besides being his minister, Matthew was Patrick MacLayne's best friend...perhaps his only true friend until Laurel came into his life. He was one man who never refused to tell him the truth, even when the truth was hurtful to hear.

"What's eatin' at you this glorious fall day, brother?"

"Can't be that obvious."

"You didn't hear one word I preached this mornin', Mac, and if I do say so, it was one of my best sermons. Wished you'd heard some of it."

"Sorry, Matthew. It's true. All week long...truthfully, for more than two weeks, I've been restless and on edge. I don't know what's wrong. I should be the most content man at Shiloh. When I got home, Laurel had the homestead suited out for winter, stocked with enough provisions for the whole community. The firewood's chopped and stacked, the barn loft is running over for what little stock we have, and the larder's brimming over with food."

"I can see why you're so worried."

"Hang it all, Matthew. Laurel's going back to school in two weeks and will be gone all day. What am I going to do with myself all winter? How much time does it take to milk one cow and feed two horses? I've been homesteading less than two months, and the interest is gone. The thought of the routine ahead bores me to distraction. What if I'm just not meant to be a farmer?"

"Mac, is this just a mood?"

"I wish. This morning, Laurel was dancing around the cabin and singing. She is as happy as I promised her papa I'd make her. She told me she never wants to leave Shiloh. You know what I was doing? I was thinking about what can I conquer next. What am I going to do, Matthew? Help me."

"Are you dissatisfied in your marriage, Mac?"

"What? No, Matthew. How can you even ask me that? Since I brought Laurel home the first of September, that part of life is good."

"Well, that's only been six weeks. How can the new be worn off so soon?"

"Hang it all, Matthew! I could spend twenty-four hours a day making love to Laurel in our four-poster. I'd love to read and discuss Scripture with her in front of our fireplace all day long. That ain't gonna happen. Laurel is going back to school two weeks from tomorrow. If Laurel, the fellows, and I could debate politics all winter, maybe I could keep my sanity until spring. but everyone except me seems to have work to do. What purpose do I have?"

"Come on, Mac. Every homesteader has work to keep them busy all the time."

"Okay. Since I'm new at it, tell me what I need to do."

"You have to keep wood cut and ready to burn all winter. You've got animals to tend and shelter, especially when the weather turns bad. Fresh meat for the table is your responsibility. I ain't telling you nothin' you don't already know."

"Have you been out to our place? Laurel ordered thirty cords of firewood cut, dried, and stacked under the lean-to while I was gone to Maryland. The forage in the loft could feed a herd of ten cows, and we have one. You know yourself that she had a hog butchered because you brought us the meat to store."

"You still have pasture to fence and land to clear."

"I've already fenced more pasture than I need for my first herd, and we have more than enough land tilled for our needs now. Laurel's father was afraid she'd be helpless when he was gone. I'm thinking she needs me as much she needs those silly glasses she perches on her nose when she reads."

"Mac, that's ridiculous. Laurel loves you."

"I know she does, but she seems more than able to fend for herself."

"Isn't that one of the promises you made to her father? You said you'd help her learn her own worth…"

"I didn't think she'd have no need for me."

"Am I looking at bruised pride, brother?"

"I don't know, Matthew."

"Patrick MacLayne, I never thought I'd see you in this state. Laurel has given you time to spend this fall getting out into the community. You'll have the opportunity to build a base toward election to the state house next fall. That's a worthy purpose."

"I told Al Stuart and the other men on the committee that I won't run this term. I owe it to Laurel to let her establish her home here at Shiloh. She is happy at the homestead. She wants to go back to teaching school. You should have seen her dancing to "O, for a Thousand Tongues to Sing" as she fixed breakfast."

"I know she is content here. She loves teaching Sunday school and helping with church families in need. She's the best teacher we ever had at the subscription school."

"If I win the election, she'd have to quit those things and travel with me to Little Rock part of the time. Laurel won't like the role of a politician's lady. My political aspirations need to wait for a few years."

"The first election is a year away, Mac. Let's ask the Lord for the answer 'cause I don't have one. I do know He didn't bring you here to become a miserable homesteader. He's designed a path where you'll find contentment and purpose for your life. We will find it when we seek the answer." In the beauty of the Crowley's Ridge fall, Mac and Matthew knelt by Lost Creek and prayed together.

The following day Mac invited Laurel to ride to Greensboro with him. She reminded him Monday was laundry day. Her wash water was heating in the kettle near the back porch. He made a solitary trip. Tuesday proved to be as unproductive. He did the few menial chores required. He spent the afternoon going in and out of the cabin, hoping to engage Laurel in conversation. Yet, she was consumed with her preparation for the opening day of school, which was a week and a half away. Roy and John were busy sorting tack in the shed next to the barn. He felt that chore was more makeshift work than a task that truly needed to be done, but he wanted to keep them both on hire until school started if he could find enough for them to do. Together with Laurel, they had done such a good job of preparing for the upcoming winter, and the homestead needed little to keep it fit through the worst the season could bring.

By Wednesday, Mac had reached his breaking point. He paced the main room of the cabin and then sat down for two minutes. He rose, grabbed his hat from the peg, went to the barn, and then returned before thirty minutes had passed. He shoved the door closed with his foot, strutted across the room, stirred the logs in the fireplace, and plopped back in his chair. He picked up a book and shortly tossed it back to the side table after hardly reading a page.

He walked to the table where Laurel was working and pulled his fingers through her hair and nuzzled her cheek. She brushed his hand away. He saw the rebuff as a challenge and continued his flirtation, pulling Laurel into his arms. "Let's go to Eden today."

"Mac! Have you lost your mind? It's nearly freezing outside. Besides, I have a hundred things to do before I can go back to school. Haven't you got some work you need to do?"

"I do, but I need you to come with me. We haven't been to Eden in a couple of weeks. The sun is shining, and it's so beautiful this time of year."

"And it's the middle of the work week. Surely, there are things on this homestead that need your attention."

"I was hoping you did."

"Patrick MacLayne. I never lack for your attention. You are a most loving husband, but I have work to do. Are you sure you don't have something to occupy your time, too?"

"What else would you have me do? I built your house. We have a barn stocked with enough forage to feed ten animals…we have five. We have a springhouse so crammed with food that we could feed a family of twelve, and there are two of us. We have a root cellar and a larder with so many canned victuals that we could feed the Shiloh community. Maybe I should cut firewood…but where would I stack it? No, Laurel. You've made this homestead as prepared as it needs to be."

"You could take the boys and build some more fence for pasture. Your herd will arrive in the spring."

"I already have more pasture than I need." Mac sank back into his armchair and closed his eyes. "You were right when you told your father you could make a go of a homestead by yourself. You more than fitted out our place while I was in Maryland with my ma and pa."

"Mac, I did it for you. Are you angry with me?"

"No. Why would I be angry? You did a fine job getting ready for winter…you, John, and Roy." The words seemed complimentary, but Mac's tone was anything but pleasant.

"What is wrong with you? I didn't do anything wrong."

"No, you didn't."

The cabin was quiet for some time. Laurel sat on the arm of Mac's chair, and he leaned back with his feet outstretched toward the fireplace. His head was back and his eyes closed. His grandmother Hayes's clock chimed twice.

"Another wasted day…. I'll lose my mind this winter while you're teaching school."

"Do you want me to stay home?"

"What good would that do? Then there would be two of us with not enough to do. I should have bought that herd already. At least I'd have something to do to fill my time."

"You know we aren't prepared to take on a herd this year. We'll grow the hay and oats we need for cattle this next spring, and then we can bring in the cattle you want to raise. Mac, I didn't realize you are bored with our life here at Shiloh."

He pulled her from the chair arm into his lap. "I am ecstatic with you. I love our time together. Even building this homestead was a great challenge, and I enjoyed that time." He stopped and embraced her for several seconds. Then he looked into her grey eyes. "To tell you the truth, Laurel, I am not sure I was ever meant to be a farmer. I wanted to please my father. He asked me to build a home and to carry on the family name. He gave me the generous gift of land and money to build a comfortable life here in Arkansas."

"How long has this been bothering you?"

"Since I realized that you were going back to school, and I'd be here alone for the next two months. There is just not much to keep a man occupied, especially with a wife as organized and industrious as you. I'm pretty useless around here right now."

"You're never useless around here. I can't survive one day without you."

"You do more than survive without me...you thrive. Look at all you did."

"And look what I did when I thought you weren't coming back. I bolted."

"And you came back."

"Mac, what do you want?" Laurel's lips trembled.

"I don't know. I want you and a family. I don't want to be the last MacLayne in America. Beyond that, I don't know what the Lord wants me to do. I'm pretty sure I'm supposed to do something more than milk one cow and take care of a couple of horses and two mules."

"I thought you were going to run for the legislature next year."

"I told Al Stuart and the committee I'll not run this election. I'm not ready yet."

"Why?"

"Just not ready."

"What is preventing your run?"

"Laurel, I don't want to talk about politics right now. Let's go down to Eden."

"Not today. It's too cold and I've work to do. Tell me why you changed your mind."

Mac wasn't interested in reopening the conversation he had with Al Stuart earlier in the week. So, he began to pull the hairpins out of Laurel's chignon.

"Stop, Mac." She pushed his hands away. He pulled out another pin, and her hair fell. "Don't tear down my hair."

"We have a lovely bed in the next room, and it's not cold in there."

"Patrick." A series of kisses stifled her complaint. "Husband, dear, you really do need something to keep you busy this afternoon, don't you? Maybe I should teach you how to twist rags for a new rug for our bedroom. I want a new rug to put in front of the hearth."

The storm blue of Mac's eyes shouted his anger. He pushed Laurel off his lap into the floor, stalked to the door, pulled his hat from the peg, and slammed the door on his way out.

"Patrick...." The crash of the door stifled her call.

# CHAPTER TWO

*Wives, submit yourselves unto your own husbands, as unto the Lord. For the husband is the head of the wife, even as Christ is the head of the church:... Husbands, love your wives, even as Christ loved the church, and gave himself for it;*
*Ephesians 5:22-23,25*

Gold and red beams streamed through the ominous clouds to the west of Crowley's Ridge. The temperature cooled considerably as the sun fell below the horizon. Laurel drew her shawl closer as she peered down the road for the hundredth time since Mac left her that afternoon. She went inside and returned to the table. Their uneaten supper remained on the table. She spooned down some of the lukewarm brown beans and a bite or two of the cornpone she'd made—A lonesome meal, indeed.

Why had she not been aware that her husband was bearing his soul to her when he spoke of his doubts about being a homesteader? Mac declared she wasn't the reason for his restlessness. Yet, the words she'd intended as playful and teasing had cut his pride to the core. Where was he? As she cleaned the kitchen, she continually turned her eyes to the door. She wanted him home.

At bedtime, Laurel turned down the lantern wick, leaving a dim glow to welcome Mac should he return. She stoked the blaze in the bedroom fireplace and laid two large logs on the grate. She pulled a warm flannel nightdress over her shivering body. Fall foretold of a cold winter to come. She crawled into the tall four-poster under a blanket and the double-wedding ring quilt, and she curled into a tight ball. All the time, she longed for the warmth and comfort of Mac's arms.

Sleep evading her, Laurel took her Bible from the table and tried to concentrate on the words. Even a comforting, familiar habit like reading Scripture left her empty without her husband's company, and even her favorite story of Ruth failed to hold her attention. She turned over to the front panel of her Scripture book where she had written her wedding vows. The words she had written eight and a half months ago jumped off the page as if she'd written the vows in letters a foot tall. I PROMISE TO RESPECT YOU AT ALL TIMES.

Laurel bolted from the warmth of her bed and knelt before the blazing hearth in the second pen bedroom. "Precious Father, what have I done? I was trying to ease Patrick's distress, and I broke the first and most important vow I made to him. I do respect him, and I love him. Please give me the chance to show him. Help him forgive me. Lord, please forgive me for being a careless wife." As she prayed, tears tracked the sides of her face until she was drained. The clock on the mantle in the main room chimed midnight, and Laurel returned to the four-poster. She again curled into a tight ball and finally slept.

In the darkest hour of the night, Laurel woke, unknowing what had aroused her. Mac was standing, shadowed by the glowing embers from the fireplace, looking down at her.

"Thank God. You're home, Patrick."

He pulled her from the bed into his arms. His forceful embrace surprised Laurel. She gasped and tried to pull away. Mac only pulled her closer. He lowered his face into a long, fierce kiss. Laurel ceased resisting. He laid his hands on either side of her face.

"Laurel, I am your husband. I intend to be the head of this household."

"I know, Patrick. Your absence worried me. Where have..."

"Hush." He continued to ply her with long, passionate kisses and drew his hands roughly down her arms and back. His touch was sensuous and demanding. He picked her up and laid her brusquely into the four-poster. His intention was obvious. Mac carried out their love-making that night with a ferocity and urgency unknown to Laurel. She'd never seen this side of Patrick's nature, and she was somewhat frightened. Nevertheless, she knew Mac loved her. That night she played the role of the submissive, willing wife.

*Help me, Father, to be understanding. Show me how to address this incident with Patrick when we can talk in peace.* Laurel's final thought before she slept was that a frank conversation would clear the air between them. That night's "event" would not become the pattern for their marriage. She was determined. She and Patrick would discuss all that happened the following morning.

When Laurel awoke the next morning, Mac was gone. Now she was more than aggravated. Her flip remark about the rag rug had started yesterday's conflict and brought on the time of separation. She didn't know what sparked Mac's strange behavior in the middle of the night, but he wasn't a coward so why did he sneak out before she could face him? Her Campbell temper was dreadfully near its explosive point at that moment. When she went to the kitchen to prepare breakfast, Mac sat at the table. A pail of fresh milk and the eggs from the morning chores awaited her on the dry sink.

"Good morning, Laurel. Are you speaking to me this morning?"

"Of course, I am. I missed you. I'm sorry about yesterday afternoon."

"Stop. We have things we need to get out, but not here or now." Laurel and Mac devoured the simple but satisfying breakfast. They spoke of plans for the next week and Sunday services the next day. "Enough small talk, Laurel Grace. It's time to chip away that boulder that's between us. Do you want to talk here or go for a ride?"

"Let's ride out to Eden."

After they settled under the giant oak they loved the best, Mac built a small campfire to mitigate the cold of the morning. He sat not far from Laurel and looked up with the storm blue eyes that she so loved.

They spoke each other's name at the same time, both anxious to lay their apology before the other. "You go first, Laurel."

"Mac, I ask you to forgive the disrespect I showed in that silly comment about teaching you to make a rag rug. I can't believe I even said that to you."

"After I cooled down, I realized after a time you were teasing. In the midst of my temper tantrum, I didn't take it that way. I overreacted."

"When you didn't come home last night, I couldn't sleep so I tried to read. When that didn't help, I opened my Bible to the page where I wrote my marriage vows, and I saw the first one. I stood convicted. Patrick, I don't ever want to disrespect you. I was thoughtless. I suppose I didn't know how to reply to your honest comment that you don't feel called to homestead. I love our life here at Shiloh, and this life seems so perfect to me that I haven't noticed you aren't as content as I am. I shouldn't be so self-absorbed that I don't see you aren't happy. My selfishness is a worse sin than the other."

"I'm not unhappy with you. Laurel. We've only started our life here. I promised your papa we'd have a home, and now we have one. I just have to find a way to make it a challenge…give me a purpose for being here. But wife, I'm not gonna make any stupid rag rugs…I don't care how much you want one. I am a man, and I will be the leader of this family."

"I know that, Patrick."

"I guess that is why last night happened, Laurel. I didn't hurt you, did I?"

"No."

"Laurel, last night the old part of my nature wouldn't turn me loose until I showed you I am the master of this house. I don't know if it was pride or vanity. I was wrong. I need you to forgive me. I didn't feel any better afterwards. I didn't sleep at all. We should have talked it out when I came home and given it to the Lord. I am sorry I was so rough with you."

"You owe me no apology, Patrick. I am your wife and I love you. You made love to me in our home and showed me I am desired. Several places the Scripture tells a wife to submit to her husband. I can't say it was the best night I ever spent with you. Truthfully, I would have liked a goodnight kiss before you fell asleep."

"Be serious, Laurel."

"All right, Patrick. I was frightened in the beginning. I don't like the role of the submissive wife; however, I will play that role anytime you come to me in anger or frustration. I will not deny you our marriage bed. I think that is scriptural, but I want to come to you as a partner and a participant. I'm not chattel. Please don't treat me that way ever again."

"Laurel, I'm sorry."

"Please darlin', I'm not finished. I hope you've noticed I enjoy our intimate times together. Being your mate is one of the blessings of my life. I didn't enjoy what happened last night. I refuse to lose the love life we've built. Please remember I want always to be your cherished mate…not…"

Mac stopped her with a gentle, lasting kiss. "I promise, Laurel. Thank you for your forgiveness."

"Patrick, you'll never doubt you are the man in our household. I love you, my darlin'. Please forgive me that I made you feel less the man of our house." Laurel placed her head on her husband's shoulder and brushed her fingers through his beard. "I am so blessed the Lord sent you to find me in Washington County."

"Let's head home. It's too cold out here."

"Wait. There is another matter concerning me. Why did you decide not to run for the state house when you want to do something more than run a homestead?"

"I told you I'm not ready to make that commitment."

"And what exactly are you going to do with your time? You didn't buy your herd because you weren't ready this fall. You have plenty of time on your hands to lay a foundation for a campaign without that obligation on your hands."

"Laurel, you don't understand the demands it will make on our lives if I get elected. We need to talk about that. We are just getting settled here. The election in '62 or even '66 will be a better time for our family. We are still young."

"Is it something about me you are not sure of, Mac?"

"No, wife. The time is not right for us. I don't want to talk about it anymore."

The rest of the day passed in an uneasy quiet. While some of the issues no longer plagued them, Laurel knew the boulder that Mac wanted to chip away was not totally gone. Later, Laurel joined Mac on the front porch as the moon began to rise.

She pulled her shawl closer around her neck. "It's a bit cool out here, don't you think?"

"A tad perhaps." Mac shuffled, turned from side to side, and pulled his hands through his hair. A long silence followed. "The time since I brought you to our home, sharing our stories and forging our lives together… it's been precious time. Then last night… I am sorry. I never want you to think I don't respect you. While I was gone yesterday, I thought about my life before you, and I don't want to return to that time ever." Mac took Laurel's hand and pulled her to the rail of the porch. "Look out there. Isn't it the grandest sight?"

Light from innumerable stars and a full moon provided a backdrop for Crowley's Ridge. Fall constellations were vivid in the clear night sky. Laurel and Mac shared the natural beauty of the night. He pulled his wife closer.

"It's been a strange fall."

"Yes, I'd say that, wife. Strange indeed." By the irony in his voice, Laurel knew they weren't speaking of the same thing.

"What seems strange to you, Patrick? I was talking about the weather, but you weren't."

"When did I lose my sense of connection to Fomalhaut?"

"What on earth are you talking about, Mac?"

He studied astronomy during his years at Annapolis. Like all good navy men should be, he was quite astute at reading the skies.

"Look up at the glory of the night sky, Laurel."

"It is beautiful…that is why we come out here every night… to look at the sky. I don't see one thing strange about it."

"See up there, to the left, over those trees …that is Aquarius, the water bearer. See how angular it seems. See those stars flowing from it?" Mac pointed toward the section of the sky where Aquarius lay. At first,

Laurel did not see any star pattern that looked like water flowing. Mac took her hand and pointed in the direction of the constellation.

"I don't see it."

Mac walked up behind her, took her head between his hands and laid his chin atop her head.

"Look straight ahead. See those..." He pointed out eighteen faint stars forming a vague, rectangular shape. Several more stars cascaded from the rectangle. "See the falling water?"

"Well, maybe I see it. What does it mean?"

"Just wait, I'll show you. Look there to the left of Aquarius, just below his bent elbow. Do you see Capricornus?" Again, he went through the same routine helping Laurel see the image of the great horned goat. Then, he told her the story behind the constellation.

"Takes a stretch of the imagination to call that a goat!"

"That's not the point. You faintly see nine or ten stars, but there are scores more that are too faint for us to see."

"Still doesn't look much like a goat." Laurel giggled.

"Silly, I'm just trying to help you find the southern fish, Pisces austrinus. See there below the other two?" Mac pointed out a series of stars that did somewhat resemble a fish, and at its tail was the only truly bright star in the sky.

Laurel immediately found the sole bright star at the tail of Pisces. "Goodness, that star is one of a kind. It outshines all the others. It's the brightest in the sky tonight."

"It is every night when it is visible. It stands alone. Sailors call it Fomalhaut, the lonely star. Since I learned about it back in school, I've felt somehow akin to that star."

"Mac, how can you think of yourself as a lonely soul? You're constantly surrounded by people who like you and respect you. You're Shiloh's favorite son, so my Aunt Ellie tells me."

"Laurel, look at the sky. Fomalhaut is surrounded by millions of stars, but none seem to reach out to it. Not one seems to encroach upon his light. I felt like that–for a long time. At my lowest time, that time when your Uncle Matthew convinced me to make a trip west, I was ready to give it all away." He swept his arm in an arc across their property.

"So, now you don't feel akin to Fomalhaut anymore?"

"How can I? You invaded my light. I am not the lonely star anymore. As a matter of fact, you've let all those other stars approach me, too."

"Mac, you are certainly in a sentimental mood tonight."

"Not at all. Look there just above the tree line. See all the stars that approach the southern fish? There to the right is Grus, the great crane, and over the trees to the left, see the rising of the Phoenix?"

Laurel began laughing. Her husband pulled her into an embrace. He had paid her the greatest of compliments, thinking she understood all he was telling her. Her laughter became contagious, and Mac too began to laugh. The happiness the MacLaynes shared on their porch echoed across the homestead. "Life is good with you, Laurel."

"I am more than pleased you are happy, but darlin', I'm cold. Haven't you noticed how the chilly the breeze has become?"

"Well, I know a remedy for that." Mac picked Laurel up and carried her to the second pen bedroom. He dropped her into the tall bed.

"God blessed me, Laurel. I don't deserve a wife like you." Mac joined her in their tall four-poster and pulled her into his arms. He kissed her with sweet tenderness. "If ever forget you are a lady, wife, you tell me, and I'll remember my vows in a breath. You have engraved them on my heart."

"Thank you, darlin'. I'll keep you mindful, Patrick. You've taught me I'm a lady of great worth. I don't mind you playing "master of the house" once in a while, but never forget that ladies have minds of their own, too. We don't like to be dominated all the time, but you'll never find a time that we will complain about being cherished. And speaking of vows.... If you want to run for office and are not doing it because of me, I think you better let me read my vows to you again. I promised to support your life work, not to help you be a homesteader unless that's your choice. I'll be watching the situation."

~

THE NEXT SATURDAY morning dawned sunny and somewhat warmer than the previous week. This was typical for late fall in Arkansas. At breakfast, Mac spoke, “Let’s ride out this afternoon. I have something I want to show you. I can’t believe summer is gone, and school will start back a week from Monday. You never stopped teaching, Laurel. You’ve worked all summer teaching Sunday school.”

“A little thing. But the daily task of teaching all those children… sometimes, it seems almost too much responsibility. They depend on me.”

“You’ve done them a world of good…them, and all the Shiloh community. But I don’t want to spend this glorious Saturday with the schoolmarm. We’re going on an adventure, so go put on your dungarees and that warm work shirt. You can even braid your hair into that horrible coronet if you want to. Hurry on now.”

Laurel was somewhat puzzled, for Mac hadn’t seen her in braids since the night he’d found her in Bolivar. She rarely wore her dungarees. Work clothes were of little use on the homestead since the crops were harvested. She always enjoyed the ease and comfort of her days in dungarees and braids. However, as she prepared to go on her adventure with Mac, she realized she didn’t want to wear her spinster hairdo. She pulled her curly mop into a long, full ponytail tied up with her green ribbon.

Both Laurel and Mac rode out of their yard in high spirits. Laurel laughed aloud as she kicked Sassy into a fast trot, urging Mac to race down the road away from their cabin. Her challenge took him by surprise, so he rode hard to catch her. Mac refused to allow Midnight, his mighty stallion, to be bested by a little mare like Sassy. At the curve of the road, Mac declared the race a draw and took the fork in the road that led off their property.

“Mac, I thought you said we were going to look over our wooded property. Well, there’s our marker, and we’ve now gotten on someone else’s land.”

“No, it’s ours. Some of the fifty best acres of hunting woods along the whole ridge.”

“Mac, you didn’t buy more land, did you?”

"Couldn't pass it up, Laurel. The land was state property, and the agent wanted to go back to Little Rock. He sold it to me for $1.00 an acre, so he could head home."

"What are we going do with it? You've got so much to take care of now. Besides when you go to the legislature..."

"When I go? That will be years off."

"Don't change the subject. Why did you buy so much more land? What are we going to do with it?"

"Right now, darlin'...nothing. We'll just leave it the way the Lord created it. No loggers will come in and cut down all these old trees. No farmer will come in and convert this wilderness into a plowed field."

Again, Laurel laughed. "You want to create another Eden for us?"

"No, but we'll have plenty of game to fill our pots all winter. This parcel is close to home so I won't have to be gone long when I need to hunt."

They rode around the new land for some time. The natural beauty of the newly acquired land was breathtaking but couldn't compare with their own private Eden near the creek.

## CHAPTER THREE

*What profit hath he that worketh in that wherein he laboreth?... Every man should eat, and drink, and enjoy the good of all his labors; it is a gift of God.*
*Ecclesiastes 3: 9,13*

As Mac and Laurel left Shiloh church on Sunday, Dr. Edward Gibson and several other men waited on the porch. They stood with their hats in their hands and serious looks on their faces.

"Mac, we need to have a private word before dinner," the good doctor spoke in a whisper. "May I escort Mrs. MacLayne over to the ladies in the grove?"

"There's nothing you will say that Laurel doesn't need to hear. Speak your mind, Ed."

"Mac, you know we've been pushing you to run as our candidate for state representative from our county. Lots of people here 'bouts are behind you. We learned that a man the Family is supporting has moved in over around Gainesville. He's not real friendly, they're saying, but he sure thinks he'll get the seat because the Family is behind him."

"Besides, he's got some health problems that will keep him closer to home," Bob Clayton added.

"What've you been hearin', Carl?"

"People are saying Mac'll win Greene County if we work hard enough to get him out so they all get to know his name."

"Whoa, fellows, I already told you I won't run this year. Laurel and I are only now getting used to life on our homestead and to living as a married couple. The time's not right for us to go traipsing about the county right now."

Mac took Laurel's arm to lead her to the wagon. They had not taken five steps from the porch when Laurel looked back over her shoulder. With the green ribbons from her bonnet blowing across her face, she flashed an impish smile at the gaggle of supporter. Mac saw the green lightening in her eyes.

"Gentlemen, thank you for the faith you have in my husband. With great pride, he will run this race. Have a blessed Sunday."

Mac's jaw dropped at Laurel's bold announcement of his candidacy. "Laurel, do you understand what this will mean for us?"

"Mac, tell them you'll run and let's go home to talk all this out." He walked back to his friends near the porch, spoke a few seconds, and returned to the wagon. He lifted Laurel to the seat, and they drove from the church yard headed back toward their homestead.

"Now, wife, will you tell me what exactly you are thinking?"

"I know you were distracted this morning during the sermon. You didn't pay much attention last week either. You have been restless at home, and you told me that you'd not be satisfied with the life of a homesteader now that you've completed the building. The last thing I want is for you to feel burdened by the life we live at Shiloh. If you need to find your purpose beyond our homestead, it should be something you love. I will support you every way I can."

"Laurel, only last week you asked me if we could stay at Shiloh always."

"We can if it is our home. This will be our place to come back to regardless of where we wander off to from time to time. To tell you the truth, Patrick, I can't stand having you under my feet all the time. I can't get my chores done with you pulling at my hair pins every minute."

Mac laughed and slapped the reins on Midnight's haunches. "Hurry on, boy. It's time to eat."

That afternoon as they sat on their front porch, Mac looked across the valley. The heat of the day belied the fact winter was near at hand. Crowley's Ridge was ablaze with all the colors of fall. Crimson, rust, orange, gold and yellow leaves cast their colors among the dark green of the evergreens. Autumn was the season Mac loved the best, and this autumn would be fulfilling and busy. He would mount a campaign, and the work ahead would be demanding and hectic. But he knew he could serve Greene County well and help to build a better future for his adopted state.

Mac sighed, and when he looked over, he saw Laurel staring at him. He knew she didn't quite believe his explanation that his restlessness was not her doing. A longer, more serious conversation about his future as a homesteader must take place. Another time.... Instead, he lifted her hand to his lips smiled. "I love you, Laurel." Humbly, Mac whispered "Thank you, Father. You have given me all any man could want."

"Are you all right?" Laurel's whispered question had been all but inaudible.

"So much so. I am more content than any man has a right to be."

THAT MONDAY no laundry would be done at the MacLayne homestead, Mac informed Laurel. Since she was going back to school in a week, he declared this week his own personal "Laurel Time." They would enjoy their last week together. Today he had promised a visit to Lorado. He made the promise when he ran into Russell Lamb at the mercantile last week. Of course, he had neglected to tell Laurel. She didn't object. A visit with the Lamb family, who helped care for her after the encounter with the cottonmouth in the Cache River bottoms, would be a fine way to spend a day. Of course, time with her husband was an extra blessing.

Mac smiled at the prospect of a day of play with his wife. They saddled their horses and made a quick trip across the way to Lorado. When they arrived, the Lambs warmly welcomed their visitors. Russell Lamb told Mac he'd had a bumper harvest so he was able to buy two more cows. He planned to sell milk to a local merchant, as well as the cheese that his wife made from the excess milk. Russell beamed when he showed Mac his new livestock and told him that he was planning to grow a herd from these cows.

~

SHIRLEY LAMB and Laurel spent some time reminiscing. They also talked about the newest member of the Lamb family who was due the week before Christmas. Shirley lowered her eyes and stammered, "Laurel, are you and Mac having a baby soon?"

"We want to, but so far we haven't been blessed. I am going to teach school again this fall."

"Would be hard to teach school with a little one to care for. You gonna keep teachin' when you got babes of yer own?"

"I haven't thought about that, but we would make some kind of arrangement to keep our school open even if I wasn't teaching. Our community sets great store in our school."

"Do ya think there'll be room in your school for my little girl, Sandy, this fall?"

"Shirley, it's a long trip for your daughter to come all the way to Shiloh. It's better than five miles."

"I know, but I'm worried that our young'uns ain't gonna get no schoolin' over here. Our farm land is good and makin' us a livin', but we ain't got no school here in our settlement."

"She'd be welcome at school, but I don't see how she'd be able to get there from here every day."

"Iffen you'll let her come, we'll find the tuition money somewhere. I may be able to board her with my aunt. Aunt Permelia lives not far from Shiloh school. She's a widow, and her young'uns are all growed up and gone from home."

"Wouldn't you miss her, if she were away from you?"

"Surely, I would, but she wants to learn real bad. Russell could bring her home for the weekends. Well, for two months, I could let Sandy try school. The term's over by Christmas, ain't it?"

"Yes, Shirley. November 2nd until December 23rd is the plan, if the weather holds."

"I'm gonna try to give my babies what I never had. I want all of 'em to get their schoolin', like you, Laurel."

~

On Tuesday, Mac rode to Greensboro to meet with the election committee. Laurel agreed to join him for the morning trip because it offered the opportunity for her to visit the general store. Mac planned to confirm his decision to run for the seat in the Arkansas Legislature. Sitting around the table in Al Stuart's office, Harold Armstrong, Mac's neighbor to the west, was the first to speak. "Mac, we all are ready to hit the campaign hard. We're danged tired of the graft, the incompetence, and them not caring one whit for us up here. I ain't sure those 'do nothin's' in Little Rock even know we're alive up here in our part of the state."

"Harold, we do have a few real concerns, but some of those folks are trying to do right by the whole state."

"Bet ya can't name me one."

"I rightly can. The governor, Elias Conway's made some progress in reducing Arkansas's bank debt. That debt's been hanging over taxpayers in this state, eating up our tax revenue for the past dozen years."

"Maybe so, but we still pay our taxes, just like the delta planters do. Yet look at our roads, the bad mail service, and the only schools in the whole region we provide for ourselves!" John Marcum spoke in a loud, angry voice.

"John, we're doing better here now, but I agree we should get better attention than we do."

Bob Clayton added, "Look at all that flooding we get over around Big Creek and on the Cache River. The politicians in Little Rock don't even know where Greene County is. How're they gonna know what kind of problems we deal with?" A chorus of 'Amens', 'You tell 'em, Bob' and 'That's the Lord's truth' followed.

"Mac, you are the choice for us. I'm not saying that 'cause you're family. You can do lots for us here at Shiloh and for the whole state." Matthew had joined the group of men.

"Thank so much, Matthew. Friends, I am ready to start any day... with y'all to help. Most of my winter's stores are laid back already, and my good wife filled our larder. I don't have a herd yet. I reckon the time is right for us to try to make a crack in the stronghold of the Family."

"Great. We'll start on Sunday evening then." Matthew walked toward the center of the circle of men. "The Shiloh congregation received an invitation to the Herndon Church's anniversary celebration. They've built a new church, and this week their congregation has been chartered for ten years. It's a good place to start. Next Sunday, our church will join with them to celebrate, and we'll kick off Mac's political campaign at the same time."

As the group of men departed, Harold Armstrong clapped Mac on the back. "We'll be seeing you at Herndon on Sunday evening, Mac. Bring your best campaignin' smile." Mac waved and returned to pick up his wife at McCollough's store.

As she left the store, a stranger who was not paying attention walked into her. She dropped her packages. Flustered, she bent to retrieve the parcels, paying little attention to the man who'd collided with her. "Excuse me, ma'am. No offense intended." He wheeled around and walked down the alley and out of her sight.

*Well, he could have helped me pick up the mess he caused!* She spotted Mac in the wagon and finished picking up her last package.

The whirlwind that would engulf the lives of the MacLaynes until the election of 1858 began in earnest that weekend. They visited friends and helped neighbors who were not as prepared for winter as they were. They stopped in small settlements Laurel hadn't visited before. In the good fall weather, they gloried in the beauty of fall along Crowley's Ridge. Campaigning proved a pleasant task. Laurel's role was simple. She kept Mac company, rode Sassy Lady in the warm autumn sunshine, and filled her senses with Arkansas's beauty. In a brief week, they campaigned in twelve different places across Greene County. All the time, the beginning of the school term loomed ever closer for them both.

Friday night as they rode from a party held in Greensboro, Laurel began to laugh aloud. "Just what is so funny, my dear?"

"A silly thing. I remembered how Papa used to say, 'Tis better to wear out than rust out.' He'd say that all the time when he got too busy. Papa's bragging in Heaven right now. Can't you see him telling all the angels how his son-in-law is working so hard to get elected?"

"This is the first time I remember you laughing over a happy memory of your father, Laurel. I love to see you laugh. I hope he would approve of me. In our short acquaintance, I came to like him. His passing is a loss to me. He'd have been a fine father-in-law."

"You forget. If Papa hadn't been so sick, there would have been no reason to marry me." Laurel laughed again. "My father would love you, but I'm not sure he would like to see you neglecting me as you have been lately."

"Neglecting you? I have not! I take you every time I go to a rally or any kind of social event. I've spent this entire week entertaining you before you return to school."

"That is true, but how long has it been since you carved out an afternoon only for me?"

"Well, I have been using the opportunity to campaign, but I do want you to be with me. That is why I always take you along."

"Mac, we haven't even been to Eden except for that one time right after we got home from Bolivar."

"I didn't know you found my attention wanting, wife."

"I'm not complaining...well, at least not much. But you did promise we'd go back to Eden. Soon it will be too cool for a day out."

"Duly chastised, wife. You do have to give me credit...I asked you to go last week. I'll plan us a trip to Eden soon. Just a day for the two of us...no politics."

The next day, nearing noon, Mac and Laurel rode into to the yard at the Widow Parker's old cabin. Laurel had only been there once since Mac took her to live at his homestead. The tiny empty cabin with its once neat yard showed signs of neglect. The daisies they planted near the steps drooped from the lack of rain in the last two months. A couple of the cedar shingles lay on the ground, so the cabin could have a leak in the loft come the winter rain and snow. The barn door stood open, a sign that others had been there since they moved away. The little homestead seemed dreary and sad with no people around to care for it.

"Mac, this was such a happy place when we were here. Now, look at it!"

"A place can sure go to waste when there is no one around to keep it up. Well, we need to get this place back into shape. I'll come over with the boys next week to do some repairs. We could rent out the place. Would that be all right with you, Laurel?"

"Me? Mac, this is a part of our overall holdings."

"Maybe so, but I'll always think of this as your place. We'd not have it if you'd not bought it."

"I would like to see a small family or a newlywed couple come here and take care of this place. I know I was happy here most of the time."

Mac and Laurel spent another hour looking over the place. They walked through the cabin and barn, checked the well, and removed debris from the widow's flower beds. "Tarnation, wife, it's hot out here today. To be the end of October, I can't believe the heat. Seems more like August than October."

"It's been warm this afternoon and so dry this fall. I don't remember it raining but once since we got home from Bolivar."

"That trip was wet enough, but you're right. It's almost parched in some of the fenced pasture. Laurel! Let's go for a swim in the creek."

"Mac, it's October. The cold nights we've had will make that creek feel like ice."

"I don't care. Let's go." So, they mounted their horses and rode to Eden. As they neared the grove of old oaks, Laurel saw her little wagon parked near a rocked fire pit. The same faded oilcloth they'd used on their trip across the state hung from three sides of the wagon. Mac had recreated their makeshift tent, and except for the empty wagon bed, the sight was a familiar one.

"You've been planning this adventure for a while, I see."

"Trying to keep my promise to you, wife. I told you we'd come back to Eden, and this may be our last weekend before winter decides to drop by. "Let's swim a while." Laurel and Mac stripped to their underclothes and ran into the clear water.

"Ohhhh...the air is warm but this water is not...Let's get out."

"Not yet, Laurel." Mac wrapped his arms around her and kissed her. "We'll be warm if we swim." And they did and played like children in the clear creek water for a short while. As the sun began to move toward the western horizon, the cool creek became a cold creek.

"Enough, Mac. My teeth are chattering, and I've got goosebumps all over me!"

"Fair enough, but what a fine time we had playing in our creek." Mac pulled Laurel from the water, swept her into his arms, and carried her back to the wagon. He pulled her yellow coverlet from the wagon bed and covered her. "You sit right here and I'll light us a fire. Already got it laid, see." In a very few minutes, a small fire turned to a roaring blaze. Mac used dry wood just for that purpose. He had planned well, knowing the temperature would drop, and Laurel would be cold in her wet chemise. "I remember another late afternoon when I wrapped you up after a swim. That time, though, you wore your coat, boots, and socks. That night, I was not so well-prepared."

"Oh, you."

"Yes, ma'am, quite a sight! Your fall in the river over near Jasper would be a fun memory if you hadn't gotten so sick," Mac said.

"I'm afraid I don't remember much of those next two days. I do remember the third day when we walked in the snow. How beautiful the mountains were--totally covered with snow and ice crystals, sparkling in the sunlight. I also remember how angry I was with you."

"We've had our share of those times, too, before we realized what fools we were acting."

"Thank the good Lord we got past all that. But Mac, if we don't get out of these wet clothes, we'll both be sick, and no one'll be here to nurse us back to health."

"You're right, as usual." Mac approached Laurel where she sat on the fallen log nearest the fire. He untied the ribbon that closed the bodice of her chemise and removed her wet lawn garment. He pulled her into his embrace and held her as they stood near the fire in the twilight. "Your bed awaits you, Laurel." Mac lay her tenderly on the pallet nearest the fire. "I never made love to you while we were on the trail. I should have." He loosened her hair and let the tresses fall across her shoulders. He buried his face in her tawny curls. "I never knew how precious life is until I knew I loved you, Laurel." Tears of joy traced a silent path across Laurel's cheeks. Their Garden of Eden at Shiloh was more than paradise for them that night.

# CHAPTER FOUR

*The tongue can no man tame; it is unruly, evil, full of deadly poison. Out of the same mouth proceedeth blessings and cursing. My brethren, these things they ought not be so.*
*James 3:8, 10.*

"We missed y'all at church this morning, brother."

"We were on a late camping trip yesterday. I guess we overslept." Laurel and Mac hadn't awakened 'til well past dawn that Sunday morning and getting to church wasn't their most pressing thought. However, they rode into Shiloh church yard in time for Laurel to greet her Sunday school class at 1:00. Of course, they stayed through the evening service, as was their custom. At the end of the service, Matt and Ellie Campbell approached the MacLaynes.

"Mac, Harold Armstrong stopped me after church this morning. He asked if we could attend another debate over in Meadow Grove next Saturday. He said the opponent from Gainesville promised to be there to debate with you."

"Laurel, do we have any social plans for next Saturday?"

"None I am aware of, but school starts tomorrow. I'll need my weekends at home."

"We'll talk about it later. Matt, tell Harold to arrange the debate. I'd enjoy one more opportunity to show our folks that I am a better candidate than that newcomer to the county." By the time they left the church about 8:30, the weather had cooled considerably. The sudden drop in temperature made the night feel like mid-fall—which it was. Mac didn't wait to ask about a fire in their room.

Laurel spent a hectic first week at school. Besides the time she worked away from home, she finished several small projects she'd started. The bedroom now had the beginnings of a new rag rug, and Laurel began a blue scarf she intended for Mac's Christmas present. She had worked up four large pumpkins to have the puree for pumpkin pies and pumpkin bread from her mother's recipe for the holidays ahead. When Friday came, she was flat too-tired, and she didn't want to go to the political rally. Being in the company of those fine folks would be a blessing any time, except on the Friday at the end of the first week of school.

When her uncle arrived to ride with them, she'd have to recruit his help or be resigned to put on her bonnet and woolen shawl and climb into the wagon seat. "Uncle Matthew, please tell me you will take care of Mac, just this once. I want some time to collect my wits. I am so tired. Besides, I can't stand the thought of nine miles on a wagon seat and half of it on those corduroy roads! Think how much faster y'all can travel on horseback."

"Niece, don't you like my company?"

"I love to be with you…just not today."

"Laurel, I want you to go with me." Mac intruded from the doorway. "We've been separated too much already. You've been gone all week."

"I am glad you want me to go, but you won't miss me for one evening. I promise I'll be right here when you get back. I'll have a fire in the bedroom, and the tall bed will be turned back and ready for you."

"I'd rather you go, but just this once, I'll relent."

~

SHORTLY, Mac and Matt rode off, headed to Meadow Grove, with high hopes the rally would put a few more cracks in the hopeless campaign of the opponent. Meadow Grove had become a thriving community since the Kennedy family arrived in the area in the late '40's. During the last three years, several other families settled nearby. The land there was somewhat flatter than Shiloh, but the area was blessed with ample water from creeks feeding into Cache River. The hard-working people labored to build levees and a ditch system to hold the river back from the fertile bottom lands, which had been made into black gold from scores of floods in the past. Even today, tracts with no levees were still prone to annual flooding. Yet the industrious, tireless settlers worked to tame the natural ebb and flow, knowing when they succeeded, the excellent bottom lands would provide a fine living for them and their children.

When they arrived, a fair-sized crowd of about twenty men and a few women had gathered in a large, new barn at the outskirts to the settlement. People sat about on hay bales, upturned kegs and on the stall railings. Some people sat in their wagon seats just outside the doors. Several lanterns were hung around to cast a dim light across the informal scene. As Mac entered, people cheered and applauded. He had become well-known in that community, and a couple of Meadow Grove families now attended Shiloh church as they had no established Methodist church in their settlement yet.

Mac was disappointed. As soon as he entered the barn, Benjamin Kennedy, the original settler, told him that Ezra Digby, the rival for the legislative seat, had taken ill and sent his apologies to them. After making the long ride, Mac would not waste the opportunity to present his case. He stood to address the people waiting to listen to the debate. "Friends, I'm not gonna stand here and promise y'all the sky. I'm not able to deliver it. I am asking you to think about voting for me so I can take your concerns to Little Rock. The only way I'll know what your concerns are would be for you to tell me. Since my worthy opponent could not be here to use his part of the time, I'd like to hear from you."

Mac pulled a barrel to the edge of the crowd and sat down to listen. He sat in the company of the people for more than two hours, and they seemed excited that someone wanted to hear their concerns. They spoke of their poor roads, unreliable freight deliveries, and limited supplies during bad weather. This community was particularly interested in getting some state help with the levee system. They were planning to grow cotton in the area soon, so they wanted to know how they could get their crops to market. Several of the people expressed concern about squatters trying to set up homesteads on their property and people trying to claim their land with false deeds being sold by land speculators, mostly originating in Little Rock.

Neville Riggs spoke out. "We're mad as hornets about the graft. Our tax money goes to line the pockets of members of the Family's political clan. Nothing gets done in our part of the state unless we do it. I ain't against hard work, but I'll be dag nabbed it I let squatters take my land that I bought with my own money and my sweat and bruises."

"Yeah, what about all those land agents the governor handpicks? He's gotta know they're stealing from the settlers."

"Are you an honest man, MacLayne?" The voice came from an area near the door.

"Yes, stranger. And that's the kind of legislator I plan to be. One promise I will make to you is that I will listen and work toward the needs of those who elect me."

"Mac, it's getting late and tomorrow is Sunday."

"We'll call it a night, folks. Thank y'all for coming to hear me out and for sharing your thoughts. We got a few miles to ride, and my wife will be expecting me back."

"Is that the same woman who used to "expect" all the boys back in Washington County? Heard she was good at entertaining all the boys, dressed only in her eye glasses." A woman near Matthew gasped.

Mac bolted to his feet. Red blotches spread across his cheeks. "Who said that? Where is the coward who attacks an innocent woman who's not here to defend her honor?" The crowd hushed and parted as Mac stalked across the floor into the midst of several men who stood along the back wall. "Where is the cad who slandered my wife?" No one responded to his challenge. "Well, I guess that's all you can expect of a low life who attacks women."

A ruddy skinned, well-dressed man pushed his way into the opening in front of Mac. Matthew rushed to his side and grabbed Mac's fist before it landed in the troublemaker's face.

"I'm no coward." The intruder threw his hat toward the wall.

Matthew Campbell stepped between Mac and the man who had defamed his niece.

"I said it. We got a right to let people know what kind of person we're votin' for."

"My wife isn't asking for your vote. I am. I won't justify your ugly slander. You'll find no more honorable woman in this state than my wife."

"She is that Campbell woman from over at Hawthorn Station in Washington County, isn't she?" The stranger continued to heckle Mac.

"If you have a problem with my wife's past, perhaps you need to ask a bully named Robert Duncan, or are you that bully?"

"No matter what my name is. You're so high and might..."

Matthew took a step toward the intruder and laid his hand on his shoulder. "Look, brother, we don't want no trouble here. The assembly was peaceful and friendly up to a few minutes ago. You'd best make your way out of here before my nephew comes over me and whips the meanness right out of you. He's usually a pretty reasonable sort, unless someone gets his dander up...or when it comes to protectin' his wife. That action won't take a second thought."

The crowd murmured, anticipating a brawl. "Don't want to see no one get hurt here tonight." Matthew towered over the other man, and the strong grip he had on his shoulder made his intention very clear. "Get out of here, now."

The man pulled his hat over his brow, and he backed toward the door. Just before he walked out of the open door, he turned to shout back into the crowd still gathered in the barn. "Better ask Mr. High and Mighty if he beats his wife. They only got married back in March, and she done run away from him once."

Those words were beyond the limit of Mac's patience, and he charged the man. He grabbed his collar just before he reached the post where his horse was tied, and he spun him around to face him.

"Who told you those lies? How do you know about my wife? I don't know you. I never saw you before. What reason do you have to attack us?"

"Let's just say I got my friends, just like you got yours. They tell me things...and one of the things they told me to tell you is you'd be better off to get out of this election now. Things could get bad, ya know."

Mac drew back his fist. His anger overshadowed his usual calm nature.

Matthew grabbed his arm just as he moved toward the man. "Mac. The Lord saith, 'Vengeance is mine.' Let it go. He'll get his punishment in due time."

"Don't you ever speak ill of my wife again. My preacher might not be around to protect you a second time."

The man turned in his saddle as he rode from the barn lot. "You've been warned, MacLayne." He jerked the reins of his horse and headed off in the direction of Gainesville.

Matthew turned back to speak. "Sorry for the disruption, folks. I think that man made it very clear why we need Mac in Little Rock. No group of people has the right to bully us out of our votes."

After saying goodbye to a couple of friends, Matthew and Mac rode toward Shiloh. They travelled a couple of miles before Matthew broke the silence. "Mac, politics is always a rough life. So far, you've been treated pretty fine, but as people begin to take your side, you know the other side will fight back. They're not used to losin'. They've had a grip on political power since before statehood. They're not likely to let it go too easy. Tonight was the first attack, but you know it won't be the last."

"I'm grateful Laurel wasn't with us. She would've been crushed by those ugly comments."

"You know they'll get back to her. Too many people heard. Sooner or later the gossip will reach home. If I were you, I'd tell her. It'd be easier comin' from you than hearin' it as gossip."

"Matthew, she's just settling in here. We've been so happy these last couple of months."

"You can't protect her from what's already happened, Mac. But you'll have to decide what you'll do."

"I should drop out of this race."

"You'd have to explain that to Laurel, too. Anyway, I know you too well. You won't run away from your duty and live happy. You know what you need to do."

"Tarnation! Laurel doesn't deserve this."

"No. That's the truth, but she didn't deserve what happened to her when she was fourteen, nor did she deserve that horrible broadside that came from Maryland back in August. Mac, she's weathered all those bad times, and look at the woman she is now. Want to trade her for someone else?"

"I'd be the loser if I did. I can't win a debate with you, Campbell. You're the one we should send to Little Rock."

"Not me, brother. I got a higher calling. I am quite happy right here in Shiloh. Life is good with Ellie and my young'uns, and me trying to be a pastor to my flock. Ain't got no doubt what God's will is for me."

"You are one lucky man, Matthew Campbell."

"Not one bit lucky...I've been blessed." They rode for a while longer before Matthew asked a question that'd been on his mind. "When are you and Laurel going to start a family?"

"Doing what we can. It's in the Lord's hands, I guess."

By the time Mac rode into his barnyard, his anger had cooled considerably. The pragmatic side of his nature had taken him back to reason. He knew politics often brought out the ugly side of men, and he had been foolish to think this race would be any different. The Family had dominated Arkansas politics since there had been a state, and they had little inclination to let even one seat go to an opponent. Their supporters--and there were some in the northeast part of the state, especially among the planters along the rivers--would do whatever had to be done to win the Greene County seat. Even worse were the unscrupulous men in every part of the state who could be bought to put barriers in the paths of others who might want to seek office. Mac was sure the man he had encountered tonight had been one of the latter.

Mac calmly promised himself he would find out about the man who had slandered Laurel. He felt sure the man's behavior had failed to discourage anyone who had decided to vote for him. He hoped he could prevent any more rumors other than those which would come from the confrontation at Meadow Grove. And he knew he would just have to deal with gossip this time.

There was a single lantern in the MacLayne's main room. It was past eleven o'clock, and Laurel had been in bed for some time. He knew his immediate problem was telling her what had happened in Meadow Grove. He dreaded the telling. He entered the second pen and saw Laurel snuggled under the wedding ring quilt in the tall bed. She had turned down his side, just as she'd said. He sat in the rocking chair to remove his boots.

The time since coming home from Bolivar had been sweet. This life was the fulfillment of the dream of home for him, and he believed for Laurel, too. She had blossomed under his attentiveness, in her new role as candidate MacLayne's wife, and as his lover. Every day they had fun together. He looked at his sleeping wife and smiled. The lost years of Laurel's youth were being returned to her to some degree. She had worked alongside of him as he built split rail fences to protect his cattle, and he dried the dishes beside her after supper. They shared prayer and study time every evening. They nestled together every night in the beautiful carved four-poster and often made love in their tall bed. Life was more than good. She had come so far to put her past behind. He never wanted to see the Spinster of Hawthorn overtake his wife again.

At the same time, Matthew spoke the truth. The damage Mac could cause to their growing relationship would be irreparable if he made Laurel vulnerable to local gossips. He knew trust had brought them to the place they were now. He would do nothing to break that trust. He wouldn't jeopardize the relationship they were building. He must his courage and tell her about the rally before she saw another person.

But not tonight.

THE AROMA of fresh bread baking in the hearth oven and ham cooking in an iron skillet woke Mac that Sunday morning. He overslept, as the sun was well above the horizon. He hurried to the kitchen,

"Good morning, sleepy head. You must have been worn out from your late night." Laurel planted a quick kiss on his cheek.

"Sorry I overslept. I'll get to the milking and gather the eggs now," he said with a yawn. "I'll be back shortly."

"Never mind. I've already done the morning chores. Sit down here and eat your breakfast while the water for your bath heats. You will have to hurry, or we'll be late for church."

"Come over here and join me. Thank you for doing my chores and fixing me a good breakfast." Laurel sat next to Mac after placing a basket of hot biscuits on the table. He took her hand, raised it to his lips and spoke a brief blessing.

"How was the rally last night?"

"Good sized crowd. Some new folks and a few familiar faces from the first social we had in Meadow Grove. You remember that log rolling for the newly-weds. I have some good support in that community and got some more last night. Digby didn't show up for the debate. He sent word he was ailing."

"I'm sure those people over there see you as a better candidate. What time did you get home?"

"Pushing eleven, I'd say. You were sleeping so peacefully, I didn't want to wake you."

"I must have been dead to the world. I didn't even know when you came to bed."

They continued eating their hot meal, but as Mac sat sipping his second cup of coffee, he knew the time had come to tell Laurel about the attack on her character the previous night. "Laurel, we need to talk before we go down to church." Mac paused to look within himself to find the right words to say to her.

"All right. You go take your bath while your water is hot, and we'll chat on the drive to church."

"No.... not a chat. We need to talk, here, just the two of us."

"Patrick, what is it? You are frightening me. Did something happen to my Uncle Matthew?"

"No, nothing like that, Laurel." An uneasy pause followed. " Laurel..." Mac couldn't seem to find gentle words so he just told her. "Laurel, last night—a stranger at the rally made crude remarks about that incident back in Washington County, the time you were attacked by that Duncan boy."

Laurel turned and looked into Mac's face and sat down in the armed chair near the hearth. She sat looking into the fire for several minutes. Finally, Mac spoke again. "Laurel, we stopped him as quickly as we could." Still, she didn't comment. "I don't know how, but that lowlife knew about our trip to Bolivar. He told the few people who were still there that I beat you so you ran away from me." Again, there was only the sound of the crackling logs burning in the fireplace. "Laurel, I know politics is a brutal business, but I just didn't think anyone would strike out at you. I'll withdraw from the race if you want it."

At the last comment, Laurel stood up, straightened her shoulders slightly, and stubbornly lifted her chin into its most stubborn pose. And she said exactly what Matthew had predicted the previous night.

"I'd not give anyone the satisfaction of thinking we would run from those lies. Now enough procrastinating. Get your bath. After we missed church last week, the least we can do is get there on time today."

Within half an hour, they were headed to Shiloh church. Laurel filled the short time with small talk. That alone was a clear indication of how the morning news upset her. She was the last person to perpetuate small talk. Yet before they drove into the churchyard, Laurel gave Mac a shopping list for his next trip to Greensboro, explained her plans for a spelling test the next morning at school, and said she hoped her Uncle Matthew would sing *Old Rugged Cross* before the service ended. Mac simply nodded, smiled, and answered "Yes, ma'am" to a question or two.

Matthew was on the porch greeting each family as they arrived. When Mac helped Laurel from the wagon seat, she immediately left him to speak with her cousin Susan. Matthew stopped Mac at the door. "How did Laurel take what you told her this morning?"

"Quietly. She told me in no uncertain terms that we wouldn't leave the race. Then she said nothing more."

"Well, that's good news, at least."

"Is it? You should have heard her prattle on–small talk all the way from the cabin. Matthew, I've got to find out how that personal information got out. Few people knew. Anyway, I'll not rest until I find out who's spreading the gossip."

"Let me handle this, Mac. We don't need any more gossip fodder."

"I'll be patient, at least for a little while."

That night, they prepared for bed, a little earlier than usual. The temperature had turned colder. Mac watched Laurel engage in busy work all afternoon. She avoided him most of the day and made no effort to keep company with him, as was their Sunday afternoon routine. She would sit in her rocking chair, but before five minutes had passed, she would rise to do some other meaningless task that crossed her mind. Mac decided to reopen the conversation from the morning before they retired that night.

"Laurel, I've watched you try to work off your nerves all day. Even now, you can't be still for a minute. Tell me what's bothering you."

"Nothing is bothering me. I guess I am just preoccupied with school." Mac turned her to look squarely into her face where he saw her resolve.

"Are you sure that is what's bothering you?"

"I said so, didn't I?" Mac knew the issue was closed, at least temporarily. He was aware of her irritation at his asking, and he knew also Laurel would be aggravated with further questions. She had closed the conversation before he'd even had a chance to open a dialog.

"Yes, wife, you did. Let's go to bed. I am tired, and you need to get your rest. School day in the morning." Laurel knew that was true, but she couldn't sleep. The nightmares and the clouds from her past just never seemed to leave her for any stretch of time. She'd hoped for a new life far from Washington County. She wanted to be the new creature her Uncle Matthew talked about. Yet, in the midst of her happiness, her past reared its ugly head again.

Hundreds of questions raced through her mind. Was the man Mac had argued with Robbie Duncan? How did he know where she was? Why would he follow her all the way across the state? Laurel saw Robbie Duncan only twice after the incident and then only at a distance. She'd thought it a real blessing the Duncan family moved from the Hawthorn settlement before two months passed. But now was he in Shiloh? Just the possibility brought all the old fears back to her.

When Laurel arose about 5:00 the following morning, she'd slept less than two hours, and because of her sleepless night, she arose with dark circles under her eyes and a noticeable lack of energy, neither of which were part of her nature. As a matter of fact, she did not want to return to school at all. The eagerness she'd felt just the previous week had disappeared.

"Laurel, you are up early. Are you so eager to get to school?"

"I suppose that is why I couldn't sleep. I didn't mean to wake you." Laurel deliberately lied to Mac. She knew her inability to sleep was not her anxiousness about a new school year. If she'd talk to Mac about what she was feeling and thinking, she'd be better able to cope. How could she tell him when she didn't know herself what she feared? If she could only remember all the events of that night, put all the pieces together...if the nightmare only made sense to her.

"Well, if you're up for the day, we might as well get started on the right foot." Mac reached out to pull Laurel into an embrace as he did every morning. For the briefest time, Laurel stiffened and pulled back from him. She'd not done that once since they'd come home from Bolivar. Laurel quickly pushed the old reflex away and moved into Mac's arms.

"Good morning, Patrick. I hope you slept well."

## CHAPTER FIVE

*A false witness shall not go unpunished,*
*and he that speakers lies shall not escape.*
*Proverbs 19:5*

November 9th was a very cold day, especially in contrast to the weather the previous week. When Laurel stoked the morning fire, she noticed frost covered the window over her dry sink. She needed to go to school earlier than usual so she could build a fire in the stove and try to warm the building. Her students would be cold since most of them had to walk some distance to school. Before they arrived, Laurel arranged the classroom with her desk to one side. Shortly, the room warmed to a comfortable level. When the clock showed eight, Laurel rang the school bell. As the students took their seats, she found one student who had not been in school the previous week. She smiled. Roy Dunn arrived with Cathy, and they both wore new shoes that morning. Cathy also carried a small covered pail with food enough for her and her brother.

"Mrs. Mac!" Cathy ran to greet her teacher. "Mrs. Mac! Grandma got her pension check you wrote for. She told us to make sure and say thank ya for helpin' us out."

"You tell her I'm happy things worked out. I'm glad Roy is here instead of coming only to Sunday school."

"If it's all the same, Mrs. Mac, I'd like to keep coming to Sunday school, too. I figure I got a bit of catchin' up to do," Roy said.

"He's a figurin' he's got some courtin' to do. That Smith girl is a real looker."

"Hush your mouth, Cathy. I'm learnin' real good in Sunday school."

"Roy, you are always welcome at Sunday school." Laurel smiled at the amiable sibling conflict.

With Roy's enrollment the second week of school, two children of recent settlers, and Sandy Lamb, Shiloh community school enrollment was twenty-three students. There had never been a higher enrollment. Some of the students were not members of the Shiloh church but lived in nearby communities. Their families wanted the children to get schooling, but teachers were not available in their settlements. Laurel welcomed all the students, but she also knew the limits of their building to serve many more, not to mention the added workload. If more students enrolled, Shiloh would need to hire a second teacher. Shiloh church would be hard pressed to build a larger building or to pay for another teacher. She looked around, took a deep breath, and shook off the thoughts of her school's inadequacies. She would have a successful school term. Her fatigue from her sleepless night was the source of her doubts. She whispered a prayer. "Lord, help me see this as a new challenge and give me the desire to make this term a good one for my students. Please forgive my doubts."

"Class, welcome to the new week at Shiloh school. We'll start the day off with our song." Most of the students joined Laurel as she sang, "Morning has broken, like the first morning…"

MAC FOUND life on the homestead too idle to suit him. The worst problem was that he missed Laurel's company all day. Due to her diligence during his absence, they were well-prepared for winter, even if it proved to be a harsh one. On Monday, Mac put John to work cleaning the barn, and he decided he needed to talk with Matthew. He saddled Midnight to ride the two miles to the Campbell's homestead.

"Mac, what brings you out so early? Something wrong at your place?"

"Not really wrong. I'd like to talk for a while."

"Sure thing. Come on up in the loft and help me stack this hay. We'll have this place to ourselves. Ellie wants no part in the laying in of the forage."

"Be glad to help. I am proud to say that mine's all done."

"I know you didn't come over here to brag, so what's taken the smile off your face?"

"Shows does it?" Matthew jabbed his pitchfork into the hay and looked into the eyes of his friend. "When I first told her, I didn't think Laurel was too upset by what I said. But all day yesterday, she seemed, well…I don't know…she wasn't herself."

"What did she say?"

"Nothing I can put my finger on. She spent the whole day making up idle chatter and busy work. She couldn't sit still for a minute before she'd get up to do something else."

"Well, you know how excited she is to be back at school." Matthew tossed another fork full of hay.

"This morning she wasn't at all excited, almost like she dreaded leaving the cabin. She went out of obligation, not the joy she usually has for her teaching."

"It'll pass. Do you think her sleeplessness has something to do with the rally at Meadow Grove?"

"Yes. Laurel hardly slept. She was restless. Tossed and turned most of the night. I didn't think much about it, but Matthew, this morning when I reached to hug her, she tensed and moved away. That is the way she acted when we first met. It only lasted a second, but I sensed those old fears return."

"I think you are right. She is more upset than we thought."

"What am I gonna do? Things have been too good between us to let it go back to the way it was."

"You know as well as I do, Mac, Laurel's never dealt with all that hurt and fear from the past. Has she told you about what happened that night back in Washington County?"

"Snatches. I don't know the whole story. I've tried more than once to get Laurel to tell me so I can help her face it. That's one thing she won't or can't share with me. She gets upset and stops talking every time I try to question her about it. The one time we seriously talked she said that some things she can't remember. She wouldn't lie to me, Matthew. She wants to tell me, but some of it she doesn't know to tell."

"I don't think she'll ever let go until she does talk, Mac. Do you want me to talk to her about it?"

"No. I'll do it. This campaign slander is something we'll have to deal with together. I'm sure the gossip will come up again. The campaign's not nearly over yet."

Mac couldn't have been more right with his prediction of more gossip. On Thursday at noon recess, the Shiloh students stayed in to be near the fire. They sat in small groups, talking or reading together. Laurel walked quietly around the crowded classroom to keep order. As she walked near the older girls, she caught snatches of conversation about the rally. Laurel heard the words 'socked him a good one' and 'protecting his wife' and 'Hawthorn'. She didn't need her imagination to know she was the topic of their gossip. Laurel also knew that kids gossiped about what they'd heard in their homes. She continued to walk around the room, pretending to be oblivious to any conversation.

A similar incident occurred the following Saturday in Greensboro as Mac and Laurel entered McCollough's mercantile. They went to Greensboro to order apples, oranges, nuts, and candy for Christmas gifts for Shiloh's children. As they stopped at the counter to talk to Mr. McCollough, Laurel noticed three women staring at her. She noticed one of them point in her direction, and the three ladies turned away when she nodded to them. Within a matter of seconds, they parted ways, two of them leaving the store. She tried to return to her shopping, but the one remaining woman continued to stare at her. Laurel fought the urge to run. Instead, she strolled around looking at items brought on a recent freight wagon. After the third time, however, Laurel could no longer ignore the stares. She walked toward the woman and asked, "Can I do something to help you? You've looked my way several times."

The flustered woman seemed helpless without her two gossip partners. She stammered for several seconds, trying to answer Laurel. Finally, she reached up to tie her bonnet a bit tighter and replied, "No. Oh, well, perhaps you will tell me your name. I'm sure we've met somewhere in the past."

"Where could that meeting have taken place?"

"Is it possible I met you in Lexington? That was my home before I moved to Macedonia with my husband."

"Since I've never been in Kentucky, I'm sure that couldn't be. You must be thinking of someone else."

"Please forgive my rudeness for staring. I was sure we had met. Please excuse me. My husband is waiting for me." She rushed through the door and down the street, knocking over a display of pumpkins and gourds. She didn't stop to help the owner retrieve his produce.

Mac walked across the room and put his arm around his wife. "What's all that about, Laurel? What caused her to rush out so fast?"

"I'm not sure. She said something about her husband waiting for her. Seemed to be late. When she went out, she met the same man who came to school the other day and called me Miss Campbell."

"You didn't tell me about a man at school who used your maiden name. Why not?"

"Oh, I don't know. It didn't seem important at the time. I'm sure it's nothing."

Laurel hoped she'd evaded Mac's question. Anyway, she felt proud that she had confronted one of the gossips. She decided she would confront anyone who chose to carry the rumors further. She did hate that the gossip had spread to another community. "If we're finished here, Mac, let's go home."

"I got one more stop to make. You can stay here and shop in the warm mercantile or you can come with me to the livery. I'm gonna meet Al Stuart and Harold Armstrong for a short meeting."

"I'll stay if you promise not to be a long time. I'd rather go home."

"Half-hour, I promise." Mac hurried across the town square to the livery where Al and Harold were already waiting for him. "Well, did you find out about Laurel's attacker?"

"We have some news. A man named Bob Duncan is the foreman at the Digby place over near Gainesville. He came here in the late spring shortly after Digby bought the land. That was before you brought Laurel here or shortly after. Do you think it's a coincidence?"

"His being here maybe, but someone told him to make that attack on us at the last political rally. I wouldn't be surprised if Digby had staged the whole thing, especially since he was too sick to show up for the debate."

Ed nodded before he spoke. "I'm thinkin' that too. The Family's supporters are afraid you are winning the people over. I hear there is some breaking of the ranks in a couple of other places across the state. Lars Anderson from the Snoddy settlement told me a friend of Sevier's may run for governor. Wouldn't surprise me if he faced Conway himself."

"Harold, I don't care about that right now. I need some concrete proof to shut that man up before he makes another public assault on Laurel. The next time, she may be with me."

"I know, Mac. We want the same thing. We'll keep looking."

"One more thing…there is a man in the community that is following Laurel. She just told me he's been at the school, and this morning he met up with a woman who was gossiping with two of the town's women. See if that's Duncan, if you get the chance. He knew Laurel's name was Campbell."

THAT NIGHT, well after midnight, Mac awoke to Laurel's screams. He'd almost forgotten the heart-wrenching cries Laurel made so often in the early days of their marriage. Laurel pushed herself toward the headboard of the tall bed and wrapped her arms around her knees. The blank stare in her eyes told him that she was lost in the terror of her nightmare. Mac reached across to pull her close to him, but the moment he touched her, she screamed again. Panic rang out in her cries and showed in the void of her eyes.

"Please, don't hurt me anymore!"

"Laurel, darlin'. You're all right. You're safe."

"No. No. Don't touch me like that!"

"Laurel, wake up." Holding her shoulders, he shook her enough to wake her. "Come on, Laurel…wake up for me. It's Mac and you are safe." Laurel opened her eyes and looked at the man who spoke to her. For several moments, there was no recognition. Mac refused to release her though she struggled in the beginning. He stroked her hair, brushed gentle kisses on her face and neck, and whispered calm words and prayed, repeating her name. She crumpled into his arms and wept as he held her.

"I wondered how long you'd keep in that fear and anger you've been holding in since I told you about Mountain Grove. You've been brave and foolish long enough, don't you think?" He continued to hold her, and he kissed her wet cheeks. "You are safe in my arms, Laurel. Nothing is going harm you. Sleep now, and I hope tomorrow you will tell me about the nightmare."

At breakfast Mac asked, "Laurel, will you talk to me about your nightmare last night?"

"Mac, I'm sorry I woke you." His response was a tender caress of her unrestrained tawny curls. "I've been so happy since we came home to our cabin. I was about to believe in happily ever after. What foolishness to think the past wouldn't find me all the way across the state!"

"We live in a very real world, Laurel. We can never outrun our past, but God has promised His grace is enough for us. He will lead us to the other side of our pain and regret, but we always have to go through the valley. There is no path around it."

"I know I promised to walk out in faith with you, Mac. I want to believe you when you tell me I am safe. I wanted to leave that ugly part of my life in Washington County. Why did it have to rear its ugly face to me again?"

"Believe me, Laurel. I will protect you, but I need you to tell me about that boy Robbie. What happened to him after he attacked you?" Laurel stiffened when Mac made his request.

"What good is bringing all those painful memories back to the surface? How can I forget them if I tell it again?"

"Laurel, trust me enough to tell me."

"What does it matter now? I never want to think of those horrible times again."

"I know you tried to bury it as best you could a long time ago. Can't you see that you can't bury it deep enough? You need to bring it into the light. We can face whatever it is we have to face...together. It is so much easier to discredit someone's slander when you know the truth."

"Do you think someone from Washington County has come to Shiloh, Mac?"

"No, not to Shiloh exactly, but to the county. Laurel, we know the man at the rally was Bob Duncan. He works for Ezra Digby, my opponent. It's not a coincidence. Someone out there is trying to push me out of the race for the State house by attacking you."

"After that night, no one ever spoke to me directly the incident. I heard talk the Duncan family left the area before school ended that year. I know Bobby wasn't at school for the end of term festival and didn't get his certificate for finishing eighth grade. My papa and our minister then, Brother Elgin, and Jedidiah Trent, one of our elders, went to talk to Robert Duncan. That was Robbie's pa. He was a big man and not one to take a talking to. My friend Rachel said Mr. Duncan laughed when Reverend Elgin told him what Bobby and those other two boys did to me. She said Mr. Duncan patted Bobby's back and said 'Guess my boy went a tad too far in his sparkin'. Then he laughed even harder. That is all I've ever been told. I don't know where they went when they left Hawthorn."

"Well, Laurel, my dear, Mr. Rob, Bobbie, Robert Duncan Jr. cannot move into our world. You put all your fears to rest. Remember we have come home to Shiloh."

In the daylight, Laurel kept up a pleasant façade so her fears did not disrupt her classes. Yet at night, Laurel cried out in her sleep and woke more often than not, trembling from her dreams. As November drew to an end, even people from her Sunday school class began to ask about her health. The lack of sleep and the anxiety were becoming more evident every day. One afternoon late in November, Cathy Dunn stopped at her desk before she left for home. "Mrs. Mac, Grandma and me been worrying about you. After church last Sunday, Grandma asked me if you've been sickly. I hope you don't get sick, Mrs. Mac. We ain't never had a teacher as good as you."

"Cathy, that is so sweet that you're concerned for me. I'm all right. Tell your grandmother not to worry. I'll try to rest more." Laurel knew she was tired. She had slept only sporadically since the political rally at Meadow Grove. There were no more nightmares, not since Mac had begun to hold her on his shoulder. Yet, she seemed unable to sleep through the night. Often, Laurel felt overwhelmed with the need to talk to her mother. Mac was at a loss for what to say when she told him. Laurel's mother had died before her thirteenth birthday. He offered to listen, but she shook her head. "Sometimes girls need to talk with another female."

One early December afternoon, Laurel wanted that talk worse than she ever had. She decided that a talk with her Aunt Ellie would help ease her mind. She left the school and headed to the Campbell homestead instead of leading Sassy home. She hoped the whole way her uncle Matt wouldn't be there when she arrived.

"What a nice surprise, Laurel Grace. Come over here and warm yourself by the fire. I'll make you a cup of tea." Laurel sat in a chair near the hearth.

"Thank you, aunt. Where is Uncle Matthew?"

"He's off in Greensboro. He told me there was some business, but I know he went over there to talk politics this afternoon. I expect he'll be back by supper if you want to talk with him."

"No, Aunt Ellie. I'm glad he's not here. I want to talk to you."

Ellie Campbell sensed the trouble in Laurel's voice. She crossed the room and sat at the hearth facing Laurel's chair. Stirring the pot on the spit, she asked, "Did you want to talk about something in particular, darlin'?"

"Aunt Ellie, do I look sickly to you? People have stopped me the past couple of weeks and asked me if I was feeling poorly."

"You do look a bit piqued, and you got dark circles under your eyes. Have you been restin' at night?"

"I know Uncle Matthew told you about the nightmares coming back, but it's more than that. I feel queasy at times. I don't have the stamina I had. By the time the school day is over, I'm tuckered, and I want a nap."

Ellie Campbell smiled, "Laurel Grace, didn't your mama talk to you about having babies?"

"Babies? I don't think that is the reason. I'm upset about the rumors, and whether I'll have to face Robbie Duncan somewhere."

"Did she tell you about what happens when you're expecting?"

"No. Not much. She died when I was just before my thirteenth birthday. She didn't have the time to tell me anything about being a wife or becoming a mother. I don't suppose she thought I was ready to know such things."

"Well, Laurel Grace, you've been married going on nine months. I'm surprised you haven't asked me about this before now." Laurel toyed with the gold band on her finger. She felt shy and awkward around her aunt for the first time since they had met. "Laurel Grace, there's no reason to be embarrassed. Most young couples start their families within a couple of months after they're married. "Of, course it takes longer for some. I got in the family way with Susan within a few weeks, but it was several years after I had Mark when we got Mary."

"I hadn't thought about expecting a baby yet. I know Mac wants a baby, but how will I know for sure?"

"Well, Laurel...early on I always was real tired, especially in the afternoons. Sometimes my stomach felt nervous when I ate in the morning. After about three months, I got so queasy in the morning I couldn't eat anything until afternoon. You told me you are feeling some of those same things now. After a few months, Susan always gets cravings for some strange thing to eat. Seems it's something different with every baby. Your monthly will stop."

"I already missed one, Aunt Ellie, but I didn't think much about it. I do that sometimes when I've been upset ...like when my brother Samuel and papa died. Do you think I am going to have a baby, Aunt Ellie?"

"Well, only one way for us to know. Let's go over to see Dr. Gibson. He'll know right away if you're in the family way."

"I do hope so. Mac would be so happy."

"Let's you and me go to Greensboro on Saturday."

"No, Aunt, let's wait a little while. I don't want anyone to know yet. I don't want to disappoint Mac if it's not so. Please don't mention any of this to Uncle Matthew. He talks to Mac about everything. Let's see what time brings."

"Well, if that's what you want. Tell me when you want to talk again or if you want me to go over to Greensboro with you." Laurel hugged her aunt.

"Thank you, Aunt Ellie. I feel so much better since we talked. I'd best be getting home. Mac'll be expecting me long before I can get there."

As she rode toward home on Sassy, she smiled to herself. Perhaps she carried the child Mac wanted. For now, she wanted this secret for herself for a little while. She would wait before she hoped too much. A week or so would tell the story. Laurel thought about the events that led her to this place in her life. How perfect that a baby comes from the wonderful times of lovemaking she and Mac shared! Laurel remembered the special weekend adventure Mac had planned for her in Eden, and she shivered! "Thank you, Lord. Has there ever been a woman more blessed than I am right now?" Her praise rang through the forest path on her way home, and she laughed. If she carried Mac's son, she'd keep the special secret until Christmas. What a wonderful present to give to her husband, and she knew exactly how she would tell him.

The sun was edging below the horizon as Laurel rode into the yard. Mac came from the barn with a pail of fresh milk. "Evening, wife. Were the kids so bad you kept them late at school this Tuesday afternoon? Everything all right?"

"Everything is fine! I had a yen to talk with my family for a spell. I went over to see my Aunt Ellie."

"You saw her on Sunday. Is there a problem at the Campbell place?"

"No, I just needed Aunt Ellie's advice about a Christmas present is all. You know we're less than a month away from our first Christmas together."

"The weather seems to be heading toward winter. That's good, because I never get in the Christmas mood until it gets really cold or snows. Here, take this milk in, and I'll put Sassy away for the night."

Laurel dismounted, walked toward Mac and threw her arms around his neck. She kissed him with more passion that she'd demonstrated in weeks. "I love you, Patrick MacLayne. You are so good to me." She took the pail and started toward the back door.

"What brought that on?"

"Nothing special. I love you is all."

"You need to visit with your Aunt Ellie every day after school."

# CHAPTER SIX

*Blessed be God...the God of all comfort. Who comforter us in all our tribulations that we may be able to comfort them which are in any trouble by the comfort wherewith we ourselves are comforted of God.*
*2 Corinthians 1:3-4*

In December, Laurel worked even harder to push her students toward the goals she set for them. The weather could force a close to the winter school term sooner than the set date of December 23rd. She wanted all her students to make enough progress to allow them to be promoted for the spring term. Four students would take the exams to complete their formal schooling at the end of the term. Foremost, she wanted each of them to feel successful.

Unfortunately, Laurel found herself very concerned with one of her best students. Francine Jackson was scheduled to graduate along with three other eighth-level students. The bright sixteen-year-old and Elizabeth Collins competed for the top score on every assignment. Until last week, their scores were so close she wondered which girl would speak at graduation.

Laurel scored Elizabeth's math exam, and she'd made an almost perfect score, missing only one problem. Francine missed seven problems, and all by making careless errors. Laurel never knew her to pay so little attention to the details of her work. When she looked over the test, she realized Francine's score should have been perfect. She made errors in silly little things she overlooked. She laid the test aside and decided to wait another day to confront her. Perhaps Francine had a bad day, and she'd not repeat the poor quality of her work.

On Friday of that same week, Laurel knew she must intervene. She took up the essays from the eighth-level students before noon recess. She dismissed the students for recess. Some of the boys went outside, even though the temperature was uncomfortably cold. Others gathered in groups to talk as they ate their meals. Laurel stayed at her desk to read the essays. Usually, she returned the papers for minor corrections, but today the first two were excellent. When she picked up Francine's essay, Laurel saw at a glance the girl had not done the assignment. Francine failed to write the argumentative theme Laurel assigned. She wrote a strong opening paragraph with one supporting point and stopped. This was the first paper of any eighth-level student Laurel scored with a failing grade. Something was terribly wrong. Laurel would have to talk to Francine because the term's end was less than three weeks away. She would not allow Francine to lose her opportunity to graduate with her class.

At 3:30, Laurel dismissed her students, all but Francine Jackson. "Francine, please remain for a few minutes. I need to speak with you."

"Yes, Mrs. Mac."

"Good day, class. Have a safe trip home. I'll look forward to having you back in school on Monday."

When the room was empty, Francine Jackson walked up to Laurel's desk. "Mrs. Mac, I know why you called me out. I'm sorry I didn't finish my work. I'll work harder, I promise."

"Francine, I am concerned, but this composition is not the only thing I'm worried about. You did a poor job on your math test earlier in the week, and you can work every problem. Your mind has not been on your studies all week."

"I can't seem to think about school right now. I am sorry. It's not your doing."

"Francine, this work is not what you've always done for me. Is something bothering you?"

"No, ma'am…not … well, no." Francine avoided looking at her. "I'll try harder. I want to do good work. I'm sorry I disappointed you, Mrs. Mac."

"That isn't the concern here, darlin'. Something has changed. You aren't taking your work as seriously as you did. That's not you. You told me you want to sit for your teacher's license."

"I do want to be a teacher. I'll try harder, Mrs. Mac. I promise I will. I want…" Tears ran down the side of Francine's face.

"Francine, can't you tell me what is bothering you?"

"I can't talk about it. My ma told me to forget it. I try, but…I don't mean to be a cry baby. Please forgive me, Mrs. Mac."

"I cry at times. Are you worried about passing your final exams?"

"No. No, I can do the work."

"I'm glad you realize that. You've always been one of the best…"

Francine blurted out, "That was before. Now my mind won't stay on my work. The harder I try the farther it goes wonderin' off."

"Can't you tell me what's changed? I'll help you if I can."

"I'll think about it. I'll do better. I promise you I'll try." Francine picked up her food pail and the book she was reading. She turned to the door. "And Mrs. Mac, thank you for wanting to help. I'll see you at church on Sunday."

Laurel didn't feel much better after the talk. Francine told her she'd try harder, but she seemed anxious and sad. Laurel knew there was more to Francine's changing school work, but the girl couldn't bring herself to say more.

That evening, Mac built up a bigger fire in the hearth, and he then went into the second pen to build a fire in the bedroom. Arkansas weather had been strange that fall. September had remained hot until the very end with temperatures more like mid-summer. He and Laurel had swum in the creek up until the end of October. Summer ended with the coming of winter, skipping autumn altogether. November was a cold month, and early December had been bitter. Laurel wanted to keep the cold away for three more weeks, but heavy frost blanketed Northeast Arkansas every morning. The area was dry, but the bone-aching cold didn't cease.

"Laurel, is the school warm enough this term?"

"Yes, Mac. The stove does a fair job of keeping us comfortable. We keep busy too, so we don't pay that much attention, I guess."

"Well, let me know if we need to look into getting a second stove. I don't want you to get sick working in the cold."

Laurel looked up from her grading at the table. "Mac, I worry more about the kids having to walk to school in the cold. I hope this dry weather holds until the term is over at Christmas." She laid an essay aside and took off her glasses. She rubbed her nose where her glassed normally perched. "Mac, what do you know about the Jackson family?"

"That's a jump--from the weather to the Jacksons. What makes you ask?"

"I'm concerned about Francine. The past two weeks her school work has been far below her usual level. She didn't want to tell me, but something has to be wrong. She said her mother told her not to talk about it. What could have happened to that sweet girl?"

"Frank Jackson is a good man. He's a hard worker and a good supporter of the church. You know his wife, Lillian. She's always making decorations for the church altar. In the summer, she cuts flowers from her yard. They have five kids, all girls I'm thinkin'. Francine is the youngest, and the only one still at home."

"Have you heard of any problems at their house? Has Uncle Matthew said anything?"

"Laurel, you know Matt won't talk about our congregation if they tell him something in private. I've not heard of any problems."

"Well, I asked Francine to talk with me on Monday. She said she'd think about it." Laurel walked toward her rocking chair near the hearth and picked up the book from the side table. She placed her glasses on her nose and began to rock and read again. Within five minutes, she nodded off. The clock on the mantle had not yet marked 8:30, and Laurel had already fallen asleep.

"Hey, there, schoolmarm. You must be working too hard. You never sleep this early in the evening."

"Goodness, I am tired. I guess it's been a long week. The extra students do seem to make the days busier than they were in the spring term. I believe I'll go to bed if you don't mind. I know it's early."

"No, darlin', I don't mind. Our room should be warm by now. I added a couple extra logs earlier."

"You are such a thoughtful husband. Bring your Bible to bed, and we'll read in there tonight."

"Go on. I'll close up the house for the night."

Laurel had already replaced her beautiful silk night dress with a long sleeved one. The lawn night dress was pretty with its flowing sleeves, tucked bodice, and lace-trimmed collar. Pretty it was, and so much warmer. Mrs. Dunn finished it, along with her gray sateen ball gown, just school started. Laurel paid her fee. The dear lady earned enough money that she was able to pay the tuition for Cathy's whole school term. Laurel took down her hair and shook it loose. Her hairbrush would get a reprieve that night. She was too sleepy. When Mac came to the bedroom, he found his wife asleep already, but not before she'd turned down his side of the bed. He smiled at her thoughtfulness, but her company for the night would be sadly absent.

The following Monday, Laurel hoped Francine had taken their conversation to heart. Instead, she found that the girl didn't come to school at all. Laurel fretted throughout the day. Before the time came to dismiss the class, she decided to ride to the Jackson's homestead on the other side of Big Creek. The trip would make her homecoming late. Mac would worry, but she couldn't go through the night without knowing about Francine. At 3:15, Laurel dismissed her other twenty-two students. They looked up at her, delighted and puzzled. Mrs. Mac never let them out early, not until the old school clock on the wall showed 3:30.

"Boys and girls, please don't forget to take your work home to study. Y'all have spelling tomorrow. Be safe."

As soon as the last student left, Laurel went to the peg on the back wall and picked up the green coat and bonnet Mac had brought her from Maryland. She turned to the door to leave when she saw Francine, standing at the foot of the porch. She shivered from the cold, and her swollen red eyes told Laurel the young woman had been crying a long while.

"Francine, dear, come in here and get warm by the fire. I missed you at school today." She took the girl's hand, icy to the touch. She led her to the woodstove and removed her coat. "Have you been standing out there very long?"

"For a spell. Mrs. Mac, I left home this morning to come to school, but I couldn't stop crying. I tried to stop, but the harder I did, the more the tears came. Can I talk to you?"

"Of course, you can."

"You gotta promise me not to tell my momma."

"I will try to honor your request, Francine. But if you tell me things that will harm you or someone else, I won't be able to keep your confidence. Do you understand?"

"It won't matter. I gotta tell someone. I trust you, Mrs. Mac. You will help. I know it."

"I hope I can." Laurel laid her arm across Francine's shoulders. "Come over here and sit down. Tell me what has upset you."

Francine looked up into her teacher's eyes. Mrs. Mac was the one person she would trust with her story, but the words didn't come easily. Laurel sat, holding the girl's hand and waited. Finally, Francine poured out her words. "Mrs. Mac, I am going to run away from home. I don't have any other choice. I don't know what to do or where to go. I've never been so scared in my life."

"Right at this minute, you don't have to do anything. Take a deep breath, and just rest here by this warm stove. Are you hungry? Did you eat today?"

"No. I'm not hungry. I have to go away from here. Mrs. Mac, Mommy told me if my daddy finds out, he will send me away because I've shamed our family. She said I couldn't tell anyone--not anyone!"

"I see why you're upset, darling. I'm sure your mother was speaking from her own fear for you. She doesn't mean you aren't welcome at home. I'm sure."

"She does. And if I have a child, what'll I do?"

Laurel sat dumbfounded by Francine's last words.

"Mrs. Mac, what can I do if I have a baby after what happened?"

What could she say to her student who was pouring out her fear and secret? What did the girl need to hear? "Francine, you're not alone. Tell me whatever you need me to know. I'll listen."

The girl broke into sobs. For many minutes, Laurel held her. Only the crackling of the wood fire and an occasional thump of hickory nuts falling outside broke the silence.

When Francine was able to control her tears, she began to talk in quiet, broken sentences. "Mrs. Mac, six weeks ago, I met up with Marcus Cramer from Herndon at the Crowley's harvest supper. I've liked him ever since we met last year at the Fourth of July dance at Greensboro. He danced with me twice that night. We've seen each other off and on at different socials. We ran into him and his pa in Greensboro on the Saturday before the party. We were standing on the porch in front of McCollough's mercantile. Marcus held my hand a minute or so, and then he asked me if I could go with him to the party. I said I'd ask my daddy.

"When I asked, Daddy told me not to talk to Marcus anymore. He said I'm not old enough to think about courting. But I am, Mrs. Mac. I'm sixteen since my birthday last week." Francine stopped her story and wiped her eyes on the hem of her petticoat.

Laurel nodded her attention, so the girl continued.

"I was so happy when Marcus asked me to meet him at the Crowley's. You know everyone always goes to the harvest festival at the Crowley's. I saw Mr. Mac and you at the party. I didn't tell Daddy I was going to see Marcus there but went to find him as soon as we got there that afternoon. Anyway, we spent the whole afternoon together talking, and when we were by ourselves, he kissed me a time or two. When the dancing started, I didn't want to go into the barn because my mommy and daddy were in there. Mommy likes to dance. I asked Marcus if we could walk over by the creek instead. We walked a while. Then we sat down on those big old rocks there at the mouth of the creek. Marcus started hugging me and kissing me. I liked it when he kissed me, Mrs. Mac." The girl looked up into the eyes of her teacher. Her tear-streaked face reflected her confusion and fear. "I let him keep on kissing me."

Laurel didn't speak to her. She smiled and tried to maintain an expression without judgment.

"Do you think I am bad, Mrs. Mac? I know I should have made him stop, but..." Her words faded from Laurel's attention. Memories from her own past claimed the present. Laurel fought hard to push back the distant memories. Francine needed her attention.

"Francine, it's all right. You are safe here. I'm not your judge. You can talk to me."

"Everything happened so fast...I don't know exactly...I should have...At first...Oh, my dear Lord, I'm a terrible person. I know it was my fault. I should've fought him harder. I am a harlot. That's what my mommy said." Tears flowed again, but not so hard this time. "I told him to stop. I know I said no...no...no...but I didn't fight hard enough. Anyway, I know it's my fault. I shouldn't have gone against what my daddy told me. I didn't have to let Marcus kiss me the way he did." Again, Francine looked up at Laurel. "Mrs. Mac...what will I do with a baby?"

"Francine, did Marcus do more than kiss you? Has your mother told you how a girl can have a baby?"

"Not in so many words, she didn't. Raised on a farm, Mrs. Mac, I know about those things.... I should have made Marcus stop. I could've if I'd tried harder. I didn't want him not to like me, I guess. If I have a baby...." Francine looked up with such fear in her eyes, seeking some reassurance from her teacher.

"Francine, it's too soon to worry about that right now. What happened when your young man heard you telling him to stop?"

"He said he liked me, and he held me closer. Marcus told me how beautiful I am. He told me that he knew I was scared, but he'd never hurt me. I don't know how I let this happen."

"Your mother hasn't told your father yet, has she?"

"She said if the problem goes away, then there is no need. She knows he'll get riled at me and Marcus even more. Mommy don't want no talk at Shiloh. You know how people gossip."

"I understand. Francine, I hope things work out for the best. I hope you don't have a baby now. But regardless of what happens, I want you to know I'll stand with you. I believe your parents will too."

"I wish that would be true, but I know my folks will disown me." Francine wiped the tears from her face once again. "Anyway, Mrs. Mac, I'm gonna make up my work. I will finish school and sit for my teacher's license."

"That's a good decision."

"You're so good to listen to me. I don't deserve it, I know. I should've run from Marcus, but I do like him. I just never thought anything like this would come from a little kissing. I'm ashamed of what happened to me."

"Francine, I know what it is like to carry a burden. You don't need to spend your young life with that shame. Pray about it, and let God forgive you. And darling, most important is for you to forgive yourself. Everybody makes poor choices at times. Not one man has lived without making a mistake, except Jesus."

"I'm glad you let me get this all out. You've been so good to let me pour out my grief to you."

"Can I take you home now?"

"Yes, ma'am. That would be kind of you. I hope mommy is not still mad at me."

Laurel closed the door and began to untie her mule. She was about to leave the schoolyard when Francine's mother approached the wagon.

"Francine, how come you stayed so late at school? It's near on to five o'clock."

"Mommy, I didn't...uh..."

"Mrs. Jackson, Francine came late to school this afternoon. We've been talking about getting caught up with her school work and getting ready for her final tests next week."

"Francie, why're you late for school? You left in plenty of time to get here."

"Mommy, I couldn't face school today. I was crying and crying. Mommy, I had to talk to someone about...well, you're so mad at me."

"What'd you do that for? I told you not to talk about your shame. We'll have the whole community gossiping about our family."

"Mrs. Jackson, our conversation will go no further, I promise you. I'll not speak a word Francine has told me. She's afraid and angry with herself that she's disappointed you. Let's wait and let the Lord work all this out. Francine isn't a bad person. She made a poor decision, but we all make mistakes at one time or another."

"Mrs. Mac, she shouldn't never have gone out by herself with the older boy."

"She knows that now. She feels sad that she disobeyed, but she can't change what's done. Right now, she needs our understanding and for us to stand by her while we wait."

"Lord, I pray I don't have to tell her pa. It'd kill my man to think something bad about his baby girl. She's always been his favorite."

"You have to decide how to deal with her pa, but girls need their mothers most when they've made a mistake."

"I know that's true...Lord, help us. Come on along, Fran. Let's go home and get our chores done. And please pray for us, Mrs. Mac. We don't need no baby now."

LAUREL TURNED her wagon toward her own cabin. As soon as she knew she was alone, her composure crumbled. Great sobs racked her body, and tears fell so hard she could not see to drive the mule. She had no idea how she managed to drive back to the barnyard. Neither did she remember leaving the wagon at the porch railing. Francine's frank confession to her had unlocked every buried memory, hurt, and shame from her own past. She could no longer deceive herself.

Laurel made her way to the bedroom, not noticing the cold there. She fell across the tall bed and continued to cry. Mac made his way from the barn a short time later and saw the wagon and mule at the doorway. Laurel didn't usually leave the stock unfettered. Mac slung the reins around the porch post and went inside to find out if Laurel was all right. As he opened the back door, he heard crying. He walked the short distance and found his distraught wife on their bed.

"Laurel, what happened, darlin'? Has someone hurt you?" Laurel was not able to speak. She clutched at Mac and he held her. After some time passed, Laurel's tears stopped.

"Patrick, I want to tell you about the night I was attacked so long ago in Hawthorn."

"Is that the reason for the tears? You don't have to tell me."

"Yes, I do. I know all the story now. I remember everything that happened that night. I know the whole ugly story."

"Laurel, I'll listen if you want me to."

"Mac, I wouldn't remember that night because I caused it. I know now that I led Robbie on and let him think I would let him kiss me and take liberties. I had no business being alone with him or letting him kiss me at that harvest party. When I tried to push him away, he got furious and lost his temper. I shouldn't have let it start in the first place."

"Laurel, stop blaming yourself, and tell me what happened."

Laurel's story burst forth. "At first, I was having so much fun. I loved the attention Robbie paid to me. Flirting and teasing seemed so harmless. I thought we were having a good time. I'd been sweet on Robbie for a while. I thought he liked me, too. I was thrilled when he chose me to be his partner on the hayride, and later he danced with me. He told his friends, Lester and Zack, I was his best girl. After we danced a couple of times, Robbie asked me to walk out with him. I knew I shouldn't go, but I wanted him to kiss me. I wondered how that would feel. I liked the kisses, Mac, and I let him kiss me over and over. But when he started to touch me and pulled me closer, I got scared and told him to stop and let me go. He started to laugh at me. Then I heard Zack and Lester laughing, too. They'd been watching us from the woods.

"I started struggling with Robbie. I slapped him, and he lost his temper. He slapped me back. He hit me again, and my eye started to swell shut. He told me I had been asking for his attention for a long time, and now I'd get all I wanted from him and his two friends. I started to scream and fight back. Robbie clamped his hand over my mouth, and the other two boys started grabbing at me. One of them jerked my hair and threw me to the ground. I screamed when I could. Robbie covered my mouth with his, and I kicked him. He cursed at me, and then they all started laughing again. They'd torn my blouse all the way down the front and jerked my skirt away. I still hear those awful names they called me. I got away and started to run, but they pulled me back and continued to rip at my clothes. Oh Lord, I hate these memories."

"Laurel, you've told me enough. I know what happened."

"I want to tell you the rest of the story. Patrick, my clothes were in tatters when they dragged me back to the barnyard. All the other kids from my class stood around. I still hear the things they taunted me with. Someone said, 'You're not so prim and proper now.' Another boy danced around yelling, 'I guess your brains didn't save you this time.' A girl I'd helped with her schoolwork smirked. 'See how proud your family will be of you now.'

"That is when Robbie saw the sheep shears hanging on the barn wall. He said, 'You won't think you're so fine when we shear you like a sheep!' Lester and Zack took my arms and pushed me to the ground, my face in the dirt, and Robbie cut off my hair. One side it was all the way down to my head. I can still hear those kids laughing and calling me names. Not one came to help me."

Laurel had stopped crying by this time. Her voice quieted and her demeanor calmed as if she understood the reason for the attack. She knew why she'd been ashamed to speak of it for more than half her life. "I thought they liked me, Patrick. I thought Robbie liked me. No one stood up for me, not one of my classmates. I had no idea they disliked me so much they wouldn't even help me. What is wrong with me?" By the time Laurel had spoken the last words, she had used the last of her anger, fear, and energy in the telling. There were no more tears.

Laurel laid her head on Mac's shoulder. Fatigue forced her to seek his support. At the same time, she felt a sense of calm, as if a weight had fallen from her shoulders.

"That is a horrible thing to happen to anyone. No wonder you decided to hide from the people who had humiliated you. But, Laurel, I can see nothing in your story that says you can accept the blame for what happened. That boy arranged to make you a laughing stock. I don't know why, but he wanted to get back at you for some reason."

"Mac, I told you I let him kiss me…"

"That is nothing to be ashamed of. All of us are curious about such things during our youth. Everyone wonders what it's like to be loved and special to one person. We all yearn to belong. And it is scary. Look how long it took me to admit that I am in love with you." Mac brushed a kiss across her wet cheeks. "Laurel, what happened when your father saw you?"

"Papa hadn't wanted me to go to that party. I had begged to get his permission. When I got home, Papa pulled me into his arms right off. I remember standing there with my torn chemise, bare shoulders, bruised face and arms, and my shorn head. Papa was my shelter. I'd have died then and there if he had rejected me. But he didn't. He took a quilt off his bed and wrapped me up and held me in his lap. He let me cry a while, and then he listened to my story. He hugged me when I finished and told me to forget the whole incident. He said to pretend it was a bad dream. He said he'd take care of everything, and he never spoke to me about it again.

"Laurel, I am glad you told me the story that has haunted you. I don't think it will have any power over you from now on."

"I have never forgiven myself. I was not just a helpless victim. I know that now. All this time I've carried the ugliness around with me because I wouldn't accept my part in the attack. God forgive my ignorance and guilt. I won't let this ugly thing cast a shadow over us anymore. I wish I had told you a long time ago."

"Why today, Laurel? Did someone make an attack on your name again?"

"No, husband. I saw my past reflected in the life of one of my students who wasn't as fortunate as I was. She is so much braver than I've ever been because she had the courage to seek out help. Her misfortune let me remember and understand that night after all these years."

"Is there something I need to do to help this girl?"

"No. I promised her we'd be patient and wait to see what the Lord would make of this. Goodness, I am tired. I can't believe how sleepy I am."

"Lie here and rest for half an hour while I care for the animals. Then we'll make us a nice meal and call it an early night."

~

FRANCINE'S SCHOOL work returned to its earlier quality within a few days, yet Laurel could see the look of concern in her eyes. She also saw a young woman's determination to go on with her plans to be a teacher. Francine sought out some opportunity most days to speak in private with her. On a Wednesday, the week before Christmas, Francine waited until after school to talk.

"Mrs. Mac, I've been meaning to tell you I saw Marcus on Saturday when I went to Greensboro with my daddy. I didn't get to talk to him because Daddy told me not to, but he acted like he was glad to see me. He smiled at me and lifted his hat. I saw him look at me more than once."

"How do you feel about that?"

"I guess I was happy. Marcus didn't pretend I wasn't there. He could've ignored me. I still like him. I guess I shouldn't, but I don't think he meant to harm me. I gave him the wrong impression."

"Francine, sweetie. Be very careful not to let yourself get caught up in a romantic dream. You are still very young."

"What if I am supposed to make a life with Marcus. I would want him to marry me if I have his baby."

"Has he told you he wants you to get married."

"Well, no. We haven't talked since that night."

"Francine, don't rush decisions in a heated moment. Life has a way of working itself out if we wait and keep our faith."

"It's good I have you to talk to. My mommy shushes me when I try to tell her things like I tell you. Sometimes I am so confused. I don't know how I'm supposed to act or feel around boys."

"Francine, that is so normal. Here I am twenty-eight years old, and I think the very same thing. For today, though, tell me you'll wait a while longer before you decide to make choices about your future. You've got lots of time."

"I promise. I will wait a while longer, Mrs. Mac."

# CHAPTER SEVEN

*Do not withhold good from those who deserve it when it's in your power to act.*
*Proverbs 3: 27*

Laurel didn't have the luxury of time. Since her last talk with her Aunt Ellie, Laurel had come to believe she carried Mac's child. Every day, she craved her afternoon naps. The past two mornings, she was queasy after eating even a couple of spoonsful of oatmeal. The idea of eating fried eggs and bacon in the morning sent her running to the back door. Laurel decided to ask her Aunt Ellie to go with her to see Dr. Gibson in Greensboro. If he confirmed her hopes, Laurel would give Mac the best Christmas gift possible. Two more days and she would know whether she would give Mac crocheted booties on Christmas morning. She so hoped she would.

The last week of the school term was the most hectic time of year. The students were excited about Christmas coming. The eighth-level students anticipated the end of their formal schooling. Nervous chatter among them was not always concern over final exams. Younger students worked determinedly. They intended to complete assignments as soon as they could, allowing them time to work on the Christmas pageant. Everyone had some role to play in the program, which they would present to their parents.

Laurel felt almost overwhelmed by the number of activities demanding her attention. At school, she had to prepare tests, to teach lessons, to make decorations, to rehearse student speeches, and to maintain discipline. Furthermore, she had to finish the stockings for all the students. Thank goodness, she wasn't doing all the refreshments for the party alone. At church, Laurel continued reading lessons with the Sunday school. She meant to keep the promise of allowing them to read after the new year began. At home, Laurel still had to finish gifts for her husband, her Campbell family and the Dunns. Of course, she needed her afternoon nap every day. All this was getting done, but she didn't know how.

After the Saturday visit to Dr. Gibson, Laurel's mind wandered continually. Carrying Mac's son brought her the greatest sense of fulfillment she'd ever known. On the other hand, not telling him turned out to be one of the most difficult things she'd ever done. Furthermore, Laurel's napping so often and her poor appetite led Mac to believe she was ailing. He began to let her sleep later than she had at the beginning of the term.

Mac woke Laurel as the sun was rising over the ridge. "Wake up, sleepyhead. I got our breakfast and food for your dinner pail ready." Laurel stretched her arms above her head, and Mac took the opportunity to grab her arms and pull her to him. He pushed back her hair and kissed the nape of her neck.

"Enough of that, Mac. No time for sparking this morning. It's a school day, and you must have a chore or two to do." Mac continued to plant slow, soft kisses on Laurel's neck.

"Chores will wait, wife."

"Well, my students won't. I've only got an hour to get to school."

"Very well, I'll wait until tonight. I'll piddle the day away until you get back. Maybe I'll ride over to Greensboro and see what's happening outside of paradise. Even if I do go, I'll be home long before you get home from school. Would you like to walk in the hills this afternoon?"

"If I get home in time, and it's not too cold."

"The trees are near bare now, and they make a pretty sight against the sunset. I don't think it'll be too cold, but even if it is a bit cool, we won't have many more nice days before we can't roam around our land."

"We'll see. Now let me up. I have to get dressed, and you're making me late."

"Well, don't plan on nap this afternoon."

The MacLaynes parted. Laurel rode northwest toward Shiloh, and Mac rode south toward Greensboro. Within the hour, he arrived at Al Stuart's office to tell him what he had learned about the man who'd attacked Laurel. All evidence suggested Robbie Duncan was the man who confronted him at the political rally. At their last meeting, Matthew Campbell promised to put an end to the talk. Mac wouldn't be satisfied until he knew how their personal lives became political ammunition for Mac's opponent. He also had a nagging concern for Laurel's safety.

"Morning, Mac. What brings you to Greensboro so early on this Monday before Christmas?"

"I wanted to talk about the campaign and share a bit of information with you."

"Well, the campaign is going fine. We've worked hard all fall, so we can take some time off through the worst of the winter. We can hit the campaign trail hard again in the spring and up through summer. Notwithstanding some strange happenstance, we got this election all wrapped up."

"You know that is not what I came to talk about. What have you learned about those men who slandered Laurel at the rally in Mountain Grove?"

"When I was over in Gainesville for court last week, I asked about the tall, rough young man who spoke out. It's pretty obvious that Digby is no farmer so he'd need someone who can run a place that large. The people at Gainesville don't think that Duncan is much more of a farmer than Digby. Seems funny."

"Anything else?"

"Not much, I'm afraid. Seems that Digby was actually sick that Saturday. Local talk is that he's been going to the doctor regularly since mid-November."

"That's still not proof he didn't set up the whole thing."

"Be patient, Mac. We'll learn more."

Mac clinched his fists. "Al, I won't tolerate any more attacks on Laurel. I'll be patient for a while, but not at the cost of her good name."

"Matthew and I told you we would find out, and we will. Have you learned anything?"

"Laurel told me her father, the preacher, and a third man from Hawthorn church confronted Duncan's father after Laurel's assault. You know that's how the discipline of our church tells us to deal with a wrong from one of our fellow church members. Duncan didn't receive the visit very well. Afterwards, his refusal to discipline his son didn't sit well with the Hawthorn church. He refused to admit his son had done anything wrong. Duncan moved his family out of the county before the next school term began in the spring."

"There's gotta be more to it than that. That was more'n a decade ago."

"Duncan is a coward, and I'll bet he blames Laurel for his crude behavior. Fool! Al, keep digging. I want to know if he is the one."

"We promised you, Mac. Give us a little time, and we will find out the whole of it."

Mac scowled as he left the lawyer's office. Al had not been able to confirm that the slanderer at Meadow Grove was Robert Duncan. Nothing he'd learned had given him any assurance that Laurel would not become a target again. He mounted Midnight and started home at a much faster gait than he usually rode. The rapid pace of the trip home did not lighten his mood. Mac was a man of action, and it was not his nature to let others do his work.

Laurel stood on the porch as Mac rode into the yard. He stepped from Midnight's back and took her arm to begin their walk in the mild winter afternoon. His sullen mood and silence overshadowed the promise of a pleasant evening. They walked toward Crowley's Ridge. Little by little, the beauty of winter and the touch of Laurel's hand brought a smile to his face. As the moon rose and the stars sprinkled the night sky, Laurel and Mac found themselves back on their front porch.

"Look, Mac. There's Fomalhaut, your favorite star."

"Not any more, wife. You've made me lose all interest in that lonely, solitary star. I can't relate to Fomalhaut anymore."

~

THE END of the school term vanished with activity. The students were busy and excited. The progress made each school day removed all doubt Laurel's her first year at Shiloh school would be deemed a success. Only two issues nagged her. Each day the temperatures dropped a bit and heavy frost blanketed the ground. Fewer students came to school. Students were sick more often, and the travel became more difficult. Laurel prayed the weather would hold. The students wanted so much to have their end of school celebration on December 23. So, did Laurel.

The second thing bothered her more. That morning she had once again caught sight of a strange man at the bend in the road just below the churchyard. Laurel felt sure she had seen him before. He did nothing but stand beside his horse and look at her. His hat slanted down to shadow most of his face. When they made eye contact, the stranger bowed, mounted his horse, and rode away from the school.

The Saturday night before Christmas, Laurel spent the evening working on the party. She made lists, sketched diagrams, and rummaged through her bureaus. She couldn't finish one project before she began another.

"Mac, darling, I am so excited!"

"What brought all this about?"

"The end-of-term party. I've got so much to do. I want everything to be perfect."

"It won't have to be. Everyone will enjoy one last party before the weather gets harsh."

He walked over to the table where Laurel was working on a holly arrangement for the church altar. He put his arms around her and pulled her closer.

"You know when the ice and snow come, we pretty much have to hibernate until spring. I know I'm gonna like winter this year."

"Oh, you. At the party, the children will sing and act out the

Christmas story for their families. My sixth-level students wrote the pageant this year, and it is precious. My Sunday school class is going to read the Scripture. I am planning to make wassail for everyone." She pulled away and went to the kitchen. "I do hope I can find an orange I can stud with cloves. I've saved cinnamon to use too. I want to..."

Mac put his finger to Laurel's mouth. "Not tonight. I'm building a fire in our bedroom and putting another blanket on the four-poster. I want to go to bed, and I want you to keep me warm. Now, put your fancies away and come along, wife. You've paid enough attention to your Christmas planning for one night. I'm thinking I'd like some of that attention, too."

AT THE CLOSE of Sunday services, Matthew invited everyone to attend the Christmas pageant of Shiloh school on Wednesday evening at 5:30. The church planned a combined event marking not only the Holy season, but also the commencement celebration of the eighth-level students and end-of-term party. Sunday morning was mild and sunny, so the congregation turned out in force. The enthusiastic applause foretold a good attendance at the party and the commencement.

Laurel was more than excited to celebrate her first Christmas at Shiloh. This pageant would be very much like the ones she remembered from her childhood at Hawthorn. A smile lit her face and green flashed in her eyes.

She and Mac had worked every night for the previous two weeks. No Shiloh child would leave the celebration without a Christmas stocking filled with small gifts, fruit, hard candy, and nuts. She reminded Mac at least a dozen times to bring home the apples and oranges they had ordered from St. Louis. Mr. McCollough told her they'd come with the freight on Monday, so Mac would make the trip to Greensboro on Tuesday.

Some students made paper decorations to hang around the church. Other students adorned pine cones with bits of ribbon and holly berries. These were to be presented as gifts, along with poems they'd done as a class assignment. The ladies of Shiloh promised a potluck dinner to rival any Christmas feast known in the area. Laurel's excitement was more childlike than that of any of her students.

Her excitement flowed over into her home as well. She walked through nearby woods searching for cedar boughs, mistletoes, and glossy holly with red berries. She'd use these natural ornaments to dress the sturdy mantles above her fireplaces. Laurel planned to encircle the red cut crystal lamps with dark evergreen and holly. Mac's mother's lamps, which he brought from Maryland, would hold the place of honor at the center of the dinner table. These were traditions from her past. Her day of searching allowed special memories of Christmases past to surface. Laurel intended to create those kinds of wonderful memories with Mac in the home he built for her. She would know exactly where to find them Christmas Eve morning when she was ready decorate her home. She planned a special breakfast when she and Mac would share their private time at Christmas. They'd promised to spend Christmas day at the Campbell homestead.

As busy as her time had been, Laurel managed to find enough lone time to make two small Christmas gifts for Mac. She planned to give them to her husband at their Christmas breakfast. She decorated two small pieces of paper with some homemade dyes. She copied Scriptures telling of angels and stars in red to finish the wrapping paper for Mac's gifts. The final detail was red ribbons she'd found during her last trip to Greensboro. She could hardly contain her excitement.

On Tuesday, the day before the Shiloh Christmas party, Mac came into the cabin from the barn. "Laurel, you take the Bolivar wagon to school today. The temperature is not too low right now, but there is a light drizzling rain. The awning will give you some cover if the rain gets worse."

"That silly looking wagon? I can't believe you've kept it all this time."

"Please, humor me, wife. I don't want you sick at Christmas time." Laurel grudgingly agreed to drive the shed on wheels to school.

Even in the bad weather, most Shiloh students tried to get to school that day. They knew activities to prepare for the celebration the next day were important. The day before, Brother Matthew said he'd hold final practice right after their noon meal. Their pastor and teacher planned a very special program and Christmas concert. They practiced for weeks. Every child in the school was playing some part in the pageant. Some were angels, and other were sheep, but each knew the part was important to the program. Brother Matthew and Mrs. Mac showed them the need for every part to insure the best performance.

Laurel did not entirely neglect the lessons, though. She listened to the younger students during their reading lesson. Then she made sure the graduating seniors practiced their commencement speeches. Those would be the highlights of the entire Christmas celebration.

The snow began falling about 9:30. Between tasks, Laurel went to the window to look out. The flakes were huge and fluffy, but luckily, they were melting as they fell. At noon, Laurel sent David out to bring in water for lunch. The tall young man came back sooner than she'd expected.

"Mrs. Mac, there's ice all over the wood stack, and the well's got a sheet of ice all over it. This water is icy."

Laurel went to the porch. She gasped at the cold and the ferocity of the northern wind gusting across the valley. The rain from the morning had now changed to sleet and ice. The ground was glazed over. Laurel pulled her wool shawl closer around her and returned to the classroom. Most of the students walked to school because their families didn't own spare animals for them to ride. A few of the parents brought the small children so they could practice for the concert, but none had stayed to take them back home.

Laurel made too many trips to the window. Her students became restless. She didn't know how to assure their safety. If she kept them at school, they could stay warm. Yet, she knew parents would worry. If she sent them home, would they all be able to get back to their homesteads? She decided to wait for her Uncle Matthew to ask his advice.

Shortly after the noon break, Matthew Campbell arrived. "Laurel, I'm sorry I didn't get here earlier. I just came from Greensboro. We've got to get these children home. This storm's not near over. No doubt, it'll last through the night. Let's pray this ice turns to snow soon."

"Uncle Matthew, some of these children live more than three miles away. We can't send them out to walk home in this ice."

"Laurel Grace, we won't let them. You take the kids that live east of here in your covered wagon. I'll take the others in my wagon and cover them with this oil cloth." They hurried the children into the wagons. Icy rain came down even harder. Laurel loaded nine students in her wagon. As she put them inside the little box on wheels, she whispered a word of thanks for the ridiculous little wagon. Even before they had gotten from the churchyard, two parents on horseback rode up to get their children. Matthew was happy to see Rafe Johnston, as his homestead set far back from the main road. Larry Gibson had ridden his plow mule to get his six-year-old. Still, nineteen students needed safe transportation through the frigid, wet afternoon.

Laurel drove at the fastest pace she dared. In about half an hour, she had delivered three children to their porches. Parents called out thanks as they rushed their trembling children into the warmth of their cabins. As the sleet continued, Laurel found more difficulty keeping the wagon on the road. Every blast of wind tried to push the wagon into a ditch. She slowed Sassy to a walk to keep her charges safe. At three o'clock, four more children were home, but Cathy and Roy Dunn remained in the box wagon. They lived the farthest from the school. They had only been able to come to school that day because a neighbor had driven them.

"Cathy, are you and Roy all right back there?"

"I'm awful cold, Mrs. Mac. I'm shakin' so hard."

"I know it's cold, Cathy." Under the tin roof, there was nothing to keep them warm. Their jackets were far too thin and threadbare to be of much comfort. "Here, Roy, take this shawl and hug your sister up real close and cover yourselves. I'll have you home soon." Laurel handed her woolen shawl back and returned her attention to the road. She dreaded the steep hill about half a mile from the Dunn cabin. Laurel would have to lead Sassy up that incline if she were to make it to the top in the rain and sleet.

At the bottom of the hill, Laurel climbed from the wagon seat. Until then, the bright yellow awning had been a god-send to her, and she was dry. Her dry coat was warm enough, but as Laurel lead the little mare up the hill, the rain and cold began to take its toll on her. Her teeth began to chatter, and chill gripped her. What if she couldn't to get the Dunns back to the safety of their grandmother? The sun was now obscured by the heavy cloud cover, and the dark began to fall much earlier than usual.

"Please, Lord, help me get these children home." With chattering teeth, she murmured. "Father, give me the strength to keep them safe."

~

BY THIS TIME, Matthew had returned to the church. While he'd had several more students to deliver, he'd made the trip quicker. When he reached the churchyard, he saw Mac riding up the Greensboro road. "Where is Laurel, Matthew? I came from our place, and she's not home yet."

"She left about one o'clock, taking the kids home down the east road. I thought she'd beat me back. She didn't have as many kids and about a half-mile shorter distance to travel."

"Which kids did she take?"

"The ones that lived the farthest would be the Dunns. You know the Widow Dunn lives up that slope from Big Creek."

"See to your family. I'm going after her. She may be in trouble."

Matthew called after Mac as he rode away, "Lord keep you." Mac didn't hear as his attention was on the road east.

~

AT 4:30, Laurel stopped Sassy at the Dunn's doorstep. She went to the wagon door and picked Cathy up and motioned for Roy to run to the porch as fast as he could. Laurel carried Cathy to the arms of her grandmother.

"Lord love you, Missy. I was so afraid for my young'uns. I didn't have no way to bring them home. God bless you, Mrs. Mac. You've always been so good to us."

Mrs. Dunn rushed her grandchildren into the cabin. She began to strip off the wet shoes and coats from them as they huddled near the roaring fire, warming themselves. "Here, Mrs. Mac, you need your shawl back. You're so wet and cold. Come over here, Missy, and warm yourself. Take off those wet clothes and let me spread them to dry. You sit there on the hearth while get your clothes dried out."

"Thank you, Mrs. Dunn, but no. I need to return home because others will come searching for me if I don't."

"Well, here take this old quilt to warm yourself then." Mrs. Dodd took the quilt from the only double bed in the cabin. Laurel feared she didn't have enough covers, and the quilt may be the only one she had for her bed.

"No, no, sister Dunn. Thank you for offering, but I have a lap robe in the wagon, and my shawl is wool and very warm. Roy, you need to get in lots of wood for the night. You will need plenty, I'm thinking."

Laurel left the little cabin, using her damp shawl to cover her head. She turned Sassy around and climbed back into the wagon seat. Now the light was gone. Heavy cloud cover and continuing rain obscured any hope of moonlight or stars to help guide her. Laurel urged Sassy into a slow walk back down the slope. She tried to ride a short distance but realized Sassy was afraid to descend the hill alone. Laurel again climbed down from the wagon seat and lead her horse down the slippery road. She didn't know what time it was, nor did she know how far from home she was, but she continued to plod onward. At least she knew the way. Mac's words from the other night came back to her. He had said that even though we live in a real world, the Lord's grace is enough for us. She pushed her cold and fear away and continued to put one foot in front of the other. To keep her mind off the cold, she began to sing the Christmas carols she and her uncle had taught her class. "Silent night, holy night. All is calm, all is bright." At the base of the steep hill, she climbed back into the wagon seat and drove toward Shiloh.

After what seemed to Laurel to be an eternity, she thought she saw a light in the distance. Was it light in a cabin where she could stop and warm herself before she started home again? She urged Sassy into a little quicker pace. As she did, the wagon began to slide on the treacherous road. Before she realized it, the wheels fell into a steep ditch, and Sassy broke from her harness. The wagon, painted in all its circus colors, lay in pieces at the bottom of the ravine. The little mare, frightened by the loose reins, stamped the ground. Sassy reared more than once. Still, she didn't run away.

"Sassy Lady, calm down, sweet friend. Be still and calm." Laurel pulled herself up from the ditch and hurried to her scared horse. She couldn't let Sassy run from her, for she well knew she could not walk all the way back to Shiloh. She soothed the mare, climbed onto Sassy's bare back, and rode again toward the light at the distance. To keep her hope strong, she started singing again. "We three kings of Orient are...."

After several minutes, Laurel heard Mac calling out to her. "Laurel Grace, please answer me if you can hear." Mac carried a glowing tar-fed torch, which provided little light in the wet cold night. By providence, there was enough that Laurel saw the glow a long way back and had ridden toward him. By the time they met, her strength had all but left her. The cold had taken all the feeling from her arms and legs.

"Thank God, you've come, Mac. I thought I'd never get home." Mac pulled a blanket from his saddlebag, covered his wife, and took the reins of her horse to lead her back home. By the time they had reached their cabin, both were near frostbite. Mac carried Laurel into the bedroom, stripped off her wet clothes, and tucked her into their bed.

"I'll build a fire as soon as I put the horses away. Stay covered and I'll be back soon."

Laurel's chills shook the sturdy tall bed. She fell into a feverish sleep and was unaware when Mac returned to the cabin. She tossed, turned, and shook for what seemed to be hours. She dreamed of a frozen waste land where she was stung repeatedly by needles of ice. She often whimpered in pain as the sensation returned to her fingers and toes. At last though, she rested. The roaring fire, several blankets, and a quilt warmed her. She lost her fear of the frozen waste land she'd dreamt of. When she was warm, she found the sanctuary she'd sought in her dream. She slept well into the morning, and when she awoke, she lay in Mac's arms. Regardless of the raging storm outside, she was safe and warm...home at Shiloh.

THE RAIN STOPPED mid-morning on Christmas Eve. The bitter cold did not. The view from the cabin porch was incredible. The beauty of the ice-clad limbs and branches sparkled as the breeze whisked them back and forth. Northeast Arkansas had dodged a major ice storm. Only an hour or so more, and the drizzling rain would have added more weight than the tree limbs could bear. The trees would have become deadly instead of beautiful. Mac and Laurel walked to the barn to feed the animals and break the ice in their water trough. Immediately, they noticed how frigid the day was. Not even the brightness of the sun permeated the northern winds, which seemed to hurl ice shards everywhere.

"Laurel, please help me spread extra bedding for these animals. I don't remember it ever being this cold since I came to Shiloh. Thank the Lord, I haven't brought a herd here yet."

"Mac, things will be all right now, won't they? I mean since the rain stopped."

"We were lucky. Another couple of hours, and the ice would have played havoc with the forest. Ice laden limbs kill."

They worked to finish the outside chores. Laurel began to shake again. Even dressed in her worn her old dungarees and flannel work shirt, the attire was no match for the extreme cold. "Laurel, grab extra firewood and get back to the house. You've not warmed yourself from yesterday's soakin' yet!"

She carried an extra load of wood into the cabin. Mac followed shortly with even more firewood.

"Mac, what are we going to do about our Christmas program and the frolic? We have all the gifts for the children."

"We'll keep them for a late celebration. No one will be out in this weather. The roads are treacherous, and the cold worse. I'm afraid the only Christmas company you'll have this year is me, darlin'."

"Well, I guess you'll do. I didn't even get my cedar boughs for the mantle or the holly berries for the table, or one limb of mistletoe. My mama always hung mistletoe over the door at Christmas."

"Don't you fret, not one little bit. You don't need it." Mac drew his dungaree clad wife into his arms and kissed her. "Have I told you today that you are beautiful?"

"Don't be ridiculous. I look like a field hand."

"It's the way you looked when I found you. Well, not exactly. That day you wore your hair in that dreadful coronet, and you had on those useless glasses."

"It seems a lifetime ago, but it's been less than a year. I'm not sure I'm even that same person."

"You are. The good, faithful, beautiful, intelligent, desirable woman I was meant to share my life with. St. Nicholas brought me exactly what I wanted, a few days to spend with you, the two of us alone."

"Goodness, sir! So bold a declaration! Remember I am a married lady."

"And I thank goodness you are. And married to me." Mac again demonstrated his affection and desire for his bride.

Mac and Laurel spent their first Christmas Eve alone but didn't notice the isolation. Mac plucked the large goose he'd shot that morning on the pond in the south meadow. Laurel blended walnuts, flour, cinnamon, butter, milk, and a precious jar of the apples into a large apple cake. At mid-morning, she mixed the yeast into her dough, making rolls to take to her Aunt Ellie's Christmas dinner. Of course, they wouldn't be able to go. Regardless, she carried the cloth-covered bowl to the hearth so the dough would rise. As they worked, she and Mac told each other stories of Christmases past. They shared tales of the people from their youth whom they loved and missed. The couple lost track of time.

After finishing the work, they sat together and read a recent copy of the Arkansas Gazette. Mac had found it in Greensboro earlier in the week. The paper, dated November 27, was a rare treat because it was a recent newspaper. Mac commented about the state of politics in Arkansas. A lead story reported widespread discontent in the southwest, northeast, and north central parts of Arkansas. The people from those areas felt ignored by the state government. Laurel asked several questions and listened intently to everything Mac answered for her. Laurel's attentiveness was not lost on her husband.

Until early evening, they laughed, talked, and speculated on their future. While they talked, they shared frequent touches and tender embraces. Mac sat back in his armed chair in front of the blazing fire with his long legs resting on the hearth. The Christmas aromas of cinnamon and fruit, the warmth from the fire, the rose-colored aura from the ruby lamp, and Laurel's touches filled his senses. He closed his eyes and basked in the atmosphere of his home. He heard Laurel's soft sigh. This day had been the living out of his dream. He had no sense of the restlessness or hint of loneliness he'd carried with him before his trip across the state. Mac felt his roots belonged at Shiloh now. The love growing between him and Laurel was the home he'd wanted. He would be home anywhere and anytime as long as his wife was part of his life. She would be with him every day until April when school began in the spring. He whispered, "My dearest Lord. Thank you. Life is so good. How can I be so blessed?" Mac napped.

About dusk, the MacLaynes arose from their Christmas Eve naps and realized daylight was near gone. Mack pulled on his heavy coat and went to the back door, planning to do his evening chores. "My goodness, Laurel. How long has it been raining again?"

Laurel walked over to join him. The cold was even more brutal than she'd remembered from the morning and a heavy drizzle was falling. The trees bordering their yard were so laden with ice that the limbs bent almost to the ground. When Laurel went to the wood stack for another arm load of wood, the sleet stung her face and hands. The wind was gale-like as the sun sank below the horizon.

"Laurel, go back in the kitchen. I'll bring in more wood when I return from the barn. I don't want you chilled again." Mac ran to the barn to feed the livestock and milk the cow. Since he'd laid more bedding that morning, finishing evening chores took only a few minutes. He made three trips into the falling sleet to lay in the wood they'd need to keep the cabin warm through the night. "Laurel, I hope you are up to eating a lot of yeast rolls. I am afraid our trip to the Campbells' tomorrow won't be happening. I am sorry. I know you were looking forward to being with your family this year."

Laurel helped Mac remove his icy work coat, and she took his frozen hat and hung the two pieces on the pegs near the door. She walked to her husband and put her arms around him. "Patrick MacLayne, I will be with my family tomorrow. As long as you are with me, that is all I need to celebrate Christmas. I love you."

"Wife, the Word is all so true. All things work for good for those who love the Lord.' This year He has provided the best for me. Today has been a living out of my dream."

Tears filled Laurel's eyes. She turned to look out the window in their sitting room. She looked out toward the ice laden trees that bordered the front of their yard. Mac walked up behind her and wrapped his arms around her. They stood in the embrace for some time--just enjoying the moment.

"Husband, read me the Christmas story, while I punch down the yeast dough for our Christmas rolls."

As the domestic scene unrolled inside the MacLayne's cabin, beyond the walls, the ice storm grew worse. The wind howled and the ice thickened on every surface outside. Laurel covered her pan of rolls with the cloth and again set them back to rise once again. She made stew for supper and baked a pan of cornbread. As content as she had been all day, an eerie feeling settled over her. The wind roared outside and a harsh staccato of sleet beat against the glass panes of their windows.

After they went to bed, a sharp recoil, followed by an extended crackling sound, came from the back yard. Laurel bolted straight up in bed. "Mac, is that a rifle shot? Do you think someone out in the storm is in trouble?"

"Darlin', those are tree limbs falling under the weight of the ice. If this storm doesn't pass soon, I'm afraid we'll find major damage all around the ridge. The forest damage will be bad. Even worse, friends may lose herds and even their buildings that are too near falling trees."

Throughout the night, the death knells of ice-covered trees echoed across the valley. Mac got up several times during the night to stoke the fire and to put more wood in both fireplaces. Laurel knew he worried about the excessive damage the storm was bringing. At dawn, no longer able to hide his concern, Mac arose and put on his heavy coat and went out to assess the damage. At first, he stood speechless in the beauty of nature that surrounded him. The ice on the bushes and trees sparkled in the bright sunlight. The snow that had fallen after the rain, now covered the ground with a pristine blanket of white. He didn't know the extent of the damage from the number of crashes he'd heard throughout the night. The sight of his undamaged barn called forth a prayer of gratitude.

He continued toward the barn and as he reached the door, he heard another crashing oak tree from across the yard. Yet, his barn still stood through the storm and all the animals remained unharmed. A quick scan of the yard showed Mac that he had so much more to be grateful for. While many of the larger trees bordering the yard had lost limbs, none of them had split or toppled. He spoke a quick word of thanksgiving and offered a quick prayer his homestead had fared so well.

"Well, darlin', the storm could have been worse. Thank the Lord, the sun is out, and the rain clouds are gone from the area."

Removing his coat, he saw Laurel had already dressed in her Sunday best. Her yeast rolls baked in the hearth oven, and the aroma of hot coffee and cinnamon wafted through the room. He heard the sizzle of bacon and watched Laurel pull fresh hot cinnamon rolls out to cool on the hearth. "Mac, go get cleaned up. I've poured you a warm bath in the washroom, and your broad coat is on the bed. Even if we have to celebrate alone, we will dress for the Lord's birthday."

By the time, Mac returned, dressed and groomed to a tee, Laurel place a huge meal on the table. She had prepared bacon, oatmeal, and eggs to go along with the cinnamon rolls. The goose was roasting over the spit in the fireplace and a pot of beans simmered. She intended that they would have their Christmas feast, even if only two shared the bounty.

They sat down to breakfast and offered thanks for the day and the Gift of Christmas. "Lord, You bless us beyond measure. Thank you for the greatest gifts, Your Son and His unwarranted sacrifice for us. Thank You for our protection in the storm last night. Bless this food, and we ask You to make us better servants for Your kingdom. Amen."

Mac reached over and kissed Laurel. Over her shoulder, Mac saw two small gifts tied with red ribbon. "Merry Christmas, wife."

"And to you. Here, let me pour you a cup of coffee."

"Let's go sit by the fire, Laurel. I saw the presents. I love presents. Have ever since I was a little tyke. Christmas morning is my favorite day of the year." He took a small box from his jacket pocket. "You liked the old things I gave you." He picked up her hand and kissed her wedding band. "I hope you like this as much."

Laurel untied the ribbon and took the lid from the small box. Inside was a beautiful gold crucifix attached to a long onyx rosary. Laurel had never seen a more beautiful prayer chain in her life.

"Laurel, I looked for something new to give you, but nothing seemed right. You aren't Catholic, but I knew you'd treasure this rosary. My mother loved it and asked me to see that you got it. Mother had two, one from her father and one from my father. I have the other in my Bible."

"Mac! How precious, you'd share your mother's rosary with me. Thank you, thank you so much."

Mac broke in… "Well, what about me. Don't I get to open one of those?"

"Such a poor gift after this priceless treasure you have given me."

"Nonsense. Let me open my present." Laurel handed him the larger of the two bundles. Mac ripped off the paper she'd spent so much time preparing. Inside, he found a long scarf, knitted from storm blue wool, the color Laurel associated with his eyes. "What a timely gift, wife. How did you know we would have an ice storm and I'd need this fine scarf? When on earth did you find time to knit such a fine scarf?" Mac smiled. He threw it around his neck and walked to the mirror above the sideboard. "Don't I look fine?"

"I have another present for you, too."

"Well, give it to me, woman. I love presents." Laurel handed Mac the tiny wrapped package from the hearth.

"Merry Christmas, Patrick."

Again, he ripped open package. Nestled in the paper, he found two white crocheted booties. For a moment, he didn't grasp the significance of the gift, but then …"Laurel Grace, are you… are we…are you telling me you are with child?"

Laurel looked into his storm blue eyes and smiled.

"My precious Lord! I don't know what to say. Thank you, wife. I've never had a more wonderful Christmas!" Mac pulled Laurel to him and buried his face in her hair. Silent tears of joy streamed down his face. The joy he felt only the previous night paled in comparison to the emotions he felt that moment. Laurel was giving him a child. His joy burst forth in laughter.

"Darlin' woman, for the first time in my life, I don't have the words. My cup runneth over! I didn't know anyone could feel such joy this side of Heaven. God bless you, dear wife. Thank you." Again, Mac's joyous laughter filled the cabin.

"When? How long?"

"Best I can figure, we'll need a cradle around the middle of June."

# CHAPTER EIGHT

*Have I not commanded thee?...Be strong and of a good courage;*
*be not afraid neither be thou dismayed: For the Lord, thy God is with thee*
*wheresoever thou goest.*
*Joshua 1:9*

When Laurel and Mac arose the day after Christmas, the sun was shining. As far as they could see, ice and snow covered everything. And while the sunlight reflected from every surface, the intense cold showed no sign of abating that day. When Mac went to the barn to feed the stock, he found the water frozen solid. He knew he'd have to thaw enough water for the animals to drink. He returned to the fire in the cabin and stood rubbing his hands before the blaze.

"This cold could be deadly, Laurel. I'm worried about our church family. So many trees fell and are still falling. I hope no one's cabin has taken a hit."

"What can we do? Should we ride over to Uncle Matthew's to see if we can help?"

"Too cold for us to ride that far. The icy roads may be too slippery for the horses. I'm not sure what we should do. Let's wait until noon and perhaps the temperature will rise."

"Someone could be hurt. Let's go in the wagon. The mules are more surefooted than the horses."

"My dear wife, you will stay here in the warmth and safety of our home. You have to take care of my baby."

"Mac! This child is months from being here. I can help and no harm will come to either of us. We can wrap in the bearskin and blankets and go to check on our neighbors. We'll only be gone a couple of hours."

"No, Laurel. I won't take you out in this cold." Laurel had never heard Mac speak to her in that tone of voice. "I'll wait until noon and then I'll go. You will stay at home." Mac took the kettle of boiling water from the spit and rushed back to the barn to melt the water in the animals' trough. He spread fresh hay for bedding, milked the cow as fast as the process could be done, gathered a half-dozen eggs, and returned to the warmth of the cabin. At least the fire was warm even if the attitude of his wife had cooled a great deal. "Laurel, I didn't mean to speak so harshly to you, but I can't let you endanger your health. You've already come close to frostbite once this week."

They passed an uncomfortable three hours, the tension between them obvious. Finally, Laurel ended the silence. "Patrick, I know you are trying to protect me, but please don't ask me to stay here alone. I can help if there's a problem. I'll stay at the church while you make the rounds. It's only one short mile to Shiloh church."

"Laurel Grace, I'm only thinking of your welfare." She lowered her eyes and waited.

"All right, you can ride with me, but only to the church. If anyone is in need, we'll bring them there." Within a few minutes, Laurel dressed in her warmest clothes, including her wool coat with an extra shawl draped over her head and shoulders. She grabbed quilts from the linen drawer of her mother's walnut bureau. She poured a canteen of hot coffee from the pot. The brew wouldn't stay hot long, but even tepid coffee would be welcome in the bitter cold.

Mac prepared the little wagon, placing the old bearskin across the seat. He hitched the mules to the wagon that had brought them across the state, hoping he was making all the effort for naught. Yet while he hoped for the best, he knew he had to prepare for the worst. In the frontier, people had to take care of each other should the need arise. Laurel approached carrying a small basket of leftovers and the canteen of coffee. Mac lifted her onto the wagon seat and covered her with the bearskin.

The one-mile trip to Shiloh was slow and treacherous. The road, even though it was one of the better ones in the entire area, proved to be a nightmare. Ice, inches thick, covered the pathway. Mac stopped three times to pull fallen branches and limbs off the road. In several areas, the mules balked at the slippery conditions, and Mac was forced to encourage them with a flap of the reins on their haunches. Even then, the mules would not pull the wagon up the hillside to the front of the church building. Mac got down and walked, tugging at the reins to lead the frightened animals the last hundred feet to the steps. They made six or seven steps ahead. Then Mac fell on the ice. He realized why the mules had balked at pulling their load to the church doors.

"Are you all right, Mac?"

"Only my pride, but I'm sure I'll have some nice bruises tomorrow." He pulled himself up and walked to the wagon to lift Laurel down. "We'll walk from here...slow and careful." He pulled her into the crook of his arm and supported her every step to the porch. Someone had partially cleared a path up the three steps to the porch. At the church, Matthew Campbell had already built a fire in the stove. The sanctuary was far from warm yet, but the room would be tolerable soon.

"I'm glad to see you, Mac. At least I know part of my congregation is well and able. But Laurel Grace, what foolishness has brought you outside this morning? Don't you know how difficult it is for Mac to have to support you and himself on this ice? It's too dangerous."

Laurel looked at Mac and saw concern on his face. She understood now why he had been so adamant about her staying home. She was almost sorry she had pleaded with him to come. In her attempt to be self-sufficient, she'd given no thought that she might need care herself. She scolded herself silently because she hadn't considered Mac's feelings and concerns.

"Is your family all right, Uncle Matthew?" She wanted to divert the attention from herself.

"We've had some damage, but our cabin and the barn are still in one piece so we were spared the worst. I pray the same is true of all the Shiloh people. I hated to cancel our Christmas program. Blessedly, the storm started early enough no one got caught outside."

"Have you heard from any of our folks?"

"Only the Stephensons. Hugh rode by earlier and said there was plenty of damage over toward his place, but his family is fine."

"Do you think we need to make the rounds? We have several older folks who may need some help."

"As much as I dread going out in this cold, you're right. Laurel Grace, can you stay here and keep a fire going? If someone is in need, I'm sure they'll try to make their way here."

"She can indeed." Mac gave her no opportunity to answer for herself, and she made no effort to respond.

"Don't forget you have coffee in the wagon, and please be careful." Laurel brushed the back of her hand against Mac's beard, wrapped his new scarf around his neck, and tucked the ends under his coat. "I love you, Patrick."

Matthew Campbell and Mac drove away from Shiloh, beginning a long circuit to visit the older members of the congregation. Matt prayed with each blustery gust of wind that their trek would be useless. Laurel, in the meantime, decided to put the time to good use. School was over until late spring when planting season ended. They wouldn't need the school materials and books for several months. She set about storing the books and other school items that belonged to the Shiloh subscription school. She placed most of them behind the pulpit and in the tiny coat room off the front door. She carefully removed the prized maps hanging near the slate board. She wrapped them in an old sheet kept for that purpose. She was so proud to have maps of such good quality to use in her teaching, and she certainly wanted to assure they would survive for many years. Shortly, the room looked much more like a church and less as the classroom she'd left. She intended to speak to her uncle about holding a celebration for the four students who finished their coursework. Finishing school deserved recognition. Perhaps, they would set aside a Sunday for them.

When the clutter was removed, she noticed the room could use a good cleaning as well. Having little else to occupy her time, she dusted and cleaned each surface she could reach. She even melted some snow and used the warm water to clean the windows inside the now warm sanctuary. The Shiloh community saved special offerings for several years to purchase the glass-paned windows in their church. She tackled the insides of all the lantern globes which hung down from the ceiling, even though it required her to stand on the desktops. She would not want her students to see that! Satisfied with those chores finished, she dusted and polished the pews and pulpit. Finally, she swept the floor. At last, she couldn't find one more thing to clean or polish. She looked through the newly washed window and saw the sun setting below Crowley's Ridge. She'd been so filled with nervous energy, she'd paid little attention to the time passing. On the back wall, she saw the school clock mark the time as 4:45. It would be dark soon.

Laurel had filled the stove with wood twice during the day, and the fire was again burning low. She went to the back porch to bring in firewood and saw the wood box would be empty after one more trip. She prayed Mac and her uncle would be back soon, but in case they didn't arrive before dark, she decided to bring in enough wood to fill the wood box on the back porch. She bundled herself well. Holding firmly to the porch rail, Laurel stepped from the back porch and walked tentatively across the yard toward the wood stacks. The Shiloh family provided for the church well by bringing wood as part of their tithes each fall. Because of the snow drifts, walking was much easier than it had been on the ice-covered path in front of the church. Laurel made three trips back and forth from the wood stacks to the back porch. She went back one more time to bring in several logs to place on the fire inside.

She was cold. She tightened her shawl around her head and shoulders, picked up several logs, and then stopped in her tracks. A tremendous crash sounded at the left side of the church. Thick ice-laden branches, several inches thick fell within inches of the log building. Laurel crouched at the recoil of the snapping branch. She whispered a prayer of thanksgiving. Shiloh Church had been spared. Even in her somewhat shaken state, she stiffened her resolve to finish her task. She picked up two of the logs she had dropped and walked back toward the porch. As she took the first step up the back porch, she heard the moaning split of another large hickory nearby. She screamed and dropped to the ground again. Several smaller branches from the much larger limb fell atop Laurel. The ice broke away and felt like shards of glass where it touched her face and neck. At first, Laurel felt pinned to the ground. Stunned, she fell in and out of awareness for several minutes. "Get yourself up, girl." That thought turned in her mind over and over. Shortly, she pushed her way back to clarity. She had to get back to the warmth of the stove inside the church. Her unborn baby was in danger. She cried out, "Lord, please help me."

Laurel began to push the limbs away. Shortly, she freed her arms and shoulders from the icy debris, but one of her knees was trapped by a larger part of a branch. She picked up one of the logs she'd carried from the wood stack and used it to beat the branch until it broke. Only then did she notice how dark it had become and how cold she felt. She pushed herself up and salvaged the two logs she'd dropped. With some pain, she managed to pull her way up the back porch to the door.

Grace had saved her. The back porch of the church had taken the brunt of the weight from the split hickory tree. Using the door jamb, she was able to pull herself up and push open the back door. Her clothes were wet from the ice that had melted from her body heat. However, to her great relief, she was able to walk with some support, and she didn't seem to have any serious injuries. Picking up the logs, she made her way to the stove and pushed both of them inside. Her knees were shaking so badly, they'd not hold her, and she sat flat on the floor, gasping at the comical fall she'd taken. With her limbs splayed wildly in all directions, she began to laugh. "Thank you, Lord, even for the humor. You have spared me and my child. Praise be, Lord, how often you take care of me!"

In a few minutes, Laurel was warm again. She arose and lit one of the lanterns near the stove. The sun had fallen below the western horizon now, and neither Matthew nor Mac had returned. Her imagination began to tell horror stories of what may have happened to them. "My Grace is sufficient for you." The Scripture brought her comfort, and she pushed the dark thoughts away. She noticed she was hungry. She took one of the yeast rolls and a few bits of the goose from the small bundle she'd taken from the basket in the wagon. She laid them on the stove to warm. She had no milk, but she drank a bit of melted snow. She rolled herself in the one blanket she'd removed from the wagon and sat down on the floor near the fire. She waited. After what seemed an eternity, she got up to retrieve a Bible from the pulpit so she could read. She opened the book to the middle and found Psalms 16. At first, her mind would not focus on the words. *Where is Patrick? Is he safe?* Deliberately, she spoke aloud, "Stop it. Laurel Grace Campbell, remember Whose you are!" She returned to the Scripture again.

> *Preserve me, O God: for in thee do I put my trust....*
> *I will bless the Lord, who hath given me counsel: my reins also instruct me in the night seasons.*
> *I have set the Lord always before me: because he is at my right hand, I shall not be moved.*
> *Therefore, my heart is glad, and my glory rejoiceth: my flesh also shall rest in hope.*
> *For thou wilt not leave my soul in hell; neither wilt thou suffer thine Holy One to see corruption.*
> *Thou wilt shew me the path of life: in thy presence is [fulness] of joy; at thy right hand there are pleasures for evermore.*

David's words brought her comfort. She felt the peace she needed. She curled up and slept, knowing in her heart that her loved ones were in God's hands.

MATTHEW AND MAC'S day had not been as productive. They made their way to the homesteads of the older members of the congregation. The people in each place they stopped reported all were safe. Damage had been widespread throughout the community, though. The Shepherd family had lost their milk cow when an ancient pine had collapsed on their barn. The Fergusons lost a tool shed. Lars Anderson reported that two of his 'stupid' pigs had gotten away from their cover and had frozen to death. The Smith's cabin had been damaged when a large oak split and fell onto their second pen. Luckily, they were able to keep warm inside the main room of their cabin. Other families told of their terrifying night. The men were plied with food and hot drinks to help them along their difficult trek. They stopped just long enough to warm themselves, eat a bit, and then return to the cold. They were grateful all were well so far and hoped to find the next family well and warm.

As the sun reached the western horizon, they saw the Dunn's cabin. Matthew lit a tar-fed torch he'd brought to provide light if they were not able to return to Shiloh before dark. At the foot of the steep hill, Mac stepped down to guide the mules to the door of the single pen cabin. Matthew also jumped down to steady the nervous, tired animals. After about four steps, Matt stumbled on a large rock on the side of the road and fell.

"Tarnation! What in the devil are we doing out here?"

"Matthew, you surprise me!"

"I'll ask forgiveness later when my teeth stop chattering. Mac, I don't see a light at the Dunn's cabin. Do you?"

"No, brother, I don't see any light." Mac threw the reins around the porch post and climbed the stairs to open the door. Both men picked up their pace as their concern for the widow and her grandchildren grew. "Widow Dunn...Roy, are y'all okay?"

There was no reply. Matthew called out, "Roy, Cathy...It's Brother Matthew. Are you okay?"

A timid voice replied from the bed. "Brother Matthew. We've been so scared. Grandma's been gone for such a long, long time."

"I went out and hollered and hollered for her, Mr. Mac. I walked around the yard until I couldn't stand the cold no more. I looked for her and called out, but I didn't hear nothing but the wind and cracking branches."

"Why did she go out, Roy?"

"She went out a little before noon. The fire was getting low, and she wanted to fix us something to eat. She told us to stay in and try to keep the fire stoked. That wood burned out a long time ago."

"Mr. Mac, can you find our grandma?"

"We'll go look for her, Cathy."

Matt and Mac took the tar-fed torches from the porch where they'd left them and walked toward the barn. The night sky was clear and well-lit with a bright moon and hundreds of starts. In the twilight, they saw dozens of ancient trees surrounding the Dunn farm. Many lay in broken heaps. Whole trees, huge branches, and a myriad of branches had fallen across the length of the yard.

"Widow Dunn, can you hear me?" Matthew's call went unanswered. He went into the barn and found the stock safe. They needed fresh water and feed, but the roof was intact. "She's not in the barn, Mac."

"I'll find the wood stack. Maybe she is there." Mac headed toward the stacks of cordwood while the preacher went to the well to bring water for the animals. He'd only finished filling the trough when Mac called to him. "Matthew, come help me."

The widow lay beneath a large oak tree, uprooted with the weight of the ice. The two men pulled the tree from the widow's body and knew immediately that she had not survived. The Widow Dunn's back was broken. Matthew believed she'd died instantly and mercifully from the blow. "Oh, my dearest Lord…this precious saint." Matt kneeled in the snow and prayed for the dear old woman. Eleanor Dunn had been the first in his congregation to welcome his family when they came to serve Shiloh church. She had always been so loving and generous, even though she had so little.

"Matthew, let's carry her in. We need to see to those two frightened young'uns inside." Together they carried the broken body of the old woman inside and laid her gently on her bed. Cathy cried out immediately, "Gran, oh Gran." Roy remained stone-faced and quiet as he took on the role of caretaker for his younger sister.

"Mac, can you put some wood in that fireplace. These two kids are near frozen." Mac nodded and went back to get the needed firewood. "Children, come over here to me." Matthew drew the children, whose worst fears had been realized, into his arms. "Cathy, Roy, you know your grandma's gone to be with the Lord now, don't you?" Cathy nodded and tears ran unchecked down her face. Roy pulled away and went to sit on the raised hearth. He turned his back. Matthew crossed the hearth to sit next to Roy. The small girl went to her pastor, and he pulled her on his lap and laid his other arm across Roy's shoulders. "You know your grandma was one of my first friends here at Shiloh. How often she talked to me about you two and said what a blessing it was to have you here with her. She loved you both more than you'll ever know." Matthew held the two orphans for some time, while Mac built a large fire in the fireplace.

As the room began to warm, the preacher pulled Cathy closer and began to pat Roy's back to the rhythm of the song he sang to them. The old Welsh lullaby brought comfort to him as a youth, and he hoped it did the same to the Dunn children.

*"Sleep, my child, and peace attend thee.*
*All through the night.*
*Guardian angels God will send thee,*
*All through the night.*
*Soft the drowsy hours are creeping,*
*Hill and vale in slumber sleeping,*
*I my loving vigil keeping,*
*All through the night.*
*Love to thee, my thoughts are turning.*
*All through the night.*
*All for thee my heart is yearning,*
*All through the night.*
*There is hope that leaves me never.*
*All through the night.*

After a while, Cathy slept and her brother took her to a pallet near the fire. He lay next to her and pulled an old quilt over them.

"Matt, we can't head back tonight, not with these kids and needing to care for the Widow Dunn. Do you expect Ellie and Laurel will be all right alone?"

"I hadn't thought to be gone all night, but we have to take care of this family. Ellie will be fine. The kids are there to help. You know John is all but grown and can do the work of a man already, but Laurel Grace is alone at the church waiting for you. I'd feel a lot better if she wasn't so headstrong. I pray she'll stay put."

"She'll fret some, but I don't see we got much of a choice."

As the night grew later, Laurel awoke as the room cooled. The fire in the stove had burned low. She worried at the hour because Mac had not returned. She shivered and knew that she had to go out for more wood. Thankfully, she only had to walk across the porch and not across the yard again. Laurel added three more logs to the stove, stoked the fire, and wrapped herself back in the quilt. Now, she was too anxious to sleep. Perhaps she should go to her aunt's house to find out if her Uncle Matt had gotten home. Laurel quickly discarded that idea. The road between the church and the Campbell's was tree-lined and untraveled all day. The road would be impassable. Even though the sun had shone brightly all afternoon, the extreme cold prevented any melting. Her mind turned over idea after idea, but due to her pragmatic nature, she rejected each one. Besides, she knew Mac would return for her as soon as he was able. After what seemed an eternity, she curled up on her coat and tried to sleep again, waiting out the night.

When the morning dawned, the sun cast streams of light through the church windows. Laurel tried to stretch her bone-weary body. Unused to sleeping on the hard wood floor and the tussle with the fallen hickory, Laurel found her leg achy and stiff. The fire had burned out again while she slept, and the church was cold. Opening the back door, Laurel was surprised to see icicles beginning to melt. As is so typical of Arkansas weather, the extreme cold had passed, and the sun was now providing heat as well as light. The landscape was still covered with ice, but at least the ice was beginning to melt. Laurel picked up several logs from the back porch. She had even thought to find some small limbs to knock the ice from so she could have some kindling to restart the fire. She wanted to have a warm place for her husband when he returned, and she hoped that he'd return soon.

She tried to push the worry from her mind, but worry crept back often. The time passed too slowly. She had done all the chores she could think of yesterday. She had not thought to bring anything to read or a sewing project. Of course, she'd had no thoughts she'd have to remain alone in the church building all night.

In mid-morning, Ralph Massey and his oldest son came to the church seeking news after the ice storm. "Goodness, Missy. What'd you do to yourself?"

"What's wrong, Mr. Massey? I know I must look a sight, all rumpled from sleeping in these clothes last night."

"That didn't cause that whopper of a bruise on your face, Mrs. Mac."

"I didn't know I had a bruise. I guess it happened yesterday afternoon. I got caught by a tree branch."

"Thank the Lord, you wasn't hurt any worse. Where's Brother Matthew and your mister?"

"I'm not sure. They went out about noon yesterday to check on the older folks in our congregation. I guess they had to hold up somewhere for the night. I'm beginning to fret some."

"Don't be a fretting. They're both able to take care of themselves. I'm sure they'll be back soon." Of course, he was right. Shortly after the school clock showed 12:00, Mac and Matthew drove the wagon up to the porch of the Shiloh church. Roy Dunn sat next to Mac on the wagon seat, and Matthew rode in the back, holding Cathy wrapped in an old blanket.

Laurel met them at the door. "I'm so grateful you are both back. I had all kinds of terrible thoughts of what could have happened to you."

"We're fine, niece. Can you help me with Cathy? We lost the Widow Dunn."

Mac climbed from the wagon and took the small, grieving girl from Matthew's arms. "Cathy, Mrs. Mac will take care of you now. Go on in and get yourself warm. Roy, you go on, too. We'll take good care of your grandma."

Laurel led Cathy to the stove and removed her coat and shoes so she could warm more quickly. Roy followed. He was solemn and withdrawn, as he'd been since Matthew and Mac had carried his grandmother into their cabin. Laurel wished she had something to feed them, but she had not thought to bring more food. She moved a chair to the fire and pulled Cathy into her lap.

"Are you getting warm, yet, Cathy?" The sad little girl nodded and laid her head on her teacher's shoulder. "Roy, you can come closer to the fire."

"I'm okay."

Matthew Campbell walked into the room, followed by Mac. Mac walked to Laurel's side and tipped her head upward to kiss her. When he saw the ugly bruise, he stopped. "What on earth happened to you, Laurel? Are you all right?"

"I'm fine. It's only a bruise. What happened at the Dunns?"

"Lots of damage from the ice storm. I'll tell you later." Mac bent to finish the kiss. "I'm so glad to be back with you. I was afraid you'd start off looking for us."

"I thought about it, but I remembered how stern you were with me about staying put."

"I seem to remember times when a thing like that wouldn't have stopped you. I'm glad it took this time. Thank you for remembering. What happened to your face?"

"A small thing. I got a bump from a tree limb when I went out to get some firewood. I'm fine really."

"We need to get home. We'll have some hungry animals and a cow that needs milking. Let me check with Matthew about his plans to care for Widow Dunn."

Laurel went to speak to her students. She grieved with them for their loss. She recalled clearly the pain of losing a parent, and that was the role Widow Dunn had filled in their lives. She also knew how the dear little lady had blessed her own life. The gift of her embroidered bread cloth always graced their table. And Laurel had never felt more beautiful than she did when she wore the pink party dress the Widow had made for her. The loss of the dear saint would touch every life in Shiloh.

She brushed her hand across Cathy's brown hair. "You warm enough now?"

The little girl wrapped her arms around Laurel's waist. "Mrs. Mac, we ain't got nobody no more. Papa's in prison for a long time. What's gonna happen to me and Roy?"

"Cathy, honey, you're not alone. You've got your whole Shiloh family here to care for you and Roy. I know you're sad for your grandma because you love her, but she wouldn't want you to be afraid. You'll not be alone. Lots of people love you and Roy. We're not going to let anything happen to you."

Roy looked at Laurel when she promised they'd be taken care of. "I ain't no baby. I can take care of us."

"I know that, Roy, but how can you look after Cathy while you're working with Mac every day?"

Matthew and Mac returned to the stove to talk to the Dunn children. "Roy and Cathy, how would you like us to care for your grandma?"

"She'd want us to lay her next to Grandpa here in our church yard. Cathy brought her best Sunday dress, so I guess that'll do. When can we have a buryin'?"

"If the weather holds, we can have her service tomorrow. Mac, can you take these young'uns home for the night? I know we could all use a hot meal and a good night's rest."

"Of course, we have plenty of room for some visitors. Don't we, Laurel?"

"I'd love to have them come stay with us for a few days."

Shortly, Mac, Laurel, and the Dunn children headed to the homestead. They made a slow trip as Mac let the mules walk most of the way. He knew the two jacks had served him well during the storm. By the time they arrived at the homestead, the temperature had risen well above freezing. The ice on the road was slushing up, and travel was much safer. Rivulets ran from the icicles hanging from the barn roof.

He stopped next to the cabin porch and lifted Laurel down to the step, and then he handed Cathy down to her. "Laurel, if you'll take care of building a fire and start us an evening meal, Roy and I will take care of the animals and fill the wood box.

Laurel and Cathy went into her cabin and set to work. "Mrs. Mac, is this your house? I ain't never been in such a beautiful cabin before."

"Thank you, sweetheart. Mr. Mac built it for us. It was my wedding present."

"What can I do? I'm used to helpin' with chores."

"For today, sit there in that big chair and wrap the shawl around you. I'll make a fire and we'll be warm soon."

The next few hours crept by. Chores done, supper eaten and cleared away, the fire built up to keep for the night... The atmosphere remained somber. Mac read the Scripture for the evening and said prayers. The MacLaynes tried to put Cathy and Roy at ease by making them a part of all they did that evening. Still, the grief and fear remained for the orphaned Dunns.

Finally, Roy spoke, "Do you want me and Cathy to sleep in the barn, Mr. Mac?"

"Goodness, no, Roy." We've got a place ready for you, or almost ready. We only have one bed now, but we'll get you a bunk built so you'll have your own. For tonight, we'll use the feather bed and make you a pallet on the floor in the loft. I guess that will do until we can make you your own bed. Is that all right with you?"

"We'll be fine on pallets down here if you want."

"No, Roy. The loft will be warmer and much more comfortable."

"We don't intend to take your space, Mrs. Mac."

"Cathy, darlin', Mr. Mac and I have our room in the other pen. You're so welcome to sleep in our loft." Laurel led the children up to the half loft above the kitchen. Laurel's bed from Hawthorn fit well beneath the eaves and was spread with a clean sheet and quilt. She took one of the feather pillows from the bed and handed it to Roy. "Cathy, this bed is for you. I used to sleep in it when I was a girl like you. I'll bring you a night dress to sleep in. I'll go get bed covers for you, Roy."

Laurel went down to get the needed covers from the bureau. In the drawer, she found a night dress for Cathy and a length of green yardage. She decided to use the fabric to divide the loft into two areas where the Dunn children would have their own space. She found a feather bed, a sheet, and a quilt in the cedar chest.

"Roy, let's lay out your pallet here next to the wall. Put the featherbed on the floor and lay the sheet on it. You'll stay warm under that quilt." As Roy worked to make his bed, Laurel hung the green fabric from a couple of nails to create two little rooms in the loft.

"Goodness, Mrs. Mac. I ain't never had a whole room to sleep in by myself."

"Well, don't be afraid, Cathy. Roy will be right here, and remember that angels are watching over you. Goodnight, you two."

In the meantime, Mac laid up a good fire in the kitchen fireplace so the Dunn children would sleep warmly through the night. Then he did the same thing in their bedroom hearth. Mac was impatient to have some private time with his wife. Laurel had hardly closed the door to their room before Mac took her into his arms. "Laurel, it's been too long since I've been able to hold you." He kissed her deeply and tenderly. She responded passionately.

"I never want to spend another night like the one I spent last night at the church. The whole night, I feared the worst had happened to you and Uncle Matthew. Thank God, you're both safe."

"The roads were so bad, we had only reached the Dunn's by dark. Then we found those kids in a freezing cabin, not knowing where their grandmother had gone. We couldn't bring them out in the dark. I am pleased you stayed at the church, like I asked you to do." Mac set Laurel on the side of the tall bed and started to remove her boots and stockings. Before he'd gotten the first one off, he saw the intense bruises on Laurel's shins and thighs. "What exactly did you say happened to you, Laurel Grace?"

"I'm fine. It's a small bruise."

"You told me a falling branch grazed your face. What about this bruise on your ankle and these on your legs?"

"Mac, I'm all right. You'll see it anyway. That old hickory behind the church split and fell when I was gathering wood for the night fire. Part of it fell on me, but most of it landed on the back porch. I pulled myself out and took the wood in. Nothing happened."

"I will take you to see the doctor tomorrow."

"No, husband. I promise you I am fine."

Laurel dropped her long-sleeved lawn night dress over her head and let it cover her bruises. She went to the side of the bed where Mac sat, and she placed her hands on his face and looked into his troubled blue eyes. She kissed him and stoked his beard. "I love you, Mac. What a good man you are."

"What brought that on?"

"You and Uncle Matthew risked your own lives to care for our church family. I've never been so proud of you as now."

"We didn't do anything that others wouldn't have done for us if we were in need."

"I'll not argue with you. I'm proud of you. What will happen to Cathy and Roy now?" Laurel asked.

"We'll see what the Lord decides. First, we need to help them get through the funeral. That's all we have to do right now. But I don't want to talk about them tonight. I want your attention. Please come to bed."

"I love you, Patrick. I'm truly happy you put the half loft above the kitchen only. I guess I'm jealous of our space."

THE YEAR 1857 ended in tragedy and in joy, much the way all years end. Shiloh community buried one of its saints on December 28 when they laid Eleanor Dunn next to her husband in the Shiloh churchyard. Matthew Campbell spoke a beautiful eulogy before commending her spirit to Heaven. Laurel and Mac stood in place of the family for the two orphaned children. The church family turned out in full number to honor their fallen sister, regardless of the cold and poor travel conditions. Mac announced that Shiloh would celebrate a wake for Sister Dunn at the end of school term celebration on New Year's Eve at the MacLayne homestead.

"Mr. Mac, you don't gotta do that for us. We ain't got no way to pay for a party like that."

"Roy, don't you worry. Your family is here to take care of what needs to be done. We will certainly honor your grandma."

The New Year's party turned out to be a time of laughter, a time of tears, a time of healing and a time of celebration. The Shiloh congregation shared stories about the life of the good Widow Dunn. Mrs. Stevenson told how Mrs. Dunn baked pies for the wakes of all members of the Shiloh congregation. Everyone from Shiloh knew at times she hardly had flour to bake bread for her own household. Ellie Campbell praised her beautiful needlework. Two younger women explained how Sister Dunn taught them Bible stories during sewing circle. Cathy closed the sharing with the simplest of eulogies. "She was our gran and she loved us."

Matthew Campbell brought all the youth together to sing the carols they'd learned for the Christmas frolic. Just as Laurel promised, three of the adults from the Sunday school read the Scripture that night. At the close of the program, the head of the school committee presented diplomas to four students who finished the school curriculum. He also announced Ann Broadway and Francine Jackson had passed the exam for their teacher's credentials. Applause and cheers filled the cabin. Every part of the Shiloh community seemed to have some claim on the evening's celebration.

"Mrs. Mac, will you let me talk to you a minute?"

"Of course, Francine. Let's go into the other room." She led the girl into the bedroom.

"My goodness, Mrs. Mac. Your cabin is grand. You've made everything so beautiful."

"Thank you, dear, but I don't think you asked to speak to me to compliment my house. Are you all right, Francine?"

"Yes ma'am. Everything is fine now. The young man I told you about talked to me tonight while my papa was outside smoking his pipe. He said he felt bad about how it happened. He said he wanted to see me again."

"What did you say, Francine?"

"I told him I would think about it, and when my Pa allowed, I'd let him come courtin'. I do like him a lot, Mrs. Mac."

"That is a fine answer then. When your papa allows."

"And Mrs. Mac, I ain't fretting no more. I'm not havin' a baby. I guess my prayers and yours have been answered."

"The Lord is good."

"I still have a few things to figure out, but I'll deal with them as they come."

"You'll know what to do when the time comes. You've got a good head on your shoulders, and I think you've grown up quite a bit."

"Thank you, Mrs. Mac. I don't think I'd have made it through all this if I didn't have you to listen to me. I won't never forget how good you've been to me. Thank you so much." Francine threw her arms about her teacher and her friend. "I'm sorry you won't be my teacher anymore."

"It's better now. We can always be friends."

The two friends returned to the party amidst the singing of familiar songs. They were just in time to watch the children receive the belated Christmas gifts. Both were especially happy women: one so grateful she carried new life and one exceedingly relieved she didn't.

When they'd finished distributing the presents, Mac stood up and walked to the hearth.

"Friends, before we strike up the music, I want to share one more piece of good news with y'all, my church family. He took the tiny booties from his pocket. "This is the present Laurel Grace gave me for Christmas." Cheers, laughter, claps on the back, and hugs filled the cabin again. Best wishes resounded.

Matthew Campbell came up to his friend, "You, of little patience. Aren't you the man who told me only ten months ago he had no use for this homestead?" He clapped Mac on the back. "God bless you, my brother."

"He always does." Mac pulled Laurel into his arms and kissed her cheek. The party continued into the late hours. They enjoyed music, storytelling, joke telling, and recipe sharing, along with some dancing—all activities common in fellowship times at the Shiloh community. At the close of the party, some families nearest to the Mac Layne's headed for home while several families stayed. Many bedded down on pallets and even in the haystacks in the barn. For those most distant families, a huge breakfast on New Year's Day would mark the end of their visits. This was the first opportunity Laurel had to serve as hostess in her home. She found the role exhilarating and satisfying. Mac's approving looks throughout the night assured her that she'd had done herself proud.

By 8:00 the following morning, the last of the guests had left. Laurel and Cathy worked most of the day putting the MacLayne home back to normal. Mac and Roy worked outdoors on the mild winter day. At lunchtime, they sat down together to eat.

"Mrs. Mac, thank y'all for the fine wake you gave our gran."

"You're more than welcome. Our entire community enjoyed the celebration. Don't ya think?"

"Well, young'uns, we have to make some plans for your futures. Roy and Cathy, Mrs. Mac and I have talked about the two of you. We're hoping you will want to stay here with us."

"You want us to live here with y'all?"

"Yes, Cathy, if you want to stay. You have your own home, but it's a long way from school."

"It'd be easier for Roy to be here to work with me, too."

"But what'll happen to our homestead?"

"Well, Roy, if you want, we'll go over now and again to keep things up. We'll pay the taxes and when you are old enough and want to, you can go back there to make a home with your own wife."

"You'd do that for us?"

"Roy, you always work hard to make your way."

"You're being so good to us, Mrs. Mac. I'd love to be here to help you and your new baby."

"Thank you for wanting to stay. I know you will be a big help to me."

That New Year's Day, Laurel and Mac enlarged their family. Cathy and Roy Dunn became permanent residents at the MacLaynes' homestead.

# CHAPTER NINE

*He sitteth in the lurking places of the villages:in the secret places he doth murder the innocent. He croucheth and humbleth himself that the poor may fall by his strong ones.*
*Psalms 10:8, 10*

The first weeks of 1858 were bliss for Laurel. She and Mac spoke often of the blessings they'd both found at Shiloh. The snowy, cold winter added to their joy as they spent many days together. The new family read before the blazing hearth, talked for hours, studied Scripture together, and played simple games. The isolation caused by the weather allowed them to become a family. Laurel often noticed her cheeks were wet whenever she thought of the tiny baby she carried. Both Mac and Laurel were at peace, their love for each other growing beyond any depth either of them ever hoped for.

February proved the most bitter month of the year. While the weather was dry, the temperatures frequently fell below zero and stayed at the freezing level for several days at a time. People in the Shiloh community were pretty well homebound for the last three weeks of the month. The homesteaders worked long hours to safeguard their live-stock in the extreme cold. Mac and Roy made several trips to the barn every day to check on the animals in their overstocked barn. The MacLayne's barn was not huge. Mac had built it to house his horses, two mules, and a milk cow or two. Roy had brought a second cow, two hogs, and several hens from the Dunn place. Keeping water available in such an overstocked barn was the hardest task. The water froze within a few minutes. The many animals housed together required many buckets of fresh water every day.

During the second week of the freeze, Mac told Laurel he must go to Greensboro to do some business with Al Stuart.

"Mac, you can't be serious. Wait for a day or two. The temperature will rise soon. What could be so urgent for you to go out in this bitter cold?"

"Don't be a mother hen, wife. I'll be fine. I've got my buckskin coat, and I promise to be home well before dark."

"I still don't see why you need to go today."

"Let's chalk it up to a bad case of cabin fever." Laurel knew Mac was aching to get word about the campaign and news from Little Rock. His lack of activity brought back some of the restlessness he'd shown before Christmas. He needed contact with his friends. Having no news about the rumored break among the supporters of Governor Conway irritated him the most. He had only seen one newspaper since Christmas, and it was from St. Louis, not Little Rock.

"Can I come with you, Mr. Mac?"

"No, Roy. I need you here to look after my wife and your sister. I'll bring back news from town. Do you need any supplies from the mercantile, Laurel? And Cathy, darlin', get Mrs. Mac to teach you how to make an apple-cinnamon cake for our supper. We have dried apples in the larder."

Mac was true to his word. He rode back into the yard about the time the sun was setting in the western horizon. The sunset with streaks of red, gold, and gray was beautiful in the crisp coldness. He put away his horse, broke open the water in the frozen trough, fed the stock, and hurried into the house. He brought home two copies of old newspapers and a new book he found at McCollough's. Besides the new things to read, he reported lots of talk from Greensboro. The best thing he brought was the mail, a letter from Elizabeth Wilson for Laurel and another from Maryland.

"Let's eat supper, then we'll open our letters. I don't want the fried chicken to get cold."

"Me neither. I love fried chicken, Mrs. Mac. You're a fine cook, ma'am," Roy added from the place he'd adopted at the table. The family time was pleasant, and the meal was a feast complete with the apple cake Mac asked for. "Mr. Mac, we got way too much livestock for our family's needs. What are we gonna do with all that extra milk and eggs from my animals?"

"Maybe you could sell some of your eggs and milk. It'd give you a chance to start saving for yourself, Roy. Someday when you are out on your own, it'll be nice to have a little nest egg saved up."

"I could take them eggs and milk to Greensboro a couple of days a week. Those town folks need eggs and milk from the store when they don't keep animals. Thanks, Mr. Mac. That's a good plan."

"Roy, you mean those eggs. Remember your grammar!" Laurel missed no opportunity to teach her students, even at the dinner table. After supper, the family settled in front of the hearth. Roy laid on extra logs to ward off the February cold.

"Mac, won't you share the letter from your father?" Laurel said.

"Gather close and let's see what my Pa has to say. Mac lifted the wax seal from the back of the letter.

*My dear son,*

*I am delighted at the news in your December 30 letter. What a blessing to know I'm going to be a grandfather this summer. Please tell Laurel how pleased I am.*

*Patrick, your news has reinforced a choice I've made. Since your mother's passing, I find our home of forty-five years to be a burden. I am lonely with my family all gone from here. I am finishing details to rent our farm on half shares. One of our workers wants to become my tenant farmer. I've had two offers to buy our house, but right now, I'm not sure if I want to sell it. I can lease it until I want to part with it.*

*Regardless, I want to come to Arkansas so I can rejoin my family. Will you both have me? Maryland no longer holds me, so I need to find my home again. If you agree with my decision, I plan to move this spring so I can settle in before my first grandchild comes. You've spoken so boldly of the opportunities in Arkansas that I look forward to finding out for myself very soon.*

*I hope to receive your response soon.*

*Affectionately,*
*Your father*

"Oh, Mac. How fine it will be to have your papa here with you. We'll have to add another pen to our cabin."

"Yes, Laurel. I want Pa here, but he will want to build his own house, I'm sure. We'll have to provide him a place while he finds the land he wants, and then he'll build a house of his own. Maybe he'll want to stay at the widow's cabin. It'd be nice to have him so close. Thank the Lord, he's decided to come join us. I've wanted him to be a part of our family here at Shiloh."

"You write to him tonight and tell him to come soon. We'll make space for him."

"I'll get a letter posted tomorrow if we go to Greensboro or the first day the weather allows."

"Mrs. Mac, you've got a letter too."

"I'd almost forgotten, Cathy, after hearing such good news from Mr. Mac's father." Laurel opened the envelope, she found two sheets of paper written front and back. In her small clear hand, Elizabeth wrote of the bitter winter in Washington County. The northwest quarter of the state suffered through frequent snow and ice storms. She wrote of three friends' deaths and the births of new babies in the Hawthorn congregation. She reported her family was well and prospering. When Laurel turned the first page over, she found news that wasn't good.

*Laurel, I wish I didn't have to tell you about this. I know Rachel wrote you that she was going to Californey with Josh and her little ones. They left with the Fancher wagon train from Hussau in Boone County. Oh, gracious, Brother Caldwell told me they call it Mount Pleasant now... Anyway, you know her mama's family was kin to the Fanchers way back. That group left Boone County about the middle of the summer, a few weeks after you already headed east. Your uncle Jarrod had only one letter from Josh and Rachel. She said it was hard to find places to post mail from the trail. She wrote that travel had been hard, but they're making good progress. She said the wagon master hoped to be in Californey early in December.*

*Last month, a military captain came to Hussau. He talked to some of the Fancher and Baker families still living in that area. He said the wagon train had been attacked by a group of Mormons and Indians some way from Salt Lake in Utah. They murdered every man, woman, and child older than six years old. He said the army didn't know why they'd done it. We knew. Those families took fine livestock and a fair sum of gold with them so they could buy good farmland out west. Jarrod said that Joshua had over a hundred dollars himself. How could they have killed all those good people? More than 120 of our brothers and sisters! Near all of them from the Methodist church. My dear Lord, how could they've got killed trying to build a good future. I am heartsick. The captain told the families that some of the babies and little ones were missing yet. He also told them that those murdering outlaws took all the goods from the wagons. Then they auctioned off all the loot to some town folk in southeast Utah!*

*We got word here in Hawthorn only a few days ago. As sad as it makes me to tell such a terrible story, I know how you loved Rachel. Besides, you're the Godmother to that baby girl, Gracie. I wish I could tell you more news of that sweet toddler. If I hear more, I'll write as soon as I hear.*

*Bless you, Laurel, my dear. I know this news is hard for you. Trust that your friend Rachel and your cousin Joshua Wilson rest with the Lord now.*

Elizabeth's letter closed with wishes for Laurel's health and prosperity in her new home.

"Patrick, my dear Lord! This couldn't have happened, not to Rachel and her beautiful family."

Mac walked to Laurel and took the letter from her hand. He pulled her to him. She began to weep. Cathy became quite upset. She put her small hand into Laurel's.

"Mrs. Mac, please don't cry so hard." Mac patted Cathy.

"Cathy, you are a sweet girl. Laurel will be all right in a while. Rachel was a dear friend, and she is grieving."

Over the next several days, Laurel broke into tears frequently. Cathy wouldn't let her out of sight. She would wipe the tears, hug Laurel, and hand her a kerchief whenever she saw the need. She became the protector for her guardian in Laurel's time of mourning. At the end of the week, Mac came home from Greensboro to find Laurel sobbing uncontrollably in her chair before the fire. "Darlin', what has upset you so?"

"Mac, how can I have so much when Rachel is gone and her entire family massacred in that wilderness in Utah? I'd probably never have seen her again because of us living so far apart, but I knew where she was and that Josh…." Sobs broke her sentence.

"Laurel, I have no words I can say to make it better. I wish I could take away your sorrow. Sometimes, we have to give our pain to the Lord because we can't bear it ourselves." He picked up her hand and brought it to his lips.

"Not to know if any of Rachel's babies still live. How scared they must be."

"We'll make every effort to get some news from the military. Laurel Grace, you have to stop grieving so hard. You've gotta take care of yourself and our baby."

February ended with one final winter storm. Snow fell for more than two days, blanketing the entire northeast corner of the state with more than eight inches of snow. On the third day when the sun finally made its appearance, Greene County was transformed. Every object, manmade or natural, flaunted its pristine cover of white, opaque crystals. This icy cloak sparkled in the sunlight and shimmered in the bright moonlight after dark. Travel was impossible for three days as the drifts were deep and, for the most part, blocked the roads. The beauty outside mocked the despair Laurel carried.

Mac tried to entertain his family. He asked Laurel to come outside and play with Roy, Cathy, and himself. Laurel half-heartedly donned her coat and scarf and joined them in a snowball fight. The Dunns were excited to be "playing" with their new family, but when Mac challenged her to build a snowman, she refused, saying she was too tired. She returned to the cabin, leaving Mac and the kids playing, laughing, and enjoying the beauty of the last winter snowfall together.

That night as they lay together in their tall, four-poster, Mac opened a touchy conversation with Laurel. "I'm sorry you didn't feel like building that snowman with us Laurel. We had a fine time, playing together. I love having a family."

"I'm glad. At least I did throw a few snowballs at y'all."

"I sorta think you only did that to please me. You didn't seem to take much pleasure from playing with the kids and me."

"I'm sorry. I'm tired so much of the time. Besides, you know I don't like the cold. I like the fire in the hearth so much more than snow down my collar." Laurel hoped her explanation would end the conversation for the night.

"Laurel Grace, you haven't been yourself since we learned about Rachel and her family. You've put up a front, but I know you well enough to see something is wrong. Won't you talk to me?"

Laurel didn't speak for some time. "I don't know what to say. I've not done anything wrong, as far as I remember."

"Laurel, I'm not blaming or criticizing you. I'm concerned is all. Truthfully, I'd not have said anything to you, but the kids asked me why you were always walking away from them. Cathy said she didn't know why you don't like her anymore. Roy told her to hush up and not to make problems. I told them you cared about them both and was very glad they were here with us."

"I am, Mac. Having the children here is good."

"I told Roy that and he said, 'Then why won't Mrs. Mac smile at us anymore.' I realized you don't smile at me either."

Mac's words convicted Laurel. She knew he had spoken the absolute truth to her. Since the letter from Elizabeth Wilson, Laurel had felt a gloom settle over her world. Even worse, she was angry with herself because she had so much to bring her joy. She was married to a good man who loved her. She was well-respected and appreciated in her new home at Shiloh. God had given her a well-defined purpose in her life.

She was warm and healthy. Best of all, she would be a mother in a few short months. What right did she have to be so low?

"Mac, I'm sorry I've caused concern for you and the kids. I guess I didn't realize I've been...well, I'll be more aware."

"Laurel, I don't want you to try to please me. I want you to be happy. I know you have been dealt a harsh loss, but we have also been so blessed this year. You know that we will be celebrating our first anniversary in about two and a half weeks. What a fine year we've had."

"You are right, Patrick. Thank you for bringing it to my attention. I do love you and both Roy and Cathy. I must live in the sunshine and let the Lord take the hurt. The blessings have so outweighed the bad. Please forgive me."

"No need to ask. I know you love me. Come over here and let me hold you for a while. You know, by tomorrow we may be able to get out. If the weather holds, we'll be able to get to church by Sunday. Being the last day of the month, I could use a good worship and praise time to start off a new month and a new season."

"I'd like that. I hope we can."

The next Sunday morning, the sun was brilliant and warm. The breeze from the south began to melt the snow from the roads, and the MacLaynes with the two Dunn children made their way to Shiloh church. The congregation was small that day, as only those closest to the church had ventured out, but the service was spirit-filled. Mac and the children seemed to be glad to be in church with the other Shiloh families. Laurel appeared glad, but the smile on her lips did not reach her eyes. She said all the right things and did all the right things, but she knew her heart wasn't in her actions. She was pretending...pretending so hard to keep Mac and the Dunns from knowing. That day she actually felt nothing at all.

For the next two weeks, Laurel walked through each day pretending, acting the part of a happy, blessed woman, but feeling the grip of sorrow trying to overshadow her blessings. As the weather turned spring-like, the number of tasks demanding her attention grew. She was glad. In her busyness, she didn't have to work so hard at seeming happy. By mid-March, the ground was dry and warm, ready to receive the seeds. Soon spring would nurture the plants and grow the vegetables and grains they would need to survive the next winter.

Laurel despised the way she looked at her life, surviving each week instead of living in the joy she should have felt. She doubled her efforts at every task she started, working each day from dawn to dark. Mac fussed and Cathy tried to take many of the spring tasks from her because they wanted her to rest more and take better care of herself. In her stubbornness, she refused to let others do what she could do...what she needed to do. When she was busy, she didn't pay attention to the gloom, and when she accomplished a task and had done it well, she felt a sense of peace and purpose. On those days she smiled at Cathy many times. And whenever she sat down for even a few minutes, she fell asleep, napping until some commotion woke her.

Laurel's slim torso showed signs that her child was growing. As her waistline begin to disappear, Cathy took over some roles that a daughter of the household could do. Cathy was so excited at the prospect that she would have a little brother or sister. She daily asked Laurel for some new task to help get ready for the baby. Laurel wanted to scream some days because she found the constant pressure to be upbeat and cheerful around the girl almost more than she could bear. On some days, she would retreat to her bed for a nap – some short and some not so short—to escape from the tension. On some days, she did not want to get up at all. Sleep kept the gloom away and let her rest from the role she had been playing for several weeks.

One afternoon while Laurel slept, Cathy went out to the barn to talk with Mac. "Mr. Mac, I am worried about Mrs. Mac."

"Has something happened to Laurel, Cathy?"

"No, sir. She's asleep again. She takes naps all the time. And, Mr. Mac, she acts like she's fine, but I don't think she is...well, I don't exactly know what it is, but she's not been her own self in a while."

"Cathy, many times when women are expecting a baby, they get tired a lot. You know she works very hard to make us a fine home."

"It's not that. Do you think she is happy? Maybe having me and Roy here is just too much for her while she's in the family way."

"Cathy, don't be worrying about that. Laurel loves you, and you are always helping her. I'm sure that is not a problem at all."

"I won't say nothing to her. I love being here with y'all. But, Mr. Mac, I hope Mrs. Mac will be happy. Her eyes are so sad."

Cathy had verbalized what Mac had been thinking for several weeks. Laurel did seem to be playing the role of happy homemaker and soon-mother-to-be. Their daily life had continued in a pattern they'd laid out since bringing the Dunn children to the homestead. They ate together, read Scripture together, and prayed together every evening. Both the kids seemed to be secure and very much a part of the family life. From the start, Mac established a strict bedtime for the household. He intended the private time he and Laurel shared was not cut short by the demands of their pre-maturely formed family. Yet, even in their private times, Laurel was not herself. She walked through the role of dutiful wife, but each day that passed, Laurel seemed more disconnected from him. His concern grew, and he knew that he'd feel no better until he talked out the problem with Matthew and the Lord.

"Roy, please see to the night chores if I don't get back before dark. I'm gonna ride over to the Campbells to talk with Brother Matthew."

MAC FOUND Matthew sitting on the front steps of the beloved log church. Matthew Campbell established this habit early in his ministry at Shiloh. After finishing the work of the day, he'd take time to read his Bible, think about his next sermon, and visit with folks who needed a word with him. That was the role he would fill with Mac that Thursday afternoon.

"You've got a long face, Mac. What's on your mind?"

"What's always on my mind when I've got a long face? Laurel."

"She's not sick, is she?"

"Not in body, but she's not herself. Even Cathy's noticed she's – well, I'm not sure what she is."

"Well, she is expecting a baby you know. Pregnant women sometimes act moody."

"Laurel's only mood right now is sadness. She seems to be pretending, acting out a part she thinks she should play. Hang it all, Matthew! We have absolutely everything in the world to make us happy. I can't think of one thing more we could want."

"You're right, brother, in your eyes everything is as it should be. What about Laurel? Have you asked her?"

"I've tried a time or two. She sees my concern as criticism. She apologizes and says she'll try harder. Matthew, Laurel was happy when she told me about the baby at Christmas. Those two days we were snowbound were as blessed a time as two people ever spent together. I know she wanted this baby."

"A lot's happened since Christmas, Mac. Laurel became a mother overnight to two kids, her body is changing, and her energy level is being sapped by spring chores. Don't forget, she's had news that her best friend was massacred. That's a lot of change happening all at once for anyone."

"What can I do about any of that?" Mac furrowed his brow and pulled his fingers through his hair. "I want her to know the same joy I feel. She deserves to share this with me."

"You're right about that. She needs to know joy, but Laurel has rarely lived that life on the mountaintop. She wants to feel it too like her mother did. Leah lived much of her life in a low mood, too. Before they moved to Arkansas, Mark spoke to me several times about Leah's melancholy. Seems that she took spells when she couldn't see the sunlight for the clouds. I seem to remember him saying that Leah's pa had dark times when he'd go off from his family for days at a time. Could be it's just part of her nature. I wish I knew more to tell you, but I don't."

"Do you think I should take her to see Dr. Gibson?"

"What could he do to make it go away? I believe she needs a good long talk with a friend. I'll send Susan to make a visit. Mac, I'm afraid the only One who can help Laurel return to living in the light is the Lord." Mac and Matthew spent a long while in prayer.

~

THAT VERY AFTERNOON, Laurel spent a great deal of time praying, too. Her prayers were cries of desperation. She poured out her anger over Rachel's death. She deplored her lack of gratitude for her own blessings. She begged for strength to keep up the façade she tried to show Mac and the Dunn children. And that day, like too many others, she didn't feel God heard her cries. And that day, like the others, she pleaded, "Lord give me a grateful heart and lift this gloom from me. Show me a sign that I am worthy of Your grace and a fit companion for Mac. Please, Lord Jesus, I can't find the light without you. I can't disappoint my family again." When she finished, she was exhausted. She lay down for a short nap. She did feel better for it when she rose to prepare the evening meal.

Susan came to visit Laurel on Saturday afternoon, and Laurel was glad to see her. They seldom had time on Sundays to talk much. Laurel knew that one thing she missed at Shiloh was a close friend—the friend Rachel had been in Hawthorn.

"Susan, how nice to see you! What brings you over our way?"

"My husband wanted to talk with Mac about some cattle he's heard about over around Sikeston. I decided I wanted to come along for the ride. It's not often we get away from our four babies, just me and Warren."

"Afternoon, Warren. Mac is down in the south pasture if you want to drive down that way. Come on in, Sue, and let's have a cup of tea, or do you prefer coffee?"

And so began a long conversation between the two cousins. Susan kept the conversation on topics Laurel would once have considered small talk. They spoke about their lives on the homesteads, told stories about the children in their world, and shared a bit of local gossip about the new teacher. Laurel began to relax and enjoy chatting with her cousin. While on the surface much of it seemed trite, Laurel relished the communication she was having with Susan.

"How are you feeling, Laurel? Being in a mothering way is not easy."

"I suppose things are going as they should. My waistline is going...or I should say gone?"

"That's a good sign–means your little one is growing. But how are you feeling?"

"To tell you the truth, I'm tired all the time. I always want to go to sleep."

"I did that too, early on. You'd better take advantage of those naps. When your time is close, you'll find it really hard to sleep because you will feel awkward and uncomfortable, sitting or lying."

Laurel smiled. To know that napping and fatigue were common with most expectant mothers made her feel somehow better. Perhaps other things she was experiencing were not unusual either. Did she dare tell her cousin about her sadness? Would Susan think her heartless if she said she felt no joy at her soon-to-be-motherhood? Could she risk saying those things aloud? Laurel decided she would ask.

"Susan, is it normal..." Her voice fell off. She looked away, unable to look at her cousin. "I mean, should I feel...shouldn't I be happy now?"

"Some days, of course, but not always. Cousin, when I carried my babies, my feelings jumped from one extreme to another. Some days I would laugh out loud, I was so happy, and other times, I'd bite Warren's head off if he didn't say good morning to me in the right tone of voice."

"I've been sad for a few weeks. Mac mentioned it, but I've been sort of pretending with him and the kids. I hate feeling like this."

"Laurel, it'll pass. Keep your eye and heart focused on June. Even sooner than that. You'll never know such joy as when you first feel that little one move inside. Sharing that with Mac will be one of those cherished memories you'll keep for a lifetime. Keep on praying. You know the Lord will carry you through. After all, you've come to Shiloh now, my dear friend!"

The two laughed, and for Laurel, the laughter was real. She hadn't lost all her gloom, but she did feel hope that it would pass. If she could continue her own prayers, the sign would surely come. Even if she didn't feel it, she knew the truth in her cousin's words. Faith would carry her to Shiloh if she would let it.

That night as they prepared for bed, Mac asked, "Did you enjoy your visit with Susan?"

"I did. I really needed someone to talk with. You know Rachel and I talked about everything when we were growing up. I have missed her." For the first time, Laurel was able to speak of Rachel without falling into despair.

"Well, that doesn't say much for me now, does it?"

"And just how many babies have you had? I didn't realize you were so knowledgeable on the subject that you can help me learn the things I don't know?"

"I concede. Susan is probably a better choice for talking about babies than I can be."

"Mac, I told her that I've been sad lately and that I've been pretending to keep you and the kids from worrying about me. I should have told how I was feeling."

"What did she say?"

"She said mothers-to-be are moody. You know I have been more than moody lately."

"I know, darlin'." Mac brushed a kiss against her cheek. "But Laurel Grace MacLayne, I'd rather be with you in any and every mood than to be without you ever again. The Lord is going to show us the sunlight."

"Mac, I need you to pray with me."

"'Til the day I die, my love."

# CHAPTER TEN

*She looketh well to the ways of her household, and eateth not the bread of idleness. Her children rise up and call her blessed; her husband also he praiseth her.*
*Proverbs 31: 27-28*

As the winter became a memory, spring on Crowley's Ridge began to strut all nature's glory. Nothing new to Arkansans...a typical Arkansas springtime! Early wildflowers sprang up across every hillside and through the meadows. The trees, which were bare one day, seemed to sport leaves in every shade of green the very next. Gardens began to show new life, pushing their shoots through the rich dirt. Mother Nature worked her magic across the northeast corner of the state.

Human efforts brought forth changes, too. Mac increased the size of his planted acreage in both corn and hay. With the new herd, he would need a bumper crop to assure adequate forage for winter feed. With his father coming, Mac needed a bountiful harvest to share with him until he could establish his own homestead. The fencing for his pastureland was finished the previous fall. He'd fulfilled his role as a homesteader.

Laurel continued to add things to their cabin to make the place more of the home Mac wanted. Cathy and she planted flowers around the front porch and lined the flower beds with fieldstones. This created a pretty border to keep animals off the sprouting plants. In the evenings, she worked with Cathy. They crocheted and sewed tiny garments for the baby who would join the family in mid-June. Laurel did not neglect Cathy's daily lessons either. She made sure the girl would be well prepared for her fourth level work when school started back in late spring. Roy came to home school on rainy days, or at times Mac had no particular chore for him to do. Laurel also began to keep a journal. Writing seemed to let her untangle so many of the things that passed through her mind. Her low moods found their way onto the page and did not resurface as often in her dealings with the people she loved. She took joy in recording the changes at Shiloh, in her family, and even within herself.

Day by day, the family grew closer as they worked, lived, played, and prayed together. Laurel worked to push away the low moods, and the time she felt compelled to escape into afternoon naps diminished. Mac basked in the warmth and comfort of his family and home. He spoke often to Matthew and to Laurel herself of the best blessing he'd ever received, next to his salvation. He made sure that Laurel knew every day how precious she was to him. Despite her swelling torso, Mac found her more desirable than at any time in their acquaintance. While their love-making took on a less vigorous nature, the passion and intimacy between them grew. These bonds were more precious than any physical relationship.

He and Laurel spent much time talking and dreaming of their future and their new son. No day passed that Mac did not thank God for allowing him to find his perfect life mate. Little by little, Laurel's prayers became more praise-filled as her grief for Rachel lessened. The Lord helped her see the light through scores of daily blessings in her life despite her loss.

On March 12, 1958, Mac and Laurel retired to their room about 9:00 as was their routine. No sooner had Mac closed the door than Laurel wrapped her arms around him. When he started to ask about her embrace, Laurel covered his mouth with her own. "Thank you, wife, for your loving welcome." Laurel laughed aloud with joy he'd not heard for some time. "What have I done to merit such sweetness at the end of the day?"

"Come over to the bed and let me show you." Laurel took Mac's hand and led him to their tall four-poster. Mac wasn't surprised. Laurel often initiated their love-making, but not in several weeks. That night was something different. Her spontaneous laughter and light-hearted playfulness brought welcome relief to Mac, who not seen her happy since they'd learned of Rachel's death in Utah.

"Wife, I'll gladly join you, but don't you think we would be more comfortable without so many of these clothes?"

"Patrick, just take your boots off and come lie by me." Mac responded as she asked. "Here, give me your hand." Laurel drew Mac's hand to her swollen belly. "Do you feel your child moving, Patrick?"

He waited. Finally, he decided Laurel was imagining things. They lay together for several minutes, quiet and waiting.

"Laurel..." She shushed him and laid her hand on top of his. Then Mac felt the gentle fluttering of his son. Almost like the brush of a butterfly on his fingertips, so slight was sensation. But that gentle movement of life his child had made forged a bond between father and child. The awareness of his pending fatherhood became real for Mac at that moment.

"My dear Lord, thank you! Laurel, thank you. What a gift you have given me!" Mac pulled Laurel into his arms, almost reverently, and held her. "Laurel, I wish I knew the words to say. This is my child."

"I could hardly wait until bedtime. When I felt our baby first move tonight during evening prayers, I wanted to share it with you. Can you still feel him?"

"Yes. Does it hurt?"

"No. It feels like a movement of a butterfly, but the baby is still so little. Later we'll feel him move more."

"I'll never forget this moment, wife. Now it is real for me. Up 'til now, I've been happy with my dream, but I'm not dreaming anymore. You've made me a father. Thank you."

"I'm happy, too." God answered her prayers and sent this precious time to help her find her way back to the light. Mac kissed her and kissed her again.

The next morning, Mac arose a bit later than normal. Laurel had been up long enough to build a fire and make fresh coffee. The aroma of the hot coffee had awakened him from what he'd thought to be a powerful dream. Laurel was singing a familiar praise as she kneaded the bread for the day. When she saw him standing in the doorway, she smiled and spoke. "Come over here and greet your child, Mac." Laurel wore only her springtime lawn nightdress and her silk wrapper. When he touched her, the gentle movement dispelled his notion that he'd dreamed it all. "Can you feel your son this morning?"

He nodded, "I thought I'd dreamt it last night, but it is real, isn't it, Laurel?"

"Yes, my love. Every bit as real as the love you gave me a year ago yesterday when I met you for the first time on the porch of my papa's cabin."

About noon that day, Matthew Campbell rode up to the MacLayne cabin with Terrell Douglas, a second member of the school committee. "Morning, Laurel Grace. How are you feeling this morning?"

"Doing well, uncle. How's your family?"

"All's well. Where is Mac today?"

"Down in the field somewhere. He said he could get the rest of the corn in today. You know he added a few acres of forage this year. If you need him, I'll send Cathy out to call him in."

"No need, Mrs. Mac. We actually came to see you. We want to talk about the next school term." Mr. Douglas seemed nervous as he spoke.

"Well, Mr. Douglas and Uncle Matt, come on in. Can I get y'all a cup of coffee or some cool water to drink?"

"Thank you. Coffee would be fine." Laurel brought two cups of coffee and offered milk and sugar.

"Laurel Grace, first we want to tell you what a fine job you did last year. You saw all four of our eighth level students finish their schooling. We'd have lost at least one of them if you hadn't worked so hard."

"Mrs. Mac, you're the best teacher we've had since we started Shiloh school."

"Thank you both for your kind words."

"That is why we need to talk to you now. Of course, we know you ain't thinking you'll be coming back in the next term with the baby due soon. Do you want to return in the fall?"

"I heard that you have already hired a teacher to take my place. That is what you needed to do so the students could continue the good work they did last year. Mr. Douglas, I haven't thought about returning in the fall. I assumed you'd want the new teacher to stay on."

"Well, we did hire someone on the condition that you didn't want to come back."

"My baby is due in June, so I don't see how I can do both things at once."

"Do both what?" Mac walked through the back door just in time to hear the end of Laurel's reply.

"Hello, Mac."

"Matthew, Terrell. What are y'all asking Laurel to do?"

"We want to talk about the next school term. We're thinking Laurel wouldn't be wanting to come back for the summer term, but maybe she'd want to return in the fall."

"Of course, she can't come back. She's got more to do around here now, and after the baby comes..."

"Mac, I've already told them I couldn't work in the spring. I am sure they didn't expect I would even consider it."

"Laurel Grace, of course, you'll want to be home to take care of the little one at first, but we wanted to ask if you plan to return to your job at school in November?"

"No, she doesn't plan..."

"Mac, we haven't even talked about whether I'll return to teaching."

"Laurel, we'll have a child in the house for several years."

"Mac, let's not discuss this in front of company. Let's think about it until we can talk it out."

"Laurel..."

"Uncle Matthew, Mr. Douglas, if you'll give me a few days, I'll give you an answer that Mac and I have agreed to. I will not teach the spring term, but I don't know yet if I plan to return. I do appreciate your asking me though." The frown on his face indicated Mac wasn't pleased with her answer to the school committee, but he didn't continue to press his point in front of the men.

That night as they were dressing for bed, Mac brought up the question to Laurel. "Wife, do you want to go back to teaching after you have our baby to raise? You do realize that in November, he will be less than six months old?"

"I didn't say I would go back, but I did come here to teach at the subscription school. I love working with the students. Teaching is a calling to me. You know that."

"I know you are a born teacher, but Laurel, I want our baby to have a fulltime mother. What are you going to do, take him with you to school?"

"I didn't say I was going back. I just hadn't thought about not teaching. We've never talked about it before."

"Don't you think you can be happy, just being a wife and mother?"

"I guess I can. Feeling this new life in me has brought me out of the doldrums. At this moment, I can't imagine being more content."

"You make your decision, Laurel. I'll support whatever you decide. I believe our children will need you home until they are old enough to go to school. You can go back to teaching then without concern for their welfare. I assumed you would feel that way too."

"I suppose you're right, Patrick. I want to be a good mother. I'll tell Uncle Matthew on Sunday."

"No, Laurel. Don't do it because I said it's what I want. You make the decision that is right for you. Take a few days and think about what you want to do. I want you to make the decision. If you think you need to teach, we will find a way, but consider all the sides of the matter and pray about it. I want you to know you are doing what you are meant to do, even if that means you go back to the classroom. I love you, Laurel, so be good to yourself as you make this life choice, wife. Whatever you decide will be right for us and our family."

Laurel looked into the face of her husband as his storm blue eyes refused to break gaze with hers. Such a depth of love she felt at that moment! In a trembling voice, she murmured, "Thank you, my love." Mac had given her a gift so rich. He'd treated her as an equal in making decisions for their family. She knew exactly what she would choose. Family now and school later.

ON FRIDAY, Mac announced at the dinner table that Roy, John Campbell, and he would leave for Missouri on Monday to buy the start of his cattle herd. He said that Warren had brought him news of a farmer in Sikeston who was selling his entire herd before he moved to Texas. Word was that he had one prize bull and at least twenty heifers, that would make a fine start for his homestead. "We finished the last section of the fencing. The next step is buying the right animals to start making us a good living here at Shiloh."

"Do you think the weather will hold long enough to make such a long, hard trip?"

"I believe it is springtime for sure, wife."

"Arkansas springtime can be very fickle, Mac. I've seen it snow on my birthday in April."

"Stop being a mother hen, Laurel. I want to be home for Easter and well into my routine with the new herd before the baby comes. I figure we'll be gone less than two weeks. The military road north is a sound path. We'll make good time."

"Two weeks isn't much time to go so far into Missouri. Do you think you can get home before my birthday?"

"I said Easter, darlin'. That is four days before your birthday this year. Laurel, I don't want you to be alone as your time nears. You're always working too hard, and I want you to be able to rest more. Besides, you are getting more beautiful every day. How could I stand to be away from you any longer than that?" Mac gave Laurel a mischievous wink and laughed as her face flushed.

"Hush up, Mac. The children are here at the table."

"They know how much I adore you, and how I enjoy teasing, don't you, Cathy?"

"Sure we do, Mr. Mac. Mrs. Mac is happiest when you make her laugh, like now."

"Roy, do you think the three of us can handle twenty head of cattle? You know I plan to buy at least one good bull."

"It'll be a snap. You, me, and John can bring back a herd that size easy. Let's go!"

"Monday morning, bright and early. We should reach Sikeston in three or four days, tops. We'll take the flatbed wagon and the mules so we can carry our supplies for the trip. Driving the livestock back will take twice as long, but that will still fit in the two weeks. Just think, when we get home with them, all we have to do is sit back and watch those cows have calves, and then we'll let them get fat and make us a fine profit. Then we'll do it over again the next year."

"Mac, please make the trip as fast as you can. I hate being separated from you. Or better yet...don't go now."

"That's an angel's song to my ears, dear wife, to hear you want me home. You can't keep me away. I'll be back for your birthday. What do you want me to bring you?"

"I don't need anything, only bring my family back safely."

That night as Mac and Laurel lay together in their tall four- poster, Mac sensed Laurel was not herself. "Darlin', are you feeling all right tonight?"

"I'm fine. Why did you ask?"

"You seem very far away from me tonight."

"How can you say that? You are practically holding me."

"You know what I mean. Don't play innocent with me." Laurel sat up and turned to face Mac. In the bright moonlight, she could see Mac's too blue eyes, staring at her.

"Mac, I wish you weren't going to Missouri right now. I don't know what it is, but I feel uneasy about you leaving home right now. Can't you go later?"

"Laurel, what is wrong? Has something happened I don't know about?"

"No."

"I don't want to be away when your time gets nearer. I have to bring the herd this spring. You know we've found that deal over near Sikeston. I won't be gone more than ten days or two weeks at the most. Then as time for the baby comes, I'll be here if you need me."

"You've told me all that before. I'm sorry. Something just feels wrong."

"Laurel, you will hardly miss me. I'll be gone so short a time, not like the two months I was gone to Maryland. You're going to say the same thing if I go in two days or two weeks or two months."

"I'll miss you for even one day. I know I am being silly. I can't be separated from you right now. Let me come along with you?"

"You can't make this trip, Laurel Grace. Our baby is due in about twelve weeks. I won't risk your health or our baby's. No."

"Mac…Ohhhh! God keep you safe, husband. I'll quit fussing. I know you have to go find the stock to start your herd. I guess it's better sooner than later."

"I'll be home so fast. I promise you. In case you've forgotten, I love you. Being away from you is the loneliest time I ever have. I want nothing more than to kiss your sweet mouth every morning, tousle those tawny curls every night before I take you in my arms and make sweet love to you. Sleeping in your arms every night is bliss." He pulled her back into his arms and kissed her. "Let's sleep now. I can see how tired you are. Tomorrow will be a busy day."

Laurel sighed and turned so she and Mac could "spoon" together. Mac pulled her closer and held her at her waist. As his arm rested across her thickening torso, Mac felt the movement of his son. In gratitude, he prayed, "Lord, I don't deserve to be so blessed!"

Preparation for the trip was only one of many things that made days pass like hours, and hours seem as minutes. The Saturday night social at Al Stuart's home in Greensboro was a must-do party for both Laurel and Mac. Each social gathering between now and October was also a campaign opportunity. Al Stuart and other supporters invited new settlers to come and meet Candidate MacLayne and his lady. Mac's natural friendliness and sincere desire to serve attracted newcomers and old friends alike. While the supporters believed Mac had the election tied up, they didn't take one vote for granted. Locals didn't believe an outsider from Little Rock could garner enough votes to take the seat from their "favorite son." Regardless, few weekends passed without some kind of social for Mac and Laurel to attend.

The eve of Mac's departure had been the most hectic of those days. Sunday services, the dinner on the grounds, afternoon singing, and Sunday night preaching took most of the final hours. While Laurel was with Mac most of the day, there had been little time for them to talk or spend any time alone. When they headed home, Mac took Laurel's hand and spoke, "You seem especially tired tonight, wife. Are you well?"

"Yes, but I am tired. Of course, I love the special music and potlucks on Sunday evenings, but we have been up and busy since daybreak. I will be happy to get home."

"Well, Cathy, Roy, and I will take care of supper and evening chores while you sit in your rocking chair. Then after supper, we'll turn in early."

"That's not necessary."

"Yes, it is. You will take care of yourself this one night." Mac was true to his word. Cathy fixed a quick supper, Roy and Mac did the evening chores, and Laurel napped in her chair. Shortly before 9:00, Mac put out the lanterns in the living room and said goodnight to the Dunn's. He led Laurel to their room, picked her up, and set her on the side of the tall bed where he unhooked her shoes. Then he pulled the combs from Laurel's chignon and let her curls tumble down her shoulders.

"I love your hair when it is unfettered and falls in curls down your back." He kissed her cheek and handed her a spring nightdress. "I hate to think of being away from you the next two weeks. I hate sleeping away from you for even one night."

"I will miss you, too." Mac arose and walked to the walnut bureau Laurel's father had carved. He opened the top drawer and picked up a small velvet box and carried it back to the bed.

"Happy birthday, a little early, in case I'm late getting home."

"Mac, what have you done?"

"Open the box and see." Laurel lifted the blue velvet lid and inside the box, a gold brooch lay nestled on white satin. Laurel gasped at the extravagant gift. The beautiful piece sparkled with every movement in the dim light of their room.

"This is so beautiful."

"A small token to say thank you and to help keep your mind and heart set on June. It's called a Gordian Knot. It's one of a kind, like you, and a reminder of how precious you are to me. I will try to be home before your birthday, but I couldn't wait to give it to you."

"You are too good to me. Thank you."

"You are so good for me." He kissed her. "Promise you will take care of yourself."

# CHAPTER ELEVEN

*For the Lord will not cast ye off forever: But though He cause grief, yet will He have compassion according to the multitude of His mercies.*
*For He doth not afflict willingly nor grieve the children of men.*
*Lamentations 3: 31-33*

At sunrise, Mac, Roy and John Campbell left the homestead headed north to Missouri. Mac turned to wave farewell to Laurel and Cathy who stood on the porch. Laurel lifted her hand and smiled to wish Mac God's speed on his journey.

"Well, Cathy, my dear, we girls are on our own. What should we do today?"

The first week seemed to vanish. Tending her garden, caring for the stock, napping in the afternoon, sewing baby clothes, and teaching Cathy filled all the time Laurel had. They even took a day to visit with her cousin Susan. Laurel wanted to nurture the new friendship they'd begun. Playing with Susan's new baby, Randall Matthew, made the day a special treat for both Cathy and Laurel. Laurel was enchanted by the strong healthy baby boy. She loved the feel of his tiny fingers as they closed about hers, and the funny way he wrinkled his forehead when he became hungry. This short preview of motherhood only added to her anticipation.

The second week began to drag though, as Laurel missed Mac more each day. She prayed the final few days of this separation would just vanish. On Thursday afternoon, Matthew Campbell stopped on his way home from Greensboro. He had picked up the mail and had brought Laurel a letter from Elizabeth. She was more pleased to see her uncle than she was to have another letter from Washington County. She hoped he'd stay to supper and keep her company for a couple of hours.

"Uncle Matthew, I am so happy to see you. I know it's not been so long since Sunday, but we haven't had a chance to talk for a while."

"That's true, Sprite. Seems people are always so busy anymore. How are you getting on now?"

"I'm doing really good. I feel fine, and I'm so looking forward to giving Mac his son. He wants a family."

"I know. He told me to make sure you are taking it easy. You have been good for Mac, Laurel. You've taken away his restlessness. He didn't even want to go on this trip to Missouri. He's been good for you. Every time I see you, you remind me more and more of that little girl who came from North Carolina back in '42."

"Mac has taught me a lot about being faithful, and he has helped me lose the nightmares that I've lived with for the last fourteen years. I am happy here at Shiloh, uncle."

"Thank the Lord, niece. I wasn't sure when you first came here that I'd done the right thing in sending Mac across the state to court you."

"God makes all things to the good for those who love Him. Mac does love the Lord, and he deserves his dreams to come true."

"Be happy, Laurel. That's what Mac wants."

"Can you stay for supper? Cathy has become a very good cook, and she is making fresh bread. I can hardly wait, it smells so good baking now."

"No, darlin'. Your aunt Ellie's expecting me back long before now. I'll see you next Sunday at church." Matthew Campbell left for home, and Laurel took her letter to the front porch to sit for a while that pleasant spring afternoon. For the first day of April, the weather was beautiful.

She sat down and looked over to the chair where Mac would sit in a few short days. She smiled, thinking how wonderful this summer would be —the three of them sitting here on their porch. She daydreamed of long talks and rocking their baby to sleep under the stars. She tore the wax seal off the letter from Elizabeth and read.

*Dear Laurel,*

*I was so pleased to learn in your last letter that you are well and about to become a mother. How happy your mother would be at this news, God rest her soul. All is well here at Hawthorn Chapel.*

*The winter has been a hard one, but now that spring is here, we are beginning to get out and about again. We drove over by your old family place on Sunday afternoon and saw that the apple trees are beginning to bud. Of course, it is too early for blooms.*

*We had news about Rachel's youngest. They gave the baby to a family in Salt Lake. The army is reclaiming all those little ones who survived the attack at Mountain Meadow. They're bringing them home to their families. They haven't given us a time yet. Ain't talked with Rachel's pa yet, but you know that he's been a widower for several years. His health's not good either. I know he'll want to do right by the baby, but I am not sure if he will be up to raising a toddler. I'll write you when I learn more.*

*I hope this note finds you well and happy. Write soon and God bless you, Laurel. I miss having you nearby. I hope the time will come when I'll be able to meet your new baby.*

*Affectionately,*
*Elizabeth*

The returning memory of Rachel's death saddened her briefly. But thankfully, Gracie, her goddaughter lived. Perhaps she would return to Arkansas soon. She'd write to Elizabeth and ask her to tell Rachel's father that she and Mac wanted to help in any way they could.

Friday passed. Mac did not return. Saturday came and passed. Even though Laurel looked toward the north road every few minutes, Mac still didn't get home. The two weeks was up the next day, and tomorrow was Easter Sunday. Mac had told her he wanted to be home by Easter. He had to return by then! He'd promised her he would.

That Sunday morning didn't turn out to be much like Easter. Instead of sunshine and gentle breezes, the weather was blustery and dark. Cloud banks sat atop each other across the entire southwest sky. The skies darkened, and the wind increased the closer they got to Shiloh church. Cathy and Laurel had brought the small wagon, but Sassy Lady had to pull them. Mac had used the mules to pull the flat wagon on his trip to Missouri. Sassy was skittish, but Laurel kept a strong hold on the reins, and they arrived at the church.

Throughout morning worship and the Easter communion service, thunder rolled in the distance. Before the special singing, the winds increased. Strong, frequent gusts whistled through the hills and pushed limbs of nearby trees against the walls of the log church. The fury of the wind prompted the preacher to look out the door.

"Lord, as we part this morning, keep us safe as we return to our homes. Thank you for allowing us to be Your Easter people and for your blessed sacrifice for us all. Bless us as we go out to serve."

He turned to his faithful congregation. "Friends, the looks of that western sky tell me a storm is comin'. I'm thinkin' it'd be wise to cancel the rest of our day's activities so y'all can get home before the storm strikes. Please go and travel in God's grace."

Sparing little time, the Shiloh families began their trips homeward. Matthew called out to his niece, "Laurel, you and Cathy come home with us until this storm passes."

"No, thank you, Uncle Matthew. We only have a short way home, and we have animals that will need our care. We'll be home before you are. Besides, Mac and Roy may be home by now. Good-bye, Aunt Ellie. I will see you in a day or two." Laurel took Cathy's hand, and they left the church. Laurel untied Sassy and turned the little mare toward the homestead. They'd hardly reached the road when a light drizzle began.

"We need to hurry, Cathy." Before they had reached the first bend in the road, the storm broke. The rain began in earnest, and the wind howled through the tops of the trees along the road. Thunder and lightning lit the cloud-darkened skies. The louder the thunder became the harder Sassy jerked and pulled at the reins in Laurel's hands.

"I hate storms, Mrs. Mac. Do you think we need to go home with Brother Matthew?"

"We will be home in a very few minutes, Cathy. Hold on to the wagon seat real tight." Laurel flapped the reins across Sassy Lady's back, encouraging her to pick up her pace. She too wished she'd gone home with her uncle, but it was too late to turn back now.

They continued through the storm, and finally, they reached the boundary of the MacLaynes' homestead. "See Cathy, our house is just around that bend in the road." The words hardly left Laurel's mouth when a crash of thunder, so loud the air around them vibrated with its strength, sounded across the valley. An arc of lightning spread across the sky. Sassy Lady sidled to the right side of the road and reared in fright. The skittish mare was rarely exposed to stormy weather, and Laurel had never ridden her in conditions like the ones they were facing on this Easter day. Sassy pulled at the lead and began to run. Laurel jerked the reins, her nerves causing her to overreact, and Sassy again reared up. Laurel rose to her feet, trying to regain control of her frightened little mare. The wagon slid sidewise and Laurel lost her footing. She fell from the wagon and landed on her back. Sassy continued to run toward the barn. Cathy screamed as she held on to the seat.

The unexpected fall stunned Laurel momentarily, but hearing the fright in Cathy's voice called her back to awareness. She pushed herself to her feet, called to the little girl, and hurried toward the barn. Sassy stopped at the barn door and stood, pawing the ground, waiting to get inside and away from the storm. Cathy jumped down and ran back toward Laurel.

"Are you hurt, Mrs. Mac?"

"I lost my breath for a minute. No, I'm fine. Let's just get in out of this weather." Laurel pulled open the barn door and led the startled mare inside. She unhooked the reins from the wagon and put Sassy in her stall. She and Cathy hurried to the porch as fast as she could manage in her awkward shape. They closed all the shutters they could reach from the porch and went into the safety of the cabin. "Cathy, let's change out of these wet clothes. We don't want to catch a chill."

"Thank goodness, we made it home. Did you hurt yourself when Sassy made you fall?"

"Maybe my pride. I don't think I ever fell off a wagon seat before." Laurel whispered a prayer that the fall would prove to be nothing more than a source of hurt pride. She sank into her father's armchair where Mac usually sat, wishing he were there to comfort her and Cathy through the stormy evening. She also prayed that he and the boys were sheltered somewhere with their herd.

The storm howled on into the late afternoon. Laurel and Cathy lit the lanterns earlier than usual and kept watch. Occasionally, a branch from a nearby tree would slap against the side of the cabin. Thankfully, none came through the uncovered windows. Lightning streaked across the sky many times during that long day. Lightning struck one of the oak trees behind the barn about dark. The tree split and the death knell for the tree shook the ground with such force a lantern from the mantle fell. Again, the Lord had taken care of them, for it was the one lantern Laurel hadn't lit. There was a mess to clean up, but they didn't have to contend with a fire.

The fear in Cathy's eyes touched Laurel. She knew the sweet girl wanted her brother home with her. Laurel walked over and pulled her close. "Cathy, dear, we are safe here in our cabin. Come over here and sit with me in Mac's chair." When Laurel reached to pull her into her lap, she felt a strong cramping in her abdomen. She cried out with pain, and for what seemed an eternity, she doubled over with the deep cramp.

"Mrs. Mac, did I hurt you?"

"No, Cathy. Please, sit here with me. I'll be okay in a moment or two." Cathy began to cry. Laurel tried hard not to grimace in the pain, as it only increased the little girl's concern. Within a few minutes, the cramping stopped, and Laurel was able to sit upright. "See, darlin', I told you I'd be fine."

The storm continued until well past six. The lightning and wind abated little by little, and the rain decreased to a sprinkling. Laurel and Cathy went to the barn to check on the livestock and to do the evening chores. When they returned, Cathy prepared a light supper. Then Laurel invited her to sleep in the tall bed with her. The little girl would not feel safe in the loft with her brother gone. Laurel didn't want to be alone either. The stressful day left her feeling anxious. She would appreciate the nearness of part of her family. Ominous thoughts refused to let her rest. She shivered.

"Oh Mac, I need you home tonight." Laurel covered her mouth with her hand. Thank the Lord, Cathy had already fallen asleep, her honey brown curls splayed across Mac's pillow.

When the sun rose the next morning, Laurel was already awake. Except for being somewhat sore in her abdomen and bruised where she'd fallen on her backside, she felt quite normal. The day had dawned fresh and cool as was so typical after a spring storm. There was not one cloud in the sky. Monday was wash day, and the task would occupy most of the morning for Laurel and Cathy. She went about stripping bed covers from the tall bed and sent Cathy up to the loft to get sheets from her bed, too. The wash would be light since the men in their household hadn't gotten home from their trip to add their dirty clothes to the day's labor.

After breakfast, she and Cathy drew water from the rain barrel and poured it into the black wash pot near the porch. First, Cathy stuffed in clothes and pushed them down into the water with her long stirring pole. She kept up a constant chatter with Laurel and did not seem to mind at all that they were working so hard. She continued to lift the heavy, wet garments from the wash water and dump them in the galvanized rinse tub. Together she and Laurel pinned the last of the newly washed linens to dry. By noon they'd finished the weekly chore. Clean linen and clothes flapped in the breeze on the line Mac had stretched between two large maple trees.

"Cathy, let's go in and fix a bite to eat and plan a nice supper. Do you think our fellows will be home tonight? Mac told me he'd not miss Easter, and he's already done that, so he must be home to celebrate my birthday later this week."

"Let's fix something special, Mrs. Mac." They reached the steps to the back porch as Laurel doubled over with a severe pain in her abdomen.

She could not stand and slumped to the floor, crying out in pain. "Mrs. Mac, what can I do? You are hurting so bad!"

Laurel was not able to answer coherently. She knew that she had felt "different" all morning, but she hadn't been in any real pain. She hadn't felt quite right since she had gotten up. The catch in her lower left side took her unaware as she'd mounted the steps up to the porch. She lay on the floor of the porch now with her knees drawn toward her chest as much as she was able. When she caught her breath, she spoke to Cathy.

"Sweetheart, I need you to go find Brother Matthew and his wife for me." Again, Laurel cried out in pain. "Cathy, don't be afraid, but go get Sassy and ride to find my uncle. Hurry but try to ride safely."

"Mrs. Mac, I can't leave you here alone."

"Go now, Cathy. I need some help." Her eyes wide with concern, she turned to obey. Laurel cried out again and pulled her knees up, wrapping her arms around them.

"I'm going, Mrs. Mac, but please be all right. I love you. Please be okay until I get back." The young girl ran to the second pen and brought a pillow and coverlet for Laurel before she ran to the barn. Within a few minutes, Cathy left at a strong gallop, headed to Shiloh church, praying the preacher would be there. His homestead was twice as far.

Something had happened to the small baby she carried. She feared as much when strong cramping began the previous afternoon, but she'd prayed so hard that nothing would happen to her child. She'd felt well enough that morning, but perhaps she shouldn't have done the washing that day. Well, afterthought was useless now. She prayed again. "Please Lord, don't take this baby from us. It's what I owe my husband for all he's done for me. I can't disappoint him, Lord, please."

Laurel tried to push herself up so she could sit against the porch post, but she couldn't get up. As she moved the pain increased, almost as if she could feel a tearing in her womb. As the pain grew more acute and frequent, Laurel lost consciousness.

~

As FAST AS Sassy could run, Cathy rode to Shiloh Church. Brother

Matthew was sitting on the front porch as she rode into the churchyard. He and his son, Mark were sharing a mid-day meal together.

"Brother Matthew, come quick. Mrs. Mac is hurtin' so bad. She's on the back porch and cryin' something awful. Please come quick." Cathy called out without dismounting.

"What happened Cathy? Did she fall on the steps?"

"Please, can't we hurry? I'll tell you, but we gotta go. She told me to get you and Miss Ellie and bring y'all back in a hurry."

"Mark, ride home and tell your ma to come to Mac and Laurel's cabin. Hurry, son."

After what seemed to be hours, but was less than half of one, Matthew and Cathy knelt next to Laurel on the porch. Laurel was not crying out in pain, but she still lay in the place Cathy had told him. "Laurel Grace, can you hear me?" Matt got no reply from her. He picked her up and carried her to the bed in the second pen. He laid her down as carefully as he was able, but the slightest movement caused Laurel to moan in pain. "Laurel, can you tell me what happened to you? Try to talk to me."

The familiar voice aroused her. "My baby, Uncle Matthew. Please pray for my baby. Don't let anything happen to Mac's son." Laurel cried out in extreme pain and once again slipped into unconsciousness, a welcome reprieve from her suffering.

He could do nothing but pray. So, he did. Later, Ellie arrived in her wagon, thinking they may need to take Laurel to Greensboro to Dr. Gibson. "Ellie, I don't know what we should do. I don't think we should move her. I wish John was here so I could send him for the doctor, but I will ride myself, now that you are here to stay with Laurel. You'll be more comfort to her than me anyway."

WHEN MATTHEW WAS able to return with Dr. Gibson, Laurel was asleep. Ellie sat beside the tall bed, her face tracked with tears. "I'm afraid the doctor won't have much to do now. Laurel Grace lost her baby. The little boy was stillborn about an hour ago."

Matt walked over to his wife and hugged her. "Dear, Lord, no. Can they stand another sorrow like this?"

The doctor motioned them out of the room and proceeded to give Laurel the care she needed. The tiny baby lay in a basket wrapped in a white blanket. Dr. Gibson shook his head in sadness. The little boy was perfectly formed. He was so regrettably small since Laurel still had about two months until her delivery time. Dr. Gibson guessed the child weighed about two pounds. He was concerned because Laurel was quite a bit older than most first time mothers. She was twenty-nine now, and most women her age had already had several children. He prayed his examination would not show damage that would not allow her to have more children. That message he had no will to deliver to Mac or Laurel.

The doctor spoke to himself. "I pray they can bear this loss, Lord. Never saw a couple wanted a baby so bad." Dr. Edwards again shook his head in sorrow for his friends. He finished his work and returned to the main room where Matt and Ellie waited.

"Doc, will my niece be all right?"

"She's sleeping right now, which is good for her. Can you tell me what happened? I saw her only a couple of weeks ago, and she was thriving and the baby was healthy. Where is Mac?"

"I'm not sure. Cathy, come and tell us what happened this morning before you came to get me."

"Mr. Mac is not home from Missouri yet. We thought he'd be home before Easter, but he didn't get here. We're sorta worried about 'em."

"Don't fret. I'm sure they had to shelter from that storm yesterday. Cathy, do you know what happened to my niece?"

"I don't know. We did the wash like we do every Monday, and when we came in for dinner, she crumpled over and yelled out so bad. She did that yesterday too, before supper time. She told me she was fine. Is she? Nothing is wrong with her or our baby is there? You know we're a family now."

"You say she was in pain yesterday, too, Cathy?"

"Yes, for a little while. She fell out of the wagon when a loud thunder scared Sassy. A lightning bolt struck the ground over at the end of our road. Sassy Lady gets feisty in storms. Mrs. Mac said she wasn't hurt except for her pride got hurt. Is that what happened? Is her pride hurt too bad?"

Matthew Campbell picked up the eight-year-old and cradled her in his lap. "No, Cathy. Mrs. Mac has lost her baby. I expect it happened because of the fall yesterday. Dr. Gibson, will Laurel be well again?"

"As much as I can tell, Laurel should heal fine. I'm thinking that in time, there will be other children."

"Praise the Lord for that. Mac is going to take this pretty hard. He and Laurel were so happy to be having this baby."

"Laurel Grace will need us here, Matthew. She may wake before Mac gets home." Ellie took Cathy's hand, and together they went in to prepare a late supper. Matthew went to the barn to do the evening chores, including unsaddling the little mare Cathy had forgotten in the stress of the day. As he was finishing the milking, he heard the hoof beats of several horses and cows coming up the Shiloh road. He also heard his son's voice at the distance. John was singing a favorite hymn as they approached the gate to Mac's fenced pasture.

Matthew left the barn with his full bucket and walked to the back porch to set the pail down. How could he tell his best friend the news he had to tell? Mac called from the gate when he saw Matthew at the porch.

"Hey, Matthew. What brings you here? Don't you have enough chores at your place that you wanted to come here and do mine?" Matthew walked toward Mac without a witty comeback. Mac knew something wasn't right.

"Where is Laurel? Something's not right here. She always comes to meet me when I come home. I know she'll be mad about Easter, but it's more than that."

"Mac, Laurel will be all right. Dr. Gibson is here with her now. Mac…Oh, Dear Lord, help me. Mac..."

"Matthew, what's happened to Laurel? Where is she?"

"Laurel had an accident. The baby was stillborn this afternoon. I hate to tell you

such sorry news, brother."

"Oh, Lord, no!" Mac started to run to the cabin. Matt grabbed his arms and pulled him back.

"Mac, Laurel's asleep now. We didn't tell her about the baby yet. Ellie and the doctor are with her."

"What else can she take, Matthew? God, please no." Matthew pulled his friend into his arms, and they cried together. After a while, Matthew prayed for Mac, asking God to give him the strength to help his wife. In sorrow, Mac called out to God, at first in anger, and then in petition. He pleaded for wisdom and courage to support Laurel through another ordeal.

Night had fallen before the men entered the cabin. Dr. Gibson met them in the kitchen near the hearth. "Mac, I'm sorry about the little one. Laurel will heal. She is beginning to rouse up some. She'll wake up soon. I'm sorry I couldn't do anything to save the baby."

"Are you sure she'll be all right?"

"She is a strong lady, Mac. She will be well again, soon. No reason y'all can't have another baby after a spell."

By this time, Roy and John returned from settling the herd. They would have been back in Shiloh before Easter Sunday had they not traveled the biggest part of the trip in the rain. They'd had to shelter the animals from the worst part of the storm yesterday. The boys had not heard what the doctor had told Mac, but they sensed something bad had happened. The atmosphere was too heavy. In tears, Cathy sat rocking in Laurel's chair. Roy walked over and picked up her hand. "What's wrong, little sister?"

"Roy, Mrs. Mac and Mac are going to be sad for a while. Me, too. We lost our new baby."

"Y'all excuse me. I need to be with Laurel when she wakes up. I should have been here. This wouldn't have happened if I'd been home. I don't want her to wake up alone...not today."

Mac walked toward the second pen like a man carrying a tremendous weight on his shoulders. His shoulders bowed, and his arms hung at his sides. Matthew realized Mac's loss was a sorrow greater than he'd ever had to share with a friend. He had stood by his flock in times of loss... more often than he liked to think of. Yet this was not just a member of his congregation. This man was like his brother. He didn't know if he could be the support Mac needed right now. And Laurel! How could he give her any comfort? He too was grieving.

As Mac entered the bedroom, he saw Laurel lying on the tall bed covered by her favorite yellow coverlet. Her tawny curls covered the pillow, and she seemed to be in a natural sleep. As he looked around, he saw a small basket on the table. Nearby, the red diamond cut lantern was lit, throwing a flickering light across the room. He saw too a small shape covered by the tiny blanket. He knew his child was lying there. He stepped toward the tiny bundle as Laurel awoke from the laudanum-induced sleep. She wasn't coherent. She moaned and called out, "Patrick."

She fumbled as she tried to sit, calling out to him. He returned to sit beside her and pulled her into his arms. "Laurel, it's Patrick. I am home now. Can you hear me, sweetheart?"

"Patrick, you're home."

"Yes, darlin', I am here now."

"I am so glad." Her head dropped to his shoulder for a few minutes.

"Laurel, do you need anything to drink? Are you in pain? Dr. Gibson is still here if you need him. Can you talk to me?"

Her lashes fluttered against her cheeks. For a second, Laurel's grey eyes opened fully, only to close once more. Her head fell back again. When Mac gazed into her face, a sole tear fell on her forehead. Cradling her face, he kissed her. Awakening from the drug-induced sleep was proving to be difficult. "I'm very sleepy, Mac. Is it night?"

"Yes, it's late...after eight. Can you rouse yourself up? Do you need the doctor?"

"No. Why would I need a doctor?"

"Laurel, don't you remember?

"I remember feeling sick and sending Cathy to get Uncle Matthew." Consciousness returned to Laurel as she remembered the pain. Other snatches of time surfaced, seeing her Aunt Ellie sitting by her bed and her uncle praying by her side. "Oh, no, please God, no. Patrick, our baby?"

He couldn't speak. The pain in his too-blue-eyes told the depth of his grief. His loss was as obvious as Laurel's, whose sobs were so deep they shook her to the depth of her being.

With nearly incoherent words, Laurel cried out to her husband. "Forgive me, Patrick. I am sorry. Please forgive me."

Patrick had no words. He clung to his grieving wife as if their very existence depended on their being together. In their dimly lit room, they wept for the loss of their first child.

# CHAPTER TWELVE

*And know all things work together for Good to them that love God, to them who are called according to His purpose.*
*Romans 8:28*

About 8:30, Mac returned from the bedroom where Laurel once again slept. Ellie and Matthew Campbell waited with Dr. Gibson in the main room. Mac looked about the room and noticed the young people were not there. “What have you done with the young’uns?”

“Don’t worry about the Dunns, Mac. I got them bedded down a while ago. Didn’t take much talking to get them both to climb to the loft directly after supper. How’s Laurel Grace feeling?” Ellie spoke to Mac as she laid her hand on his shoulder.

“She’s sleeping again. I guess that’s a blessing.”

“Mac, she will be more alert in the morning. That laudanum is strong.”

“Tell me straight, Ed. Will she be all right? Do you know?”

“Mac, when I saw the baby, I knew exactly what happened. I’ve seen it before. When Laurel took that spill on Sunday afternoon, the cord began to tear away from her womb. Cathy said she’d had a pain after they got home. Laurel didn't think anything of it, and so on Monday, she went about her regular chores. By noon, the rupture finished. I see no sign that she's suffered any permanent harm. The little boy arrived too early to survive."

"A boy...." Mac put his face in his hands. He sat still and silent for some time. "I wanted a son." Matthew came across to Mac's chair and knelt down in front of his friend. He gripped Mac's arm at the elbow. Mac, in turn, clutched the support he clearly needed.

"Mac, I got no words that can start to comfort you, but if you'll let me, I'll grieve with you." Mac looked up at his friend and nodded.

Dr. Edwards rose from the armchair. "I'll check on Laurel once again, and then I'm headed home. I'm thinking she'll sleep through the night. I'll check back in a day or two, but send for me if you need me before then." He placed his arm across Mac's shoulder. "I am so sorry, my friend. God keep ya."

Within ten minutes, the cabin was quiet. Ellie and John had left with the doctor, all headed home. Only Matthew remained behind.

"Mac, you need some sleep. I'll stay here to see to the kids and chores tonight. Why don't you go back to Laurel Grace and try to rest a while?"

"Matthew, I can see God punishing me for my sinful past, but Laurel doesn't deserve this kind of loss. She's already lost so much."

"You know that ain't so, Mac. Our Lord is not a God of vengeance. You got no punishment due. You lost claim to all that past life more than four years ago when you gave it to Jesus. What'd make you think such a thing?"

"She's a good woman, been through hurt after hurt in her life. I figured it had to be me. I deserve it, but not her."

"Losing that baby was a natural result of Laurel's fall. Accidents happen. God will work this all out. There will be other babies, I know it."

"We were so happy for a while. I am not sure Laurel can take another loss right now. You know how hard she took the news about Rachel. I never seem to be around when things come to hurt her. I should have waited until after the baby came to bring those cattle here. She asked me not to go."

"Don't do no one good to try to second guess the past. You don't know that anything would be different if you'd been home." Matthew walked over to the side table where the crystal lantern was lit and picked up Mac's Bible. He thumbed through the well-worn pages of the book for a moment. "Here, Mac. Listen." Matthew read Romans 8:28. "God didn't take your son, Mac. Not to punish you or to punish Laurel Grace. He loves you both, and he will turn your grief to joy in time."

"I know in my mind what you say is true, but my heart is too heavy right now. I don't know what I need to do."

"One thing at a time, brother. Let me pray with you and then you try to rest awhile. You go on in and lie down with Laurel. Your being close will comfort you both, and then you will be there when Laurel Grace needs you."

Mac returned to the bedroom and saw Laurel sleeping. He walked to the chair near the window and began to remove his clothes. Only then did he realize how dirty he felt from the grit and dust of the trail. He removed his shirt and sat down to pull off his boots when the little basket caught his eye again. He rose and took two steps so he could see into the basket. He lifted the little white blanket, and he saw the still, perfect child–so tiny and so beautiful–his son.

Silent tears flowed. "Dear Jesus, help me. This sorrow is too great to bear alone." Mac turned and looked at the infant for a moment longer, and as he did a sense of peace began to sooth the pain he felt. He released the soft blanket, no longer able to look at the tiny boy.

Mac walked to the window and stood looking over Shiloh for a long time. How beautiful the sunrise was! He wept, and then he tried to praise. Count your blessings...Count them one by one...And again he cried in his grief. After a time, he turned to remove the rest of his dirty clothes and walked to the wash closet to clean himself of the grime. The cool water refreshed him, and as he cleaned himself, his anger began to ebb away. He returned to Laurel's side and quietly lay down beside her. He cradled her close to his chest. He breathed in the scent of her curls. Within moments, he slept.

STREAKS OF SUNLIGHT flowed through the windows of the bedroom as Laurel awoke. She felt as if she had not slept at all. Her limbs mimicked massive stone columns, which defied lifting. The drug-induced sleep left her world fog-filled and hazy... so vague and impermanent. She didn't remember ever feeling so tired. Then she realized Mac lay next to her, and for the briefest of moments, she was happy to be in his arms. Her joy was short-lived though when she recalled the last words she'd spoken to him the night before. "Forgive me, Patrick." Their son had not survived. She failed to give Mac his baby.

"Laurel, you're awake early. Do you feel all right? Are you in any pain?" Mac sat up and put his arm around her shoulder. He brushed her hair back from her eyes. "Forgive me for not being here when you needed me. Do you need anything now?"

She shook her head and buried her face in his shoulder. She could not look at him. The loss in his eyes would be too much for her to deal with that morning. "Patrick, I'm sorry I failed you. Please forgive me."

"Laurel, there is nothing to forgive. You could've been killed when Sassy threw you. I should have left you a mule for that wagon. Sassy is dangerous. We're getting rid of that silly mare."

He arose from the bed and noticed that the basket was gone. Matthew must have taken it from the room to spare Laurel the sorrow of having to cope with the loss if she woke before Mac. He jammed his legs into his trousers and pulled his shirt across his shoulders. Not bothering with the buttons, he rushed back to sit with Laurel. "Laurel, oh Lord help me...I wouldn't want to live if something had happened to you."

"Was the baby a boy?"

"Yes, Laurel, a son."

"Oh, no, please God, no. Patrick, how can you forgive me? I wanted to give you a healthy baby, your dream of a family of your own. I never wanted to fail you. I am sorry." Laurel's lashes lay on her cheeks. Her arms locked around Mac's shoulders. She clung to him as if she was afraid he'd disappear if she turned him loose. She didn't look at him even once. How could she stand to see the pain she had caused?

"Your Uncle Matthew is here. We need to decide how we want to lay the baby to rest. Do you want me to have Matthew take care of the burial?" Still clinging to Mac's shoulder, Laurel shook her head.

"We'll do it ourselves. He is our child."

"Laurel, you have to rest. The doctor…"

"We'll do it tomorrow."

"If that is what you want. Do you think you'll be able to be up that soon?"

"Yes. Can we take him back to Eden? I'm sure that is where he was conceived… that beautiful fall afternoon that we made love in our special place. We need to take care of…" Laurel could not finish what she had started to say. Tears again overcame her words and mingled with those on Mac's cheeks.

"All right now, Laurel. We will be all right. We have each other, and the Lord will take care of the rest." She didn't answer. She wanted to go back to sleep, back to the dark peaceful haven where she felt no pain and her worse fears and sorrows had no place. She didn't want to think about Mac's sorrow or deal with her own shame and anger toward herself. Nor did she want to confront her sense of abandonment and bitterness that God had let this tragedy happen to her and especially to Mac. She knew her faith was not strong enough to merit his intervention for her, but Mac was such a loyal, true disciple, how could God have let such a hurt fall to him?

"Mac, I want to go back to sleep for a while. I am so tired. I'll get up in a while, and we'll finish what we were planning. I need to sleep now if you don't care."

"Of course, you need to rest." He rose from the bedside where he'd been holding his wife. She turned to the side and lay back into her pillow. Mac pulled the yellow coverlet over her and bent to kiss her. "Laurel, I love you. I thank God for you." When she made no response, he left the room and closed the door behind him.

When Mac returned to the kitchen, he found Matthew sitting at the table drinking coffee. He sat down beside his friend.

"Is Laurel awake?"

"She was for a few minutes. She said she had to rest a while longer."

"Did she agree to let me take the baby to the churchyard for burial?"

"No. She says it's our task to handle. We are his parents. She wants to lay him to rest here on our land."

"Is she up to doing this herself?"

"She said she wanted to do it. I know she helped to lay out her mother and brother. I saw her and a friend take care of her father. She says it is her family's way to take care of their own."

"When can you lay him to rest?"

"Laurel wants to have a quiet family service tomorrow. Can you be here?"

"Yes, brother. I'll stay as long as you need me."

"Right now, I need to be alone. Matthew, will you stay and watch over Laurel for me? I want to ride out for an hour or so."

"If you're sure you want to be alone."

"Thanks, Matthew."

Mac went to the barn and saddled Midnight. He then headed out toward the lower part of his homestead, passing his newly-stocked pastures. He was oblivious to his surroundings. He rode, kicking the stallion into a fast gallop. He crossed the open field and headed for Eden. When he reached the glade, he jumped from Midnight's back and fell to his knees. He cried out in hurt and bitterness, "Lord, how can you let this happen to us? Jesus, please help me understand! Was I not living out the plan you had given me?" Mac wept and continued to cry out to God for what seemed an eternity. Eventually, he sat down with his back to the large oak tree where he had made love to Laurel in October. He cried again, but this time he wept for his loss. His anger again drained away, and he didn't feel alone. In his grief, he'd struck out, but in his faith, he'd asked for help, and he felt the peace of Christ's love surround him. "Father, please forgive my despair. Give me the courage and wisdom to help Laurel get through this loss. We will have our family in your time. I have no doubt of your promise." Mac didn't know how long he stayed in Eden, but he was hungry. He also felt a strong pull back to the cabin, hoping that Laurel might want him.

When he returned, he called out to Matt. "Did Laurel wake up yet?"

"No, Mac. She was still asleep a few minutes ago, and it's near noon.

We should fix a noon meal and get her up to eat. She doesn't need to sleep all day."

"She's been asleep a long time. Do you think I should get the doctor?"

"No need. She will be well when her body has a chance to heal and her spirit has a chance to grieve. She is only hiding in her sleep right now."

Laurel didn't want to wake up when Mac offered her the meal he'd helped prepare. She told him that she wasn't at all hungry but so tired she had to sleep.

"Laurel, I don't want to cause a spat, but you need to try to rouse yourself. Darlin', you haven't eaten anything in more than two days, and you've been asleep almost twenty-four hours. We need to talk to Matt about tomorrow. Do you want me to ask him to come in here so we can talk together?"

"Why do we have to do this now? I 'd like to go back to bed."

"First eat, and perhaps you'll feel like sitting up and talking to me for a while." Laurel sat up and sat on the side of the tall bed. Mac walked over to her and sat down. She would not look at him, but she did lean against him for support.

"I am so sorry. I hope you can forgive me. I did want to give you that baby."

"Laurel, I told you. You haven't done anything for me to forgive. You can't blame yourself for an accident."

"I couldn't give you the one thing you wanted."

"You didn't fail me. We have a family. We are a family already."

"I appreciate you for being so kind to me."

"I'm not being kind. Don't you have any idea of how dear you are to me? If you don't know that, I'm the one who's failed."

"Mac, let's finish your plans for tomorrow. I am too tired. I wanna go back to sleep."

"Let me take you into the front room. There is a nice breeze coming through the windows in there. We can talk and let Matthew help us make our plans."

"If that is what you want." He picked her up and carried her to her rocking chair. He went to the dry sink and poured a glass of water and picked up the plate he'd prepared for her. Laurel took it and began to pick at the food.

Shortly, her uncle Matthew came in from the porch, walked to where she sat and kissed her forehead. "I'm happy to see you awake, Sprite. I am heartsick about your baby, Laurel." She didn't answer and wiped a tear from the corner of her eye. "Do you want me to bring Ellie to get the little one ready?"

"I can do it."

"She'll want to be with you."

"Whatever you think."

"Do you want a service at the church, Laurel?" She shook her head. Mac walked up behind her and placed his hands on her shoulders. Though silent, both tear-streaked faces told of grief they could not voice. "What do you want, Laurel?"

"I want a healthy living child in my arms. I want to give my husband joy and not sorrow. I don't want to feel I'm being punished for some terrible wrong I've done. I want to know why..." Her voice trembled and once again she cried.

"Laurel, I wish I knew what to say to comfort you. I hate seeing you in pain. Please try to keep your faith, darlin'. God will give you the answers you want."

"I don't want a sermon right now, Uncle Matthew. Mac said we have to make plans before I can sleep again. Let's do what we have to. I'm tired." No anger tinged her voice, nor even a great deal of pain. Laurel's voice was devoid of emotion. Matthew looked up into the face of his friend and saw the loss he'd expected to hear in the voice of his niece. Laurel brushed the tears away with the back of her hand and squared her shoulders. She intended to hide her hurt and fear instead of face them. Laurel intended to retreat behind her protective wall, a place where she wouldn't feel Mac's grief or allow hurt to enter.

"Laurel Grace, Mac told me you want to lay the baby to rest here on your own land. We can do that if you want. We'll prepare a place this afternoon. Do you want to give him a name?"

"Whatever Mac wants."

"Laurel, are you up to doing this right now? Let me go get your Aunt Ellie to stay with you."

"Mac, it doesn't matter. Do what we have to do. If you want, we can give him a name."

"He deserves a name. I want to call him Campbell MacLayne. He is a part of us both. I'll have a maker carved so everyone will know he belongs to us."

"That's a good name. I'll get him ready in time."

"Do you want to do that yourself?"

"That's always been our way. I'll do what I need to do."

"You don't have to do it alone. Ellie is part of the family, and she will want to help. When do you want to have a service, Laurel?"

"You and Mac make the rest of the decisions. I am going back to sleep." Laurel rose from her rocking chair and started back to her bed. "Where are Cathy and Roy?"

"They're over at our place. I'll go bring them home this afternoon."

"Good."

Mid-afternoon, Ellie shook Laurel's shoulder. "Laurel Grace. It's time to get up. Can you rouse yourself for a while?"

"Aunt Ellie? What time is it? Seems like I hardly put my head on the pillow, and now you are trying to get me up."

"Laurel Grace, you've been asleep more than three hours. I know how hard it is to lose a loved one, but darlin', you can't sleep your sorrow away. Come on, girl, let me help you up." Almost as a child would obey, she stood and moved to sit in her Grandmother Wilson's rocking chair? "Do you want me to help you dress? You want a nice cool bath? It has been so warm all day."

"Aunt Ellie, do you think Mac can forgive me for losing his son?"

"Laurel Grace, such a thought! Mac's not blaming you. He loves you as much as any man can love a woman. He knows your fall was an accident. Together y'all have to grieve and then heal. Let the Lord take away the pain. You and Mac will have another baby in time."

"Don't you understand, Aunt Ellie? Mac didn't marry me because he loved me. We have an arranged marriage. He promised to take care of me, and I promised to give him a home and a family. I didn't live up to my side of the agreement."

"Laurel, it may have started out that way. For the life of me, I don't see how you can think Mac still feels that way. He loves you. True, he wants children, but you are no broodmare to him. You are his wife. He'd want you if there was no chance of ever having another child. He'd love you regardless, girl."

~

AT DAYBREAK THE NEXT MORNING, Laurel awoke, left her bed, and dressed for the day. She braided her hair and pulled the braids into a large coil at the nape of her neck. She walked to the kitchen and began to prepare breakfast. The noise of Laurel's stoking the fire in the hearth and filling the kettle with water woke Mac, who slept in his chair.

"Laurel, should you be up this morning?"

"I'm all right. I have some things I must do." She went on about the task she'd set for herself.

"Let me help you."

"I am capable of preparing this family a breakfast. You can do your own chores if you want something to do. I'll have food ready for you and the kids when you return." From her voice—that no-nonsense, matter of fact, I-mean-business-tone—Mac knew she wanted no reply. Laurel had retreated into the fortress she knew so well…just so she could survive the day. She wasn't angry or rude. Neither was there any warmth or life in the words she spoke. Mac pulled the blanket off and tossed it on the chair, leaving the room to go to the barn. Shortly, Cathy and Roy came down from the loft, dressed in their Sunday clothes, ready to stand beside Mac and Laurel at the burial of the little one.

Laurel said good morning to them. She laid out a hearty southern breakfast of bacon, eggs, biscuits, gravy, and grits. She sent Roy to the springhouse to bring back butter and milk to complete the meal. Mac's coffee was heating on the spit, spreading its aroma around the entire room. Except for the uneasy quiet, the scene was one of a typical morning, like so many others. The ominous silence marked the sadness of the place where the clicking of two spoons together seemed somehow irreverent. Mac returned and placed the milk pail and several eggs in the dry sink. He washed his hands and took his place at the table next to Laurel. Mac asked Roy to say grace. The four ate without a single word spoken until they were almost finished.

"Cathy, girl, will you fetch me another cup of coffee, please?"

"Yes, Mr. Mac."

"Thank you, Laurel, for the fine breakfast. I'm pleased you are up and able to be with us this morning."

"Mac, will you bring him to the bedroom so I can dress him?"

"Laurel, wait for Ellie to come so she can help you."

"No need. I've tended to my people for a long time. I know what I need to do."

"Very well. I will help you, then."

Laurel went to the old walnut bureau her father had carved. She removed all the things she had made and laid them on the bed. From the many items, she took a white christening gown, a pair of tiny white booties, and a blanket, knitted during the worst days of winter. Laurel had made these things to serve a much different purpose. Mac returned to the four-poster with the basket, which held the tiny son they'd so wanted.

"These clothes will be far too big for him."

"They are beautiful pieces, Laurel." Laurel took the baby from her husband and laid him on the bed. She looked at him for the first time.

With downcast eyes, Laurel spoke. "He would have been perfect–even so still he is beautiful. I am sorry, I couldn't give you a healthy child, Patrick." Tears flowed down Laurel's face. "Please go bring me some warm water."

She took a piece of soft flannel from the clothes on the bed and washed the tiny infant. With her fingertips, she smoothed a small strand of dark hair. She looked at the long lashes, so much like Mac's as he slept. She put the christening gown on the little boy and reached for the booties. "I remember how happy you were when I gave you a pair of white booties like these last Christmas." She wrapped the baby in a small blanket meant to cover him in his cradle, the same cradle his grandfather MacLayne carved for his own two sons. When she finished, she laid him on a large feather pillow that would be placed in a small casket her Uncle Matthew would bring. Dry-eyed, she turned and left the room.

When she entered the kitchen, she asked Cathy to open the windows. At 8:00, the heat was oppressive, so common in mid-June, but rare so early in April. She sat in her chair to wait for the rest of her family to arrive. Mac came in, dressed in his finest attire, and sat next to her, concern etched across on his face. But his own grief would have to wait, for his greater concern was to help Laurel get past the day's ordeal. He needed her at Shiloh but feared she was again living in the fortress where he'd met her.

The burial was a very brief ceremony. Surrounded by their family, Laurel and Mac laid Campbell MacLayne beneath the beautiful old oak tree in Eden. Matthew Campbell spoke a few comforting words and closed by singing the Wesley hymn, *How Happy Every Child of Grace.* Laurel remained calm, dry-eyed, and silent throughout the short service. Mac led her away, back down the path home, while her cousins and Roy covered the small wooden casket. At the distance, the thunder began to roll, and a flash of lightning showed over the top of Crowley's Ridge.

# CHAPTER THIRTEEN

*But by the grace of God, I am what I am, and His grace, which was bestowed on me was not in vain, but I labored more abundantly than they...*
*1 Corinthians 15:10*

Laurel's Campbell family remained most of the afternoon. The heavy rain kept them from traveling home. While she was restless in her hostess role, Laurel was relieved that there was no large wake to attend. Her uncle must have told the church family that she was not well enough to deal with a crowd. If he hadn't intervened, the Shiloh community would have surrounded her with love and support. The last thing Laurel wanted at that moment was to put on a mask and carry on her social responsibilities. She wanted nothing more than to return to her bed and sleep.

But that night when she did retreat to her bedroom, Laurel could not sleep. In her sadness, she knew she had to find some way to compensate Mac for his loss. He'd told her he didn't blame her, but she knew how much effort he'd put into their homestead, building a home for his family. She couldn't live feeling that she'd failed to live up to her part of the obligation. She resolved to put everything she was into making Mac's homestead the best in the district. Some things were under her control. She could work hard. She was no stranger to the long hours of effort required from a homesteader's wife. Mac would never be able to fault her for her role as a homemaker. She vowed to herself she'd be the best, hardest working, least demanding helpmate any man could ever have.

Laurel resolved to work her way to Mac's forgiveness. The very next morning, she arose at 5:00 a.m. and immediately began the morning chores. Before 6:15, Laurel had prepared a large meal for Mac and the children. The family gathered at the table to share the huge breakfast. Mac and Roy left to tend the cattle in the pastures, and Cathy dressed for a day of work with Laurel.

When Mac returned for lunch, he noticed all the work Laurel had done that morning. She had done as much that one morning as would normally have taken all day. Bread baking, weeding the garden, cleaning the windows, removing ashes from both fireplaces, and cleaning the hearths to lay new fires from scratch that day were only part of the things she'd accomplished. Her hair was straggling out of its usually neat bun, and she had smudges of soot on her cheeks and nose.

"Laurel, you shouldn't be working so much. The doctor said you'd be fine, but the healing takes time and rest. I'll bet you haven't sat down since I went out this morning."

"There is nothing wrong with me. You know we have lots of things to do this time of year."

"You don't have to do it all in one day, nor do you have to do it alone."

"Keeping this homestead is my job. I want to do my share of the work around here. Anyway, I wasn't working alone. Cathy has been with me all day."

"Laurel, I want you well. You have to rest this afternoon. Let me get you a book to read. You go in, lie back on the bed, and read a while …or take a nap."

"I will sit here in the rocking chair, but I intend to get to the mending. Roy has ripped two of his shirts, and Cathy needs the hem taken down in her brown skirt."

"That doesn't sound much like rest to me."

"It's easy work, then. You go on about your business, and I'll do mine."

"I am going to be around close if you want me. I'm going to move a few of those new heifers to another part of the pasture. Then I'll get to that storm damage from Sunday."

Mac had continued telling Laurel of his plans for the afternoon, but she had hardly heard a word. By suppertime, Laurel had finished dusting and sweeping the walnut plank floors of her house. She had churned the cream from the morning milk into fresh butter and sat down with the mending. She finished every chore, just as she'd told Mac. For supper that night, she baked a blackberry cobbler after finishing the bread. Laurel sent Roy to bring Mac in a bit early for supper.

After supper, Mac got up to hitch the wagon. "Laurel, will you be ready to go with us to Matthew's in a few minutes? I told you this morning, they were celebrating Mary's birthday with a cake."

"You go and take the children with you. I'm not feeling well, and I'm very tired. Y'all go on without me tonight."

"If you're not well, I'll stay here with you."

"I don't need you here to watch me nap. I overdid it a little today. I am going to rest. Besides, I still have a little work to finish before I can go to bed. Please go on and make sure the kids get to the party." She slumped into the rocking chair near the hearth and picked up her darning.

Laurel repeated her odd behavior the following Sunday. She told Mac that she was too tired to go to church, and she needed to rest. She continued to isolate herself more and more, but he couldn't bring himself to confront her so soon after losing Campbell. She withdrew from the children as well, and she had begun to shut herself away from him. Every time he'd tried to find an opportunity to comfort her, Laurel moved to avoid his touch. If Mac reached out to caress her hair, she'd pull away, and then provide him with some good excuse. By the end of the first month after losing the baby, Mac's concern and frustration pushed him to his breaking point. When neighbors dropped by to visit, Laurel was always 'resting' or 'not at home', yet she hadn't left their homestead once. She avoided contact with everyone, even her Uncle Matthew. Mac decided to intervene before Laurel slipped away completely.

The community planned a barn dance in the preacher's homestead for the Saturday. With spring planting behind them, now was the time for socializing. This provided a perfect opportunity to have a late spring party. Mac told Laurel about the dance on Tuesday, and he explained it was a good opportunity to renew his campaigning. He asked her to wear her green gingham dress he loved. The rest of the week the subject didn't come up.

Mac asked her again that Friday morning, "Wife, what time do you want to go the dance tomorrow?" Again, she didn't reply.

"Did you hear me, wife?"

"What? Oh, yes, I heard." Laurel looked up from the stack of dishes she had picked up from the table. "Mac, I don't want to go to the dance. I have a book I want to finish reading. I'm not up to going over there.

"Laurel, what is wrong. We've gotta talk about this. Do you need me to go get Dr. Gibson?"

"I don't need a doctor."

"Then what is it? You work like you're demon-possessed all day. Then every night you are too tired or not feeling well enough to go off the place. You haven't been to church in more than a month. You've started to avoid all our company. You ignore the kids, and you have been avoiding me too. What's the matter, Laurel?"

"I've not ignored this family. I've prepared meals--kept the laundry done. Our house is clean and tidy."

"No one could fault you on your work ethic. You know that is not what I meant. I am your husband, Laurel. If you can't talk to me, who can you talk to? Please don't shut me out. I miss you. We don't talk anymore. You won't let me touch you. I've forgotten the last time you let me hold you. We have slept apart since the accident. Did I offend you in some way? Are you angry with me?"

"No, Mac. Please don't push me. I'm not ready yet. I don't want to deal with people. Can't I take the time I need..." Tears ran down Laurel's cheeks. She tried to wipe them away before Mac saw. He recognized how hard Laurel was working to keep her emotions contained. Even a small bit of stress broke through her resolve not to feel.

"Please don't cry, Laurel. I don't want to add to your grief. I am here when you are ready to talk." Mac picked up his hat and left the cabin. He didn't know how to reach her, and each day she was building back the wall he'd worked so hard to breach. He had to talk to someone. He wanted to talk to Laurel, but she wouldn't let him. He went to the barn to saddle Midnight and rode off toward Matthew's cabin. He prayed his friend could help him find some answers or at the very least, let him vent some of his frustrations.

The Campbells were sitting on their porch enjoying the spring weather. Matthew was holding Ellie's hand and kissing her palm. Their flirtation ended abruptly as Mac rode into their yard.

"Evening Mac. What brings you out at this hour? Is Laurel Grace all right?"

"Good evening, Ellie. Matthew. I hate to bother you, but I hoped you'd have some time to talk."

"I do, brother. Sit here with us on the porch."

"If it's all the same with you, I'd like to walk."

"All right." Matt rose from his chair, bent, and kissed his wife. "Won't be too long, Ellie." Together, the two men walked back down the road. "What's eating at you, Mac?"

"Probably nothin' really. I just feel so darn so helpless. Laurel is... well, she's...Damnation!"

"She's what?"

"You know she won't leave the homestead. I haven't been able to get her to come to church or ride with me to Greensboro. She won't see friends who drop by the cabin to visit with her. During the day, she works like she's demon-possessed until she's about to drop by nightfall. She won't talk to me beyond the most basic answer to a question. She shies from my touch."

"It's only been a few weeks. I'm sure she'll come around."

"Laurel's not spoken one word about the baby since we left the burying. I am at a loss. Did I lose both of them...Laurel and my son? What can I do?"

"Brother, be patient."

"She's shutting us all out again, Matt. Even you, when you came out the other Monday when she'd missed church, she said almost nothing and left the room."

"I noticed, but you said she's working to exhaustion. I didn't get there until after supper."

"Since when does being tired excuse rudeness? She refused to see Ellie yesterday. She hardly speaks to Cathy and Roy—or me."

"You really are worried. Have you talked to Dr. Gibson about it?"

"No. He said she'd be sad for a while, but then she'd get back to normal. Physically, Laurel's well, but she seems to be walling herself away again. I don't have a clue of what I need to do to help her." There was a long silence between the two friends.

Matthew shook his salt and pepper hair back from his face. "Mac, I don't know if it's my place to talk about Laurel, but did she tell you about that attack when she was about fourteen?"

"Yes, she told me the whole ugly story. She finally remembered most of it. I thought we'd put that behind us."

"You know that was the first time she closed herself away. Her pa wrote to me about some of it. When she was attacked, she learned if she didn't let people get close to her, they couldn't hurt her. She took on the role of serving her family, but she never felt loveable or accepted by anyone. She works to earn her place. She did it with her father in Washington County, and now she is doing it here with you. Don't you see? Laurel Grace doesn't know anything about grace."

"If that's true, no wonder she runs from us all."

"Mac, you should have another baby right away."

"That ain't likely to happen. Laurel moves away when I reach out to her. I can hardly get her to look at me when I am talking to her. She's sleeping alone in our room."

"Are you telling me you two haven't shared a bed since before you went to Missouri?"

"That is not the issue. Laurel needs time to heal."

"You've gotta hold her now, just like before. She needs you to. She may push you away, but it's the last thing she truly wants."

"How am I supposed to know that?"

"Drat it, Mac! What did she say to make you think you're not welcome in your own bed?"

"She's not said anything. We haven't talked, but she's so tired that she goes to bed after cleaning up from supper. We don't spend family time together in the evenin' anymore. She moves away from me whenever she thinks I am going to reach for her."

"What is she saying?"

"She says nothing about anything. She gets very defensive when I ask her things. The one thing she says every day, more than once sometimes, is please forgive her."

"Lord help her. I don't know what to say that'll comfort you, Mac. I'll come out tomorrow and try to talk with her. Do you think she'll talk to her old uncle?" They walked on for a while longer. "And brother, you need to return to your place in that four-poster. Laurel needs you there, even if she doesn't know it."

After praying with Matthew for some time, Mac returned home. All the way back, he tried to convince himself that Matthew was right in telling him to reclaim his side of their bed. At least, it would show Laurel he had no intentions of giving up on her. When he entered the cabin, the clock on the mantle showed the time to be 11:00. Laurel had left the diamond cut lantern lit for him. The room was quiet, as the Dunn children had gone to the loft long ago, and Laurel was in the second pen. Mac picked up his Bible and sat down in his chair to read awhile. He hoped to find some direction, some encouragement, and an answer in the Word. He found what he was seeking when he read Ephesians 4. *"But unto every one of us is given grace according to the measure of the gift of Christ."* Mac knew his life began when he knew grace...His gift had been great beyond measure. *"Let no corrupt communication proceedeth out of your mouth, but that which is good to use for edifying; that it may minister grace unto the hearer."* Laurel must come to understand grace. She must learn she owed him nothing, except to allow him to love her.

Finally, he read the last two verses of that chapter. *"Let all bitterness, and wrath, and anger, and clamor, and evil speaking be put away from you, with all malice. And be ye kind to one another, tenderhearted, forgiving one another, even as God for Christ sake forgave you."* Mac knew above all that God's love for him had allowed him to love again. The grace God had afforded him was carrying him through the grief of losing his first child. He must help Laurel learn that, too. He would lay his fear in God's hands, and he would go back to his role as Laurel's loving husband. He laid his Scripture book on the table and blew out the lantern. He walked into the second pen, removed his boots and clothes and slipped into the right side of the tall bed. Laurel roused when she felt him lie down beside her.

"I'm home, Laurel. Goodnight, wife. Sweet dreams."

The next morning, Mac awoke before Laurel. He had decided that life at the MacLayne household would return to normal. He was sure Laurel would balk at the idea, but he also knew she would do what he wanted if he insisted. He bent over and kissed his sleeping wife.

"I've missed you, Laurel. I'm so happy you're well again so I can return to our bed. Did you sleep well, darlin'?"

Laurel roused herself and pushed her hair behind her shoulders. Rubbing her eyes, she realized that her husband had spoken to her. "Well enough, I guess." Mac pulled her into his arms and ran his hands down the length of her hair. He felt Laurel stiffen and attempt to pull away from him. He didn't respond, nor did he let her move away.

"It's a beautiful morning, and I am back with you." Mac again kissed Laurel. "You are beautiful this morning, wife. I know you are feeling better." He picked up her hand and kissed her palm, a slow, lingering kiss. "What time can we leave for the barn dance at Matt and Ellie's?"

"I'm sure I told you I'm not up to going out yet."

"Nonsense, wife. A social is what we both need…to be back with people who care about us…a place with music and fun."

"Mac, please, take the kids and go without me. I need a few more weeks."

"No arguments, woman. We're going to the party. We'll leave at five so make yourself beautiful. Wear that pretty green gingham I like so much and leave your hair down."

"Mac, I'm not going."

"Yes, Laurel, you are. Now I have chores to do, and you've got a couple of kids to feed."

~

MAC WAS true to his word. He took his family to the community dance and enjoyed himself—meeting and politicking until midnight. He never allowed Laurel out of his sight. He danced with her, romanced her, and made sure she was in the center of his attention the entire night.

In the middle of one of the waltzes, Matthew approached the MacLaynes. Mac appeared to be having a fine time. The smile on his face was a welcome sight for his friend after the stress he'd seen there only the day before. Yet, Matthew could easily see that Laurel was playing out her role as a dutiful wife. The anxiety on her face told him she'd rather be home—alone.

"Can I have the rest of this dance with my niece, brother?"

I will give her up for a few minutes only. She's mine, but I'll let you cut in." Matthew took Laurel in his arms and danced away with his niece.

"You aren't having much fun tonight, are you, niece?"

"It's been a lovely party, Uncle Matthew. Thank you for asking us."

"You didn't answer my question, Laurel Grace."

"No. I didn't want to come. I'm awfully tired is all. Don't seem to have much energy."

"Why are you tired?"

"We've been so busy tending the orchards, weeding the garden, and keeping the kids ready for school. There is a lot to do this time of year."

"Nothing out of the ordinary that all the other women aren't doing. Are you sure that's all or are you lying to your uncle?"

"The dance is over, Uncle Matthew. I need to get back to Mac. He'll be looking for me."

"He knows I'll take care of you. Let's go sit on the porch for a spell. I got a couple of things I need to talk over with ya." Laurel looked over her shoulder, hoping Mac would come to take her back to the dance. She didn't see him, so she followed her uncle.

"Here, sit in that rockin' chair."

"Uncle Matthew, I don't want to show you any disrespect, but I don't see that we have anything to talk about."

"Well, you don't have to talk. I want ya to sit down and listen! I got some things to say to you." Laurel sat in the chair, resigned to the situation. Matthew Campbell intended to have his say.

"Laurel, Mac was over here last night. He's worried to distraction about you since you lost the baby."

"Please, I can't talk about that."

"I told you that you don't have to talk, only listen. Laurel Grace, Mac loves you. He wants to build a home with you, but he can't do it alone. When you shut him out, he feels helpless, not able to help you or share in your grief." Laurel closed her eyes and wished she could close off the words her uncle was saying. She knew she'd failed Mac. Her uncle didn't have to tell her. She told herself—every day.

"Laurel Grace, you ain't the only one lost a child. Look around you. Mac lost his son. Cathy so wanted to help raise her little brother. Have ya even hugged her and let her tell you what she's feelin'?" Laurel shook her head. "The ladies of Shiloh church have tried to reach out to you. They are all so sad for you. They wanted to comfort you in some small way. They care about you, Laurel, and are so grateful you started the Sunday school to help them learn to read and write. You shut them out. No one grieves alone unless that's the way they want it."

"Uncle Matthew, please let me be. I know it's my fault. I'm doing everything I know how to show Mac I care about his dream of a home. I work from before sunrise until way after dark. If I can work hard enough, it'll repay him partly for my failing. I do all I know how to do."

"Laurel Grace, you are right. You have failed-- at being a good wife." Laurel felt as if her uncle had broad-slapped her across the face. "And I have failed at helping my friend find the wife he'd hoped for." Laurel began sobbing at Matthew's last comment. "Those tears ain't gonna make up for your faults, niece."

Laurel stood up. "I'm going home."

"I'm not finished yet. Laurel, when I suggested Mac come across the state to meet you, I believed you were dedicated to the faith. Mac told me he never wanted to be unequally yoked. The most important thing he wanted was a wife who shared his faith. You don't understand a thing about grace."

"How dare you criticize my faith. Can you see into my heart? How can you say I don't believe in God? I know Jesus died for my sins. I was baptized in the Methodist church, the same as you and my papa and our grandparents, too."

Matthew hid a hint of a smile behind his hand. Laurel had taken up her own defense. Perhaps his words were getting through to her. At least, she was showing a little spirit.

"Laurel Grace. I'm not trying to hurt you. I love you dearly, as much as I loved your father. Mac is my friend and brother in faith. He doesn't want a housekeeper or a servant. He wants a relationship with you. He loves you, but you won't let him show you he loves you. Love can only happen, niece, when we tear down the walls and give our being over to the one who loves us. That's God's way, and that's the way it is with Mac. Laurel, that is grace. What Jesus died to show us. He loves us like that, but he wants a relationship with us, not works and obedience."

"Not with me. I'm not good enough, not for Mac, not for anyone, especially not for the Lord."

"Goodness, then aren't you the arrogant one!" Laurel moaned in frustration because her uncle hadn't understood what she'd tried to say. "Laurel Grace, I've said all I'm able to say. I want you to think about what I've said tonight. I know it sounds hard. Sister, no one has a past so bad or a sin so great that God's love can't cover it. If you believe you are beyond His love, then you have a mighty big pride. Think about it. Don't be your own worst critic. There are those in the world who are more than willing to do that for you. We put daggers in God's heart every time we judge ourselves as unworthy of love or when we hate ourselves. Go home and read Romans 3:20-26. You will see. When you believe—really believe those words, Mac will have the wife he wants." Matthew Campbell pulled his niece into his arms and prayed, "Lord, help her see." With those words, he walked away and left on the porch. He returned to his guests in the barn.

Within a few minutes, Mac found Laurel where her uncle had left her. "It's getting late, Laurel. Are you about ready to go home?"

"Yes, Mac. I'd like to go home. I'll find Roy and Cathy if you'll bring the wagon." She felt such an uneasiness as she considered what her uncle had said to her. Had she only pretended to be a faithful follower and deceived her husband? Her uncertainty left her in a quiet, pensive mood.

Mac drove to the Shiloh church before anyone in the wagon spoke a word.

"Are you all right, wife? Did your uncle Matthew say something to trouble you? You've been mighty quiet since we left the social. Didn't you have a good time?"

"It was nice to see my family again. The party was good. I am tired. You know I told you earlier that I wasn't ready to go out yet."

"I enjoyed having you with me all night. You are a big help in my campaigning. People like you, and they tell me I'm a lucky man."

Laurel let the last statement go by without comment. She knew Mac was trying to make her feel important. She doubted anyone had actually said those things to him, especially since she'd failed to carry his son to term.

"I hope you're not too worn out. We have a social event every weekend between now and election time. I'll be proud to have you on my arm at each one of them."

The next morning, after a fitful night's rest, Laurel arose earlier than usual. Before she began her morning chores, she would search the Scripture her uncle had pointed out to her. She knew she'd feel at odds until she understood why he had attacked her faith. She'd remembered that her husband had done the same thing once before. She stoked the embers in the hearth and laid wood there so she could prepare breakfast soon. She sat down near the hearth to read her Bible.

# CHAPTER FOURTEEN

*Be not forgetful to entertain strangers:*
*for thereby some have entertained angels unaware.*
*Hebrews 13:2*

While the study helped comfort her, she continued to search for answers to her questions, but time didn't stop. The routine of socializing and campaigning went on right up to the end of harvest time. In the MacLayne household, an uneasy peace carried her through the days. Laurel spent her days gathering crops, canning, and preserving food for the winter to come. She made deliberate attempts to carry on conversations with Cathy and Roy.

Not one Friday or Saturday night passed that the MacLaynes were not invited for some event. Mac continued his attentive wooing of his wife. He escorted her to every pot luck dinner, dance, and debate as if he were paying her court instead of campaigning for the legislature. His devoted attention to his wife endeared him to the ladies of the community. His impromptu hugs and kisses made them the topic of a great deal of gossip, too. He continued to share their bed. He was always affectionate in his contact, but he made no effort to make love to his wife. He never shied from her touch, yet he continued to treat her much as he had in the early days of their marriage when they were friends, not lovers.

Laurel continued to seek peace and answers in Scripture. Her uncle's words gnawed at her for several weeks after the barn dance. Laurel wanted to believe the promises her uncle had told her about, but she couldn't. Grace was a concept that seemed far beyond her understanding. After telling Mac the details of her attack, Laurel no longer blamed herself, and the nightmares from her youth had stopped. Yet, how could Mac forgive her when she had failed to give him the one thing he'd wanted from her? She lost the son he was expecting in June. The more she thought about Matthew's words, the harder she worked. The MacLayne's homestead would be the best in the area, and he'd never find fault with her attempts to make it a showplace. The meals she prepared were beyond ample and always pleasing. Once again, she'd filled her larder to overflowing as she harvested the food from her garden. As she cleared one garden patch, she'd plant a fall crop to take its place. The children were always clean, and she had made them new clothes. All thrived under her constant care, all except Laurel. She worked from sun rise to well beyond dark with the intention that no chore would ever remain undone. Her uncle had reinforced the fact that Mac had lost his child, and he grieved for that loss. Laurel aimed to make sure Mac was never disappointed with her again.

After the night of her uncle's reproach, Laurel made deliberate efforts to talk to the Dunn children. She wouldn't let any day pass without telling Cathy how much she loved her. She found something to praise her for each evening at prayer time. She also sought out opportunities to ask Roy about the egg and milk business he'd started. She teased him on occasion about the young girl he seemed to be sweet on. She took special care to smile at them whenever she was aware they were watching her. Yet, the smile never quite reached her eyes... not with Roy or Cathy or even Mac.

Laurel knew she was acting out the role her family expected of her. She wore a mask for everyone to see. When they campaigned, she played the candidate's lady. At church, she was the favored son's devoted wife, and at home, Laurel was the industrious homemaker. She thought no one was aware of her pretense. Her grief and guilt had all but destroyed the intimacy she'd once shared with Mac. The trite reserved conversations between them left them both hungry for real communication. It wasn't that they didn't talk.... They talked a great deal about the routine things: needs around the farm, campaign schedules, community events, and the Dunns. Laurel realized she had become quite adept at small talk in hopes of filling the void her sorrow created. She played the role of Laurel Campbell MacLayne pretty well, but she hated the way she was living.

Mac tried to woo Laurel back. He brought her wildflowers he found in the woods, or he'd surprise her with an afternoon picnic alone. He was the most attentive husband at every social they attended in the early summer. He never left her alone at any campaign rally. People not knowing the circumstances believed they were watching two people devoted to each other and who were very much in love. Mac knew all too well the wall had gone back up. Laurel told herself he wasn't aware of the breach between them, but she could not lie to herself. She could not reach out to him, so every day she felt further from Mac than the day before. Mac had returned to her side in the tall bed, but he had not made love to her even once since Campbell died.

The Fourth of July was fast approaching. Mac planned to attend several campaign events over the three-day period set aside as a special holiday. As in all rural areas, Independence Day was always the major social event in Greensboro. Mac decided this would be the perfect opportunity to open his home to friends and supporters. Laurel had made it a showplace with her hard work, and he would be proud to bring his friends in to visit their home.

"Laurel, my dear, I hope you are up for a celebration. I want to have the th Fourth of July party here at our house this year. We've not had a real celebration here since the log rolling back in April of last year.

Within days of Mac's sudden announcement, the mood in their home changed. The last Saturday in June had been a hot, humid day. The wind blew in hot gusts from the southwest all day. A bank of dark, heavy clouds rushed across the skyline above Crowley's Ridge. Heat lightning flashed across the sky often, but there had been no rain. The blustery, dark sky was an ominous parallel to the mood inside the cabin that afternoon.

"I'll do what I can to help." Laurel's tone told Mac she felt little enthusiasm for the idea.

"What's wrong, wife? I thought you liked our Shiloh family."

"Nothing. I want to be a part of your campaign."

"You'll do it for me...whether you want to or not. Is that what you are thinking?"

"No, Mac, I'll be happy to help you plan an Independence Day party. If it's something you need to do, of course, I want to help you."

"Laurel, I don't need to do anything. Have you ever thought that maybe I want to do it? Don't you want to have a party?" Mac's comments were direct and edging on confrontation.

"Please forgive me, Patrick. I didn't realize it meant so much. You haven't mentioned it before today."

"You still haven't answered my question. Do you want to invite our friends and family to our home?"

Laurel knew she had to give him an answer he would accept and one that would move him away from the issue. "Mac, I just hadn't thought about it. If you want this, we will have a party." She had tried to evade a direct reply, yet she didn't want to have to lie to him. If she told him the truth, he would not let the issue go, and she knew it.

"Do you want to open our home?" Laurel looked down at the floor. Several seconds passed and no acceptable answer would come to mind. She walked over to the window and peered outside into the fading sunset. Silently, she prayed, "Lord, give me an answer, so I cause no more hurt. Please tell me what to say." She lifted her eyes to meet his. As she was about to say no, a loud crash of thunder resounded so loudly that objects in their cabin shook. Mac turned to look at the clouds that had moved into the area. "A storm is coming. I have to put up the shutters before the worst strikes." Laurel sighed in relief.

At dusk, Mac came in from the barn. "Laurel, where are the kids?"

"Cathy is in the loft cleaning her room. I sent Roy to the springhouse to bring milk and butter for supper. Why? Is something wrong?"

"Could be nothing, but I don't like the look of those clouds to the southwest. Something in the air just doesn't feel right."

Roy came in the back door and put the pitcher of milk and the butter bowl in the dry sink. "Gracious me, it's hot out there. It's hotter than it's been all day. Storm coming, Mr. Mac?"

"I don't know, Roy, but to be on the safe side, let's keep a watch. It's hard to know what's happening with the shutters up. At least we can leave the windows open to have some flow of air in here." They walked to the front porch to watch the storm. The wind blustered and thunder continued to roll across the valley. Cathy came scrambling downstairs into the main room.

"I don't like it when the winds come up, Mrs. Mac. Are we going to have a tornado?"

"Don't worry, Cathy. We're safe here in our cabin. Let's get supper finished. That will keep our mind off the weather." A few minutes later the family gathered around the table to share their Saturday supper. The rain began to fall in torrents, and the wind howled. The conversation around the table was forced, a natural result of the focus on the storm.

A time or two Mac rose from the table to go out to the porch to look at the cloud bank. The last time, he returned quickly. He was wet from the blowing rain. He said, "It's so dark out there I can't see the cloud bank any more. Only when the lightning flashed could I even see the barn." The storm came in waves over the next two hours. For a time, the rain would slack or even become deadly still for a few minutes only to have the full thrust of the wind and rain return even stronger an hour later. During one of the lulls about 9:00, a loud knock sounded on the front door of the cabin.

"Who in tarnation would be out on such a night as this?" Mac approached the door and found his father standing on his porch... his hat dripping streams of water.

"Well, son, I almost beat this storm but not quite."

"Pa! Welcome. Get in here out of this storm." Mac threw his arms around his father and drew him across the threshold. Behind his father, Mac noticed a small, bashful lad wrapped in oilcloth, holding to

Thomas MacLayne's coat tail. "Well, who do we have here? A stowaway?"

"I'll get around to introductions in a few minutes, but first I have two men waiting outside. They helped me haul my property from Memphis. Do you have a place to shelter my wagons and my draught animals until this storm passes?"

"I do… Laurel, can you take this little fellow over and dry him off some? I'll help get Pa settled. And can you rustle up some supper for our company?"

"I'll find enough to fill them." Laurel took the boy's hand and led him to a chair at the table. She brought him a towel to dry his hair. "Are you hungry?" The boy looked up at the strange lady and nodded.

In a hardly audible voice, he answered, "Yes, ma'am."

Outside, Mac motioned to the freighters and led them into the barn. The third wagon, driven by his father, wouldn't fit in the space, so Mac led the mule team to the lean-to. It was a sturdy shed and the wagon, covered with heavy canvas would be well protected. The black freighter by the name of Zeke unharnessed the team of draught horses and stored their harnesses.

"Is there room for the two teams of jacks and my horses in there?"

"It'll be a tight fit, but we'll double them up in the stalls until the storm passes. Come on in, men. You'll be more comfortable in my house than here in the barn. Besides, my wife lays a fine table. I'm sure you'll want to eat."

"Thank you, son. Come Joe, Zeke. Let's get in out of this wet."

"Mr. Thomas, sir, are you sure I should come in? I'll be fine here with the stock."

"Zeke, you are welcome in my house. Any friend of my father can put his feet under my table."

Laurel laid out an ample meal of brown beans and ham, corn pone, and creamed corn from her larder as the men sat down around the table. She had about half a cake left from their supper that she would serve with coffee later. "Coffee will be ready soon."

"Pa, I am so happy to have you here at Shiloh finally. I was hoping you'd come earlier, but I didn't expect to see you until fall."

"I had some things to take care of on the way across the country. I took the train to Nashville and then on into Memphis. I was lucky enough to find Zeke and Joe in Memphis to pick up my goods from the train and haul them across the way. We did real good until we ran into the rain the other side of Greensboro. Patrick, this is Joe Browning and Zeke Miles. They have been fine companions the past four days."

"Glad to meet y'all. My friends here call me Mac."

Joe Browning was a stout middle-aged Tennessean who owned his own freight business. He made a fair livelihood carrying goods from the train in Memphis. Zeke was a freed black man who earned his living picking up whatever odd jobs he could find. Thomas explained that Zeke had been born a slave in Georgia, but he had been emancipated in his former master's will. Zeke worked hard to support himself, as he constantly moved north.

"Son, do you have a place for these men tonight? In this storm, I wouldn't want them to head back to Greensboro."

"Of course, we'll keep everyone dry, even if some of us have to sleep on pallets on the floor."

"Now, introduce me to this darlin' lady you stole from Northwest Arkansas."

Mac rose and walked to the end of the table where Laurel had set a pitcher of water and glasses. He took her hand. "Pa, this is my wife, Laurel Grace. Wife, this is my father, Thomas MacLayne."

"Gracious, she is a beauty, son. How'd you ever get her to marry you?"

"The good Lord gave her to me. And yes, I know she's too good for me." Laurel was uncomfortable with the attention. She returned to the hearth for the coffee.

"And where is that wee babe? My first grandchild must be nigh on to a month old by now."

Laurel stopped in her tracks. The look on her face suggested her father-in-law had plunged a knife in her chest. Mac saw the pain on her face and walked over to her, pulling her into his arms. He a brushed a kiss on her cheek and whispered, "He didn't get my letter, Laurel. He didn't mean to hurt you. Pa, we lost our little boy in April. He was born too early."

"Please forgive me, Laurel. I am sorry for your loss, son. I didn't know."

"I wrote to you the second week in May."

"That's about the time I left Maryland headed west."

Silence became heavy for a while. To break the tension, Mac spoke. "Pa, I want you to know the rest of our family. This is Cathy and Roy Dunn. Kids, this is my father." Cathy made a stiff curtsy while Roy extended his hand to the somewhat older version of his boss.

"I guess that is everyone except this young lad. Pa, who is your young friend?"

"Laurel and Patrick, this is Andrew. I met up with him about three weeks ago. He's staying with me for a while. Laurel, that supper was fine. I see you have apple cake. That's my favorite, well except for blackberry cobbler."

"Well, come sit down at the table and let's finish off that cake," Mac said.

Laurel, Mac, and the Dunns sat down while their company ate their fill. They spend the next couple of hours talking about the trip from Franklin to Memphis and then from Memphis across the sunken lands of Arkansas. They told stories about the hazards they encountered.

Zeke said, "The most scared I got was when we got on that danged ferry. They was way too many wagons, mules, and people on that flat barge. I thought it'd sink ever time a swell washed over. Surely was glad when we got to the Arkansas side...Then we found that town...Esperanza. Thought we oughta stayed on the ferry."

Laughter rang out around the table.

"Patrick, I thought you'd told me there is a road across the sunken lands when it's dry. All we found was a barely marked path. At times, I'm not sure we even found that." Thomas continued.

"Well, Pa, it was raining most of the day."

"But it wasn't raining yesterday." Everyone laughed in the easy company. Laurel played her role as the waitress, filling their coffee cups and serving second slices of cake until only crumbs remained.

Andrew sat in Thomas MacLayne's lap the entire evening, only occasionally looking out under his lashes at the people who sat around the table. He didn't speak once until he'd eaten every morsel from his plate. Then in a quiet voice, he said, "Thank you, Mrs. MacLayne. That tasted real fine." Everyone laughed at his unexpected praise. He stood up and squared his shoulders. "Well, it did. I tell you that's the best-blamed vittles I ever ate." Again, laughter filled the room.

"Well, Andrew, I told my Pa that my wife can cook. I'm thinking you agree."

Thomas and Mac seemed to have no end of things to talk about. Laurel sat and listened as her father-in-law told stories about Mac's childhood on their farm in Maryland.

"Laurel, I see you wear Patrick's mother's wedding band." Laurel looked at him with some concern, and then she looked down at the beautiful wide gold band on her finger.

"Yes. I hope you're not offended."

"No, heavens no. I was thinking how happy my Ann would be to see it there. I hope you wear it with pride for many years, daughter."

"I love this ring. I've not taken it off since Mac put it there in August of last year."

"August? I was thinking Mac told me y'all got married in March."

"It's a long story, Pa so let it lay until later. It's getting late, and I know y'all have to be tired. Let's get everyone bedded down for the night."

"I'll bring in things from the linen chest," Laurel said.

"Son, we don't have to disrupt the routine here. We'll be fine in the barn. You've got a sound roof."

"I won't hear of it. My first visit from family won't start with you sleeping in the barn. Cathy, go collect your night clothes and come down here with Mrs. Mac and me. Pa, you'll find a double bed in the loft that you can share with your ward, Andrew. Now let me think...." Mac pulled the chairs and side table away from the middle of the room, making plenty of space for two grown men to stretch out on the rag rug in front of the fireplace. Laurel brought two covers and two feather pillows from the second pen and gave them to the freighters. "It's not exactly a fine hotel, but maybe it will serve."

Zeke stood, looking at Laurel as she offered him a pallet on her cabin floor.

Joe nodded and spoke, "Thank you, ma'am."

"I hope you will sleep well enough here on the rug. At least you don't have to go back into that downpour." She turned to talk with Roy, and then she took Cathy's hand. "Good night, Mr. MacLayne. We're pleased you've come to live near us. Mac has been looking forward to this day for months—ever since we got your letter telling us you'd decided to come. I hope you find a good life here."

"Thank you, my dear. The best part has been meeting you. Mac told his mother and me about the gift he'd found in Washington County, but it didn't seem real until I met you tonight."

"Thank you, sir. Sleep well."

"None of that sir stuff, Laurel. I know you lost your own father some over a year ago. I can't take his place, but I'd be happy to have you call me Pa as Patrick does."

"I'll try to do that. I called my father Papa, so I don't see it'd be unfeeling to call you Pa."

The storm rose and fell throughout the night. The family awoke more than once as the wind downed entire trees, tearing deep roots from the rain-soaked soil. The strong wind pushed debris into the sides of the cabin. With one particularly loud crash of thunder, Laurel startled. She sat up in the bed, trembling. "Laurel, you are safe, sweetheart. You know these kinds of thunderstorms are pretty common here in this part of the state. Come on over here and lie down next to me. The house is strong, and we put all the shutters up. We're not in harm's way. See there on that pallet, Cathy is sound asleep."

"I know. I'm sorry I woke you."

"Will you let me hold you until you fall asleep again?"

"If you want."

"I want so much more."

"Hush, Mac. Cathy's there on the rug. It's not time to talk."

"Will it be soon?" Mac pulled Laurel into an embrace and lay back into his pillow, her head on his shoulder. "Goodnight, darlin'. Thank you for being such a sweet hostess to my pa."

"You're more than welcome. Now hush up so we don't wake Cathy."

The following morning Mac's father was sitting at the kitchen table when Mac came from the second pen. The storm slacked some, but the rain was steady. "I'll help with the chores in the barn, son. Seems the right thing as half the stock there belongs to me." The animals' care was not the first priority for Thomas, though. He wanted a way to talk with his son alone without the audience there'd been every minute since he'd arrived.

As they opened the barn door, they saw the animals safe and dry. Several tree limbs had fallen on and around the barn, but no major damage had occurred. Only routine morning chores needed to be done. Mac attended to the milking for both cows. Thomas gathered more than a dozen eggs.

"Can we talk for a few minutes, son?"

"Sure, I'll be finished in a couple of minutes, and we can go in and talk over a cup of hot coffee. Laurel will have a big breakfast ready soon."

"Patrick, I'd like to talk with you alone, here in the barn."

"Is something wrong, Pa?"

"I hope not. Patrick, is there a rift between you and your wife?"

"What do you mean, Pa? Laurel never spoke a harsh word in the cabin last night--not to me or to anyone else."

"That's true enough. The two of you seem strangers, though. When you were back home last year, you spoke in such high praise that your ma and I thought you'd made a love match."

"Pa, I love Laurel. She's made this place a real home. What has she done to make you dislike her?"

"I like her very much, but there is a breach between y'all. You don't touch each other. You don't talk like sweethearts do. Laurel's body is here, but her mind and her heart seem far away. From the outside, you seem pretty content, you and Laurel and the Dunn kids. I'm not sure about the inside. I am heartsick about the little one. Laurel is taking all this pretty hard, isn't she?"

"I'd never lie to you, Pa. We do love each other, but we've had some hard days of late. Especially Laurel. Too much loss too fast. When our baby died--well, I guess you could say we are still grieving."

"Grieving is less hurtful when it's carried between you instead of each carrying his own piece of the pain."

"I know that."

"You've built a good home here, son. Sturdy cabin and barn with quite a large fenced pasture done all ready. You've made a lot of progress toward the plans you told us about. I hope the two of y'all find some peace for your loss soon. I want to see your marriage as steady as this homestead. I'd like to see you happy, son. Laurel seems to be a fine woman."

"She is that and so much more. I know I love her now, Pa. She is the only woman I ever loved. Made our separation and my trip back to Maryland worth it... I never knew what love between a man and a woman was supposed to be. I can't imagine living without her."

"Your ma would be happy to hear you say that."

"Don't worry about us. The Lord is taking care of us. I love her more than I knew I could love another person. Even in her pain, I know she loves me. We'll find our way through this valley. And there will be another baby."

"I'm hopin' it's soon."

"Let's go get some breakfast."

During the morning meal, Thomas and Mac fell into an easy conversation about Shiloh and the community surrounding the church. Mac was more than glad to praise the area, now that his father would be looking for a place to build a new home. Thomas often told his son the best times of his life had been when he built his farm and the family home in Maryland... when he and his wife were newlywed. Mac's mother had been a strong motivation to help tame his father's wandering nature. The opportunity to help settle a new state might be enough to keep Thomas MacLayne nearby. Mac wanted to rebuild the bond he'd shared with his father before his wasted years.

"Patrick, do you know of any available land in this community? If I am going to settle here, I have to build me a place before winter, and tomorrow is July 1. Half the year has passed. I need to get started."

"Land for sale? We'll have to look into that. But for a temporary place, Laurel owns a small, but strong cabin, not two miles from here. We were hoping to put someone out there soon to take care of the place for us. There are only thirty acres there, but it'd give you a place to live while we look for some good land."

"Is the cabin like this one?"

"No, I'm afraid it's pretty small. Laurel and I lived in the Widow's place while I was building this one. It's got a fine fireplace for cooking and heat. It's stonework, not mud and wattle. Has a nice loft with room for a double bed and a small bed built into the alcove near the hearth. It'd be plenty big enough for Andrew if he'll be with you a while."

"He will."

"How did you come to find that boy, Pa?"

"He's a relative. His family lived over near Franklin, Tennessee, but now he's alone. His ma died a year or so ago, and his grandfather passed back in the winter. He'll be my ward for the time being."

"He seems to be a fine boy, very polite and respectful to everyone."

"He's a good boy, but he's had a hard life. He's never been to school, and no one in his home tried to teach him to read or write. Of course, he's only six, so he won't be too far behind if I can get him enrolled in school somewhere."

"That is an easy one to solve. Our subscription school will begin the first of November. Laurel taught there last year, and we'll have another teacher before harvest ends."

"Would you like another cup of coffee, Mac or Mr. MacLayne?" Laurel began to collect the dishes from the breakfast table.

"None for me, daughter. You don't mind me calling you daughter, do you?"

"No, sir."

"I am hoping you'll come to call me Pa when you're ready, Laurel. And thank you for opening your home to me and for being an excellent mate to my son. He loves you very much." With Thomas's words, her guilt and grief surfaced unchecked.

"Excuse me. I have something I need to do." Laurel went out the back door and headed toward the spring house. She wanted a place to be alone. How strong could she be? Now there was another family member to batter at her defenses.

"Did I say something to offend her, Patrick?"

"No. Laurel has never taken to compliments. I'll talk to her in a while." Easy conversation continued between the father and son as they made plans to ride to the widow's place to check for storm damage. Mac also invited his father to attend the July 4th celebration at Herndon with his family. By that time, the two freighters came into the kitchen to eat and settle up accounts with Thomas MacLayne. They planned to leave by mid-morning.

"Mr. MacLayne, I appreciate the job. The trip across the sunken lands between here and Memphis was pretty easy until that last day and a half. Mr. MacLayne, thank you and your wife for the hospitality, mighty good food, and a dry bed." The freighter stood with his hat in his hand.

"You're welcome, Joe. I hope you'll drop by and visit us if you pass this way again." Joe nodded, picked up the small pouch of silver and gold coins and left to prepare for his trip back to Memphis.

"Well, Zeke, what plans do you have?

"Heading on North. I got no future in the South."

"I'd like to offer you a job here, helping me build up my new homestead." Thomas shook his head in regret. "But Patrick told me they passed a law in the last legislative session here in Arkansas that would put you back in bondage if you stay in the state."

"That's one law, I'd like to see changed when I get to the state legislature. Any honest man should be able to work for his living in Arkansas."

"Mr. MacLayne, don't fret about me. I been a slave down in Alabama, and I been a freeman now for three years. Got no hankering to find myself in shackles ever again."

"How can we help?"

"You done enough already. You're the first white man ever invited me to eat at your table and sleep in your house with your kin. I won't be forgettin' you."

"Cairo, Illinois, would be your best route north from here. You'll find no welcome in the boot heel of Missouri, but a three-day ride northeast will get you to a ferry crossing the Mississippi. The other side of the Mississippi, you'll land in Cairo. You'll be safe there, and can go wherever your itch takes you."

"Mr. Thomas, I am beholdin' to you."

"No need for that. You earned every cent of your wages. Here take this horse and your wages for the haul. Here's a paper saying you own the horse outright, if you do get stopped. God's speed, Zeke."

"God bless ya, both." After a glance back from the Shiloh road, Zeke headed north to Missouri, looking for his own dream of a better life.

# CHAPTER FIFTEEN

*There is no fear in love made perfect, but perfect love casteth out fear because fear hath torment. He that feareth is not made perfect in love.*
*I John 4: 18*

The morning of July 4, 1858, proved to be a beautiful summer day. The azure sky was strewn with large, fluffy clouds and trailing wisps of bright white. The day would be a warm one, but a gentle easterly wind provided a delightful reprieve from the heat and humidity of the past week.

Mac had accepted a challenge to debate in Herndon at the noon hour. He was proud his father would accompany his family to the celebration. Thomas never before witnessed a debate like those performed in their part of the country. He'd heard of them in some of the rural areas around Baltimore, but he'd had no interest before. This debate held a great interest for him because his son would speak in detail about his plans for the seat he wanted in the state legislature. Thomas knew the man he observed that day was the person his son could always have been. Patrick was a different man. The wastrel created from his tragic love affair with Marsha had been changed… first by his encounter with the living Lord and then by his love for a good woman. He didn't know if Laurel shared the feelings, but he had no doubt whatsoever that his son had given his life to the quiet, sad young woman.

The Herndon community had turned out in good numbers. They had prepared a large bar-be-que pit where the men roasted two hogs. The ladies had laid out a spread of vegetables fresh from the garden and so many desserts that no one person could sample them all. Andrew walked around the churchyard, eyes the size of some of the plums. He seemed to drool over tomatoes and fresh peaches.

"Jimminee, Mr. Mac. Is this town the richest place in the world?" Andrew looked around the churchyard in awe. "Where did all this food come from?"

"These hard-working folks grew most of the food you see. Like me, they're mainly farmers. Pretty normal for this part of the state. Didn't you celebrate Independence Day in Tennessee?"

"Me and my ma, we didn't go out much. Granddad did bring me a row of firecrackers the year before ma died. Those crackers was really loud and scared our mule. Ma wouldn't let him bring me no more."

"Well, we're going to have a good time today. I hope you have lots of fun. Just stay with Cathy and Roy, and they'll show you what's happening all day." And Mac's promise was wonderfully fulfilled. The children had a fine day, playing games, running races, and too often eating more than their fill. After a time, even Andrew began to join in, and he made two new friends with kids who didn't attend Shiloh school.

The adults also found the day special. Mac won the debate easily because his knowledge of the district was so much stronger than the newly settled candidate, Mr. Digby. Only one question from a bystander caused a moment of discord. A well-dressed man in his middle years removed his hat and stroked his fingers through his long gray hair. He looked Mac squarely in the eye as he raised a direct question to him.

"Mac, we all here know you for the most part. We like you. Most people think you're an honest man, but one thing we need you to answer. Will you vote for secession, if it comes to that?"

"That is a bill I hope I don't have to vote on at all, Cort. I know everyone has been talking and speculating all across the state. I've been thinking about it and praying about it ever since the people from this county asked me to run for this office. They know I believe in state's rights. My pa here was born in Virginia where his family owned a few slaves, but he never owned any. We built our Maryland farm using paid labor. Most of us here in our district make our livelihood without forced labor. I'd say more than half the folks here don't believe in slave-keeping."

"So, would your vote be against secession?"

"Yeah, MacLayne. Come out with a straight answer."

"If I am forced to make a choice, I'd vote my convictions. I'd vote no. Arkansas has too much to lose if we break our ties with Washington. I believe I speak for most of my supporters." The reaction from the crowd was mixed. Many people cheered and applauded Mac's words, and some others heckled and booed. The group became restless and a bit loud.

The man who had asked the question stepped up and said, "Mac, I thank you for your honest reply. We may not all like what you said, but we can't fault your honesty."

Another yeoman farmer, dressed in his work clothes, spoke up. "Our preacher from over Okean way said the government is making laws about our wives and our children. These new laws will weaken our family ties with all this abolition nonsense. You want them northerners telling you how to deal with your wife and kids?"

"Sir, I don't think we've met."

"I heard you talk over at the barn raising a few weeks back. I'm Hal Marcum."

"Well, Mr. Marcum, I'd never be one to talk against another's religious belief, but I've done a lot of study about the laws being proposed from other southern states. I have never seen even one that suggests that slavery has anything to do with my marriage or my family. I sure don't see my wife as property or a bondservant. I took vows before God to respect, support, and care for her as a part of myself. I'm sure most churches see marriage like that."

"You telling me the preacher is lying to us?"

"No. I didn't say he lied to you. People look at things from different viewpoints. I've not found anything in studying this issue that ties slavery to marriage. That's all I'm saying. I would welcome anyone to show me some bill or resolution that links these two things."

Mac stepped from the porch of the Herndon Church where the debate had been held, and he took Laurel's arm. His father stopped him. "Son, you made a good showing for yourself here today. I'm glad I got to see it."

"Thanks, Pa. It's good to have you here to support me. You know we need to make an appearance at the Shiloh dance tonight before we can head home. Laurel, are you very tired?"

"Yes, I am, but we will do what we need to do. The worst part is the thought of that long wagon trip back."

"Let me fix that, daughter. I've had enough celebrating for one day, and the kids are about played out too. Let me take them home in the wagon while you and my son ride the horses cross county. It'd make for a shorter trip. Besides, you don't need three kids to look after at a dance."

"I wouldn't want to impose, Mr… I mean Pa."

"I'd like to spend more time with the kids so I can get to know them better. Besides, I'd like to turn in a bit early tonight. I'm thinking tomorrow may be moving day if the weather cooperates."

Mac and Laurel set off for the second Independence Day celebration, just the two of them. This was a rare occasion as Cathy and Roy had attended most social and campaign events the entire season. Mac noticed after they got to the Shiloh party, Laurel seemed more relaxed, enjoying the social more than she had the debate. "You seem to be having a good time tonight, wife, especially since we got back here with our Shiloh friends."

"It's pleasant. The singing has been good all evening, all the old hymns and the patriotic music. Nice to hear you sing, and Uncle Matthew surely showed off his fine voice tonight."

"No doubt... the Lord gave him a gift—more than one really. I've been on the receiving end of several. Matthew saved my life five years ago. He's become the best friend I've ever had. And thanks to him, I have you next to me right now, and I hope always."

Laurel began to feel uneasy with the subject of the conversation. She was in control of her life this way. "It's beautiful out here tonight, isn't it? Look at that huge moon!"

"So, you are trying to change the subject. I'd like to talk about us, not the Arkansas weather."

"I was trying to make conversation."

"You're the one who's always despised small talk. Lately, that is all we do. I know the house has been crowded, but Pa is planning to move to the widow's any day. I want to talk to you the way we did before we lost Campbell. I miss our real conversations."

Laurel didn't answer. Had she been mistaken thinking things were fine at home now? Daily life at the cabin had been pleasant. Mac was attentive and made frequent attempts at wooing her. He often made romantic gestures, like tousling her hair or bringing her bouquets of wildflowers he found on their land. He smiled at her often and held her every night. Laurel had begun to think Mac was satisfied with their arrangement. She felt comfortable and at peace because he made no demands on her. He hadn't asked her to consider having another child. Only when the topic became too personal or brought back her fear of losing people she loved did Laurel retreat. Yes, she could deal with her life most days.

"Laurel, are you happy with me?"

"You're a fine mate. It's been a good day. Let's don't get serious and spoil the evening."

"Laurel, do you know how long it's been since we have shared a personal conversation?" She knew he intended to open up an area of discussion she didn't want to deal with.

"Listen to that music, Mac. I'd love to dance, again."

The conversation was closed for the moment, so he dropped his question. Mac followed his wife into the churchyard, and they joined a group in the reel. When that dance was over, he drew her into his arms for a waltz, played by the area's best fiddler. The dance was slow and rhythmic. Mac held his wife close to him and lowered his head to her ear where he could whisper endearments to her. A time or two, Laurel blushed and tried to move a step back. The distance never held more than a step or two until Mac had pulled her back into his embrace. For the next two hours, the MacLaynes danced—the reels, the square dances, the polkas, and every waltz. Mac picked Laurel up by her waist and whirled her around to the beat of the music. She felt dizzy more than once and found herself clinging to him for support. Finally, the band played the goodnight song, and the party began to end. By the time they mounted their horses, Laurel was smiling, a real smile that lit her eyes for the first time in months.

"Thank you, Patrick. That was fun."

"For me too. It's so good to see you smile, to see you happy. Before we get home, I'd like to finish what I started to tell you earlier. We don't have time at home, not with Cathy sharing our bedroom now."

She reined in the horse she'd borrowed. Laurel knew she'd rather not open this talk again, but she didn't know how to avoid it. "Yes, Patrick. What do you want to say to me?"

"Laurel, I want us to consider having another baby." That was not what she had expected him to say. She found herself at a loss for words to answer Mac. "I miss our lovemaking. Laurel, I want you."

"I am sorry, Mac. I love you. I do, and you've been very patient with me these past two months. I have never had a friend like you. Please forgive me. I am so very sorry."

"Your friendship is a gift I am so grateful for. Laurel, I am not blaming you. I don't want an apology. I want you to want to be with me again. We found such pleasure together. I don't know how long you need to heal and feel comfortable with me again. But dear heart, I hope you will want to return to your role as my lover soon."

Again, she could find no words to respond.

"Laurel, don't you want another child?"

She struggled to find the answer to his frank question. "I don't know, Patrick. I'm sorry you asked me because I want to tell you the truth."

"I see."

"No, you don't understand. I am so grateful for all you've done for me. You've made me a better person. There is so much I need to repay for all the goodness you've shown me."

"Laurel, I don't want your gratitude. I don't want you to feel an obligation to me. You don't owe me anything."

"Yes, I owe you my life, a new start here at Shiloh. I try so hard to be your helpmate on the homestead. I try to prepare good meals for you and keep your clothes neat and clean. I try to keep my chores done well so as not to add to your workload. I tend the kids, and I do want to be a good homemaker for you all."

"Laurel, I don't want a bondservant. If I did, I could buy one, even one to serve me in bed. I want you back as the passionate lover who found as much pleasure in our joining as I did. I want that hunger we had between us again. I want a child of my own, but even if we never have more children, I want you to need me and want me again, just like I need and want you."

She knew those last words had come from the very core of Mac's being. She hesitated to respond. She could see in the moon bright night the hurt on his face when she had failed to respond to his plea. The last thing she wanted was to inflict more pain on this good man.

"Patrick, I am afraid." Laurel paused. "I failed you already. I don't think I can stand losing one more person that I love. Not now."

"Thank you for telling me what the problem's been. Your telling me helps me deal with our breach somewhat. For tonight, we'll let it be. This conversation is a start to regaining what we had. We're almost home anyway. Let's get on."

"I hate disappointing you, Mac. I do it too often, I know."

"Wife, this talk is not over. I spoke vows to you. They said, 'as long as God wills it,' and He hasn't given up on us yet."

Mac continued to pay court to his wife. Almost daily, he brought her some small trinket for no reason. At night when he pulled her into his arms, he would give her long passionate kisses. Mac frequently pulled the pins from her hair. When he did, he teased her, slowly and sensually running his fingers through her curly tresses. No night passed that Mac did not pull Laurel into his arms to sleep. He reveled in her closeness, but he didn't make love to her. That would wait until she came to him—of her own volition.

~

THOMAS MACLAYNE FOUND life at the widow's cabin satisfactory. The small one pen log cabin was a far cry from the spacious two-story Georgian home he'd left behind. Yet, he and Andrew settled into a comfortable routine for a time while he made plans to rebuild his life in Arkansas near his son. He found much to like along Crowley's Ridge. There was good timber, more than ample water, and rich soil in the valleys at the foot of the ridge. Together with Mac, Thomas rode across the entire district seeking out land to buy or claim through homesteading so he could rebuild a home.

The MacLayne's homestead had fallen back into its usual daily routine. Laurel worked every day to keep the mood light, and her husband pleased, but she noticed Mac was away from home more than he had been. Of course, she knew he spent a great deal of his free time helping his father search for land. Often their trips would keep them away two or three days at a time. Whenever he was gone, though, he assured his chores were done by John and Roy, telling them that Laurel was never to do his chores. In some ways, the early fall of '58 seemed the best of times. Yet Laurel and Mac knew that what seemed to be was not always real.

About two weeks before the election, Al Stuart arranged one last political rally. Neither he nor any of Mac's campaign supporters thought it was necessary as Mac had a large base of support across the county. Besides that, word from Little Rock suggested quite a bit of dissension among people who at one time supported The Family. There were rumors that a former friend might even oppose Elias Conway for the governor's office. Regardless, Al Stuart insisted they go on with the rally. He had chosen to hold the event at the home of a newlywed couple who needed a new barn raised. The Whitesides lived at Bettis Spring near Lorado. Saturday was "water day" when locals came to draw crystal cold water from the natural spring there. The barn raising was an added incentive to draw a crowd, and provided Mac one last opportunity at campaigning. People from several Greene county communities showed up to build a barn, to eat good food, and to celebrate the end of the harvests of bumper crops that year.

Laurel, Mac, the Dunn children, Andrew, and Thomas MacLayne

arrived early at the barn-raising. Laurel spent hours the previous day baking and cooking to provide her share of the food for the dinner on the grounds. The drive over to Bettis Spring was a pleasant one, as the mid-September day was beautiful. There was the hint of autumn among the trees that filled the rolling hillside. Yes, the day promised to be a perfect one.

Mac was in high spirits as he looked forward to his final debate before the election. He was confident and proud to have his family with him that day. He burst into song a time or two on the trip across the county.

"Do you remember this one, wife?" Mac proceeded to sing in his rich, robust voice his own version of *Annie Laurel* that he had made up for her as they'd traveled across the state.

"It's been a long time since you sang that song to me. I'd almost forgotten it."

"It's been a while for a fact. A lot has happened in the time we've shared during the last eighteen months. Can you believe we have been together that long?"

"Sometimes it does seem hard to keep up with the time. We've had some difficult things to bear, but there has also been a lot of good things to remember."

"Well, I thank you, wife, for being a fine campaign companion this past year, and the help mate any man could want. I'm proud of you." Mac reached across the wagon seat and kissed Laurel briefly. The two Dunn kids who'd been listening to their talk began to giggle.

"What're you two doing back there, laughing?"

"Oh, Mr. Mac...all that lovey-dovey talk seems so silly!" Cathy covered her mouth with her hand to hide her grin.

"Well, Miss Priss, we'll see how silly you think it is a few years on when your beaus come to call." Laughter rang out as Cathy's face reddened with Mac's comment.

"Honestly, Mac, I am glad this is our last campaign social. It'll be nice to stay home for a while and get back into a normal routine before winter sets in."

"You're forgetting, Mrs. MacLayne, that after the election, things will get hectic. When we win this election, we'll have to travel to Little Rock. Not only that, but we have to make plans to keep our own homestead going."

"I've been wanting to talk with you about that, Mac. I'd like to go back to teaching when the spring term begins."

"I don't see how that can work out, Laurel."

"Well, you know Anna Broadaway's getting married around Easter. Her young man's place is well beyond Lorado, so she won't be able to teach at Shiloh."

"Laurel, I want you to travel with me when I go to Little Rock. I don't want to be separated from you for weeks at a time. Since we married, we've already spent too much time apart."

"Mac, please reconsider."

"I don't want to talk about this now in front of the kids and Pa. We'll talk about it later. There's the Whiteside place anyway. Let's go help build a barn."

The day was a huge success. The crowd was even larger than usual. Many familiar faces dotted the yard, but also there were several strangers who arrived throughout the morning. With such a large workcrew, the Whiteside barn was up and awaiting its roof when Polly Whiteside rang the dinner bell.

By 3:30, the building stood, completed. Mac and Harmon Digby took their places on the front porch. Al Stuart served as the moderator. He announced the format would be question and answers, so those present could voice their concerns to representatives. Mac favored that format because it gave him a chance to talk about the real issues in the northeast. He addressed the lack of adequate levee systems that made much of the sunken lands unusable for crops, herds, and travel. He talked about the lack of passable roads. He quoted a recent surveyor who had reported Arkansas had practically no roads. In the newspaper the surveyor had written that Arkansas's idea of a road system was hundreds of suggested paths to get a man from one settlement to the next. The strongest statement Mac made, though, brought the audience to their feet in applause.

"Friends, we have to get a handle on the unscrupulous land agents who are stealing from many honest settlers. These frontiersmen come to Arkansas to make a better life for their families, only to have their stakes taken by fraud. Every person here has been or will be impacted by these crooked land deals. Dealing with this problem is my number one priority."

Digby did a tolerable job responding to questions about the state issues. Good for Mac's case, he knew little about topics dealing with local problems. Everything he said clearly showed that he supported the Family line. He received polite applause at the end of the debate.

Mac was about to step down from the porch when one of the strangers he'd seen earlier called out to him.

"MacLayne, do you think we should break off our ties with the government in Washington?"

"No, stranger. I don't think we should break our ties with the federal government."

"What if they keep pushing the slave issue?"

Mac heard the taunting tone in the voice of the man. "Sir, this dispute is about more than slavery. By the way, I don't believe we've met."

"I'm new to the area. Will you answer my question, please?"

"All here who know me are aware that I think the United States are better together than apart. I will work hard to keep Arkansas in the union. Our state has much to lose without Washington's support. Money for our levee projects, road building, and funds for education comes from the federal level. Little, if any, state money comes to help us with these huge issues. We can talk out our problems without dividing our country."

"So, you don't hold with slavery."

"I don't think I made that statement today, but no, I keep no slaves, and my father has never held slaves. I've seen problems that bondage has brought to families, states, and even my own church. The Methodist church divided more than ten years ago over this issue. I pray it doesn't happen to our country, too." Mixed applause came from the quiet gathering.

A second man from the back called out another question. "Is it true you married that harlot from Hawthorn over in Washington County about a year ago?" Mac turned to search for the man who had blatantly demeaned Laurel in public in her own hearing. Only then did he realize that some of Digby's supporters came to push him into a brawl. A violent attack would not do his campaign much good, and he knew it. But Mac was irate! He jumped from the porch and headed toward the back of the crowd from where he'd heard the voice. Matt caught one of his arms before he could reach the edge of the gathering.

"Mac, stop. This won't help Laurel. Let me handle it. Go to her."

Mac shouldered his way past Matthew. "Where is the coward who attacked my wife?"

"Can't you answer his question? These good people got a right to know what kind of person she is." A second man called out.

The blood drained from Laurel's face. She turned her back and lowered her head. Mac walked to her side and put his arm around her, but she wouldn't look at him. The crowd murmured and shuffle around, obviously embarrassed for the genteel lady they saw on the porch. Laurel shuffled as if she wanted to run from the scene, but she stood for several moments…not speaking or moving. Then, she squared her shoulders, turned to face the crowd, and walked to the front of the porch, her hand in her husband's. Mac saw the stubborn jut of her chin and the vivid green in her eyes. Mac stepped behind Laurel. The attacker would have his answer, but not from him.

# CHAPTER SIXTEEN

*And ye shall know the truth, and the truth shall make you free.*
*John 8:32*

Laurel stood before the gathered community for a short time. A passage from the book of II Corinthians came to her in a very calm, loving voice. The words she heard were *'My grace is sufficient for you'*. These words from the same book Mac had read the previous evening, *'You are a new creation, the old has gone,'* filled her heart, and reassurance replaced her shame and embarrassment.

"My name is Laurel Campbell MacLayne, in case some of you don't know me. Who may I ask is concerned with my virtue?" The crowd was deadly quiet, people looking to see if the challenge would be answered. After what seemed an hour, the man who had called her a harlot stepped from the crowd.

"My name is Robert Duncan. In the past, we knew each other pretty well back over in Washington County." Robert said 'knew' in a way that insinuated that Laurel deserved the name he'd called her.

She took two steps closer to where he stood. "Yes, Bobby, that's what we used to call you. Would you like to tell these fine folks that story?" Some of the women standing nearby gasped. "We're among friends and family here, aren't we?" Laurel's voice didn't waver. From the look on Robert Duncan's face, he'd not expected Laurel to speak out in front of a crowd.

"No? Let me tell y'all how I know Bobby Duncan."

Mac approached her. "Laurel, you don't have to do this."

"Yes, I do." She turned to face her family, friends, Mac's political supporters, and the newcomers at the rally. "I'm not usually the one to talk in front of large groups. My husband is the spokesman in our family, but tonight is the last time I plan to play the victim. Being a victim is a terrible burden I don't deserve.

"Friends, and those of you who aren't, the title I had in Washington County wasn't harlot. They called me the Spinster of Hawthorn. I actually earned that name myself because I let fear and shame overwhelm me at the age of fourteen. That was the time I wouldn't stand up for myself.

"You see, when I was fourteen, Bobby Duncan and two of his friends attacked me at a party one night. I was sweet on him back then, and perhaps I flirted too much, but at that party, this boy became too forward. I rejected him as a suitor. He and two of his friends tore my clothes, hit me with their fists, and knocked me down. When I tried to run from them, they pushed me into a thorn bush. I still have a scar on my arm if you want me to show you. I scratched Bobby's face, and he became very angry and told the other two boys to hold me down. I screamed fearing what they'd do. One of those other boys put his dirty hand over my mouth, and I bit him. That was when he hit my face with his fist. Bobby took a pair of sheep shears from the wall of a barn and cut off one of my braids, leaving my hair only a couple inches long. With the blood on my face, my eye swollen shut, and dressed in practically nothing, Bobby and his friends dragged me before my schoolmates. Their laughter was as bad as the beating. Those kids must have been scared too. Is that what you remember, Bobby? I don't think I'll ever forget. My husband will tell you that I have nightmares still."

"You're a liar! You went home and told your pa those lies, and he brought the preacher over to our house to tell my pa those same lies. I don't know what they said, but they ran us out of Hawthorn. My pa lost our homestead because people wouldn't trade with us anymore."

Laurel wanted to scream out in revenge, 'And whose fault was that?'. Again, she sensed the calm voice saying, 'Vengeance is mine.' She turned and faced Robert Duncan. "Mr. Duncan, if I were as good a person as my husband, I'd forgive you. Seems I'm not strong enough in my faith yet, so I'll have to pray for enough grace."

For one brief minute, he stared at the woman who'd spoken to him. This was a person he didn't know. He skulked away as those standing around cheered and applauded in support of the woman who had the courage to defend herself.

Laurel turned around. She saw her uncle Matthew smiling at her, and her aunt Ellie wiping tears from her face. Mac pulled her into a strong, comforting embrace. "Mac, I want to go home."

"Yes, sweetheart, I am sure you do." But before she left, she turned to speak to those who were still milling around the yard,

"Friends, I won't speak of this again. My husband, Patrick MacLayne, is a good man. He walks in faith with the Lord and is teaching me to do that, too. Mac wants a better life for us and our children here in the northeast part of our state. He doesn't care one whit about the political machine that runs this state. If you have any sense, you'll elect him to the state legislature from our district." The crowd broke into shouts.

Laurel walked back to Mac's open arms where he enfolded her and kissed her boldly. He whispered so only she could hear, "I know your father is looking down in pride and is at rest now. He is seeing the sprite he raised and who knows her worth. I love you, Laurel Grace." Nothing had changed, but everything had.

Hours later, when they reached Shiloh, the sky glittered with a myriad of stars. Laurel made her way to the privacy of her washroom. She changed into the white silk nightdress Mac brought her from Maryland. She lit the crystal lantern and turned the wick low. When Mac entered their bedroom, Laurel stood in front of the fireplace holding her hairbrush.

"Mac, would you brush my hair for me?"

"I would love to." Mac pulled the pins from the chignon at Laurel's nape and began to make long strokes to untangle her curls. Laurel reveled in each delicious sensation of Mac's touch. When he pulled her hair behind her shoulder and kissed her neck, chills ran down her back. She turned to face him and took her brush from his hand. She laid it on the mantle and then wrapped her arms around his neck and moved her body next to his. Mac's kisses revealed the need he'd felt for so long.

Laurel laid her head on his collarbone and moved her lips near his ear. In a soft, sensual voice, Laurel spoke. "Patrick, make love to me."

FOLLOWING THAT CAMPAIGN SOCIAL, Mac found joy in rising each morning, anticipating the good each day would bring. The nights with Laurel were bliss. She once again became the passionate lover and sweetheart she'd been before they had lost Campbell. She was at peace during the days, going far beyond her role of homemaker, parent to the Dunns, and devoted companion to him. With Thomas MacLayne and Andrew settled in the Widow's cabin, life settled into a new normal. In this familiar routine, people laughed, shared stories, and worked together.

September was nearly gone and less than two weeks remained until Greene County would elect their new state legislator. Digby, Mac's opposition, saw how popular the local candidate was among the residents of Greene County, even in areas well beyond Greensboro. The candidate sent by the Family realized only an attack on Mac's character brought any hope of his winning the vote. Digby began to spread stories, twisted versions of stories about Mac's youth in Maryland. The stories were so perverted that they were lies. Mac easily dispelled the malicious stories until Digby found out about the duel and his years of wandering in Kentucky and Tennessee. Mac had no way of knowing how his opponent had access to that information from so long ago and far away. The omission of a few facts made these stories very damning, and Mac knew he could not defend himself by labeling them as lies.

Mac knew some of the stories were not far from the truth. He was not proud of those seven years of his life spent womanizing, gambling, drinking too much, and wasting his life. He couldn't change the past, but he would do what he must to protect the life he sought. He spared Laurel from the rumors and innuendo being spread around the county as best he could. When they were in public, he refused to leave her side. He'd avoided the topic of a conversation when the talk headed to some of the rumor around the community. His life was sweet now. After they'd walked through the sorrow, they deserved a time of happiness and calm.

Mac continued to play the ardent suitor. Frequently, he teased her with unexpected kisses and whispered endearments, leaving Laurel blushing. The words, "Laurel, I love you" or "Wife, you are the best part of me" or "Darling, I want you" found a way into Mac's conversation on a regular basis. Laurel thrived under his constant attention.

Shiloh's promise was rising again. The times when Laurel's eyes reflected sadness and grief were fewer and less frequent. The time she spent with Cathy and Roy became healing, happy times for her and the children. There were days when this shared time included Andrew who would come from the Widow's to visit. In a short time, Andrew came to feel quite at home with the MacLaynes.

When Laurel could find a few spare moments, she continued to read her Grandmother Wilson's worn old Scripture book. She continually searched passages to help her understand the loss of her child. She hungered for words that would explain her failure and push away the guilt she felt. Since the talk with her Uncle Matthew, Laurel realized her own self-absorption was the root of most of the pain she felt and the pain she'd caused Mac. Could it be that all sin was nothing more than putting self in the center of existence? These questions brought her to read and reread many familiar passages, thinking and hoping she would finally find the answers she sought.

The last week in September, Laurel returned to teaching her Sunday school class. Because her students had developed basic levels of word recognition, she moved into teaching Bible stories. When she did this, a few more people joined the small group to study with her. She'd missed teaching, which she'd come to see as her gift, a gift that brought satisfaction and a true sense of purpose.

~

How blessed September had been! October and the election were only three days away. Before noon that Friday morning, Thomas and Andrew rode into the front yard. His pace was too fast to suggest that he'd come for a visit. Laurel met her father-in-law on the porch. "Good afternoon, Pa, Andrew. You're in a hurry."

"Not really. I want to give Tartan a bit of a workout. He was a racer when he was younger. You are looking pert today, daughter."

"Thank you, and I am feeling like a bit of a sprite. Won't you come in and sit a spell? Mac'll be home for lunch soon. He's up in the north pasture looking after his herd."

"I'll ride up to meet him. But if you'll have me, I'll come back to share your meal. I know what a fine spread you lay. You keep feeding my son like you do, he'll be the fattest man in the county before he's forty." They laughed at the idea. "Would you mind if I leave Andrew here to play with Cathy?"

Now alone, Thomas turned his horse toward the pasture where he knew Mac kept his two prize bulls.

"Hello, Pa. Good to see you."

"Patrick, I need to talk with you. Are your hands around?"

"No. I sent Roy and John to Greensboro to bring back some supplies. You sound worried, Pa. What's happening?"

"Digby and his group of hired henchmen are getting desperate. I know you heard some of the rumors about the life you'd led before you came to Shiloh."

"I'm not worried about that talk, Pa. People around here know I wasn't a saint, but they also know I'm not that man anymore. Matthew Campbell uses me as an example of a life renewed in sermons all the time, and himself too."

"I know you're a different man now, but some people aren't as forgiving as others. They look for dirt to throw when they don't measure up.

"Let it go, Pa. I have discounted every lie they've spread about me in this campaign so far. Those trumped up stories only hurt Digby when the people hear the truth."

"Can you discount a rumor that may be true?"

"Pa, what are you talking about?"

"I should have told you this when I came here in June. Patrick, do you know a woman from over between Nashville and Franklin, Tennessee? The name is Tollison?"

"That's an odd question, considering what we were talking about. I won't lie to you, Pa. I knew several women during those wasted years. I'm not proud to say I don't remember the names of most of them. Why?"

Thomas rose from the stump where he'd been sitting and turned his back to Mac. Rubbing his hands through his hair, he carefully considered how he would continue. "Patrick, I got a letter back in early May from a lawyer in Nashville. According to the letter, a woman named Dorcas Tollison claimed you are the father of her child. Andrew is that child, Patrick."

Mac did not utter a word. Memories from his seven wayward years flashed through his mind. None of it seemed real now. "Pa, what made you wait all these months to tell me this?"

"A neighbor from Baltimore wrote that some men were asking questions about my leaving Maryland. He told me some rumors around Ann Arundel County hinted I was trying to hide a grandchild born out of wedlock."

"Why now?"

"Son, I intended to tell you the night we arrived, but when I got here and heard about the miscarriage, I couldn't bring myself to add to your troubles. When I waited those first few days, I could see things between you and Laurel were uneasy. I saw your concern for her."

"That much is true. We've had some low times, but thank the Lord, we are finding our way back to each other. You saw how Laurel stood her ground against Duncan at the barn-raising. Anyway, the name Dorcas Tollison doesn't mean anything to me. Andrew could be anyone's child. You'd think I'd remember a name like Dorcas?"

"Maybe no weight to the claim at all, son. But Patrick, when I went to see the lawyer in Nashville on my way across, he brought Andrew to meet me. I was dumbstruck at the first sight of him. It was like turning back the clock thirty years. Andrew is the image of you and Sean at that age. Have you looked at him? He's got the same chestnut-colored hair and our MacLayne blue eyes. His chin is square like ours, and his eyelashes are long and full. I couldn't believe the resemblance to my own six-year-old in 1830."

"Pa, are you telling me you think that boy is mine?"

"I'm only saying what the lawyer told me. You told me yourself when you came home to Maryland, you'd spent a good many nights with women during your travels."

"That part is true, but six years ago? I can't recall knowing anyone named Dorcas. I am ashamed to say I didn't know most of their last names anyway."

"We don't have to deal with this now. I only told ya because I didn't want you blindsided by one of your opponents in case it came up between now and the election."

"I can't say I am glad you told me, but I appreciate that you want to protect me. Right now, I don't know how I'm going to deal with this. I've got to talk with Laurel. I wish I knew more."

"For now, let's leave things as they are. Andrew will stay with me."

"Does his mother want money from us, Pa?"

"No, son. According to the lawyer, she died about two years ago in a typhoid outbreak in her county. Her father took the boy in until he passed. Mr. Tollison left his property to Andrew with the wish for the lawyer to find the boy's family. He had your name and the county where we lived."

"You said there's a letter. Can I see it?"

"I'll bring it to you at church on Sunday. I put it away for safekeeping. Actually, there are two letters, one from the lawyer and another one addressed to you."

"Pa, please don't mention this to Laurel. Let me talk to her first."

"That would be best, Patrick. If you've finished your work down here, your sweet wife asked me to share dinner with y'all. It'll give

Andrew a little more time to play with Cathy. He said she is his best friend. To tell ya the truth, she may be his first friend."

When the MacLayne men arrived at the cabin, they found Laurel pouring milk for Cathy and Andrew. "We were about to give you two up. You've been with that herd a long time. Sit down and have your dinner while it's hot."

"Let us wash up, and we'll be back." Mac put his arms around Laurel as he passed by and kissed her. "You're looking mighty fine today, wife. It's the smile!"

"Oh, you."

The afternoon proved to be a long, uncomfortable one for Mac. The conversation with his father brought back things he wished he'd never done. Still, Andrew was a reality. Perhaps, the small young boy was his son. He knew he would not rest easy until he talked to Laurel. At the same time, he feared her reaction to the news. Mac told himself that Andrew may not be his child. His conscience told him Andrew's paternity didn't matter because the boy was an orphan and deserved a home. A nagging doubt told him not to bring up problems that may damage his relationship with his wife. Unsettled, Mac could not stay seated. He found himself staring at the six-year-old often during the afternoon. Andrew didn't seem to notice.

"Andrew, would you like to go out on the front porch with Cathy? We'll read a book together."

"No, ma'am. I can't read no how."

"Didn't you go to school in Tennessee before Mr. MacLayne brought you here to Arkansas?"

"Nope. We ain't got no school where I lived with my grandpa in Davidson County. Some in Nashville, but that was a long way. We wouldn't had the money for it no how."

Mac looked up and watched the boy for a few moments. When Andy mentioned Davidson County, he remembered a two week he stayed in a village between Franklin and Nashville. He'd worked for a week or so with a local smith to earn some traveling money.

"Andrew, do you have any family left in Tennessee?"

"No, sir, nary a soul. My mama died when I almost four. Lots of people near us got the typhoid, even me, but I didn't git it so bad as some."

"Where is your papa, Andrew?" Laurel's heart went out to the small, quiet boy. There seemed to be so much sadness in his eyes but also such a maturity for his six years.

"Don't got no Papa I know of. Only my mama and grandpa. Both of them's gone now, so I guess that makes me an orphan. Mr. MacLayne's been good lettin' me stay with him. We got us a fine cabin over the way."

Mac continued to look at Andrew throughout the family talk. He finally felt he had to ask. "Do you remember very much about your mother?"

"I remember she's real pretty. She had big brown eyes. Her hair smelled good--it was the color of straw at cutting time. My mama was Dorcas Tollison, but no one called her that fancy name. Everyone called her Dorrie. Mama smiled all the time."

When Andrew mentioned the nickname Dorrie, Mac lost any doubt of Andrew's paternity. He wished he could recall the face of the petite daughter of the smith he'd worked for in Davidson County. Mac looked at Andrew again and saw himself in the boy's features. Dorrie had been a very sweet, lonely girl who slaved to maintain her father's household. Mac's conquest of the girl had been too easy. Shame and regret brought a darkness to his mood not usually present during family time. To contain the bleak mood, he picked up his Bible.

"Andrew and Cathy, come over here and sit by me. I'll read you a story. Andy, next month when school starts back, you'll go and learn to read for yourself." Though his intentions were kind, the tone of his voice was flat, almost emotionless. Laurel looked at her husband with a question in her eyes. "Every man needs to be able to read for himself. I expect soon, you'll read to us."

Mac began to read the story of Noah and the flood to the children who were now his charges. How strange things happen. He'd wanted a family, but he hadn't expected his children to be older than his marriage. He knew Laurel was a good woman, but would she accept his illegitimate son as her own? If only Campbell had lived, this news would be easier to share. He must tell Laurel about Andrew. What he didn't know was when he could do it. Not that night, but he knew he had little time.

~

In Sunday's announcements, Matthew Campbell reminded the congregation election day was the next day. "Y'all know our own brother Mac will be a good servant to us all, so don't forget to go out to vote. Even if it rains, you're not likely to melt so get to the polls nearest your homesteads. Y'all tell that clerk that MacLayne is your choice. Of course, that isn't the gospel, but your preacher would consider it a favor." The congregation laughed and clapped Mac on the back as they were leaving Shiloh church.

"Pa, we'd be very pleased if you and Andrew will join us for Sunday dinner. We're having chicken and dumplings and fried potatoes. We opened a jar of blackberries and made us a cobbler," Laurel said.

"How could I refuse an invitation like that?"

The entire family joined in the blessing and consumed every morsel of food Laurel brought to the table. They also drained the coffee pot when she filled cups half full for Cathy and Andrew. Of course, she added as much milk and sugar as they had coffee. The family talk was pleasant, and the home was comfortable with a small fire burning in the hearth.

"Pa, having you here has made Shiloh even more like home now."

"Thank you, son. Being near enough to see you often helps me not miss your blessed mother quite so much. Beginning work on the new homestead has even taken away some of the homesickness for me. But Andrew and I have to get that new house started. I'm missing the space of the old home place. How did you and Laurel live in that tiny cabin all those months?"

"I guess it did bring us closer—out of necessity." Laughter again rang out around the table.

"Mac, will you ride over to look at a piece of land I'm thinking of buying? It'd make a nice place to build."

"Sure, Pa. Laurel, do you mind?"

"No. Of course, not. We'll clean up the dishes, and the kids and I will find something to fill our afternoon."

Not long after, the father and son rode from the barnyard. Thomas said, "Patrick, I don't mind if you'd rather not ride all the way to the Lawson place. I wanted to talk to you alone."

"We can ride and talk at the same time, can't we?"

"Talking is one thing, but reading is another." Thomas took two rumpled envelops from his coat pocket and handed them to Mac.

"Let's stop there in the glade. Laurel and I call this place Eden. This is where we laid our son." They rode a few hundred feet and dismounted. "Pa, this is our little boy, Campbell. He was a beautiful perfect baby, but he was born two months too soon."

"What happened, son? You'd told me in a letter that Laurel was feeling good, and the doctor said the baby was growing."

"Lousy weather and a freak accident while I was away bringing in my first cattle from Missouri. Laurel and Cathy got caught in a thunderstorm on the way back from church. Sassy Lady shied at a lightning strike, and Laurel fell from the wagon seat. She miscarried the next day."

"Is she all right now?"

"She's getting stronger all the time. Dr. Gibson told us that Laurel will heal completely, and we can have another baby after a spell." Father and son sat on the fallen hickory log near the giant oak in Eden. Mac took the official-looking envelop and saw it was addressed to him.

*Mr. Patrick MacLayne*
*Ann Arundel, Baltimore, Maryland*
*May 1, 1858*

*Sir:*

*As directed in the will of the late Andrew Tollison of Davidson County, Tennessee, I am charged to reunite the minor child Andrew Tollison MacLayne with his family. There is no legal proof said boy is your son. Mr. Tollison's daughter Dorcas recorded his birth in their family Bible, which I will deliver to you when you come to take him, should you choose to do so. The notation reads,*

*'Andrew Tollison MacLayne, born November 12, 1852. Mother: Dorcas Tollison. Father: Patrick MacLayne of Baltimore.'*

*If this boy is not your child, you may place him for adoption or in an orphanage of your choosing. The sum of $100 gold is the remainder of his grandfather's estate after the expense of locating you. I'll place the sum in your hands at such a time as we can meet. Upon delivering the boy, I have discharged the duty assigned to me in the will mentioned.*

*Respectfully yours,*
*B.K. Lymon, Attorney*

"There's not much to go on in this letter. Not even the name of the town where he was born. The lawyer says Dorcas wrote your name as his father. That's not legally binding."

"Did Lyman tell you if the county recorded his birth?"

"No, son. Our meeting was brief. He gave me the letter I gave you, and a pouch holding $70 in gold, what remained after he took his hefty fee. He also sent Andrew's family Bible.

"I don't need more proof, Pa. I know Andrew is my son. While you napped after dinner on Wednesday, Andrew told me about his mother, at least what he remembered as a four-year-old. He called her Dorrie. I remembered a girl named Dorrie. After he described his mother, I looked at him. I mean I seriously looked at him. I have no doubt that he's mine."

"He does bear a strong family resemblance. In the short time I've had him, he's been a good boy. He needs some security and a place to belong. He also needs an education. He can neither read nor write."

"Let me read this other letter." Patrick took the crumpled, dingy paper sealed with wax from his pocket. The small glob of white sealing wax was still in its place. The writing on the single folded sheet of paper was poor and showed the writer hadn't been exposed to much schooling. It read:

*My der Mack,*

*I am ritin you today a tellin you ar baby was borned las nite. I called him fer my pa and my famle name. His name is Andrew Tollison MacLayne, and its his christyen name.*

*I wrote it in the Bible. I'm gonna post this here leter to ya the nex time I go to town, hopin yule come bak to us. He's a purty chile, Mack, and I stil love ya.*

*Love fourever,*

*Dorrie*

With downcast eyes, Mac folded the tiny letter and returned it to his pocket. The sweet words Dorrie wrote brought a flood of remorse and shame. He'd used that young woman whose face he didn't even remember. He knew God had forgiven his reckless past. What he couldn't fathom is how he could have ever been that man? At the same time, he felt a tremendous tenderness for the small boy. Mac sat on the fallen log, running his hands through his hair for some time before he spoke.

"Pa, I'm sorry I brought this shame on you. You acted as honorably as any man could. Thank you for taking care of my responsibility. I will bring Andrew into my home and raise him as my son. I'll explain it all to him the best I can, but I can't until I have time to talk with Laurel. Knowing the goodness in her, she'll accept him into our home. I only have to make her see this doesn't change anything between us."

"In your time, son. I'm happy to have Andrew as my ward, and I'll adopt him if you think it would be best for your marriage."

"Pa, you're good to offer, but I will raise my son along with Cathy. God willing, Laurel and I will bring them up with any other children He blesses our marriage with."

"I knew that would be your decision, Patrick. Andrew has a place with me until you and Laurel are ready to bring him into your home."

# CHAPTER SEVENTEEN

*With good will doing service, as to the Lord, and not to men: Knowing that whatsoever good thing any man doeth, so the same shall he receive of the Lord...*
*Ephesians 6:7-8*

October 4th proved to be a fine fall day for the election. No rain or unseasonable cold would keep men from the polling sites. Mac loaded his whole family to drive to Shiloh church, where he would cast his own vote with the local justice of the peace. When they arrived, a number of Mac's supporters and friends from around the community were there waiting to welcome him. Even Thomas MacLayne had ridden over from the widow's place.

"Morning, Mr. Representative. Could I ask you who you intend to vote for?"

"Bob Clayton, don't be ridiculous. If I didn't think I was good enough to vote for, how could I ask my friends to vote for me?" The men laughed and clapped each other on the back in good fellowship. They were excited that one of their own would undoubtedly speak for them in Little Rock.

"Mr. MacLayne, ain't you gonna vote for your son?"

"Call me Thomas, friend. I'd dearly love to be able to do just that, but

I've only been a resident since June. I don't think he'll need my vote anyway. All of you have worked very hard to elect an independent representative. I'm sure all the hard work will elect Patrick."

"We didn't vote for Patrick MacLayne. None of us here even know him...we all voted for Mac." Cheers and laughter again erupted across the churchyard. The crowd mingled around the area until Mac returned to his wagon.

"I thank you for your friendship and confidence in me. Whether I win or lose, I've already had my victory. No man with such friends can ever be thought a loser. See y'all soon."

Election day came and went. Tallying the vote would take some time as there were nine precincts and dozens of communities with polling sites reaching all the way to the state line to the north, to the Cache River on the west, the St. Francis on the East and down to the Poinsett county line in the south. Due to the distance, election results often took three or more days to collect. Then the election committee made up of several justices of the peace were charged with certifying the vote before they could announce the winner. Mac returned to work on his homestead. He'd done all he could to earn the legislative seat. Besides, he had to find the right opportunity to talk to Laurel. He had to tell her that Andrew was his son.

The next few days offered no such opportunity. A steady stream of visitors came to the cabin for the next week...people coming to congratulate him or to ask a favor when he went to Little Rock or just to be in the midst of the goings-on. Laurel spent endless hours preparing tidbits for people to snack on and made frequent trips to the spring house for cool water and fresh milk. On Friday afternoon, Matthew and Ellie arrived with Mary. Thomas MacLayne rode up with Andrew, and several of Mac's supporters from Greensboro just dropped by. Al Stuart, Harold Armstrong, Bob Clayton with his wife Linnie Jeanette, and John McCollough just happened to stop by for a visit at the same time.

"All of you know something I don't know?" Mac asked.

"Just wanted to be here for the announcement. J.P. Davidson should be here any time," Al replied.

"Could be he's going to Gainesville to tell Digby."

"No need. We all know how the vote went." Bob Clayton clapped Mac soundly on his back. "Come on, wife...Let's get to that fireplace." He took his wife's arm and led her into the house. About three in the afternoon, the J.P. arrived at the MacLayne homestead. The friends standing around the yard and sitting on the porch cheered as he rode up. Mac and several others came outside at the noise. Davidson took his time dismounting in all the official dignity of his office. Straightening his hat and retrieving his tally sheets from his saddlebag, he turned to climb the steps where Mac stood.

"Mr. Patrick MacLayne, I am right sorry for the delay in reporting the result of the election. Two of the polling sheets never got to the committee in Gainesville so we could count the votes. One from over at Lorado was missing, and the election monitor from Chalk Bluff never turned in his tally sheets. I hope this will not cause any difficulty in seating you as our duly elected representative from Greene County. You got more'n seventy percent of the votes, and if Digby got every vote from Lorado and Chalk Bluff he couldn't top your total. Congratulations, Mr. Representative! Go to Little Rock and serve us well."

A huge cheer rose. Mac waved to his friends and then pulled Laurel into his arms and kissed her. Laurel felt the pride and excitement around her. Mac could now serve, just as he'd dreamed he would.

"Well, Mrs. MacLayne, we'll be busy now! You know we have to be in Little Rock by November 1. Are you ready for another adventure across the state?" Before she could answer, Mac's friends pulled him away to congratulate him and to talk about concerns they wanted him to address in the legislature. Laurel returned to her role as hostess at the impromptu party.

When they were able to retire to their bedroom, the time was late--well past ten. Laurel was exhausted, but Mac was so keyed up from the events of the day, he wanted to talk. "Laurel, we've got to make plans to travel to Little Rock. I wish there was an easy way to get there, but there just isn't. What would be the easiest thing for you?"

"Wouldn't it be better if I stayed here to take care of the homestead? You'll only be gone a few weeks."

"No. I don't want to be separated from you again."

"I need to be here to take care of Cathy and Roy. Our animals need tending. My Sunday school class needs me here."

"I need you there. I've already asked Matthew and Ellie to keep Cathy while we're away. She'll be in school then. Roy is nearly grown. He and John will do the chores. Matthew said he'd teach the Sunday school class."

"I'm not sure..."

"Well, I am. I want you to share this time with me. I'll enjoy some time for just the two of us, and I need you there to talk over the things going on in the legislature. Please just humor me. Let's pretend we are newlyweds on our wedding trip."

"But I don't have the right clothes for city life. I'm not ready to...."

"We'll be fine. We are headed to Little Rock no later than the twentieth of October. We just have to decide how we're going to make the trip. None of our options are easy, but I seem to remember a much longer trip that wasn't easy either. We made it just fine."

"At least it's a comfort to know your Pa will be close, looking after things. Tomorrow, I'll start pulling together a wardrobe suitable to accompany the new representative from Greene County."

"You, my dear wife, will be the belle of the city."

"I think you forgot whom you married."

"That'll never happen. I married the girl the Lord gave me, and I am blessed by her every day of my life. But enough talk for one day. Come to bed and let me show you how much I appreciate the gift I've been given."

The next several days Mac investigated the travel options from Shiloh to Little Rock. He immediately ruled out overland by horseback. There were far too few inns or other safe places to shelter in the late fall. He wouldn't make Laurel sleep outside on the ground for a week in October. Besides, horses couldn't carry what they would need to take for a month or more. The second idea held more hope. He'd learned that a stagecoach made regularly scheduled runs from Memphis to Little Rock. The route stopped in Francisville. The leg from Francisville took less than thirty-six hours, almost non-stop. The ticket price was reasonable enough, but Francisville was almost a three-day ride from Shiloh. Besides, the coaches were often overfilled and dirty. The worst part would be to arrive in the city with no transportation for the entire time of their visit.

Mac chose travel by steamboat, but knowing little about schedules or costs, he decided to go into Greensboro to talk to local freighters. He knew he could learn all he needed to know.

"Laurel, my darlin', how would you like to travel to Little Rock on a steamboat?"

"That would be an adventure, but I didn't realize we had dredged our creek. I doubt if even the smallest boat could get within fifty miles of our house."

"You've always had a sharp tongue to match your sharp mind, my dear. Let me tell you how we can get to Little Rock. We'll take a short two-day ride to Hopefield. I've been there so I know a good way. There's not been heavy rain this fall, so the lowlands won't be flooded. From Hopefield, we'll take the paddleboat down the Mississippi to a little town called Napoleon. We can take our horses on board, too. In Napoleon, we'll change boats and go up the Arkansas River right to Little Rock. We'll have transportation while we're there so we can explore the central part of the state and go anywhere we have a mind to."

"If that's your wish, Mac. The whole thing sounds like it'll cost a lot of money."

"It's the least dangerous route and most comfortable. If we meet the schedules, we can be in Little Rock in about six days."

"If the rivers not too dry or the boat doesn't explode, we should have a fine adventure." Mac laughed, picked Laurel up and swung her around the room and plopped them both down in his chair where he began to kiss her.

Just about that time, Cathy walked in the front door. Laurel pushed Mac away, and she rose from her seat in his lap. She began to smooth her hair and skirt.

"Don't be concerned about me, Ms. Mac. I like it when you and Mr. Mac act like kids sparkin' because you always smile and act so happy.

Never mind me. I just came in to get my shawl. It's a bit nippy out today." Laurel flushed a bit at being caught by Cathy, but Mac roared with laughter.

"She's a smart little girl. I like the sparkin', too, because seeing you smile is a blessing of its own."

The final week was filled with more activity than Laurel ever dreamed could be pushed into one week. She and Mac made a trip to Greensboro to purchase a few additional pieces of clothing they'd never use in Shiloh. Mac also went to Harold Armstrong's livery to have Midnight's shoes checked and to pick up a small one seat buggy he'd borrowed from Al Stuart. The trip across the sunken land in dry weather was more than possible in the small buggy. Besides, the boot in the back would allow them to take a trunk for all the clothes they needed for several weeks.

Laurel also had to pack things for Cathy's stay with the Campbells. School would start before they could return, and Cathy's two-inch-growth-spurt during the summer left most of her skirts woefully short. Laurel managed to let down the hem in one of them, but the other two had already been lengthened. Laurel bought fabric for one new dress for Cathy and a length of ecru lace to add a ruffle to her brown skirt. Of course, that added hours of sewing to other things she had to do.

Luckily, Roy's needs were fewer. He would stay at the MacLayne homestead with John Campbell so if his clothes were clean and in good repair, they would serve him well. Laurel found only one split seam in Roy's blue plaid shirt and a small hole in one sock. As she sat darning the sock, she thought to herself… *Thank goodness for boys.*

The afternoon before their planned departure, Mac and Laurel planned a family dinner with their two wards. They ate dinner quite early because Roy had promised to take Cathy to gather the wild pecans that were falling all over the ridge. Mac planned to have some family time so he could have a serious talk with his two wards.

"Kids, you know Mrs. Mac and I look on you two as if you belong to us. Leaving y'all behind for several weeks isn't easy for us, but we couldn't do it if we didn't know you'd be well-cared for here at Shiloh."

"We know that, Mr. Mac." Cathy grinned impishly.

"We are planning to be home for Christmas if we can get back. No one ever knows exactly how the legislative session will go, but if for some reason we don't get back, celebrate with my pa and the Campbells. We'll have our own celebration when we get home," said Mac.

"Well, you try. It won't be the same without y'all being home," Cathy responded.

"We want you to know, both of you, that we love you. Cathy, mind Aunt Ellie, and study hard at school. Roy, I hope you will go back to school in November," Laurel added.

"Maybe, Mrs. Mac."

By 4:00, the Dunn's had left the homestead. Laurel began to clear the table when Mac took her hand. "Laurel, let's walk out to Eden to visit Campbell before we leave. The leaves are changing all over the ridge, and the valley down by the creek is about the most beautiful place on earth right now. We'll worry about a dirty kitchen later. Right now, we need to spend a while in the glory of Crowley's Ridge and in God's creation."

Laurel needed no convincing. She had visited the grave of her son several times and had always found peace and solace, kneeling there by the tiny grave. As they reached the glade, Laurel saw the reason Mac wanted to make the trip today. He had placed a new grave marker at the head of the little mound at the foot of the ancient oak tree. The carved fieldstone was in the shape of a cross set on a solid base about two feet wide. At the foot of the cross, a tiny lamb rested among a field of daisies. The inscription was a simple one.

**Campbell MacLayne**
**April 5, 1858**
**Beloved son of Patrick and Laurel.**
**'Suffer not the children to come onto Me'**

"What a beautiful marker, Patrick. Thank you for bringing me here today."

"Campbell is a part of our home here, Laurel. I am grateful you wouldn't let me build our cabin in this place. To change this glade would be a desecration of a holy place. Because our son is here, this ground will always be holy to us as long as we live. We'll never change it." They knelt beside the grave and offered a silent prayer. Mac's prayer was one of gratitude that Laurel had been able to grow beyond her grief, and Laurel made a petition that God would allow her to give Mac a healthy child soon. After a few minutes, He helped her up. Hand in hand, they began their walk home.

"You are happy about leaving for Little Rock tomorrow, aren't you, Mac?"

"Yes, wife, I am. I feel like I've been given a chance to make a real contribution to our part of the state. We may be able to make a real contribution to our county and the state."

"I know you will, Mac. I am proud to be the wife of the representative of this county."

"With all the visiting we've done around the district and all the people we've talked to, I believe I have a good feel for what our folks want. And those things are not unreasonable. Our people are pretty practical in what they want if you take the time to listen to them."

"What do you think should be done first?"

"Not that I'll have any say about that, but you know their big concerns are not what I thought they'd be before I started the campaign. So many of them worry about what'll happen if Arkansas leaves the union. Not much support for that right now. People are more concerned about being able to pay their taxes. Some of the women have approached me about the law that won't let them take ownership of their property if something happens to their husbands. Farmers want roads that don't flood in every rain so they can get their crops to market. Lord knows we need schools all over the state, not just in Little Rock and in the northwest.

"Sounds like a huge task to take on. Do you think one man can make a difference?"

"One man can try, but I'm betting I'll find others of a like mind. I can do anything if I have you there to support me and listen to me and to keep me straight... if need be."

"I've never been south before. It'll be interesting to see the capital. I'd like to see a legislative session, too. Do you think they allow spectators?"

"We'll sure find out when we get there."

"Patrick, I will try to be an asset to you while you serve in the state house."

"Laurel, you don't have to try. You are my most valuable asset, just because you are who you are."

"I see myself that way when you look at me. Your eyes have been the best mirror I've ever had. I'm glad you broke that looking glass in Jasper all those months ago."

On October 20th, Laurel and Mac were ready to leave. Matthew and Ellie had come early to see them off, even though the Shiloh congregation had given them a fine send-off party after church the previous Sunday. Mac had been particularly touched when Matthew had called the brothers of the church to the altar at the end of the service and asked them to lay hands on Mac while they prayed together. They asked a blessing on his service to the state and to their community. Matthew's final words that morning came from Romans 8:28, the Scripture Mac had taken as his creed. At the end of that day, Mac felt he'd truly been called to serve, and he was more than ready to take on his new role.

"Don't worry none about Cathy, Laurel Grace. We'll get her to school and promoted to the fourth level before you come home at Christmas."

Matthew Campbell helped his niece into the buggy. He kissed her on the cheek and said, "Keep him honest, Sprite, as we send him into a pit of vipers." Then he turned toward Mac. "God bless you, brother. Don't forget the purpose the Lord has called you to...Be a statesman for us because we don't need no more politicians down there. Vote your conscience as to what's good for the people, even though some of it may not be the easiest thing for you." Matthew pulled Mac into a strong embrace, a thing he'd done only one other time, the day they'd grieved the loss of Mac's son. "Father, bless this man. Mac, I thank the Lord for our friendship every day. God's speed."

Mac and Laurel headed toward Greensboro in the borrowed buggy, easily pulled by Midnight. Sassy Lady was tied to the back. The path down the old Military Road toward Bolivar was a familiar one. Luckily, the road was dry and firm, although it was cold outside. Mac had told Laurel they would make the river in two days. He tried to make them comfortable as they rode by covering both of them with the hide of a bear that had been his grandfather MacLayne's prey many years ago. Some heated bricks, a quilt, and the old bear hide provided a comfortable sanctuary.

"Well, wife, how do you feel about being on another adventure with me?"

"I'm a little nervous. I'm not sure I will fit into the polite society of the city, but I look forward to the time we'll have together. I've often wondered what a trip on a riverboat would be like. I've heard they're quite luxurious."

"Some are, and some are just basic. I don't know which we'll find in Memphis, but I know we'll make good time traveling down the Mississippi. Those paddle wheelers average six miles an hour. Can you imagine that?"

"Sounds almost impossible."

"Do you remember the day we left that cabin with Lonnie Thomison after that three-day rainstorm, and we traveled only nine miles the whole day?"

"Yes, I think you and Lonnie spent more time clearing trees from the road than we did traveling down them."

"For all the hardship of that trip, we have some good memories of that journey. And the outcome has been a true blessing."

"I agree. Even with the sad times, the Lord has continued to bless us."

Before dark, Midnight had brought them to Bolivar, and Mac stopped him in front of Lee's boarding house. The drive from Greensboro had been a long cold one, but Mac and Laurel had enjoyed the time together. Mac's high spirits had put him in a teasing mood throughout the day. Together they recalled so many silly, awkward moments they lived through in the last fourteen months since they had last been in Bolivar. Once he had chided her about wrecking the cabin on wheels that had brought Laurel home to Shiloh. "Laurel, you know I could probably have sold that elegant vehicle back to the smith. He'd certainly want it back, especially with that bright yellow awning and the built-in bed in the back."

"Mac, you're ridiculous. You know you're happy as a beagle in huntin' time that I turned that cabin on wheels into kindling last December. It's made a fine flatbed wagon ever since."

"Do you think Lizzie Lee and her mister will remember us?"

"You probably. I seem to remember she was going to have you arrested the last time we put your feet under her table."

"No. That was at supper, not breakfast. I'm sure looking forward to eating Lizzie's breakfast again."

"When the MacLaynes entered the parlor, Lizzie Lee met them as old friends. "Miss Grace and Mac, what brings y'all back south and in this winter cold?"

"We're looking for a warm place to sleep and a couple of hot meals."

"You come to the right place. You want that same room at the end of the hall?"

"That'd suit us just fine. How is Mr. Lee, Lizzie?"

"Right good, but he's working more'n ever. We opened us a hardware line in our mercantile. Supper's been over a while, but I know I can rustle ya up some grub if you want to sit down."

"Sounds fine, Lizzie."

"Miss Grace, you sure look different."

"Lizzie, please call me Laurel. I am just a more polished version of the old me. Mac has been elected to the state legislature from our district, and we are headed to Little Rock. I guess I have to look the part of a lady."

After a filling meal, Mac and Laurel took their leave and headed to the end room they'd shared when Mac had come to find her. "Lizzie, I'm looking forward to another grand breakfast, and please pack us a good lunch for the trail. We'll leave early in the morning because we want to be at the Mississippi by tomorrow night."

# CHAPTER EIGHTEEN

*I am my beloved's, and his desire is toward me.*
*Song of Songs Chapter 7:10*

True to her reputation, Lizzie Lee laid out a breakfast fit to please: eggs, ham, gravy, oatmeal, biscuits, grits, and coffee. Mac ate more than he needed. Laurel too enjoyed the well-prepared southern breakfast. Lizzie packed a large basket with enough food to feed a small regiment of soldiers. As the sun began to tint the eastern sky in shades of pink, red, and gold, the MacLaynes left Bolivar and started across the miles and miles of sunken land. Mac noticed how sparsely populated the area was. At times, they would drive several miles and never see a man-made structure anywhere. Strangely, no defined road joining northeast Arkansas to the Mississippi River had ever been laid out, or if so, survived the flooding so common to the area. Mac put his trust in his compass and a path the local freighters said took them to Hopefield. Even that path was a gift of the Indians who inhabited this part of Arkansas before the coming of the homesteaders. At Hopefield, a ferry would take them across 'Big Muddy'.

"I can't believe all this fertile, valuable land sitting here empty for a lack of some proper levees. This sunken land could be some of the best cropland in the state if we controlled the flooding."

"Is that what you want to do while you are in the legislature, Mac?"

"Yes, one of the things. All the secession talk won't help any though. Most of the levee work around here comes from the federal money. Our state doesn't have that kind of resources. It costs a fair amount of money to build good levee systems."

The nearer they came to the St. Francis, the more desolate the land looked. The annual flooding had driven many a strong farmer beyond his breaking point. So many of them gave up the fight with Mother Nature and went to Texas, hoping to find a better life. Travel was hard that day, but Mac drove on, stopping only a brief time to allow Midnight and Sassy to drink and rest. The distance between Bolivar and Hopefield was much more than a one-day drive. Thankfully, the moon was full, and the sky was so clear that millions of stars helped to light the badly rutted path. When the MacLaynes reached the town, the main street was dark...only one faint lantern lit a window in a small tavern. Mac pulled Midnight to a halt and entered the ramshackle building much in need of paint. He hoped to find some kind of shelter for the night. Much to his surprise, the tiny lobby was tidy and clean. A middle-aged clerk dozed in a chair behind the counter.

"Excuse me, sir. Do you have an empty room so late in the evening?"

"Ah...caught me catchin' forty winks...Yes, sir. The riverboat left Memphis two days ago and ain't another for a couple days."

"Please, give us the best room you have for my wife and me. We'd be very pleased to have a bath in the morning."

"This here is Hopefield, not Boston. If you want a bath, it's only a short trip to the river."

"We'll take the room. Is there a livery where I can board my animals?"

"Right on down the street, behind the saloon on the corner. Doubt if they'll be anyone around this time of night."

"We'll take our chances. We'll return for the night directly." Mac found the clerk was right. He entered the livery stable through a side door and lifted the bar to allow Laurel to drive inside. He attended to the feeding and watering for the two horses and then locked them in a stall with clean hay. Taking Laurel's hand, they walked back to the tavern. The clerk escorted them to a large room on the backside of the hotel. Nestled together, the couple fell asleep as soon as their heads touched the pillows.

They slept well into the morning. At 8:00 Mac entered the reception room to find several people gathering luggage. "Seems to be a lot of people ready to leave this fine town. When will the next ferry cross the river to Memphis?"

"The clerk told us we had to be on the dock by eight if we want morning passage. The second ferry wouldn't leave until one o'clock."

"Thank you, sir. Do you know if a riverboat is due to leave Memphis in the next day or two?"

"Rumor has it that the Eclipse is landing on Friday, headed south. That's a mighty fine side-wheeler if you can afford the passage." Mac knew they were in no hurry after he'd talked to the man in the reception room, so he let Laurel sleep. They would take the afternoon ferry to the east side of the river, and they would bide their time in Memphis.

After breakfast at the tavern, Mac and Laurel returned to claim their animals and buggy. Laurel watched with a bit of amusement as Mac explained to the flustered livery keeper how, why, and when he earned the double fee Mac placed in his hand. Laurel saw Mac, the politician, using his gift of words and persuasive personality with the confused man. Soon they drove the few yards down to the landing where the ferry would take them across the Mississippi to Memphis. Mac would use the time to open a serious conversation with Laurel.

"Well, dear one, it's a beautiful day, not nearly as cold as yesterday. Are you enjoying the adventure so far?"

"Except for the cold weather, this journey has been pleasant. You've been in fine spirits, and we've had so much time to talk. Seems we rarely have much private time at home. How could I not enjoy this time?"

"I know you and small talk."

"Patrick, we've not been making small talk. Nothing we've talked about has been trivial. As a matter of fact, I was pretty impressed with that little conversation you had with the liveryman. I was beginning to think you could bargain your soul away from the devil."

"That's not my job. Someone else did that for me several years back. But Laurel, I do have something I need to tell you. I should have done it three weeks ago, but everything has been so hectic at home since the election. We've had hardly a minute to ourselves when we weren't dead tired. Frankly, I still don't know exactly how to say what needs saying."

"Patrick, is something amiss at home? You're frightening me. Tell me what's bothering you."

"Laurel Grace, you know I love you. I thank God for you every day. You are the best wife a man could want, and I don't deserve you. You have to believe what I am saying. Nothing will ever change the bond between us." Laurel's face turned pale. Anxiety showed across her brows. Green streaks in her grey eyes told Mac his attempt was clumsy and too melodramatic. All the words he'd spoken to reassure Laurel brought more concern. Mac reigned Midnight in and pulled the buggy to the side of the road beneath a small stand of trees to shelter them from the gusty winds. "Laurel, Andrew is my son."

For a time, Laurel didn't grasp what her husband had told her. She sat still, looking at Mac as if she could somehow discern from his face what the words had not explained.

"Laurel, please say something."

"Andrew … your pa's ward…Andrew is your son?"

"Yes."

An awkward silence followed. Some time passed before she spoke again. "Seems a strange time to break this news to me. I didn't know you'd ever had a wife and child. Did you forget to tell me that little inconsequential fact?"

"I hear the sarcasm in your voice. You do it whenever you feel vulnerable. Darlin', please don't pass judgment before you hear me out."

"Why did you decide to tell me now?"

"I had to, Laurel. Andrew needs to become part of our family."

"I see."

"No, you don't see. Laurel, I didn't know anything about the boy until my father came to visit that day before the election. He told me

Andrew was orphaned when his mother and grandfather died. Andrew's mother's name was Dorrie. She was one of the women from my past. We weren't married, and I never knew about Andrew."

"How do you know he's yours?"

"His mother named me. I can't deny it's possible because I took advantage of the poor, lonely girl. My pa said Andrew is the very image of both Sean and me at that age. I have to acknowledge him, Laurel. It's the right thing to do."

A heaviness settled around Laurel. The one thing she could have done to repay Patrick MacLayne for his goodness to her had been done by another. Mac had the son he'd wanted. His first son was not hers. "Was she young and beautiful, Mac?"

"Laurel, believe me, I hardly remember her. She was one of too many I used to fill the void I felt when Marsha betrayed me."

"I understand."

"Can we take him into our home and raise him as our own son?"

"Of course, you'll take him into your house." Patrick had never heard colder words from the mouth of his wife.

"Oh, precious Lord! Laurel, I've hurt you again. I never meant to suggest that Andrew will replace Campbell. Please forgive my careless words."

"Nothing to forgive, Mac. Andrew is a MacLayne and a part of the family. We'll raise your son right along with Cathy and Roy." The stoic tone of Laurel's voice and the rigidity of her posture told Mac he'd failed to deliver the message as he'd hoped.

"Laurel, I know I've hurt you again. I wanted to tell you in a much better way. The time, place, and the words never came together. I should have waited for the Lord to help me tell you, so I could have spoken more gently. Keeping this from you has been hard."

"Mac, we'd best move on, or we'll miss the ferry to Memphis." Laurel's voice was flat and emotionless. Mac heard no sarcasm, anger, or expression of any kind. The lack of life in her voice was more frightening than the reaction he'd feared.

"I've only one more thing to say. Laurel, I meant every word I spoke before I told you about the boy. Please believe me. God always has a way of working things out for the best, but He never promised that we won't have to deal with the consequences of our past sins. Andrew is a good boy, Laurel, and he needs us. He deserves a family who loves him. I can make reclamation for my sin. It's not Andrew's sin. But wife, I can't give him a home without your help."

"For better, for worse. We will make the best of it. I see no point in talking about the inevitable. Now let's get on that ferry. It's much too cold to swim this muddy river." She placed her hand on Mac's arm and moved closer to him. She was determined to play her role as a politician's devoted wife to best of her ability until she could understand what had happened. No one ever said she had to feel love, security, and worth. None of that was in her vows. She tried to push away the old doubts and griefs that ate at her security once again. She had failed to give Mac a son, and now another woman had given him a son. In her mind, she cried out her failure.

Mac drove up and stopped at the door of the saloon that stood near the path leading down to the dock. "Laurel, it was right here on that last bench that I discovered what a poor provider I was for you. When I looked in my saddlebag for a clean shirt, I found the money pouch I'd meant to leave for you when I went to Maryland."

"I've not given it much thought, but it is interesting to see where you spent your time."

"Miss Sass! You know that it's these places where travelers can find a hot meal. See down there, below the rise...they're loading the ferry. Looks like we made it just in time." Mac drove down to the ramp and onto the ferry. He hoped the Eclipse would make landfall before dark.

"Howdy, MacLayne. Seems you was here a while back." The ferryman had remembered Mac from the trip he'd made north. "You headed back east again to see your family?"

"No, Roscoe. This time we're headed south. Not looking for a train this time, but a steamboat. Have you had any news of the Eclipse?"

"I suppose that floatin' palace is as on time as those vessels ever are. You never know when they'll get stopped by a log jam or a sandbar. You brought your lady with you this time."

"Indeed, I did. Laurel, this is Roscoe. He runs the most reliable ferry on the Mississippi. Roscoe, this is my wife, Laurel. We're Little Rock bound so I can take my seat in the Arkansas House of Representatives."

"Danged, if'n you ain't a politician. I thought you was too smooth to be a farmer." Other passengers laughed at the sarcastic jibe aimed at Mac.

The river crossing was easy and took a very short time. Mac paid Roscoe a five-dollar fee and drove up the bluff. The Eclipse had laid anchor a short way down the riverside at a much larger wharf. The white double-decker reminded Laurel of plantation homes she'd seen in South Carolina. Except for two tall stacks, rising high above the top of the boat, the vessel had every characteristic of the stately old mansions along the river. On the second deck, the passenger area, the Eclipse had white columns and wide verandas on both sides. This ship also had a lower deck for storage, transporting cotton, animals and the passengers' wagons, buggies and even a coach or two. The buggy they drove onto the deck was one of the smallest rigs stored there. Mac saw to Midnight and Sassy and paid a steward to take their luggage upstairs. Their cabin was on the outside of the boat and was very small, no more than ten feet square. However, its furnishings were luxurious. The curtains and bed linens were of the most ornately embroidered forest green brocade. The room held a massive carved mahogany bed, an armoire, and a chair covered in rich dark green velvet.

Everything she saw convinced her, she was living a dream. The news Mac had shared in Hopefield, the luxury of the Eclipse, and the ambiguity of her feelings convinced her she would eventually wake up to her real life. "My goodness, Mac. Have we gotten into the captain's quarters?"

"No, my dear…It's your own private palace for two nights. Enjoy it while you can. By the afternoon of the third day, we should be in Napoleon where we will have to take a smaller boat up the Arkansas to Little Rock. You won't find much brocade on the packet, I'm afraid."

"This had to cost a year's wage…Are you…" Mac stifled her complaint with his lips.

"Hush, sweetheart. Let's enjoy the moment. Take a while to clean up. I'll order you a hot bath, and then I want you to wear something beautiful. After supper tonight, we are dancing in the Grand Ball Room to the music of a whole orchestra."

"Will the boat leave soon?"

"I'd imagine an hour or so. The cotton's aboard. Seems they are takin' on more wood. It takes a lot of steam to move that forty-two-foot paddle at more than six miles an hour."

Laurel's first night on the elegant paddleboat was one of the most unique experiences of her life. Mac had asked her to dress for dinner. What did a lady wear to dinner on a floating palace? Her dungarees wouldn't do, and the brown linsey-woolsey skirt and jacket she wore to teach school seemed a bit plain. She'd worn her green wool traveling suit the past two days and had it on, so Mac must want her to wear something else. That left her with two choices. She had brought a dark blue serge skirt and white lawn blouse and her silver-gray sateen ball gown. After all, a travel trunk was only so large.

"Mac, what do you mean when you say "dress" for dinner? You know my wardrobe is not exactly 'social attire'."

"Put on the most beautiful gown you own, leave those tawny tresses down you lovely back, and put this trinket on to complete your outfit." Mac handed Laurel a small box he'd kept in his pocket. Laurel gasped as she opened the box. Lying on a bed of black velvet, she found a gold and emerald brooch in the shape of the infinity symbol. She looked up into her husband's eyes with questions in her own.

"Laurel, before you complain about the extravagance, I want you to know this gift of love came from my parents. My mother wore these emeralds to the governor's Christmas ball during her wedding trip. Pa asked me to give it to you as an early Christmas gift from him and my mother. He told me to say, 'God bless you, daughter, for helping bring his son become the man he was born to be."

She continued to look into Patrick's too blue eyes, speechless. "Oh, my Lord. Thank you. Thank your Pa. His words are the gift I don't deserve, and I'll treasure this beautiful 'trinket' because your mother wore it."

The evening seemed to be a dream. When they entered the Grand Salon at the bow of the boat, more than a dozen other couples were seated in the gilt and cream room. The room was more than a hundred feet long and a quarter that wide. The grand hall was lit by three massive, crystal chandeliers hung down the center of the room. Each held as many candles as Laurel would use in a year to light their cabin. Not one was unlit. At the far end of the hall on a small dais sat members of a full orchestra. The tables were laid with tablecloths and napkins the color of freshly fallen snow. Each place was set with translucent porcelain, crystal goblets and silver flatware. Once again, Laurel stood in awe, as she took in the opulence around her, but Mac seemed to be quite at home in the setting. She wondered if he lived in this manner at the MacLayne house in Maryland. She realized there was still so much about her husband that she didn't know.

As soft ambient music played, the head waiter, a tall regal black man, dressed in a black tailcoat and crisp white shirt, pulled a chair out for Laurel. Mac stood at her side and then took the chair to her right. As soon as Mac chose his chair, a second waiter removed the items from the two empty places at their table. The table became the perfect site for two lovers on their wedding trip. The crystal wine glasses, filled with red wine, and the water goblets awaited them. Within two minutes, bowls of creamy chowder sat in front of them, although neither had ordered. The service continued as steaming rolls, shaped like crescent moons, appeared on the table along with a small pot of butter.

"Try the butter, Laurel. You'll like it on those hot rolls." Laurel dipped her silver knife into the small pot and dabbed the light, frothy spread on a piece of her roll. The spread for the bread had an almost undetectable sweetness, but enough so the bread became a feast of its own. "That's honey butter, wife. The chef hand whips the butter and honey together."

Within a few minutes, an elegant waiter brought them steak, new potatoes, fresh asparagus, and cream sauce. This kind of food was never available so late in the fall at home. The homesteaders had already begun to use their canned, dried, and smoked foods to feed their families.

"Where do they get these kinds of fresh vegetables this time of year, Mac?"

"In New Orleans, for the most part. They have access to imported foods at all times of the year. How do you like the wine?"

"It's nice."

"Why did you wrinkle your nose then?"

"To tell you the truth, it smells of rotten fruit and tastes worse. But, Mac, everything else is so perfect. Such a wonderful meal to start my first riverboat trip!"

"That's all right, Laurel. I don't like it much either. It's a part of social life. I'm going to drink my water with this fine steak."

The entertainment in the Grand Salon that evening was a two sette ball with music supplied by the orchestra. The captain of the Eclipse announced the evening's ball would begin with a grand march. Walking by her side, Mac took Laurel's gloved hand in his and walked around the gilt and cream ballroom to the lively rhythm of *Dixie*.

"You are the most beautiful woman in the room tonight, wife. Your silver sateen ball gown is almost too elegant for the occasion. In that ballgown, you'll make an awe-inspiring entrance at our first social event in Little Rock."

"Thank you, Mac. Mrs. Dunn did beautiful work, but I wish she'd made the bodice a bit more modest."

"The dress is perfect, and I've never seen you more aptly attired than you are tonight. Laurel, you were meant to lead the life of a fine lady."

"Gentlemen, lead your ladies in the opening waltz." Mac took Laurel into his arms and swept her through a series of turns that landed them in the center of the dance floor beneath the crystal chandelier. Everything there--the beautifully dressed women and handsome men, the room with cream satin walls and golden sconces, and music from an orchestra—swirled around Laurel as she danced with Mac. The scene appeared to arise from the pages of books she'd read. She smiled without knowing, pressed herself close to her husband, and giggled. Mac looked at her in surprise.

"None of this seems real."

"Laurel, it is real, and we are only getting started." The waltz ended, and the leader announced the Virginia Reel. He divided the couples, only about twelve or so into two groups, each lead by the head couple.

The familiar tune was lively, and the quick steps added to the excitement of the ball. The music hardly ended before the Broom Waltz started. The couples stepped back into a wide circle as the captain walked to the middle with a tall broom. He danced around the room a time or two with his broom partner before he stopped in front of Mac, offered him the broom, and took Laurel as his new partner. Mac nodded to her so she danced away with the captain. Mac danced with the broom a few steps and then chose another partner from the women around the room. This continued until the broom lay in the corner, and all the people were dancing with new partners. At the end, applause rang out through the room. The last two dances of the sette were the Patty Cake Polka and an Irish Quadrille, which ended with an intermission. Couples walked back to their tables or to the buffet, set up tiny cakes and puddings. The dancers were served lemon water, warm cider, or other libations. After the refreshment break, the second sette would begin.

"Laurel, would you like to stroll the promenade and see the river at night? It may be cool, but we won't stay out long."

"Yes, I'd like that." Mac placed a warm shawl around Laurel's bare shoulders. Together they walked out to the ornate deck, which surrounded the main level of the Eclipse. No one else had ventured out. The MacLaynes walked hand in hand to the stern of the boat. The constant slapping of the huge paddles in the fast-moving current of the Mississippi produced a rhythm in the frigid night. The night was clear, and the moon and stars, too many to count, lit the night sky. Standing near the white railings, they made out some features of the shoreline as they passed. Much of the terrain was still virgin land, places where no man had changed the Lord's creation. Even in the shadows, the promise of Arkansas fascinated them both.

"Mississippi is over there, and that state looks about the same as our state. There is so much room to grow. Laurel, the future of our state holds so much promise. There is more opportunity here than any place I've ever seen. I am so grateful I get to be a part of what Arkansas is becoming."

"Yes, Mr. Representative. You are fulfilling your dream, but sir... right now I'd like to find someplace warm. It's very cold out here."

"I thought you'd never ask." Mac drew Laurel into his arms, wrapped her in an embrace and kissed her cheek. "Wife, dearest, let's go to our little stateroom. I've shared you with other men long enough for one night." He'd hardly closed the cabin door when he pulled Laurel into his arms again. "Every day I love you more. I didn't know it was possible to crave a woman the way I desire you." His kisses were tender and lingering. "Laurel Grace, I pray you know how much a part of me you've become."

"I know what you mean to me. Can one person ever know what another one feels?"

"My dearest wife, that is the mystery of God's plan." Mac swooped Laurel into his arms and carried her to the large mahogany bed. He reached for his Bible and read from the second chapter of Genesis. "See, Laurel, God ordained they become one flesh."

"Becoming one flesh doesn't mean they instantly become of one mind, husband." Laurel didn't know where that argumentative reply came from.

Mac's mood changed immediately. He dropped his hands from her shoulders at what her rebuff of his attempt to pour out his admiration for her. That night Laurel's appearance and demeanor enchanted him. The weight of her arm lying on his as they danced, and the heat of her soft breathing on his neck were intoxicating. The vision of her dancing with other men and the enticing swish of her silver sateen gown painted images so vivid he could almost see them at that moment. Had she not felt the same passion arising in her? Did she yet doubt that he loved her? Had her behavior the entire night been an act...the politician's lady playing her role?

"Laurel, how is it possible you've no sense of how I desire you, hunger for you? I have no words to tell you. I can't believe how badly I failed you."

Laurel realized her coy reply to his declaration was so misplaced. She wanted to take back the words she teasingly said. She wanted him to see the growing pleasure she took from their shared dreams, hopes, and purposes. Their time together was forging a bond beyond their spoken vows. Everyday Mac and she became more like-minded with each adventure they shared. Yet her words hurt him...all too often. Was this the result of the news he'd shared with her at the ferry landing that morning?

"Mac, please forgive that witless comment. I'd be dull-witted not to see your devotion to me. Every inch of my being screams out how blessed I am that you love me. I still can't believe you chose me. You are my intended mate. I know that from the core of my being. How could I not know that the Lord planned for us to be together? I'm sorry I hurt you."

"You KNOW these things, wife, but you still don't feel them, do you? I've reached your mind but not your heart."

"Please Mac, let's not fight tonight. The night has been so wonderful, exciting, and so pleasurable. Let's keep the memory beautiful and not mar it with ugly words. Please forgive my thoughtless words."

Mac walked away from the bed where he had been sitting next to Laurel. He had little room to pace in the small room. He pulled his fingers through his hair, the gesture Laurel had seen often during their marriage—Mac's sign of extreme frustration.

"We're forever asking each other for forgiveness. The last part of that verse in Genesis says something like the two of them were naked, the man and the woman, but they felt no shame."

"Mac, I don't understand."

"I know you don't. That is why I am at a loss right now. Dearest Lord in Heaven, I want you to understand. I want you to feel what I feel. I want you to experience love the way I know it. I hoped you would find the security, the wholeness, the oneness that will bring you joy, Laurel. Is it because of Andrew?"

"Patrick, forgive me."

"Damnation, Laurel! Please stop apologizing as if you had done something wrong. How did this enchanting night turn out as it has?" Patrick took his coat from the chair. "I'll be back in a while. I've got to clear my head." Before he opened the door, he grabbed her and crushed her to him. He kissed her with a fury, so unlike the man she knew. The kiss was hard, brutal. Laurel felt the savage anger in his kiss. Mac left her shaken. "I won't be long."

As the door slammed behind him, Laurel sunk to the floor at the foot of the bed. She never felt so alone in her life, almost as if part of her was missing. Every ounce of strength left her. Outside on the deck, she heard the pilot call out, "Mark twain..." Later he called out again "No bottom...fair passage." She had no idea of how long she lay alone. When she heard "Three-quarter twain..." she realized a great deal of time had passed. She pulled herself to her feet and removed the silver ball gown. She pulled her winter nightdress over her head, turned down the bed covers and reached for her hairbrush. About the time she began to brush her hair, Mac returned. The look on his face told Laurel that he'd lost his frustration and tamed his anger.

"I'd like to do that if you'll let me." Mac reached for the brush.

"Please get ready for bed first. It's cool in here, and I'd enjoy it more in the warmth of the bed."

Shortly, Mac sat next to her, pulling the boar's hair brush through her long curls. They didn't speak. He laid the brush aside. Then he pulled Laurel down to his shoulder, embracing her as he often did in their tall four-poster.

"Laurel Grace, you enchanted me again tonight. I spent the eternity we were apart walking the promenade, looking at Fomalhaut, and feeling no connection with that old constellation at all. Then I prayed as I walked, and I couldn't sense God's presence either. He was showing me that I belonged here, next to you. Even in our separateness, we are more than we'd ever be apart. The time will come when we will have what we are seeking." He reached to the bureau and picked up his Bible again.

"Read me the marriage story from Genesis again, Patrick."

"Not tonight. I going to read you a love story–one I tried to share with you before, but we weren't ready then." Mac turned to the middle of the well-worn book and read from the seventh chapter of the *Song of Songs*. He read as if the words were his own, not Solomon's, and each word seemed a caress. At times, he would pause and reach out to touch Laurel, each action affirming the words he spoke. After he read, *"Your palate is like excellent wine...",* he stopped reading. He kissed Laurel with reverence. "Will you read these words to me, Laurel?"

*"Flowing smoothly for my love, gliding through her lips and teeth. I belong to my lover, and his longing is only for me."*

"Read that last verse again."

*"I belong to my lover, and his longing is only for me."*

"That, my dearest wife, is the true expression of oneness. It is truth, the truth I crave for you ...not to know it but to feel it in every fiber of your being."

No more words passed between Mac and Laurel that night. They lost themselves in the reality of that world where two people cease to exist and only their union remains.

# CHAPTER NINETEEN

*Who can find a virtuous woman? .... The heart of her husband doth safely trust in here, so that he shall no need of spoil. She will do him good and not evil all the days of her life.*
*Proverbs 31: 10-12*

The passage down to Napoleon was swift and for the most part uneventful. Only once did the captain noticeably slow the paddleboat. The lead man shouted out "mark twain" several times before they reached the notorious Arkansas landing.

"What's all the ruckus, Mac? Why is he shouting 'mark twain' so often this morning?"

"Water level is in question, dear. You remember hearing the lead man call out 'no bottom'. He's done it frequently on this trip. His main job is to gauge the river depth all along the way so the boat can pass safely. You'd never know this whole area flooded last winter. This fall has been pretty dry so the river is more shallow than usual in some places. Mark twain is a signal that the river is only about twelve feet deep. The captain is being cautious, I'd say."

"That's good news. How much further is Napoleon?"

"Still a distance. We should be there by noon tomorrow." Mac and

Laurel continued their walk around the promenade and returned to their cabin. Because of the cold, much of the trip down river was spent inside. The communities of Helena and Tunica, growing up along the Mississippi were passed, unseen. Mac made quick trips down to the lower level a few times to see to the care of Midnight and Sassy. They went together to dinner and for evening entertainment in the Grand Salon, but for the most part, the small ornate cabin was home for the two and a half days.

The luxury of idle time was new to Laurel. The life of a pioneer wife was seldom free of tasks that required her attention. Cooking, baking, sewing, gardening, canning, cleaning house and the barn, washing, tending the hearth, carrying firewood, fetching water, milking, feeding animals and attending to her husband all took part of a frontier woman's day. In addition, seasonal chores were necessary to maintain a homestead. Laurel's work load included hog butchering days, candling days, tending sick family and neighbors, teaching Sunday school and helping with the harvest as the need arose. For Laurel, to have so much time without a task to perform seemed almost wasteful. She did enjoy being able to read without interruption. The conversations with her husband had been a blessing. She enjoyed the afternoon naps, wrapped in Mac's arms in the mahogany bed, but she was very much out of her element and found herself looking for a worthwhile activity to occupy the time. She supposed that planter's wives with servants to tend to the daily chores would be more at home than she seemed to be.

On the third day out from Memphis, Laurel dressed in her wool suit. Mac told her the landing was a short drive from the dock where they would board another steamboat that would take them up the Arkansas River to Little Rock. Actually, the sun had warmed the day to a tolerable level so Mac and Laurel walked around the promenade after breakfast. The river was far from straight in this area. They'd heard the deck hand talking about the horseshoe curves and the hazards around Beulah Bend. They saw a strip of land jut out below the mouth of the Arkansas. Then upon rounding the bend, they saw Napoleon.

The MacLaynes looked out at the bustling port, not sure what to make of the contradiction they saw before them. Not far from the shore was a grand three-story brick and mortar building. Not a stone's throw away were several dilapidated structures that could be thrown up overnight to house the vagrant population. Some buildings looked as if someone had started them and decided to abandon them. Sound log buildings without doors and windows appeared to be abandoned. Yet from time to time, someone would come outside. A large, sturdy pier, capable of accommodating several boats, stood at the confluence of the rivers. Yet the warehouses along the dock showed none of the same care. Across the way, they saw several strong log buildings that might have been houses or stores. Across a dirt path stood ramshackle structures that may have sheltered animals. Oddly, one of the animal huts had loud tinny sounding music and raucous laughter coming from the open door. This place turned out to be a saloon.

Laurel shook her head. "This town is strange."

"I wouldn't have imagined it so, but I've heard Napoleon is the second largest town in the state. Only Little Rock is bigger and more prosperous."

The new state representative from Crittenden County who'd eaten breakfast with them intervened. "You're right, Mr. MacLayne. This town is booming with all this river trade."

"I'm not sure I'd call this a prosperous town."

"You wait four or five years, Mrs. MacLayne. People are saying in no time, Napoleon will rival St. Louis or New Orleans as the best port on the Mississippi." The Crittenden County representative continued to boast of the future metropolis in front of them.

Laurel and Mac took many of his comments with some doubt. Napoleon seemed like a dirty, rowdy settlement, not nearly as well-built and civilized as Greensboro. "What about the floods here? You can still see damage from the last flood. See that breeched levee and the debris that's scattered along the shore?" Mac pointed out damage scattered along the shoreline as far as they could see.

"No doubt, the place needs work, but that is one of the things the legislature can help with. The federal government must have high hopes for this place. Look up there at that fine Marine hospital they built a couple of years ago."

"We'll see. I guess time will tell the fate of this town. It'd be good for the state to have a fine port city."

Within the hour, they disembarked and met the groom who unloaded their buggy and horses. Mac stowed their bags. They drove through the streets, looking at the odd assortment of structures that made up the town of Napoleon. People, many of them black, crowded the streets. Laurel had seen slaves before, of course. A few farmers in Washington County had two or three slaves who worked their orchards and fields. Even a farmer or two in Greene County kept a slave or two, but Napoleon's population had to be as much as one-third black. That number surprised Laurel.

"Mac, did you know there were so many slaves in the southern part of the state?"

"Laurel, this is the delta. The Mississippi floods have made this the richest soil on earth. The planters who live here hold huge blocks of land where they grow cotton. Cotton demands hours of labor. That's why you see the slaves in large numbers here. Not all the black people are slaves, though. Many of them are freedmen, usually a craftsman or a small business owner."

As they drove through Napoleon, the MacLaynes fanned and swatted at the hordes of insects. Napoleon seemed to be home to more buffalo gnats and flies than people. The incessant swarms made the drive unbearable. "Let's drive on over to the boarding area on the Arkansas. I've seen as much of Napoleon as I care to see, wife. I'm glad we aren't staying overnight here. Our packet to the capital is leaving by mid-afternoon. Let's go see if we can get settled in and get out of these blame bugs. I'm thinking it will turn cold again by sundown anyway."

They made the short drive to the Arkansas River. The boat they found waiting was much smaller and lacked much of the elegance of the Eclipse. The Rock City was only 127 feet by 28 feet, less than half the size of the other ship. This boat was almost flat bottomed. The boats on the Arkansas were shallow draft vessels. The boat's freight area was already loaded to capacity with barely room to store their buggy.

This small boat had only ten cabins. Some of the rooms were as small as six by six feet, hardly staterooms. The tiny room they had was somewhat larger, but not much. However, the room was clean and warm so it would serve for the short trip up river. The smaller boat would not match the speed of the paddle wheeler. The boat seemed to crawl several times the first day because of the low water levels on the Arkansas. Regardless, the trip of two and a half or three days would be more comfortable than an overland trip.

Mac was restless and impatient with the inactivity. The Rock City had little in the way of entertainment, so they spent most of the trip in their little cabin. A group of men sat huddled around a table in the dining room, playing cards. Gambling was a common pastime on the riverboats, but games of chance held no attraction for Mac. Conversations with the other representatives proved disagreeable at times because they held large differences in their views on the political scene. So, he didn't enjoy their talks. Once or twice, the discussions bordered on conflict. Laurel watched Mac rise from a chair and walk three steps across the room. Shortly, he'd return to his chair only to repeat the pointless behavior within a few minutes.

"Mac, you're acting like a caged animal. Don't you have something to read or a letter to write? You're driving me to distraction."

"I hate the confinement."

"Travel is more than half over. Next week you'll be so busy at work in the legislature, you'll wish for some of this quiet time."

"I suppose you're right. Things may be very hectic at the capital. Now might be a good time to talk about home."

Laurel had dreaded the conversation she knew was coming. Mac hadn't brought up the subject of Andrew since their wait for the ferry at Hopefield. She knew her husband was doing the right thing by bringing his son into their family. Laurel wanted to embrace Andrew as the son Mac wanted. She told herself she was happy for Mac and his son. Yet each thought of the shy six-year-old made Laurel feel her tremendous failure. She wondered if she'd be able to accept the lad as her son and not feel her inadequacy as Mac's wife. Even before their marriage, Laurel knew Mac's expectations of her. He'd told her he wanted a companion, a friend, and a mother for his children. Now he didn't need her to bear his son.

"We left everything at home in pretty fair shape. I do hope we can get home before Christmas, though."

"Laurel, that's not what I want to talk about." Outside the cabin on deck, the leadsman called out 'quarter twain', indicating safe passage for a while.

"I'll be happy to hear whatever you have to say to me, my dear." The coquettish lilt of her voice told Mac she didn't want to talk about anything serious.

"If I didn't know you so well, I'd say, fine…let's get to it. Instead, I'm going to check on our horses." Mac pulled on his coat and left the cabin. Laurel almost immediately felt his disappointment. She scolded herself, knowing her self-doubt had once again hurt her husband. She returned to her sewing, a new dress she was making as a Christmas present for Cathy. As soon as Mac returned, she would raise the topic he'd wanted to share, and they'd talk about Andrew.

But Mac didn't return until past midnight. Laurel went to bed long before he came back. She wasn't asleep, but she didn't speak, waiting to see Mac's mood. He disrobed and slipped into his side of the bed without a word, making every effort not to awaken his wife.

The next day, Mac arose and spoke to Laurel as if the previous day had not happened. "Good morning, Laurel. Are you ready to go down for a bite of breakfast? I could use a cup of hot coffee."

"Yes, I'll be ready in a few minutes."

"I know you won't want coffee, but I had some last night while I was talking to a couple of other men headed to the legislature. Coffee was really good. We talked for several hours. One of the fellows is the senator from Poinsett County. He's a friend of the representative, and they had a lot to tell. His name is Jones."

"Sounds like you had a pleasant evening."

"Sorry, I didn't get back sooner. I didn't want to wake you so late." In the small dining room, Mac introduced Laurel to the men he met the night before. They sat down to a modest, hot breakfast of ham, oatmeal, and coffee. Laurel asked for a glass of milk, but the steward said they'd not have milk until the next stop in Pine Bluff.

The two other men at their table were traveling alone. Mr. Jones said his wife didn't care to travel in the winter, and she had remained in Helena, caring for her children. Mr. Sanders was a bachelor. The three men picked up their conversation from the previous evening. Laurel sat and listened. Occasionally, one of them would direct a question or comment to her. She would respond as she thought a representative's wife should. She would do anything in her power not to disappoint Mac again. Laurel curbed her fears and self-doubt, determined nothing would cost her the life she'd come to love at Shiloh. She would reopen the conversation with Mac at the first opportunity.

Much to her dismay, the opportunity never arose while they traveled up the Arkansas on the Rock City. They talked with the new friends when they were in public areas. When they were alone, Mac talked about his growing excitement about the work that face him. They bemoaned the difficult travel conditions on the Arkansas. They complained about the cold. They never had time to talk of home. The only time Laurel brought up their family, a knock interrupted before she could even mention Andrew.

"Pier ahead–Little Rock to the port side. We'll prepare to disembark in half an hour." The announcement brought most of the passengers to the port side of the boat to see a true city in their state. Little Rock was home to more than 3,000 people. While many log structures remained, newer buildings were wooden clapboard. Brick covered a few stately structures. From the bank of the river, one would never guess the elegant building on the bluff that served as the State house was brick covered stucco. Even the tall, elegant pillars on the front façade would fool most people into thinking they were marble. Little Rock did indeed seem to be a city. Laurel had never seen another to compare.

As the Rock City neared the dock, Laurel saw a line of covered carriages attended by formally attired drivers. "Mac, is someone important arriving with us? I've never seen such a parade."

"Of course, the state representatives and senators arrive in the capital this week. I'm sure they are meeting every boat. Important people are coming to town. We are some of them." One of the porters met them as they stepped ashore.

"Sir, are you one of the representatives a-comin' to the State house?"

"Yes, I am. How did you know?"

"You all dress more serious than those gambler fellows, I guess. Do you need a hack to the Anthony House?"

"What is the Anthony House?"

"Only the best hotel in the whole South. All our gov'ment folks stay at the Anthony House."

"Well, I guess it is good enough for us then, Laurel. No, we don't need a ride. We have our own buggy. Can you tell me the way?"

"Sir, follow me, and when we get there, I'll tend your horses. We got us a fine brick stable for our guests' animals."

Thus, they found themselves amid Mac's peers at the Anthony House. Laurel felt somewhat out of place, though, for she saw only one other representative with a woman by his side. The Anthony House was indeed an elegant, luxurious place. The building had at one time been a large private home recently converted to a public house. The Overland Stage Line had designated this hotel as an overnight stop. Mac learned the building housed twenty-two private guest rooms and a sleeping loft. He also learned the cost for a night's stay was dear, $1.50 a night.

Mac paid for the room on the second floor for one night only. He also paid the groom to board the horse and store their buggy. Porters carried all the luggage upstairs, following the MacLaynes to their spacious room. The hotel room was the size of three cabins on the Eclipse and every bit as posh. The furniture was dark mahogany, and the finest horsehair fabric covered the chairs and sofa. Gilt mirrors adorned the walls. Crystal prisms hung from porcelain lamps placed around the room. The heavy blue brocade curtains and bed covers gave the room an opulence which awed both Mac and Laurel.

"Sir, dinner is served at 7:00, and music will be offered in the ballroom. Governor Conway and his niece have arranged this welcome for our new legislators. Will you be attending tonight?"

"Yes. We'll dine at 7:00. Can you tell me...is this a formal event?"

"Indeed, it is, sir."

When they were alone, Laurel moaned. "I told you I wasn't prepared to come to the city. I have one ball gown, too dressy for this affair, and a couple of schoolmarm dresses that aren't fine enough."

"Laurel, come over here and kiss the representative from Greene County. He's the only one you have to impress here, and you won his heart months and months ago."

Laurel dressed in her gray sateen ball dress once again, and Mac wore his Sunday best...the very suit he'd worn at their wedding. Together they went down to the dining room of the Anthony House. The room was every bit in keeping with the nature of this hotel. Snow white table linen, porcelain dishes, and stemmed crystal glasses graced each place. Laurel knew the flatware was silver, even though she'd never seen it before this trip. The gleam from the knives, forks, and spoons appeared exactly as described in novels she'd read.

A waiter led them to a table among several other well-dressed men and two other couples. Within minutes, the hostess joined their assembly. She introduced herself as the governor's cousin, Mrs. Prescott Montgomery. She asked the group to pardon her family. Neither the governor nor his niece would attend the reception. They had been called away on family business. The meal was served by a large staff of waiters all dressed alike. The meat was somewhat familiar, but not quite the chicken they sometimes ate at home. A senator's wife, seated next to Laurel, whispered Governor Conway had ordered pheasant for his guests. She seemed quite impressed by the menu. Laurel thought the bird had a somewhat gamey taste, much like the ducks Mac often shot in the winter. Unfortunately, that was one kind of game that Laurel didn't care for. She ate a few bites so as not to embarrass the hostess.

About 9:00, the small orchestra began to play. Mac led Laurel to the dance floor and began to waltz. The other two couple joined them, and the representative from Crittenden County asked Mrs. Montgomery to dance. With such a disparity between the number of men and women in attendance, Laurel and the other ladies had a new partner at each change of the music. In the beginning, Mac was concerned about how Laurel would react, having to dance with so many strangers. Within a few minutes, though, he relaxed as he watched her play the role of a legislator's wife. She smiled, talked, and danced as long as the music played. Mac watched with such pride. Laurel once again had held her own with the people he'd come to work. He knew she'd made a good impression on all she'd met that night. Before midnight, Mac reclaimed Laurel for the last waltz of the evening.

"My dear Mrs. MacLayne, I didn't know I'd brought the belle of the ball with me tonight. I haven't had a partner for more than three hours."

"Oh, Mac. Don't be so silly. With only four women to dance with, even the plainest of wallflowers would have danced the night away. Not that I would be that wallflower, mind you."

"Indeed not. You look every bit the part of the grand lady you are. How surprised these ladies would be to know your gown was not the latest fashion from Paris or London. Yard goods from Jasper and a local dressmaker from Greensboro turned you into a princess." They laughed together.

The next morning was Sunday. They had only a few days before Mac would begin his work as a representative. The MacLaynes started out early so they could begin to explore the capital city. After a small breakfast, they walked around the city's center. The weather was nice...a mild southern wind brought the temperature to the mid-forties. After walking only a few blocks, they found the Methodist Episcopal Church. At 8:30 in the morning, no one was there yet. They decided they would return to worship in the pretty brick chapel later that morning.

"Are you enjoying your honeymoon, Laurel?"

"I've enjoyed being with you. The new experiences have been interesting, but having to dance with all those different men last night was a bit overwhelming. I hardly knew what to say to most of them."

"You played your part very well, wife. I am surprised there are so few wives here with their husbands, though."

"I'm not. You know how hard the travel is, and this time of year the weather is so unpredictable. Besides, people have to keep their homesteads going."

"Laurel, most of these people are planters or professional men. They have overseers and slaves to take care of their property. There are a few yeomen here and a few craftsmen. Most of the elected officials are involved in the Family."

"Oh, I guess I didn't think about that." They walked for a few more blocks. Some of the streets were cobblestones, but most were dirt and rock. In their brief walk, they saw that some effort had been made to lay out streets in a grid. Many streets were straight and connected at ninety-degree angles at the corners. The houses they encountered fit almost every description imaginable. Some streets had many houses with small yards, while others sat in the midst of large green expanses. Some of the houses were clapboard, a few were brick, and they even saw log cabins that appeared to be quite old. One street near the church held only three large, almost palatial houses encircled with wrought iron fences. Laurel knew these houses belonged to wealthy men. She'd seen no others to compare with them, except the huge plantation houses they'd passed along the river. These houses didn't seem warm, welcoming places. The largest, a three-story red brick structure looked like a fortress. There were even two turrets at the ends of the front porch. Perhaps that residence was supposed to look like a castle.

"That is an interesting building."

"Yes, I'd say interesting, but not very inviting. Let's walk back toward the river and look at the State house. From what we saw at the docks, that building is quite a sight."

"Mac, if we go much farther, we will be late for church."

"We'll turn back when we get to the Capitol." A block from the State house, Laurel spotted a placard on a gate in front of a large clapboard house. The sign said, "Rooms to Let."

"Look, Mac. Let's check to see if we can get a room in this boarding house."

"Laurel, don't you like the Anthony House?"

"No, and neither do you. That place is so formal, I don't think I'll ever feel comfortable there. Besides, the expense is outrageous. Do you realize in one week's time, we'd spend the price of a steer to rent a place to sleep?"

"My practical, thrifty mate! Are you sure you want to board here?"

"The place is clean and well-kept on the outside. See how close it is to the capitol. You could walk in a few minutes. At least, we could talk to the owners and see if we'd like to stay here."

"Yes, ma'am. Let's talk." Mac and Laurel didn't know they'd come upon a boarding house that rented rooms to legislators every session.

The large house had eight rooms to let. Because of its location, men who came to serve in the state legislature rented more than half the rooms.

When Mac knocked on the door, the owner opened it. "Good morning, sir. What can I do for y'all on this cold morning?"

"My wife saw your sign on the fence. We are looking for a place to stay during the legislative session."

"Welcome to y'all. Name's J.W. Scott. My missus and I run this lodging, and we often host members of the legislature. Can I show ya one of our rooms?"

"Yes, Laurel and I will be here until Christmas at least, and perhaps until the end of the session. Weather will probably determine how long we'll stay." Mr. Scott directed them to a large sunny room on the second floor. The room, being a corner room, had two large windows, one facing the river and the other facing a forested plot of land. The room was filled with light, and there was a fireplace. The accommodations were modest but clean and well-tended. The room held a walnut bed and dresser, two chairs and two small side tables with two glass lanterns. The bed was spread with a hand tacked quilt made up of nine square blocks of many kinds of fabric.

"This looks much more like home to me."

"Yes, Laurel. We'd be much more at home here. Mr. Scott, what is your fee?"

"We ask five dollars a week and that includes three meals a day and the use of the stables. I guess you have an animal or two with you."

"That's a fair price. If you'll agree, my wife and I would like to move after church this morning."

"You're more'n welcome here."

Mac paid Mr. Scott the lodging fee, and he and Laurel walked back to the Methodist Church. As they approached the building, Mac recognized a couple of the men he'd meet the previous night.

"Morning, MacLayne. Didn't know you were of the Methodist persuasion, or I'd have invited you to join us this morning."

"Thank you, Mr. Quillman. I'd like you to meet my wife, Laurel."

"I had the pleasure of a dance with this lovely lady last evening. Good morning, Mrs. MacLayne."

"Yes, thank you. I enjoyed the dance last night."

"We'd like to have you join us in our pew this morning. My wife, Rosalind, and our son, Harmon, are already seated. I'll show you the way." Harmon Quillman, Sr. ushered the MacLaynes to the pew and made the introductions. He then returned to the front door.

"My father wants to speak to the governor before church starts. He's always so keyed up before the new legislative session starts." Harmon Jr. rolled his eyes "Politics is a dull way to spend a life, don't ya think?"

"I take it you want a different kind of life, young man. What are you planning to do?" Laurel's curiosity had led her to enter into a conversation with the sixteen-year-old boy.

"I'm going into the army. I'm headed off to West Point next spring. My older brother, Howard, is there now."

"That's one way to get a good education. Does your mother approve of your chosen vocation?"

"My grandfather was a military leader during the war with the Indians. Mother's worried, but she knows I want to carry on the family tradition. Besides, there is no war now. I'm no more likely to get wounded than if I was a legislator. You know there was a duel in the State house a couple years back."

"No, I didn't know."

The Sunday morning service was familiar, but it wasn't. The hymns were the same, the pastor read Scripture and followed the Wesley tradition of singing the Gloria Patria and reciting the Lord's Prayer. The spirit of the service seemed more subdued and more formal than any Mac and Laurel were used to. The small brick chapel was furnished with finely carved pews and chairs on the dais. One of those pews remained empty. The empty seat seemed strange as the small church was filled to capacity, and some men stood in the back of the sanctuary.

"Mrs. Quillman, why is the pew there unoccupied when there are a few people standing in the back?"

"Why, Mrs. MacLayne, that's the governor's place. The family pew always remains ready for them. The governor's mother was one of the founding members of our congregation. That chair there is her place. She doesn't come as often as she did--her health and age, you know."

Laurel didn't know. She had no idea the governor was a Methodist or that this pretty brick church was home to such prominent members. At the close of the service, Senator Quillman pulled Mac aside to tell him about the opening session the next morning. He reminded Mac to bring the certificate of election from the justice of the peace in Greene County.

"You know, MacLayne, we weren't expecting an unfamiliar face in our midst this year. You must have run a whale of a campaign."

"I had a lot of help from friends and family. My wife has been a great help in meeting and talking to our folks back home. Do you know Mr. Digby?"

"We have a passing acquaintance. He's been a supporter of the Conways for some time."

"As far as we know, he's returned to Little Rock."

A frown crossed the senator's face. "Oh, I haven't heard." Quillman turned to escort his wife from the church. Mac and Laurel walked back to the Anthony House to claim their belongings. By 2:30, they had made the move to their pleasant second-story room at the Scott's. Midnight and Sassy Lady found a new home in the stable behind the house.

"Well, darlin'. I hope you are up for a new adventure. I've never pictured you as a lady of leisure. What will you do to keep yourself busy?"

"I have a few things in mind. I'll finish the children's Christmas gifts, take long naps, go to Mr. Woodruff's circulating library, and read every book I want to read. I hope I can come to the State house once in a while to watch the legislature go about the business of making laws."

"I'm sure there will be social events we can attend. Little Rock has a theater, and I'm told they conduct interesting discussions and debates at the lyceum. We'll need to look into that."

"I'm happy we've moved from the Anthony House. This place seems so much more like home. I suppose I can deal with anything for seven weeks if you are here to keep me company in the evenings."

"Would you be very disappointed if we can't go home until the end of the session?"

"Yes, Mac. I want to be back in our home for Christmas. It'll be our first family Christmas with your father."

"And my son?" Laurel looked up into Mac's eyes. She saw his uneasiness at the direction of the conversation about Andrew.

"Patrick, I want to apologize for making light of this discussion when we were on the Eclipse. I acted very childishly. My sarcastic reply to you was wrong. Please forgive me."

"I understand Laurel. I know I'm not asking a small thing of you. The task of raising another woman's child when you've already taken on two others will not be an easy one. I should have been more tactful when I told you."

"Mac, Andrew is your son, regardless of the circumstances. You told me you know he belongs to you. You couldn't deny him; it's not who you are. I could not respect that decision if you made it, even to spare me. Andrew can't grow up an orphan when he has a father."

"Laurel, my pa has offered to adopt Andrew if you don't feel he belongs in our house."

"That's good of him to offer. What do you want?"

"Can I do less than accept responsibility for my past actions? I must try to provide a good life for him. But, darlin', I want nothing more than I want you to be happy."

"You know people will talk when you acknowledge the boy as your son."

"Yes, but the only opinion I care about is yours. God promised to walk with us through our trials. Nowhere in the Bible does He promise to erase the consequences of our own making. Andrew is here because I ignored God's guidance in my past."

"I've thought about this every day since I have known about Andrew. There is no decision to make. I love you, Patrick. I will love your son. We will raise him as our child. He deserves a family. You've wanted a son as long as I've known you. Don't fret about my feelings. I'm learning to be a big girl."

"Laurel, you're thinking about Campbell, aren't you?"

"Of course, I am. He's in my thoughts every day. I am trying to live beyond my grief and failure to give you a healthy baby. I will be the best mother to Andrew that I can be. That's the only promise I can make."

"God bless you, wife. You add to my joy daily." Mac embraced Laurel. "I want to be home for Christmas, too."

# CHAPTER TWENTY

*Behold, how good and how pleasant it is for brethren to dwell together in unity.*
*Psalms 133:1*

November 2, 1858, proved to be another mild, beautiful autumn day. Mac had never felt prouder or more excited than he did walking Laurel the short distance to the beautiful Greek Revival mansion, built to house the two legislative bodies. When they reached the porch, he stopped and looked at the impressive façade for some time. "You know, Laurel, I still can't believe I am here. Maybe you should pinch me to see if I'm dreaming."

"You worked very hard to be here, Mac. Scores of people have put their trust in you, hoping an honest man can make their lives better and this state a better, more prosperous place to live. Always remember what you promised them. You'll be a fine statesman if you do. I much prefer the idea of being wife to a statesman than to a politician."

"Let's go see if they'll let me in."

When they entered, they were met by a clerk at the door who directed them to the visitors' gallery up a grand staircase. Mac left Laurel seated there, and he returned to the main floor and approached the desk at the front of the house chamber. As he walked into the room where the work of the Arkansas House of Representatives would be conducted, he realized he'd never even thought about the reality of the day to day routine that would take place. His conversations about the role of a state representative had always dealt with the what and why, but never the how or where or when of governance. The house chamber was a real place. Mac took several minutes to take stock of that new reality. He looked up to the gallery where he had left Laurel. The area was supported by several small cream-colored columns, miniatures of the four huge columns that supported the portico outside. He couldn't see Laurel seated above. The chamber room was large and open. Light filled the room from the floor to ceiling windows flanking two sides of the room. Mac also noted that each desk had its own lantern or candle, a sign that work did not always end early for the Arkansas legislature. The room was filled with ten rows of identical desks, dark brown wooden slant tops each with a very straight ladder-back chair made with a solid wood bottom. Comfort had not been the key concern of the furniture maker. At the front of the very large room, Mac saw groups of men standing near the two marble-looking mantles. Both fireplaces had been stoked and lit. Although both fireplaces had been filled, the fully engaged fires did not adequately heat the huge chamber. The tall ceilings and many large windows would make that task difficult. Mac wondered what it would be like in this room in January. Efforts had been made to give the room a sense of order and dignity. Two very large chandeliers made of brass and crystal hung above. All the candles in each had been lit, although the light source was certainly not necessary that morning. Mac walked toward the front of the room where he saw a clerk seated at a rectangular table that faced the other individual desks in the chamber. He recognized that the marble around the fireplaces wasn't real, but painted wood made to resemble quarried stone. He grinned as he thought of the ingenuity that had added that touch of pretention. Were other things in this place not what they'd appeared to be?

"Can I be of service to you, sir?" The clerk seated behind the table had waited for some time for Mac to speak to him.

"Oh, excuse me. My name is Patrick MacLayne from Greene County."

"I assume you are one of our new delegates. Do you have credentials?"

"I do. Is it all right for my wife to be here this morning?" The clerk looked over the letter Mac presented to him for a few seconds.

"Seems in order. Yes, visitors are welcome in the gallery until the swearing in if she's a mind to stay. Visitors have a right to watch anytime in the open gallery, but I'm afraid she will find most of the day's agenda deadly boring." The well-clad, bearded man knew his role well. He explained to Mac the order of business for the day. He said all the representatives would be sworn in to serve as each of them were either newly elected or re-elected to sit at the twelfth legislative session. He told Mac what was expected of him, and then led him to the desk that had been assigned to the Greene County representative. "Just follow the others. There are few of you newcomers, so things will go well if you just do what you see the rest of the men do. Most things are pretty routine around here."

Mac thought to himself that was probably the cause of the slow progress of the state. The leaders were used to just doing what they saw others doing around them. They towed the party line to keep the peace. Perhaps he would not take that advice when it came to things that mattered. He thanked the clerk and returned to Laurel until the session was called to order. He led her to the front of the gallery and pointed out his place to her.

"This place reminds me of a classroom. Only your tables and chairs are a bit nicer than our wood pews and table at Shiloh, but at least, your seats are all lined up in straight rows. Makes it easier to keep order, I guess." Laurel said.

"The clerk said anyone can stay, but you'll probably get bored by the rest of the day's work. Seems like the first day is pretty much a formality of getting ready to do the work. I'll walk you back to the Scott's at lunch."

"I am more than capable of retracing those two short blocks when I'm tired of being a spectator."

"I'm very aware of that."

The clerk rapped the gavel on the table, and Laurel returned to her chair among several other visitors, mostly men. The elected officials rose by their desks, and the minister from the Methodist church they'd attended the day before opened the first session with a brief prayer asking a blessing on the work of the men before him. The clerk returned, directing the men to raise their right hands and to swear to the oath of office they'd been elected to.

Laurel didn't take her eyes from Mac. She knew how pleased he was to be taking that oath. She saw the pride in his face. He was living out an important part of his life plan. He would be an excellent servant to the people in Greene County and to the citizens of their growing state. Today was a very special day. After about an hour of listening to the housekeeping activities, Laurel slipped out the back door of the gallery. In the lobby, she asked a clerk at the door if he knew the way to the circulating library owned by Mr. Woodruff, the editor of Little Rock's most respected newspaper. She found it was in the same building that housed the Gazette, not far from the Methodist church. The walk would be a short one, just down on Cherry Street.

As she entered the impressive two-story brick building, she was met by a white-haired bearded man who looked to be near seventy years old. His long beard and silver hair were well-groomed, but his white shirt showed ink spots, telling her that he was a working printer.

"Morning, ma'am. How can I help you today?"

"I'm new to Little Rock, and I was hoping to find the circulating library."

"You're in the right place. I've got more'n 300 books back in the salon there. Got anything in mind?"

"I'd enjoy anything. My husband is here to serve in the legislature, and I'm afraid I have a lot of time to fill. I couldn't bring the homestead with me, I'm afraid."

"Where might that homestead be?"

"We're from Greene County. Do you know the northeast part of the state?"

"Traveled there some, but getting around up in that neck of the woods is no easy task."

"That's true. We came by steamboat, though, and that trip took more than a week. However, it was so much more comfortable than the wagon trip from Washington County to Greene County that we made last year."

"Missy, you have been a travelin'! I'm William Woodruff. I publish the Gazette. Have you read my paper?"

"Indeed. We get a few copies up our way once in a while. We always enjoy reading about the happenings in Arkansas, even though the events are often ancient history by the time we read about them."

"I'd like to hear about your travels across the state. Maybe you'll tell me more about them the next time you come."

"How much is the lending fee, Mr. Woodruff?"

"I usually ask for a deposit from newcomers, but since you are here with one of our legislators, I'll trust you. By the way, how will I register your subscription?"

"Laurel MacLayne, Mrs. Patrick MacLayne of Shiloh, Greene County, Arkansas. We are lodging with the Scotts over near the state house."

"I'm very pleased to meet you, Mrs. MacLayne." Laurel paid the sum of three dollars for the three months subscription fee. She spent several minutes browsing through Mr. Woodruff's impressive collection of books and settled on a new novel by a man named Hawthorne. "Please return it within fourteen days, and they'll be no other charge. I look forward to hearing about the trek across the state by wagon."

When Laurel returned to the Scott house, dinner had been called. She'd thought Mac would come back to eat, but she decided to eat with the Scott family and two other boarders when she saw he'd not returned. After lunch, she went to their room, mainly because she didn't know what else to do. She decided to take a few minutes to finish their unpacking and see if she could find some way to make the plain room a bit more like home. She didn't have much success, though, for they had brought little except necessary clothing and a few grooming items, like her hairbrush, Mac's razor and scissors, and his well-worn Bible. Laurel did place the brush and Mac's grooming things on the bureau next to the large water pitcher and bowl Mrs. Scott had brought them the day before. Mac had already placed the Bible on one of the side tables near the fireplace. That was all she could do.

She decided to read a while. Mr. Woodruff said that Hawthorn's book, *The Scarlet Letter,* had been well received when it was published in 1852. He'd told her the story told of a scandal in a Puritan village in Massachusetts. Laurel added a log to the fire and sat in the armchair nearest the heat. She began to read the chapter called, "The Custom House", but her mind drifted back to Mac. She wondered if he had eaten and if he was warm enough and what he was doing that moment. After a while, she laid the book aside because she realized she'd read the fourth page three times over and could recall very little of what she had read. Perhaps a nap would help.

About 4:30, Mac unlocked the door to their room. He smiled when he saw Laurel napping under the brightly colored quilt. He was hoping she'd learn to rest some away from her chores and obligations at Shiloh. He also noticed the fire had burned very low, and the room had taken on a chill. He tended the fire, and then he went to lie beside Laurel. When he pulled the blanket over his shoulder, she woke.

"Mac, dear. I'm glad you're back. I tried to read, but Hester Prynne just couldn't take your place."

"Who is that?"

"Never mind. I just kept thinking about you. Did you have a busy day at the legislature?"

"Busy, yes...but did we accomplish anything? Not much, I'm afraid. I think you saw the best part of it. You were still there when we elected Representative Otis to be the speaker. We also elected a recording secretary, whose name I don't recall. We were assigned to committees. I am going to sit as a member of the appropriations committee. The group is assigned bills that determine how the state uses taxpayers' money."

"That sounds like an important job. You may be able to help with our road needs and maybe get some funds for schools."

"I hope... but we spent nearly three hours discussing whether or not we should hire a chaplain for the House chamber. What a waste of time and money! I rose to speak out. I said any of our professing members could offer a benediction. I wasn't alone in my position. The resolution was defeated with a 22 to 35 vote."

"You were on the right side of that discussion. Good for you, speaking your mind. Your supporters at home would be pleased you are doing what they sent you here to do."

"Well, I'm glad we adjourned early. There were so many times today I couldn't keep my mind on the tasks in front of me. I found myself wondering about you... what you were doing. I'm afraid the clerk was right. Much of the housekeeping process is boring and seems quite useless. If the subject had been more interesting, maybe I could have paid more attention, but you are quite a distraction. And when I got home, what did I see? You were snuggled up here in our bed."

"Oh, Mac! Let me tell you what I did this morning. I walked to Mr. Woodruff's circulating library. He's a very interesting man. You know he's the editor of the Gazette. Anyway, I paid for a subscription and borrowed a book to read."

"That's fine...perhaps we can read it together. But not right now. I have something much more appealing to do right this minute." He pulled her into his arms and kissed her again and again.

The next day, time seemed to creep for Laurel. As it was quite cold outside, she didn't walk out to see more of the neighborhood. She worked on Cathy's new dress for a long while. Before lunch, she had finished the hem. She went down to the mid-day meal when Mac had not returned before noon. Just as she was about to sit down, he opened the door and joined her at the table. The house had recessed an hour and a half. Having Mac at the table made Laurel more open to talking than she had the day before. Mac's friendly disposition made it so easy to start conversations. Before he returned to the chambers at 1:15, they learned that two of the other boarders were Irish miners and two other rooms were rented by Arkansas congressmen, one of whom was a Senator from Carroll County. They talked of travel to the capital, and Laurel told them about their passage on the Eclipse and Rock City. Just as he left the room, Mac told Laurel that on Friday afternoon a reception for the wives of the legislators would be held in the representatives' chamber of the State house. Each wife would be presented, and a tea would follow in the Grand Salon when the leader of the Senate called their sessions back to order. With his announcement, he left her.

Laurel spent the next two days dreading the social affair ahead of her. She knew she would be called on to accompany Mac once in a while, but she would have been more than happy to miss these events. On Friday about 1:00, Mac arrived to walk with her back to the State house. They had a long talk the previous night about Laurel's meager wardrobe. As much as he had reassured her she would be appropriately attired, she doubted him. That afternoon, though, he beamed with pleasure when he saw how nice she looked. Her dress was her Sunday dress, a nice dark brown wool, long sleeved with a lace collar and tiny buttons down the bodice. She'd arranged her hair in an elegant chignon with small tendrils curling at her cheeks. She'd pinned her gold Gordian knot brooch just below her collar. She looked every bit the lady he'd known she would.

"Mac, I'm not dressed well enough to attend a formal reception or a lady's tea."

"You're stylish enough to go anywhere or meet anyone, including the governor."

Mac had not told her that Governor Conway would preside at the reception, and he knew she would be surprised. Regardless, he was proud to have Laurel on his arm. The event proved to be very formal and stately. A receiving line met them at the door to the house chamber, the larger of the two rooms. When they reached the governor, Mac shook hands and spoke, "Governor Conway, my name is Patrick MacLayne from Greene County. I'd like to present my wife, Laurel."

"I'm pleased to meet you, MacLayne. Always good to have new blood in the governing halls. It's a pleasure to meet you, Mrs. MacLayne."

"Thank you, Sir."

"MacLayne, I read in the minutes from the opening session that you opposed having a chaplain. Are you a non-believer, sir?"

"No, sir. I am a strong supporter of the Lord's church, regardless of the denomination."

"Why the opposition then?"

"If all the remarks had been recorded, you would see I'm opposed to hiring a minister to do what any believer can do. Back home at Shiloh Methodist Church, our preacher often asks members of our congregation to pray."

"Is your church of the Episcopal South body?"

"Officially, it's part of our name, but we conduct service very much as it was done before the church separated in '42."

"Hope you'll visit us at Cherry Street soon. Hello, Senator Quillman. Nice to see you." The governor ended the conversation with Mac by turning to greet the Senator they'd sat with at church the previous Sunday. The reception lasted until about 3:00, and Mac and Laurel spent that time talking to the men who sat near him in the chamber. Two of them were accompanied by their wives. When the leader of the Senate called the legislative session back into session, the ladies retired to the Grand Salon for tea. Their hostess was the niece of the governor, who had not been able to attend the dinner on the day they'd arrived.

"I apologize for missing our welcome dinner on Saturday evening. My aunt, Governor Conway's mother, has not been well. I hope we get acquainted this afternoon." After they were served with tiny porcelain cups of tea and small finger cakes, which had been iced with white frosting and decorated with miniature leaves in gold and green, the lady sitting next to her remarked, "Aren't these Petit Fours just beautiful?" Laurel thanked the Lord she'd always been such an avid reader. How else would she have known she spoke of the tiny cakes? These were the first Petit Fours Laurel had ever seen.

In a short time, the women in the room began to introduce themselves to the group and eventually drifted into small groups of four or five. Laurel found herself sitting with two planters' wives, a bank president's wife from Pulaski County, and a newly married eighteen-year-old from Hot Springs.

When she was asked to speak, she said, "My name is Laurel Campbell MacLayne. Patrick is the representative from Greene County. We are on our wedding trip, also, although we've waited for a year and a half to make the journey."

"Goodness me...what has kept you so long? When we married in '48, my husband and I spent our first month as man and wife in Washington City. It's a fascinating place to visit."

"We just had a lot to do. We've built our cabin, I taught two sessions of subscription school, Patrick had to return to Maryland when his mother died, and we were busy campaigning a good deal of the time."

"You are a teacher?"

"Yes, I am."

"How do you find time to work outside your home?"

"It has been difficult at times, but we've managed. It's rewarding to teach children. Most are so eager to learn. When I came to Shiloh from Washington County, I'd already promised to teach at the Shiloh school."

"You met Mr. MacLayne when you came to teach then?" Laurel realized she had said more than she meant to. She didn't plan to get "that acquainted" at the first meeting with these ladies, especially when she understood they had very little in common. She didn't see herself becoming fast friends with them. Thankfully, before she had to answer, Mrs. Johnston stood and thanked the ladies for attending her tea. She also invited them to attend future socials as the session went on.

"Your escorts are waiting in the foyer. I am afraid I went beyond the time for adjournment."

AND SO, the time passed...very slowly for Laurel due to her inactivity and at a very hectic pace for Mac. Within the first two weeks of their stay, Laurel had finished Christmas gifts for Cathy, Roy, and even Andrew. She had read *The Scarlet Letter* the first week she'd borrowed it. Practically every day, she napped, more from boredom than tiredness.

When Mac was able, he would return to the Scotts' to eat lunch with her, but those opportunities became less frequent as committee meetings and discussions with state government staff and even appointments with a few constituents of Greene County were scheduled for lunchtime to keep the business of the legislature from dragging out longer than necessary. Speaker Oates had hinted that he would like to be able to adjourn a few days before Christmas so delegates who wished to travel could be home for the holiday. Of course, adjournment for Christmas would depend on finishing certain tasks on time. Some days, Mac would return by mid-afternoon if the house adjourned early, but more often he would not return in time for supper. Laurel learned quickly she did not like being a "lady of leisure."

Even though early December was cold and at times rainy, Laurel began to explore the city of Little Rock. On some days, she would take Sassy Lady from the stable and ride into the countryside, not far from the city. She made her way back to the circulating library every two or three days. She would not waste the opportunity to have access to so many books. She also enjoyed the conversations with Mr. Woodruff when he happened to be in the print shop. He also seemed to enjoy the conversations with the bright young woman from the rustic northeast part of the state. One afternoon, Laurel told him about the journey from Washington County. He was fascinated with her tale, and he asked her if she would consider writing her account down for him to print in the Gazette.

"I'd never thought it'd be of much interest. I will ask my husband. If he thinks it is appropriate, his being in the legislature, I would enjoy seeing our story in the paper."

"Tell me about your husband, Mrs. MacLayne. How did he get here with no connection to the political family that has governed this state almost since statehood?"

"Please call me Laurel. Mac had to work very hard, going out to meet and listen to our neighbors across the whole county. He travelled nearly every weekend for almost two years. We went to more parties, barn raisings, community debates, revivals, harvest festivals, hog-butchering days, and log rollings than you can count. Mac likes people, and they like him. His opposition was never much of a threat to him. He didn't live in the county very long, and he didn't make much of an impression up our way. People felt like he'd been sent up there just to get elected. Too many of our folks feel like we have little to say in how things happen for the state."

"Guess Conway's bunch overlooked the voice of the people. 'Course it's no secret there is bad blood between the Gazette and the governor.

It's heartening to see citizens stand up and demand their voice be heard. Your husband must have wanted the seat pretty badly to work so hard."

"He has a servant's heart. He believes he was called to serve, just like some men are called to preach the gospel and some led to be doctors. Mac is a good man. Yes, we are aware you are at odds with the governor. We get copies of the Gazette fairly often, usually two or three weeks later than here, but we still know some of what happens."

"Does your husband support the governor, Mrs. MacLayne?"

"Mac—my husband Patrick is called Mac by most of our friends—came here to support our people back home in Greene County. He hopes to find ways to build better roads in the northeast and fund schools. He is trying to learn why our levee systems get washed away with every heavy rain. We have a problem with land speculators selling already deeded land to new settlers in our area. Those are some of the things our people want Mac to work on."

"Yes, I see, but does he support the governor?"

"Mr. Woodruff, Mac will support anyone that works to make Arkansas a better place for our families. He wasn't sent to Little Rock to support the governor or anyone else. He promised to help the people of our county.

"I'll wish him God speed then. We need some shaking up. Have you read Mrs. Stowe's book?"

"I've read about some of the stir the book's caused. Mac and his father get the newspaper from Baltimore so they can keep up with things from Maryland. The abolition community has gotten really worked up about it, but I've never seen the book, myself."

"Does your husband own slaves?"

"Mr. Woodruff, few people in our part of the state have slaves. We don't grow much cotton along Crowley's Ridge. Too many rocks on the ridge, and we need our valleys to raise our food and livestock."

"Well, I'd be interested to hear what you think of the book then. Hope to see you soon. And I hope to have the first installment of your journey to print soon."

When Mac arrived at the boarding house, Laurel bubbled over with things to tell him. He'd been concerned because she'd seemed low for several days. "Mac, he wants me to write a story about our journey across the state. He wants to print it in the paper. Do you think I should do it?"

He was relieved that she had found an interest and something to occupy her time in the capital. "That's a wonderful idea, Laurel. I'd like to see you write our story...parts of it anyway. I know Mr. Woodruff and his readers would enjoy a firsthand account of our travels in northern Arkansas."

"I'm so happy you want me to do this. I want something to do."

On weekends when the weather permitted, the MacLaynes rode outside the town. On Sunday, they crossed on the ferry to the north side of the Arkansas River. They found a few cabins and homesteads, but nothing that looked like a community. They also found land that resembled the sunken lands of northeast Arkansas. One of the homesteaders they came upon said the area had to be rebuilt every couple of years because the flooding on the Arkansas was so common.

The next weekend, Mac came home after an early adjournment to tell Laurel they were going out for the evening. Two of Mac's fellow legislators had asked him to attend a lyceum at St. John's college. The lyceum was quite the social event around the state capital. Laurel was curious to attend one of the intellectual discussions she'd heard about from the ladies at the tea and from Mr. Woodruff. She also was curious to see a college. St. John's College was a fledgling institution of higher learning which had been organized in that decade. The first wing of their building had recently been completed. How wonderful to have a designated place where young men could study for their professions or to serve the church. She recalled that John, Matt's son, had hopes of going on to study for the ministry. Maybe he would come to Little Rock to study at St. John's.

When they arrived at the grand ballroom, Laurel was pleased to see she was not the only woman in attendance. Many prominent looking gentlemen had companions. The large auditorium was filled with many rows of chairs that would allow the audience not only to see, but to hear the discussion as well. The topic for the evening was one that caught Laurel by surprise, though.

Two men came to present what they claimed to be reasonable plans to deal with the "problem" of Arkansas's peculiar situation of trying to govern two contrary viewpoints held by the planters in the Delta and the yeoman of the hill country.

"Mac, I didn't know we had a problem between two contrary parts of this state. What are they talking about?"

"It's a polite way to talk about secession, Laurel. We seem to talk about it every day in the house chamber, some way or another."

As the men presented their viewpoints, Laurel became agitated. They talked about economics, transportation, crops and political districts, but they ignored the concerns of the people. At the close of the discussion each side was allowed to present a proposal to be discussed at a later time and which would be printed in the newspaper for the public to consider. The first speaker rose and simply stated, "Arkansas should have been two states from its time of statehood. I propose that the legislature consider dividing the state diagonally to separate the western mountains from the delta cotton land." The second speaker rose, and in a strong, nearly belligerent tone, he proposed that Arkansas remain unified so all citizens could benefit from the resources of every region. He said the mineral rich western part of the state was not a step-child to be tossed away at a planter's whim.

"Mac, I can't believe some people want to carve up our state."

"Secession is a serious issue here in the capital, Laurel. There is a lot of talk that Governor Conway will step down after his term because of the intense dissention among the counties."

As they were leaving St. John's, Laurel and Mac met Senator and Mrs. Quillman on the front steps.

"How nice to see you again, Mrs. MacLayne. Are you interested in political discussions?"

"Yes, we always talk about politics at our house. I can't say I particularly like all I heard tonight, though."

"Sometimes tempers do flare a bit. Surely, they both overstated themselves. I hope to see you soon."

Two days later, when Laurel returned *Uncle Tom's Cabin* to the circulating library, she asked Mr. Woodruff about the controversy that had been raised at the lyceum. "Yes, my dear, some of our leaders are quite serious about dividing the state. Many of our planters fear Arkansas won't stand with the other southern states if this abolition talk threatens them. Large numbers of folks in this state think more like westerners than southerners. They're a stubborn, independent lot... Some of them elected your husband, didn't they? The planters need to keep close ties with other cotton states."

"Surely, it won't come to that. There must be a better way."

"Perhaps a sensible solution will be found. Did you enjoy *Uncle Tom's Cabin*, Laurel?"

"I don't know if enjoy is the right word. The book did give me many things to think about. Some of it seemed exaggerated and sensationalized. I am sure some slave owners are like Simon Lagree, but I know people who treat their laborers well, just like I've seen bosses who treat their free labor very badly. We can't generalize everybody into a few categories. I basically agree with Mrs. Stowe. I don't believe in human bondage, but on the other hand, she does present a very biased picture."

"Very astute observation, young woman."

"Anyway, I came to bring you the first story about our trip to Greensboro. This part is about our three-day-stay in a cave when were snowed in by a March snowfall."

"I hope it will be the first of many."

## CHAPTER TWENTY-ONE

*If ye were of the world, the world would love his own: but because ye are not of the world, I have chosen you out of the world; therefore, the world hateth you. Remember the word that I sent unto you, the servant is not greater than his Lord. If they have persecuted Me, they will also persecute you;...*
*John 15:19-20*

The first week in December brought with it the first true winter weather. In the center of the state, they experienced miserably cold rain and bitter north winds. Laurel wondered if the northeast may be having their first snowfall of the year. In the one letter from Mac's father, he said all was well. The winter supplies of wood and fodder for the livestock were laid by. He also wrote that Andrew had taken to school and was reading pretty well even in one short month. Of course, he credited Andrew's progress to Laurel's giving him a head start before she left with Mac. Matthew had written that Mark and his bride would be making him a grandfather again by mid-summer. He told Laurel she needed to hurry home because teaching the Sunday school class was a chore. He wanted her to take the load off his shoulders.

The same day Mac brought Matthew's letter, he handed Laurel a soft cream-colored envelope, addressed to Mrs. Patrick MacLayne. The penmanship was artistic, filled with swirls of ebony on the elegant stationery. The seal on the back was impressed with a bold Q in the gold sealing wax. The envelope held a single sheet of paper, inviting her to attend a holiday tea with the legislators' wives. Mrs. Quillman planned the afternoon tea for the Friday afternoon before Christmas recess.

"Well, my dear wife, another party."

"I wish it wasn't my duty to attend. The last two were trying enough. I'm not much of a socialite, you know."

"You always do me proud, Laurel. Let's walk down to the emporium near the newspaper office on Saturday. We should think about getting a few "store bought" Christmas gifts."

"I guess it would be one way to spend an afternoon and a lot of money. From what I've heard, the goods they bring in on the steamboats are dear."

"But we have so little selection for nice gifts back home. We can splurge this once."

December 7th was a particularly gloomy day. Laurel was shut in all day by the heavy rain and bitter cold. Keeping warm was difficult with the small fire in her room. She wrapped herself in a blanket and read most of the day. The last time Laurel visited the circulating library, Mr. Woodruff recommended a new novel. He said the author was a man named Dickens, and the story was a ghostly Christmas tale. She'd also taken a small book of Plato's writings.

About 2:00, Mac came into their room in a foul mood. He slammed the door and threw his coat and hat onto the bureau and sat slumped in a chair near the fire.

"Tarnation! It's cold in this room, Laurel. Why didn't you put more wood on the fire?"

"I've been covered as I sat here reading. You are in a miff. Did things not go well today?"

"Such a wasted day! Speaker Oats has resolved that he will recess for the Christmas break when he has a final report from the apportionment committee. He wants to present it to the governor."

"Well, you said last week you were making good progress. Weren't you asking for funds to investigate land speculators and the misappropriated levee money? Those are very important things to our part of the state."

"I know that's true, but putting the recommendation down isn't good enough. We have to form a consensus. That will take a lot of bargaining and persuasion—serious talking to be done by serious people. But do you know what we debated today on the chamber floor? How much would we pay for new stationery for the House chamber! We discussed that little matter for more than two hours! We were ready to bring up the land speculation bill. The speaker recognized a representative from Garland County, instead. He asked us to consider an act of relief for a planter in his district. An act for relief is a bailout for people who can't handle their own finances. That ate up the rest of the afternoon. I am so frustrated."

"Mac, you'll get your work done."

"I told you and the kids we'd be home together for Christmas. You know that even a fast trip home will take more than a week. If we could plan to leave here on the 17th, we may be able to get home. But we can't plan anything because we don't know when we will recess."

"Mac, everything will work out fine, one way or another."

The next evening, the MacLaynes attended a dinner hosted by the St. Francis County delegation. The entire assembly was in high spirits at the elegant dinner served in the Anthony House dining room. The first section of railroad tracks from Hopefield to Helena was finished. The Memphis/Little Rock would be the first railroad to operate in the state. The segment of eighteen miles was now complete. Laurel knew the people back home would like that news. Having a rail line as close as Hopefield would help with travel on the eastern side of the state.

On Thursday, Mac arrived at the boarding house in the best frame of mind he'd had all week. He came into the little room, picked Laurel up, swung her around and kissed her firmly before he spoke one word. "Hallelujah, Laurel! Today I did a fine thing. I got a resolution to limit debate on any one topic to twenty minutes passed by our committee. My colleagues clapped because a lot of the trivial comments stopped. After we limited discussion, we actually arrived at a consensus on one of our recommendations. We are asking for charges against two land agents. They're accused of defrauding settlers with false claims to land designated as swampland. You know, Laurel, nearly every acre of the land in our area of the state is classified as swampland." Things were looking up. Lord willing, they would get home for Christmas.

The trip to the Emporium on Saturday was quite an experience for Laurel. She had never seen so many goods displayed in one place. For the most part, the general stores in Washington County and Greensboro contained basic necessities. Nowhere had she seen the broad array of merchandise she found in this city store. She gasped aloud when she saw the exorbitant prices. Yet, her eyes sparkled and a broad smile lit her face. This new experience would be something to talk about back home.

Before they left the store, they'd bought special Christmas gifts for their entire family. Mac asked the clerk to hold the purchases until he could return with the buggy.

"Well, husband, that was a nice way to start our Christmas celebration."

"We didn't get you a gift."

"I've gotten so much since I've been here. I don't need anything else."

"I think you do." He led Laurel to a display of ladies' dresses. "Let's see, you need something elegant and warm to wear to that fancy tea next week. How about this nice gray wool afternoon dress with the black lace insets and trim at the sleeves? This dress has one of those more-shapely skirts, not so bell-shaped."

"Mac, it's far too showy for back home. I have my lovely green travel suit to wear."

"And you've worn it to the last three social events we've attended. You even wore it to the theater the other night when we saw King Lear. You felt uneasy most of the night because the other woman had on evening dresses."

"Nonsense. Once that wonderful play began, no one paid attention to what I was wearing."

"Never the less, I want you to have a new dress for the tea…and a new hat. No argument. We are finishing our Christmas shopping."

On the walk back to the Scotts' house, they stopped by the Anthony House for supper. Mac tipped his hat to several men at the door, and the two of them walked to a small table in a secluded area of the elegant dining

"Mac, what plans do you have for our trip home?"

"Since we don't know exactly when the recess will be called, I haven't been able to book passage down to the Mississippi. Some of the representatives are leaving early, even before the recess, so they will be able to get home. I guess we could do that. My biggest fear is not getting those last two recommendations into the appropriate report. We still want to ask for an investigation into the levee system fraud and to ask for a report about the funds that were meant to go to school support. When swamplands are sold, a designated percentage of that money is meant for building schools and supporting teachers. Shiloh never received any money."

"Those are important issues. I don't think you'd feel you'd done your job if that isn't done."

"Laurel, you have been a great support and comfort to me the two months we've been here. I know you haven't enjoyed this adventure as much as I have, but you've made it possible for me to do the work I was sent here to do. You've made this time a pleasure for me because you are here to share it. Thank you, wife."

"I am glad you wanted me, and I am grateful you are allowing me to go home where I can be useful."

"If we do recess this next Thursday or Friday, I'll find us a place on a riverboat headed south. Likely, we can book passage from Napoleon back to Hopefield. If the weather is fair, we can make the drive home in two days or less. Maybe we'll be home for Christmas day."

"I'll pray it's God's will. If not, we'll have a late family Christmas this year."

The week did not go well. Arguments erupted over school funding. Another group of legislators thought the recommendation toward land speculators was too harsh. By Thursday, Mac knew the report wouldn't be complete, and the recess would not take place the next day. Red-faced and scowling, he reflected his frustration all day. When called on to defend one of the recommendations, he drew himself up, his arms pushed against his desktop. His jaw twitched twice before he calmed himself enough to speak.

"Colleagues, we weren't elected to protect unscrupulous men at the expense of settlers they cheat. What would we do to a common thief in our towns? I call for passage of this bill."

Debate continued. One red-faced representative from the southcentral part of the state interrupted the report being given by the chairman of the Appropriations Committee. He called him a blackguard and a fool. The bailiff stepped in to stop a scuffle from erupting on the floor. Blessedly, the session adjourned before a more physical confrontation took place.

LAUREL DRESSED in her new dove gray wool afternoon dress on Friday. She fastened her gold Gordian knot to her high collar. She put her stylish new bonnet atop her chignon and tied the broad gray silk bow at her chin. She looked every bit the society lady Mac wanted her to be. He arrived at lunch to drive her to the tea at Senator Quillman's home. The streets were very muddy due to the excessive rain the first part of December. Laurel put on her social face and greeted her hostess, Mrs. Quillman, as she answered the door.

"I'm glad you are able to join us, Mrs. MacLayne. Since your journey home is so long, I was afraid that you and Representative MacLayne may have left for home early."

"We'd like to be home for Christmas. Our family is expecting us, but Patrick will not rest easy until he sees his work done. I hope they make good progress this afternoon."

"Come, let me introduce you to some of the other wives. Several of them have come to Little Rock to spend the holidays with their husbands. Laurel met some of the planters' wives and wives of the socially elite. Most of these women were from wealthy or at least well-to-do professional families. She met the wife of a minister from the central area of the state who had lived the pioneer life she knew. Of course, many legislators from rural parts of the state, yeomen farmers or craftsmen, could not afford to bring families to Little Rock.

The conversations eventually turned to the work of the legislature. Wives were always eager to share what'd they'd been told by their husbands. One lady from the southeast part of Arkansas asked Laurel if Mac enjoyed his first year in the State house and the work he'd done.

"He's happy about some things they've recommended, but he is concerned they may not be able to recommend funding to improve the roads in the northern part of the state. He also wants to find funds to support schools. Those are two big concerns for us in the northeast."

"My dear, Governor Conway says Arkansas is blessed with an abundance of good solid dirt roads about anywhere we need to go."

"Mrs. Bowers, have you ever traveled north of Little Rock?"

"Of course. We've gone to Memphis a few times. We've even been to St. Louis. The riverboats are quite comfortable now."

"I agree. We came here on the Eclipse, a luxurious side paddleboat. Still, how do you get around if you must travel inland where there are no riverboats?"

"We have little need to travel inland. The travel by coach or horseback is dangerous and very difficult."

"That's exactly the problem. My husband and I drove a wagon pulled by two jacks more than three hundred miles across Governor Conway's good dirt roads. At least, we traveled the roads when we could find them. Except for the military roads, built by the federal government, we mostly have paths suggesting the way between settled areas."

"I can't imagine it's as dire as that."

"We made the trip in about five weeks, traveling long distances nearly every day. Arkansas is a beautiful place, but we must have better roads if we are going to progress as a state."

"I never realized the hardships in the wilderness," a second woman commented.

"Do I remember you said you are a teacher?"

"Yes, Mrs. Quillman. I teach in the subscription school held at our church."

"Oh, then I assume your area of the state has yet to develop a public school. You know we have recently opened our boys' school and our girls' school here in Little Rock. They provide such an advantage to our children."

"Yes, Mac and I visited the boys' school one afternoon. Such a nice building and so much material to use in teaching! I understand that Little Rock had funding from the state to help build those schools."

"I'm sure I don't know about that."

"Well, the use of money from the sale of federal lands is supposed to support schools. In our region, though, we wouldn't have a school at all if our church congregation didn't support our school through subscription. The swamplands are all over the state. The funds should be shared that way, too."

"You seem so aware of state politics. Is your family involved in local politics?"

"No, only my husband, but we do like to talk about his work. He is very serious about the job our community sent him here to do."

"What a lovely dress you are wearing...." Laurel realized most of the ladies there had little interest in her political discussion. She knew and cared so little about clothes and hairstyles that the conversation around her lost its appeal. With a breath of relief and a tiny smile, Laurel greeted Mac when he came for her at 4:30. She'd had her fill of social life in the capital and prayed Mac would tell her they were leaving for Shiloh.

THAT WAS NOT THE CASE. Once again, the report was delayed. Speaker Oates called for a session on Monday so the work of the committee could be finalized. Mac and three other legislators worked long hours all weekend and on into Monday night to complete the apportionment report. With fewer people there to object, the committee drafted the report with all three of the issues Mac promised to include. He could go home, knowing he'd served Greene County as well as he was able.

Finally, at 12:00 on December 21, speaker Oates recessed for Christmas break. He told the legislators they would reconvene at 9:00

on January 17, 1859. The 12th Legislative Assembly still had much business to complete.

When Mac arrived at the Stones' following the recess, he'd missed supper. Laurel became concerned when two other legislators returned at dusk. Another had already headed back to Searcy County. Neither told Laurel they'd seen Mac after the closing session. A state senator praised his work. "Congressman MacLayne was just like a bulldog. He's a stubborn one, that husband of yours. We tried to settle this thing on Friday. Because we'd not recommended a plan to deal with land speculators, he kept after us. He wouldn't quit until he pushed the appropriation report through the committee."

"That's one of the promises he made to our folks back home," Laurel explained. "Travel safely home. It was nice to have known you."

"Won't ya be here when we come back in January?"

"I am going home where I am needed. Merry Christmas to y'all."

"Yes, Ma'am, and the same to you."

Well after dark, Mac came through the door to their room. "I am sorry to be so late. When I was able to get away, I went down to the wharf to see if we could get passage back to Napoleon."

"That's all right. Did you have anything to eat?"

"No, not since breakfast, but I know I'm too late to get supper now. I'll be fine 'til morning."

"No. You get your coat and scarf off and sit down to rest. We had ham and beans for supper, so I'll get you some heated. I know Mrs. Scott won't mind."

Mac was bone tired. He didn't remove his coat, scarf, or boots. He lay down across the bed to wait for Laurel to return. His head barely touched the bed before he slept.

Laurel found Sandra Scott finishing the kitchen chores. Together they heated a large supper of leftovers for Mac. Laurel scooped mounds on the plate and finished with two large squares of cornbread on top.

"Y'all headed back north in the mornin'?"

"Honestly, I don't know yet. Mac returned from the riverfront, but he was hungry so I wanted to find him some supper. I didn't find out if he'd been able to find passage."

When Laurel returned, she carried the overfilled plate to the hearth, along with a large cup of steaming coffee. As much as she hated to wake Mac, she knew the meal would be good for him. Besides, she didn't want to wait until the morning to learn of their travel plans. "Patrick, wake up and eat while this food is hot. I brought you a cup of coffee."

"I hadn't meant to fall asleep. I'm more tired than I knew." He moved to the chair near the fireplace and began to devour the beans, stewed potatoes, and pone. "This is about the best meal I've had since we got to Little Rock."

"You're hungry. What did you learn about passage?"

"Darlin', you know we can't get home before Christmas. That's my fault. I pushed and argued and bargained until we got those three points in the report, but it took me two days longer to do it. I'm sorry you will miss your family Christmas this year."

"It doesn't matter. We'll celebrate together when we get home. It doesn't have to be on Christmas day."

"We do have some options. Senator Quillman invited us to stay with them during the break and return home when the session is over. It may only take about three more weeks."

"Are you sure the session will end so soon?"

"You know how it's gone so far. I'd say we have five or six weeks of work to do, but the tentative adjournment day is set for the end of January."

"You mean after you reconvene the third week of January? That would take us to the first of March."

"I knew you wouldn't like that plan. You can't blame a man for trying. I'd love to keep you here with me."

"Mac, I am so useless here. At home, there are so many things that I need to be doing. It may be gardening time before you can get home. Who will tend to that?"

"Who will tend to me if you go?"

"There is a difference between need and want, my dear."

"Sometimes I can't tell the difference...." He reached for her, but she sidestepped him.

"You said we have options. Did you find a boat headed to Napoleon?"

"Yes, but not a very big one, and certainly not as comfortable as the Rock City. If you can be ready to leave at sun up in the morning, we can head home. There is no guarantee we will find a connecting passage when we get to Napoleon. Can't you even imagine us spending our Christmas in Napoleon?"

"I'll be ready. I already stowed most everything in our trunk. I want to go home to Shiloh. The Lord will provide our passage. He'd never make his children spend the Lord's birthday in a place like that river-front nightmare of a town."

"I know you wanna go home. I'll do what I can to get you there."

As the sun rose on December 22, Mac and Laurel loaded their two horses and the borrowed rig. The boot of the buggy held their trunk and the extra boxes of things they'd bought for presents for the family back home. The Johnny Mack was a tiny aft-paddle steamer and much flatter to the water than any boat they'd ridden. This boat had only two decks, a lower one for cargo and a second promenade deck with six minature cabins. The central area of the boat, "the salon" was a boxy room about eighteen by thirty feet, centered by a wood stove. A half-dozen tables and chairs completed the furnishings for the room. The tiny cabin Mac had been able to secure was at the aft, a few steps from the captain's bridge and quarters.

Next to the bridge rose the one stack, coming up through the deck. In the cabin, a small bunk was attached to the wall on one side and a table with a water pitcher and bowl sat beside the door. Luxury was not the description of their room on the Johnny Mack. Little did it matter. The boat had a reputation for being a fast vessel and heading down river was easier than going north. This boat was going in the right direction, and that was what mattered to Laurel. If the weather and river cooperated, they would be in Napoleon by nightfall on the 23rd. The river was high because of the recent rains so travel should be swift and safe.

During the day, the MacLaynes managed a few short walks around the promenade, but the cold made the trips brief. They did watch as the boat took on more cargo in Pine Bluff, a growing settlement along the shores of the Arkansas. Lumber seemed to be a big part of the wealth of that area. After a meager dinner of stew and hot bread, the MacLaynes retired to their tiny cabin to stay warm. Spooned together in the small bunk, they knew it was too early to sleep. Mac took the opportunity to open a long-postponed conversation.

"Laurel, the time we've been away seems short to me. I know the time has moved much slower for you. We've had good times and met some interesting new people during our stay. We've had some much-needed time to talk about a lot of important things. I want you to know I'll always cherish these memories, but we haven't spent much time talking about home or family."

"You know people on their wedding trip rarely talk about their children."

"Yes, I guess that's true. Few newlyweds have a son, sixteen; a daughter, almost nine; and a six-year-old son to worry about before their second anniversary."

"I enjoyed being the pampered bride the first few weeks. It has been nice to be the center of your attention when we had time together."

"This seven weeks has been good for me, too." Mac finished his thought with a sweet kiss. "Laurel, we have some things we need to think about before we get home. I am grateful you said we'd take Andrew to raise, but we've not spoken about him since our trip downstream. Are you sure this is what you want?"

"Patrick, I don't see much that needs discussing. Andrew deserves a home with parents who love him and will raise him well. I will learn to love him because he is yours."

"I told you my Pa will raise Andrew if you think taking him on is too much for us to deal with."

"Andrew is only a small boy, Mac. I'm sure I can handle him."

"Laurel, Andrew doesn't change anything between us. I am ashamed to say I have no feelings for his mother. I hardly remember her, but I do have feelings for the boy. I want him to grow up as our son."

"I will be the best mother to him that I know how to be. I won't tell you that I didn't want to give you a son first, but if it's God's will, we will have a child one day."

"I pray so. I asked about legal issues of taking him into the family. Seems Arkansas doesn't have any formal procedures to adopt children. All I have to do to acknowledge him and Cathy is to put their names in a will or another legal paper, like a deed."

"That should be simple enough, then."

"Laurel, what would you say if we acknowledge both of them at Christmas?"

"At Christmas? Can we do it so quickly? What about Roy?"

"Roy will be seventeen in the spring. He already wants to be his own man. He's been talking about going back to the Dunn homestead and making his own way. I doubt he'll want to become a MacLayne, but I know Cathy does."

"Mac, I want our family to be happy and feel as if they belong to us. We should ask them when we get home, and if they like the idea, we'll acknowledge one, two, or all three of them. We will record their kinship in our family Bible. That is better than a legal document anyway."

"We'll do both. I want things right and legal."

"I hope this puts your mind at rest."

"I'm quite content, if you are sure you truly want to make this commitment, Laurel."

"Patrick, if you'll think back, I made the commitment in March of '57. Do you remember the vows I made? Nothing's changed. As long as God wills us to be a family, I'll do all in my power to keep my vows to you."

"Our cabin is going to be very crowded with three children there."

"Three? I am thinking about six or seven. There are lots of logs on our property."

"I'll raise another pen whenever you say. You tell me when you want it, and I'll make the space."

Late the next afternoon, the Johnny Mack arrived in Napoleon. The high river and light cargo load allowed this trip in record time, slightly more than twenty-nine hours, not counting the stops. The rustic river port was alive with people, coming and going along its docks and dirt walkways. Loud, tinny music came from two or three ramshackle saloons. Of course, few loiterers stood outside the notorious establishments this time. The cold pushed the idlers inside to the relative warmth of the highly stoked wood stoves. Even though they were fully ablaze, the stoves could barely keep the freezing temperatures at bay.

A deep scowl settled on Mac's face. When he asked about a connecting passage to Memphis, he heard that no boat headed north was at anchor. One freighter, waiting with his load, told Mac the Delta Queen out of New Orleans was due the next evening. Of course, that created a problem. He would have to find suitable shelter for Laurel, himself, and their animals. He was not sure such a place existed in this town.

"Can you tell me, friend, is there a hotel here that will be a safe place for my wife? I can't let her spend the night outside in this freezing cold."

"Honestly, mister, they ain't no place here in Napoleon I'd want to take a gentlewoman."

"I guess any place would do. I doubt we'll see this night through without more rain."

"I usually stay in a loft above one of the saloons. Sad as it is to say, they're lots of saloons and fancy houses hereabout but ain't no school nor decent lodging house in Napoleon. The Catholic church is up that way, but the priest's not in town right now. Drive on down the shore a piece. You'll see a place that looks like a derelict boat. Well, that is actually what it is. They have a few guest rooms, but you won't find that place exactly peaceful or comfortable. With you there with her, I suppose you'll keep your wife safe for a night or so until the Delta Queen can make land."

Mac returned to his seat and drove the short distance down the shoreline, and he found the boat beached not a hundred feet from the Mississippi. "Laurel, this may be the only shelter we'll find for tonight. Come with me to ask. I don't want you to be out here alone."

They entered what seemed to be a reception room, poorly lit by a few dirty oil lamps. Ancient settees and a well-used chair or two sat near a blazing fire, which did little to dispel the cold. A haggard clerk sat behind a counter, thumbing a dog-eared newspaper.

"Excuse me. Do you have a room for tonight and a place to shelter my horses?"

"Could be, if you have the price. We've had several askin' but not all are willin' to pay what we're asking."

"I don't think I asked the cost. I need a room for my wife and myself. We also need a hot meal if such a thing is to be had."

"We got three rooms left on the upper floor. They're real nice cabins. You'll have a place to sleep."

"Fine, I'll take one. What about shelter for my horses?"

"We got a lean-to out back, that's about all."

A man lounging on the faded settee wisecracked, "Yeah, but it's full of the people who couldn't pay the room cost." Others around the room laughed at his crude, but true remark.

"Is there a livery near?"

"Yeah, a way up on the bluff. You'll have to go up there any way to find a place to get a meal."

"Please give me one of those rooms you've got. We'll be here until we can make passage to Memphis."

"Yes, sir. You plant a five-dollar gold piece in my hand, and I'll be happy to give you the best room we got left."

"What would the worst room you have cost?"

"Five dollars, like I said." Mac took the coin from his pocket and took the key. Together he and Laurel carried their belongings to the second level of the boat-turned-hotel and locked them up. The task of finding shelter for the animals remained.

Mac and Laurel took Midnight, Sassy and the buggy up the bluff. As they got to the center of the town, the noise level increased and piles of debris and trash grew at every corner. After driving through the streets, they found what seemed to be a fairly sturdy livery stable. At least this one had an intact roof and walls capable of holding off part of the blistering wind. The stableman was an old German who told the MacLaynes his name was Wagonner, which he pronounced with a 'V'. He told Mac the fee was 'von' dollar to shelter and feed the two animals for a day. He also told them he lived up in the loft so he could keep watch on the animals in his charge. "Ain't nobody gonna steal 'von' of the animals, I keep. Truth of it all, I have to keep my belongings up there to be safe. The only way I can stay in business in this town. Napoleon is a rough town and too much mayhem goes on here. Gentlefolk don't usually stop here unless they are forced to stay overnight."

"Well, I'm sure we'll be fine for the night, Mr. Waggoner. I appreciate your taking care of these horses for us. They are like members of the family, not work animals."

"I wish you rest, madam. I'd make sure you get settled in before the sun sets about 5:30. At least you'll have a fascinatin' tale to share someday... about a night you spent in Napoleon, only about three hundred feet from hell. This here is a fine little town with twenty-three saloons, hardly no churches, and a murder every night." Waggoner bellowed with laughter.

"Thank you, sir. I appreciate your advice. Is there a café nearby where we can eat before hiding away for the night?"

"Best cafe in Napoleon is in the next block, right near the Marine Hospital. Mrs. Ellis sets a pretty fine table. She'll make ya a nice sack of vittles that could give you a supper and breakfast, if you like plain cooking. She don't fix much fancy stuff, but it's filling."

"Sounds like what we need. We'll see you in the morning."

Mr. Waggoner had spoken the truth. The food was filling, plain fare and at a reasonable price. Mac and Laurel took the extra meal with them and returned to the hotel, arriving as the sunset. The crowds had already become more rambunctious.

During the night, as they slept in their not-too-warm four by six cabin, the MacLaynes heard gunshots at least three different times. "I suspect that is one of those nightly murders Mr. Waggoner told us about?"

"Don't fret, Laurel. Most river ports are like this at first. Civilization hasn't made it here yet. Sleep if you can. With a bit of providence, we'll be headed home tomorrow."

~

The Delta Queen docked at 1:00 the next afternoon. Mac was able to book passage to Memphis. The boat left Desha County before sundown. The accommodations aboard the Delta Queen were even more luxurious than those they'd found on the Eclipse. The Grand Parlor was lit with several gold and crystal chandeliers. The large room was well-heated by high gloss black wood stoves, ornately decorated with gilt grills. The stoves sat throughout the room assuring all the guests were comfortable. Whether they were dining, dancing, gambling, or simply lounging in the rose velvet upholstered chairs. No one would complain of the cold.

That night was Christmas Eve, and the captain hosted a celebration to start the holiday. The music swelled across the room. The candles and evergreen provided the wonderful aroma of Christmas. The British chef prepared a feast of roast goose, hot-cross buns, and flaming pudding. These were dishes made in all the best homes in London. Mac remembered his mother serving them at Christmas.

Mac and Laurel joined the celebration for a time. "Laurel, are you well? You don't seem to be enjoying all this finery tonight."

"Yes, dear. I'm fine. The food was wonderful. The music and atmosphere of this room are unbelievable, but I was thinking about the Christmas we'd be having at home."

"Keep that dream in a safe place for a few more days. We'll have our family Christmas, I promise."

"I didn't intend to spoil your evening, Mac."

"How could you? I am sitting here with the most wonderful gift I ever got."

"Thank you. I do love you."

"Do you?" Laurel looked up and met his stormy blue eyes. "Come and show me. Let's go to our room and have our own private Christmas celebration, a party for two. That is the reward we get for having to sacrifice our family Christmas. I have a few more days I don't have to share you with anyone."

For two long, cold rainy days, the Delta Queen pushed its way up the river toward Memphis. The cold persisted and the rain continued. The hostile weather made captives of most passengers aboard the Delta Queen. People went outside only to hurry to the Grand Salon or to look after their cargo on the lower deck. Laurel and Mac did not seem to mind. They had good books, a warm comfortable bed, and each other.

Passage upriver took a day longer than the trip downriver. The rain was causing floods all along the shore where the land was lowest. Excess water drove a stronger than usual current. Mac told Laurel of his concerns about their trip from Hopefield to Bolivar. The path that had been dry and well-defined in October could be under water if the rain had been as heavy in the north.

"Mac, we can't do anything about the weather. God will provide us a way home. Relax and enjoy our last night on board this floating palace."

"Well, if you insist." He drew her close and forgot about the world outside and the difficult travel that lay before them.

When they left their cabin the next morning with their baggage, they were delighted to see dry land. The temperature was below freezing, but the area didn't experience the intense rain they encountered below Helena.

"Thank you, Lord!" Mac raised his hand in praise. "Laurel, you were so right. He has made sure we can get home."

By midafternoon on the 28th, they were back in Hopefield, traveling north and east toward Bolivar. Once again, Mac covered the front seat of the rig with the heavy bearskin, and he purchased several heated bricks to lay at their feet under the skin. They would provide some relief from the cold. The road was frozen but not icy, and they made good time, but Mac knew they could not reach Bolivar by nightfall. He hoped he would be able to find someplace to shelter along the way.

About halfway across the sunken land, the Lord provided for them again. At a distance, Mac saw a barn outlined against the horizon. The building was on a slight rise above the floodplain. He drove on about half a mile and drove into the barn lot. Mac realized the homestead was long abandoned. The cabin had burned to the ground, but the barn remained intact and would provide shelter from the wind and a place for their animals to rest.

Once inside, he scraped out a clearing to build a fire. He took the bricks from the buggy floor to heat in the fire during the night. He managed to find enough forage to feed Midnight and Sassy Lady.

Finally, he settled down next to Laurel under the bearskin. They shared bread and cheese she'd saved from the breakfast on the Delta Queen. They fell asleep in each other's arms, fed and warm.

The following two days were long, difficult, and cold. They spent one night with Lizzie Lee in her boarding house before they began the last leg of their trip home. The second day out, they drove from sunrise until well past sunset. The twenty-six miles between Bolivar and Shiloh wasn't going to keep them in the cold one more day...not if Mac could prevent it. What a blessing! The night sky was cloudless and filled with moonlight and stars. They covered the last four miles between Greensboro and Shiloh well after dark. At ten o'clock on New Year's Eve, Mac and Laurel drove into their yard. The house was dark, and no smoke arose from the chimney. It didn't matter. They were home!

# CHAPTER TWENTY-TWO

*Neither shall thy name any more be called Abram,*
*but thy name shall be called Abraham...*
*Genesis 17:5*

The rising sun didn't awaken the MacLaynes the next morning, but Roy and John did. The shouts and cheers they made could have awakened the county. The boys found Midnight and Sassy in their stalls when they went out to do morning chores. Mac rose, donned his travel clothes, and went to the kitchen to greet them.

"Welcome home, Mr. Mac. We're right happy you made it. We've been looking for y'all since the weekend."

"Morning, boys. Good to be back. We made a fast trip, but couldn't get home in time for Christmas."

"My ma and pa will be glad to see you two."

"John, will you run a message for me?"

"Sure, I will."

"Please tell your pa we're home. Then invite the whole family over. This afternoon, we're having a New Year's Eve supper, celebrating our delayed Christmas. Roy, I want you to ride over to the Widow's place and ask my pa to come over and bring Andrew. Make haste, fellas. It's time for a party at Shiloh."

Laurel came from the second pen, dressed and ready to prepare for the family celebration. She was happy to be back in her home. She fairly danced across the walnut plank floor to her husband. "This is the most glorious home in the world. Nothing we've seen in our travels can come close to our home."

"Good morning, wife. Merry Christmas."

"The same to you and Happy New Year, too. Good morning, boys. So good to see you both."

"Run on now boys. Let's get started." Laurel returned to the kitchen to begin breakfast. How fine a thing to be able to knead bread and cut out biscuits! A simple task, like separating cream from the morning milk wasn't work, only pure pleasure on this last day of 1858. Mac built a large fire to heat the hearth oven so Laurel could bake bread. The spit stood ready to roast the meat that would complete their delayed Christmas dinner.

After a quick breakfast, Mac took his rifle from the nook behind the fireplace. "Wife, I'm off to find our Christmas meat while the boys go gather our family. Would you prefer a turkey or a goose?"

"It doesn't matter. Whatever you find first will be fine. I'm so pleased to be home, I'd cook ham and beans and think it a feast today."

Work to transform the cabin into a festive place where a family would celebrate Christmas a week late began. Laurel planned to combined the New Year's celebration into the same event, so she set a large kettle of black-eyed peas with several pieces of pork from the smokehouse to cook on the spit. An extra pone would add little to her workload and would make the Christmas/New Year meal complete. She went to the woods after the meal was on the hearth. She searched beyond the fenced pastures for small branches of holly, an evergreen bough or two, and a few sprigs of mistletoe. When she returned, she displayed the greenery and the red holly berries across the mantle and the dining room table with lengths of red ribbon. She placed candles in her mother's pewter candleholders among the evergreens. The final touch to the table was Mac's mother's red crystal lantern with red bows placed here and there about the room. The cabin took on the atmosphere of Christmas, the sights and smells Laurel remembered from her childhood. She was happy.

Shortly before noon, Roy returned with Cathy. She ran into Laurel's arms. "Mrs. Mac, I am so glad you are home." The girl wrapped her arms around Laurel's waist and pranced in her excitement.

"I have missed you, Cathy. We have work to do to get ready for our family Christmas tonight. Can you help me hang this mistletoe over the doors?"

"Oh, yes! I was afraid we missed Christmas with you and Mr. Mac this year."

"Did you have a nice holiday with Brother Matthew and Miss Ellie?"

"Yes, even Mr. MacLayne and Andrew came to dinner. Miss Ellie made a fine dinner, and we got our presents, but it wasn't the same without your being here."

"Well, we're here now, and we're going to celebrate together. We're going to pretend it's Christmas Eve."

"Wow! Two Christmases! I love that idea." She hugged Laurel again.

Shortly, Mac returned with a large goose he'd found down by the creek. The bird would make a fine centerpiece for their Christmas meal the next day.

"Cathy, girl! How pretty you've gotten while we've been gone!"

"Oh, Mr. Mac! I've not changed one bit. It's only that you're glad to see me."

"Right you are, darlin'." Mac planted a kiss on Cathy's forehead.

At sunset, Thomas MacLayne rode into the yard with Andrew on the front of his saddle. They had come to spend the night and the next day at the homestead. "Welcome, Pa and Andrew. I'm glad you're both here. Now we can start the holiday celebration."

"Are we a-havin' a New Year's Eve party, Mr. Mac?"

"No, Andrew. We're celebrating our family Christmas – a little late this year, but we are celebrating...none the less."

"Goody! We'll eat then 'cause at the Campbells' we had such good eats at Christmas. We even had gingerbread cookies Aunt Ellie made. Them was scrumptious."

"We'll have more tonight and tomorrow. Christmas is a special time for our family...whenever we celebrate it," Mac assured the small boy. As the sun sank below Crowley's Ridge, the entire MacLayne family sat down to their Christmas Eve supper on that New Year's Eve. Heads bowed as Mac offered thanks for the season, for his family gathered around his table and for the birth of a Savior who had led him to salvation.

The sent of cedar and cinnamon, the crackling logs in the fireplace and the wavering light from many candles made the room sound and smell like Christmas. The family enjoyed the hot beef stew, black-eyed peas, cornbread, and bubbling blackberry cobbler that Laurel and Cathy had prepared for their supper. Sitting at the head of the table, Mac laughed, interjected comments, and blushed a time or two as his father told stories of Christmases past and of his childhood back in Maryland. He was more relaxed and rested than Laurel had seen him in a long while.

"Patrick was always the worst at Christmas time. He always wanted to know what he was getting from St. Nicholas. He'd start nagging at me and his ma the first day of Advent. When he was seven, he got it into this head that he'd get a horse. His ma said no because he was too young to be responsible for a horse at that age. We had decided he had to wait a couple more years, hoping a growth spurt would kick in. He was not very big at that age, though you'd not know it now. Anyway, Patrick's brother Sean was near grown, and he did need a new horse to ride to school, so we got him one.

"That Christmas morning, Patrick sneaked to the barn in the early hours and found Sean's horse. What a fuss he made when we told him the saddle horse was Sean's! He tried to climb on the bareback of that stallion, and the feisty animal threw him into a haystack. Wonder he didn't break his neck! He got up, brushed the hay from his hair, and told his brother, 'Sean, that old horse is too brown to suit me. I want a black stallion. That horse is a nag!"

Everyone around the table laughed. Mac nodded, "It was true! Sean agreed with me when Lancer threw him the very next week, and he got a broken arm." Again, laughter filled the room.

The small boy spoke up. "It's fun having Christmas at New Years. This is the best time I ever had."

"Andrew, Christmas is the best holiday every year. See how Laurel and Cathy decorated our cabin? We had a special supper tonight with all our family. It's Christmas Eve."

"It ain't really though, is it?"

"The date doesn't matter. For us it is. Didn't you celebrate Christmas when you were with your mother and grandfather in Tennessee?"

"Not as I know.

"Well, it's high time you got to know about Christmas then. Pa, would you read the Christmas story to us?" Mac handed his father the Bible from the side table.

"Which Gospel do you want to hear?"

"Let's start with Matthew, and we'll read the others tomorrow and the next couple days while I'm still home." Thomas read the first account of the Nativity story from the Gospel of Matthew. He told them about the birth of the baby in a stable, the bad king who wanted to kill the new baby, and the visit of the wise men, bringing gifts. Andrew listened intently. More than once, a confused look crossed his face, but he didn't stop listening.

"You tell it so nice, Mr. MacLayne. Did you like the Christmas story?" Cathy looked at her new playmate. The six-year-old nodded.

"Well, it's time to sing Christmas carols now, Mr. Mac. Can we start with *Silent Night*? It's my favorite."

"Yes, Matthew, lead us in *Silent Night*." Matthew Campbell rose and led the carol Andrew listened again as he watched the family sing about Christmas.

"That story is the same as Mr. MacLayne read to us, ain't it?" Mac felt a pang of shame. His son knew nothing of Christmas or Jesus' love or even family life. His wasted years had hurt many people besides himself, and he hadn't even been aware of the pain he'd caused. Silently, he prayed for forgiveness for the damage he'd done. He would spend the rest of his life trying to make up for the six lost years of Andrew's childhood. He pledged that not one more day would pass before this small boy began to experience all the things he'd missed.

"Yes, Andrew. The story is the same story."

"What's frankincense and myrrh?"

"Precious gifts for the Christ child, the very first gifts of Christmas. Now, St. Nicholas brings gifts to children on Christmas Eve."

"Brother Matthew said something about that on Christmas morning, but I didn't ask about him. I guessed he was a friend from Shiloh church."

"Well, boy, come over here and sit with me. Let me tell you about Saint Nicholas." Mac pulled him up and began to explain.

"You're jokin' me, Mr. Mac. No one gives away things for nothin'."

"Andrew, didn't you have any kind of Christmas at all with your family in Tennessee? Didn't you get fruit or candy or new clothes?"

"No, ma'am. I don't think we have that holiday over in Franklin. I'm pretty sure St. Nicholas don't live over in our neck of the woods. We did have a fine Independence Day every summer, but I don't remember nothin' about a winter celebration like Christmas. In the winter, we mostly stayed in and tried to keep warm."

"Didn't you hear about it at church, Andrew?" Cathy couldn't believe he hadn't ever celebrated Christmas, even at church.

"No. My grandpa didn't hold much with church."

Laurel looked at the small boy who was so much like her beloved Patrick. Her heart ached, knowing he'd never experienced a real family or the joy of Christmas. Learning to love him would be easy. She smiled at him sitting in his father's lap. Andrew saw her and he smiled back.

"Well, Andrew. We put a lot of store in church here, and it's because of Christmas and Easter and the wonderful gifts Jesus gave us. Those things are better than any gift St. Nicholas could ever bring. You'll learn about those things with us here at Shiloh."

The family sang *Joy to the World* and *Oh, Little Town of Bethlehem*. The night had been very special for them all. Laurel sighed. *Even a week late, this is a perfect family Christmas.*

"Family, before we turn in for the night, I want to do more thing. Cathy, Roy and Andrew, you three young people have been a blessing to us. Thank you for becoming a part of this family."

"Gee, Mr. Mac. You're the ones been good to us. I don't know if

Cathy and me could've made it alone when Gran died. You took real good care of us."

"Roy, son, you've worked hard as any hand I ever had. You've more than earned your keep."

"But Mr. Mac. I ain't done nothin' to help. I ain't earned nothin'."

"Andrew, families don't have to earn their place. They belong because they're loved. Laurel and I love all of you."

"But, Mr. Mac, I ain't family. That ole lawyer left me with your pa. I don't know why."

"He left you with your grandfather. Andrew, I am your pa." Mac stopped and looked into the face of the small boy in his lap. Andrew didn't move or say anything. "Is that all right with you?"

Laurel looked on with tears filling her eyes. Andrew looked first at Mac and then at Thomas MacLayne and back to Mac. He didn't speak. Mac sat, hope showing in his face. He wanted this boy to accept his place in the family. Clearly, Andrew was at a loss for an answer. She walked across and laid her hand on his shoulder.

"Andrew, your father and I want you to be our little boy. We hope you'll want to grow up here with Cathy and Roy. If you want us, we will be good parents to you. We'll be one family, all of us here in this room."

"Is this for real, Mr. MacLayne?" Andrew looked across the room to the man who'd been his guardian for the last six months.

"Lad, I think you should call me granddad. Would you like that?"

Andrew slowly raised his head to look at Mac. Shyly, he made eye contact. "Mr. Mac...are you my for sure papa? For real?"

"Yes, Andrew. I'm your for sure papa. That is, if you want to be a part of my family."

"What'd I have to call you, Mrs. Mac?"

"You can call me whatever you like. I'd be proud to have you be my son."

"Well, golly geez, now I got me a new granddad and a papa of my own. If I call you mama, that won't be slightin' my ma, would it?"

"No, Andrew, I don't think so."

"Can I give you a hug, Mama?" The boy leaped from Mac's arms and ran to embrace Laurel.

"You can do this anytime you want, son."

Mac looked on as his son embraced his wife. Andrew's face was pink, and his eyes were the size of jaw breakers, his favorite candy. His smile stretched across the width of his face. Watching his son's joy, brought tears to his lashes. Was it less than two years ago he'd all but given up on the idea of ever knowing this life? God had given him his wish, and Laurel had made it all happen with her love. A tear traced a path down his cheek. Finally, he spoke, "Kids, we are a family. After Christmas, Laurel and I will do what it takes to make this all legal. Cathy and Roy, we want to adopt you both, if that is what you want."

"Mr. Mac, you want to be my papa, too?"

"That's right, Roy. We want to be your parents."

Andrew all but danced. "Gracious me! Christmas is a special time, ain't it?" With those words, Andrew walked over to Mac who bent down to pick up the boy. He put his arms around Mac's neck and whispered, "I'm glad you're my Papa."

Patrick's father took the small boy from Mac's arms. "Andrew, the Indians and even people from the Bible had a custom of giving folks a new name when something special happened in their lives. Tonight, you decided to become a MacLayne. We oughta give you a new name. Would you like that?"

"Ain't thought about it. Kinda used to Andrew."

"Your papa has a special name. His friends call him 'Mac', but his real name is Patrick. Cathy's name is Catherine, but we all love her so we call her a sweetheart name, Cathy. I'd like to call you Andy. You are a newest MacLayne, and we want people to know how glad we are to have you. If you'll let us, from now on, this family will call you Andy MacLayne. Is this something that you'd like?"

"If I do this, will Papa adopt me too, like Roy and Cathy?"

Laurel took a couple of steps over to where her father-in-law stood by the fireplace. "No, Andrew. You belong to your father already. I will adopt you because I want you to be my son, too."

Andy leaned over and kissed Laurel's cheek. "You can call me Andy, Mama."

The night couldn't have been any better. The spirit of love filled the

MacLayne home that New Year's Eve. The celebration ended with a family prayer, and Matthew and his family headed back to their cabin. Near ten, the children were in bed.

Thomas walked over and embraced his son. "Patrick, I've never been prouder of you than I am tonight."

"That means a lot to me, Pa."

SQUEALS AND LAUGHTER WOKE FAMILY. Cathy and Andy had slept on a pallet on the floor near the fireplace in the second pen, but they crept into the main room about the time the sun rose. They found the rewards St. Nicholas had left. Cathy tried to quiet Andy, but her shushings were as loud as his 'gollies' and 'no ways'. Mac and Laurel joined them, and a few minutes later, Thomas MacLayne and Roy came down from the loft.

"Papa, lookee here...Cathy says this has my name on it. How does St. Nicholas know my name?"

"It does say Andrew – see this?" Mac showed him where his name had been written on the package. "See, everyone has gifts. This one says Roy, and that one is for my pa."

"Everyone gets presents at Christmas?"

"Since the first one. Remember the story from last night? The wise men brought gifts to the baby Jesus. Well, St. Nicholas shares that love still today. Do you want to eat breakfast first or open presents?"

Both Andy and Cathy screamed together, "Open presents!"

The adults, including Roy who considered himself too grown up to be excited about presents, sat together around the hearth. Thomas added logs to the fire and took a seat there.

"Well, children, let's see what St. Nick decided to bring you."

Cathy tried with great care to untie the ribbon that held the wrapping paper around the box in her lap. That was not the case with Andy. He yanked the ribbon off the package, letting it slip to the floor. Then he ripped through the paper. He found a copy of a 1st level reader, like the books he'd seen in school.

"I guess that fella knowed what I needed."

"Keep looking, Andy. St. Nick always brings something we need and also something we want." Cathy squealed with delight when she removed the paper from the box holding the porcelain doll with brown banana curls. She was in awe of the doll that looked very much as she did. The doll wore a pretty green gingham dress covered with a bright pinafore. "Gracious, Mrs. Mac. I've never had a real store-bought doll like this. She's wonderful."

Andy looked at the doll and shook his head. "This St. Nicholas must a pretty rich man to bring such fine things."

"Go ahead, Andy. Look to see if there is something else for you." Mac urged him on.

He picked up a second small package. "I don't think this one is for me. See, the name don't match."

"You're a smart boy. See this one says Roy."

"Here, Roy. Looks like St. Nick didn't think you are too grown up." Everyone in the room laughed at Andy's gentle gibe at his new brother.

"What a fine knife. Thank you, Mr. Mac. I've been wanting a new whittlin' knife, ever since I lost my old one in the creek."

"Are there more?"

"Oh, yes, ma'am. There's lots left." Roy picked up bundle after bundle, handed them to Cathy who read the names and gave them to Andy to pass out. When they finished, Cathy had two more, Roy had two more, and Andy had two more. Even the adults had a gift apiece to open on that first day of the new year.

When Andy opened his last bundle, he stopped mid-way. His mouth fell open, and his eyes popped as he saw the new hat nestled in the paper. "OHHHH, my goodness! Surely, this ain't for me. I never saw a finer hat...Mr. Mac, I mean, Papa. It's 'xactly like yours!"

"Yes, Andrew. It's made like mine, except a bit smaller. See here on the hat band? The golden clasp has the letter M. It is our initial, Andrew and Patrick MacLayne."

"Oh golly, goodness! I love Christmas. I can't believe such a wonderful day has been ever year, and I never had it before. Now I got me a new shirt, a fine readin' book, and a brand-new hat! Ain't this the best time ever?"

Laurel walked over and picked the boy up. She carried him to her rocking chair. "Andy, Christmas is the best time of the year. Every year to remember Jesus' birthday, families come together to share. It's because we love each other that we have such a wonderful time. Our Christmas has been very special this year because you are here to be a part of our family."

Mac watched as Laurel told the young boy how he blessed their family, and he smiled. Laurel had done exactly what he'd hoped and prayed she would. Of course, he'd had little doubt she would. Still, he was grateful for her loving nature.

The packages were soon opened, and the children rushed around to clear the room of the strips of paper and ribbon they'd torn from their gifts. Mac reached out and took Laurel's hand and pulled her to her feet. "Thank you, wife. You've made me a happy man once again. Seems you do it every day."

"This has been a fine holiday, even if we did celebrate it a week late. This has been a real family holiday, like the one I'd dreamed we'd have. My only regret is that I didn't give you a healthy son. I made another pair of booties that I wanted to give you this year, but I guess it's not time yet." Mac saw tears in Laurel's eyes. He tilted her head up so her eyes met his.

"Laurel Grace, you've given me a home. That is what I wanted and needed. In His time, the Lord will give us another child. I know he will." He kissed her. "Thank you for this wonderful holiday."

About noon, Laurel's Campbell family arrived. They feasted on the fat goose Mac had found, along with a large array of holiday dishes, including steaming cups of wassail at the close of the day. Laurel's uncle Matthew led them in singing every Christmas carol they knew. Mac's Pa closed the day's festivities by reading the version of the Christmas story from Luke, Chapter 2.

After the Campbells and Susan's family departed, Laurel gathered the rest of her family around the fireplace. She recited for them Dicken's ghostly Christmas tale she'd read while she and Mac were in Little Rock.

"Do you think everyone in Arkansas has a Christmas as fine as this one?" Andy asked.

"Well, I don't know, Andy. But the only thing people need to make Christmas time wonderful is to be with the people they love. That's why we've had such a fine holiday."

"Well, anyway, I'm real glad to be here in Arkansas with y'all. I'm sure they ain't nothing half this good in Tennessee." Again, the MacLayne family laughed at his surprising remarks.

"Son, I'm glad you are here in Arkansas, too, but I'm sure most of the good folks in Tennessee have fine Christmases too. You kids need to think about calling it a night. Tomorrow, we'll have lots to do."

"Yes, Pa. Goodnight, Granddaddy." Andy walked over to Laurel and motioned for her to bend down so he could whisper to her. "Is it all right to say I love y'all yet?"

"Of course, it is." He turned around and put his hand in Laurel's.

"I had a grand day! Thanks so much, and...well... I just want..." He lowered his too blue eyes and whispered, "I love all y'all." Then he shuffled across the room to the loft where he would sleep with this grandfather in Cathy's loft bed.

That night as they lay in the tall bed, Laurel and Mac spoke of the wonderful holiday they had with their family.

"The past two days couldn't have been any better, Mac. I was hoping we'd have exactly this kind of family holiday. Even our late celebration was wonderful. You enjoyed the time, didn't you?"

"How could I not have? To have my father here and Andy. I've been with my excellent wife and fine Dunn children—now our children—to have my best friend and his family to share the time. Nothing could have made the holiday more perfect." Mac then realized what he had said. "That was thoughtless of me, Laurel. I wasn't thinking. I'm sure you missed your own pa and our son."

"No, Mac, I understand what you were saying. You weren't slighting others. I know you too well to think that. You're like me, sort of overwhelmed by the blessings we've seen since we got home."

"I am happy, Laurel. This cabin has become a real home. We laughed and shared our stories and our gifts. We worshipped together, and we played together. Everyone is safe and warm and well-fed. You have given me all that, Laurel. The time we spent having our late Christmas far outshined any dream I ever had for the life we would share here."

"I am happy, then. Mac, how long can you stay home before you have to go back to Little Rock?"

"Speaker Oates told us we would reconvene on the 17th, so I've figured that I can stay at least until the 10th."

"Can you get back to Little Rock in only a week?"

"Yes. I've decided to go across country, Midnight and me."

"Mac, it's the worst time of year. I'm not sure I like the idea of you riding across the state alone in the dead of winter."

"I've considered the good and bad of it. In my buckskins and taking only the most necessary clothes and such, it's the best way. The route is direct. I won't have so much boggy land to deal with. There are settlements where I can get shelter during the night. I think I can ride to the capital in five days if the weather stays good."

"Mac, this time of year the weather is so unpredictable!"

"Laurel...All things work for good..."

"I know."

"I want to spend as much time as I can with you and the kids. If I go any other way I will have to leave by the end of the week."

"I won't argue. I can see you've already made up your mind."

"I know how to take care of myself, wife. What I don't know is how I will survive without you in Little Rock. I'm rather spoiled having all your attention for those two months. I know the days were long for you, and you didn't enjoy the trip as much as I did, but our political adventure is a time I'll never forget, wife. We shared so many experiences. We'd never done those things here at Shiloh."

"That part of the journey, I did enjoy. Where will you stay when you get back to Little Rock?"

"I hope the Scotts will have room for me. Anyway, if you will write to me there, I'll pick up letters, even if I have to board somewhere else. I hope you will write. I'll be less lonely if you do."

"I will."

"Now come over and let me love you, wife."

Mac made excellent use of the nine days he had at home. Every day he worked with his herd and made small repairs and improvements around the homestead. Mac also worked with John and Roy who would once again take over the homestead when he had gone. The evenings, he spent time with his family. He began to build strong ties with his son. Each night they would spend a time sitting together before the fire playing checkers. Andy was quick to learn the game, and he thrived in the attention of his father. After supper, Mac took the slight boy into his lap and held him as he read the Scripture. At 8:30. the children climbed to the loft to sleep. The extra cot made the space very crowded, but Mac promised to remedy that problem in the spring.

By nine, Laurel and Mac would retire to the privacy of their own room. They safeguarded the little time they had to spend together. The fire in their fireplace provided a comfortable, romantic place for them to share the few nights they had left to them. Mac's return to the capital on the tenth of January would separate them for an unknown time.

On the day before Mac had to leave, he told Laurel he wanted to return to Eden. "I want to visit Campbell before I leave for Little Rock." Mac, Laurel, and the two children drove the short distance to the glade the next morning. The sight was a stark contrast to the lush green of the spring afternoon they'd laid the baby to rest in Eden. When they reached the knoll, Mac helped Laurel and Cathy down from the wagon seat. Andy jumped from the wagon bed.

"Papa, why did we come here?"

"Here, take my hand and come with me." Mac and Laurel walked together the short distance. Within a few minutes, the MacLaynes stood before the tiny granite cross where their baby lay. Laurel placed a holly and cedar bouquet tied with a red ribbon at the grave. Mac took her in his arms as her silent tears fell.

"We were so happy this time last year, Mac. Remember it was Christmas morning I gave you those tiny booties. I am so sorry I didn't give you a healthy child." Mac wiped the tears from her face.

"In time, Laurel. I am not afraid."

*I am....*Laurel pushed the negative thoughts away. She would not bring darkness on Mac's last afternoon at home. She looked into his eyes and smiled.

"He already has. He brought us Cathy and Andy." Laurel brushed Mac's hair back and walked over to Andy.

"Papa, why did we come here?"

"Hush yourself up, Andy. Jerking on his arm, Cathy hurried to silence him.

"It's alright, Cathy." Laurel patted her check. "Andy, this is Campbell, our little son here under this great oak tree. Jesus is keeping him for us in heaven. We stopped here to say Merry Christmas and that we love him."

"Is that why you are sad, Mama?" Andy patted her hand. She hugged him and ruffled his hair as she'd seen Mac do so many times in the week they'd been home.

Mac, Laurel and the two children knelt at the foot of the tiny grave. Mac spoke, "Lord, we grieve the loss of our baby, and we know sad things happen. Even in our sadness, we thank you for the love that created this precious son. We praise You for Your goodness to us, that we are healthy and comfortable and safe. We enjoyed our family celebrating Your birth this year. Thank You for the love we have found here at Shiloh. Bless all our family and friends through the year, and Lord, please keep my family safe while I'm gone. Amen."

# CHAPTER TWENTY-THREE

*Every man's work shall be made manifest for the day shall declare it, because it shall be revealed by fire; and fire shall try every man's work of what sort it is. If any man's work abides, which he hath built upon, he shall receive a reward.*

*I Corinthians 3:13-14*

January 10, 1859, was a mild, sunny day in Arkansas. Laurel almost felt ashamed of the fear she'd felt since Mac said he would ride across country back to Little Rock. More time reading the Psalms would have been a better use of her time. Yet, she couldn't help but remember the words of Mrs. Gert, the wisest woman in the Shiloh congregation. Only the day before, the dear old woman had bemoaned the terrible winter yet to come. Every weather sign she knew had pointed to it. She told of the spoon shape in the persimmon seed. She also said her husband had brought home a rabbit on Wednesday with the thickest fur she'd ever seen. Laurel's Aunt Ellie showed them a yam with skin so tough she needed a knife to pierce it. Worst of all, the previous night, Laurel herself heard a screech owl crying like a lost woman.

"Ain't no doubt about it. We got us a monstrous storm a-comin'."

Mrs. Gert warned all who would listen. "Y'all need to prepare for a blizzard, the worst I ever seen."

Laurel pushed the negative thoughts away. That morning as she prepared to say goodbye to Mac, she felt the dread more than she wanted to admit.

"Well, my dearest, I guess I'd best make way. I hate to go and leave you here." Mac walked across the room to have one final embrace, one last kiss. Dressed in his buckskin as he was, he seemed so much bigger… so different, almost invincible. She prayed his wilderness clothes would keep him safe and warm until he was back in their home again.

"What, woman? Have you no farewell for your lover, your mate? Do ya not have one more kiss for a man who wants to carry you off across his saddle so he won't have to face the next long weeks alone?"

"Mac, you've forgotten we're not alone." Before the words were out of her mouth, three others hurried from the loft to say their goodbyes.

"Kids, you'll do as your mama tells you, and don't let her overdo while I'm away." Mac picked up Andy and brought him up to meet his eyes. "Andy, son, I'm glad we have you with us. I expect you to mind your mama, just as you would me. Be a good boy. I'll be home as soon as I can."

Mac picked up his overstuffed saddlebags and placed his Bible inside his coat. He opened the door, walked to the porch, and set Andy in his rocking chair. Cathy and Roy followed. Then Laurel came out to the porch. Her blue shawl draped her shoulders, and her curls tumbled down her back. Mac pulled her into another embrace and sank his face into her hair. He inhaled deeply and whispered, "Dearest wife, at this moment, I have no want to go, only to carry you back to our tall bed and make love to you all day. You are so much a part of me, I can't think of being parted from you. Please take care of yourself. Know I love you." He drew her into a kiss, so stirring, so tender, so intense that tears ran unchecked down Laurel's face.

"Mac, please take care to get home safely, as soon as you can. I love you."

He threw the saddlebags across Midnight's rump. He mounted the tall horse and rode away. As he reached the road, he turned to look at his family one last time. The image he saw he'd carry with him until he could be home again. Hand in hand with Andy, Cathy waved her hand high above her head. Roy sat on the porch rail, his hand sheltering his eyes from the light of the rising sun. At the center of this image was Laurel, curls askew and her cheeks touched with tears. She'd touched her fingertips to lips and lifted her hand above their family for one last farewell. Mac turned and rode toward the west.

As Mac rode beyond their view, Laurel looked at his family and ushered them inside. "Kids, we have a new day to start." The first three days were beautiful…mild and sunny. During the daytime, Laurel enjoyed being at home where she had things to keep her busy. From time to time, she'd stop and wonder where Mac was and how far he had travelled toward the capital. Often, she whispered a prayer of gratitude that Mrs. Gert's forecast of a winter storm proved wrong. Mac would not be in much danger if the weather stayed as nice as that second week of January had been.

Laurel found that falling back into a familiar routine did not take long. All day, she had many tasks to occupy her time. Only at night, when she went to her tall four-poster did she find time lay heavy. She wasn't able to sleep without Mac beside her. In her sleeplessness, she found herself brooding about Mac's wellbeing, fearing he'd not been able to find shelter for the night. After three wakeful nights, she went to her knees and turned her fears to prayer. That night she slept. When she awoke, she scolded herself for her lack of faith. "Laurel Grace, you know better. The Lord sent Mac to serve. He will take care of him. Romans 8:28...Mac believes it with all his being. Time for you to take heed, woman!"

The weather was beautiful the entire week. On Friday, Laurel found herself drawn outside into the fresh air and sunshine. She decided to ride. Sassy seldom got much of a workout in the winter, so a ride would do them both good. She called to Cathy who stood on the porch, saying that she'd be gone a while, but she'd return long before dinner.

Laurel flapped the reins, and Sassy trotted down the road toward Shiloh church for no particular reason. The entire time, Laurel found herself thinking about Mac. He must be near Little Rock after five days.

The farther south he went, the less likely he'd get caught in a bad winter storm. Yes, he was all right, but she missed him.

"Great day for a ride, niece." Her uncle Matthew called out from the porch of Shiloh church as she rode into the churchyard.

"It is that, Uncle Matthew."

"Come on in and sit a spell with me. Tell me how things are going." They walked into the sturdy log church. "You and the kids making it okay at home?"

"Of course, we are. You know we'd already laid out the stores we'd need for the winter. The day is too pretty to stay inside."

"Yes, the weather is nice. Somewhat of a surprise for this time of year."

"I'm so grateful for Mac's sake. I didn't want him to ride across country, but he wouldn't listen. He said it was the shortest and fastest way. I thought he'd have a bad time, but I fretted for nothing."

"All fretting is for naught, niece. You know that."

"I do, uncle. I remembered this morning."

"Do you wish you had gone back with him?"

"No. I didn't like the idleness I had in Little Rock. Mac had work to do, but I invented things to keep me busy. I'm better here, but I miss Mac. If we'd known the winter would be so mild, we could have had a couple more months of school this year. I have plenty of time to teach this term with Mac gone."

"Don't count 'old man winter' out just yet, Laurel Grace. You know how fickle Arkansas weather can be. I'm not sure the jonquils are ready to bloom yet."

"Did you have a chance to talk to Mac much about our time in Little Rock?"

"A few things in passing. He wanted to spend time with y'all more than he wanted to talk politics with me. He did seem pleased that they'd made the recommendations he'd asked for. He seemed to think the new bill could mean more attention for our part of the state. If the bills pass, we may get a few road improvements and put a stop to the illegal land deals going on around here."

"He worked very hard on those bills. A few senators and one or two representatives weren't happy with his influence on the appropriations committee. I know he loved the work he did in the legislature, but he didn't seem to have much of a heart to leave on Monday. He's torn between his work in the legislature and our family."

"I know that's true. Mac will do his duty, no matter what. He told me Sunday he dreaded spending so much time apart from you. He's smitten, niece. Every time I see him, he has fallen more under your spell."

"Uncle Matthew...you know that's not so."

"It is, niece. You forget that I knew him when he swore that no woman would ever own his heart. Both of you must have forgotten that silly notion of a marriage of convenience."

"I admit, there is nothing convenient about a marriage when the person you love is so far away. A part of me is gone."

"How do you feel about raising Mac's son in your home?"

"He's a sweet boy, and he needs a family to care for him. He's fitting in fine."

"And how do you feel about raising Mac's son in your home?"

"He's Patrick's child. He loves the boy. How could I love Mac and not accept his son? Andy will always be a welcome part of our family. Anyway, he may be the only heir Mac will have."

"Laurel Grace, you don't know that."

"No, but I haven't had any sign of giving him another child."

"Don't lose your faith, darlin'. It's not quite been a year since your accident. We'll keep praying."

"I'll try, Uncle Matt. I'd better head back home. I told the kids I'd be back long before dinner."

MAC'S PREDICTION had been accurate. He had ridden to Little Rock in about five and a half days. Thanks to Midnight and the extraordinary weather, this winter trip was the easiest one to date. Mac returned to the Stone's boarding house and asked for a room for the reminder of the legislative session. The Stones welcomed him back but weren't able to give him the bright room he'd shared with Laurel. After he had unpacked, he still had a day and a half to prepare to return to work.

The next day, Mac walked the short distance to talk with William Woodruff at the Gazette. Laurel had spoken so highly of the pioneer of Arkansas journalism, he wanted to make his acquaintance, too. Besides, he promised to deliver another of Laurel's stories about traveling across Arkansas. As he entered the newspaper office, he met two representatives from the Delta region.

"Mornin' MacLayne. Did you have a nice holiday?"

"Yes. Good to be home with the family. Travel made the recess pretty short."

"I'd thought maybe you and the Mrs. stayed in the capital for the holiday."

"We wanted to be with the children. Besides, Mrs. MacLayne wanted to return to the homestead."

"I guess I misunderstood. Someone told me you were newlyweds. Of course, I thought that may be an error. Your wife's not exactly a filly. I didn't realize you'd married a widow."

Mac bristled. A furrow appeared across his forehead. His face turned to stone. "People often talk about things they know nothing about. Excuse me, gentlemen. I have business with Mr. Woodruff."

"Meant no offense, MacLayne. I heard you and a few of the fellows got those recommendations to the appropriation report sent up for a vote before adjournment. You know a couple of them can't make it to the Senate, don't you?"

"I was under the impression that debate on those bills won't start until the house is called back into session on the seventeenth. Good day." He turned and walked to the counter as his colleagues left the building.

"I overheard your conversation, Mr. MacLayne. One of the hazards of being a professional journalist…can't seem to keep my ears out of other folks' conversations. I'm William Woodruff."

"I won't introduce myself since you already seem to know who I am."

"I had the pleasure of knowing your comely wife during the first part of the legislative session in the fall. I'm sorry she didn't return. I enjoyed our talks. She has quite a hand with writing, too. I printed one of her stories about your trip across Arkansas. She promised me more."

"That is why I came." Mac pulled several sheets of folded paper from his coat pocket. "Laurel asked me to give you this. It's her second story. She'll mail more if you want them."

"Indeed, I do. Please give her this for her work." Mr. Woodruff handed Mac coins worth two dollars. "I will pay for any stories she wants to send me."

"She didn't do it for pay."

"Any craftsman is worth his wages...or hers." Mac and Woodruff talked for some time, and Mac learned why Laurel like Woodruff as much as she did. They didn't agree on everything, but the old journalist was straightforward with his opinions. He allowed his company the same liberty.

"I'll head back to the boardinghouse for dinner now. I'm glad we met."

"Before you go, MacLayne. Watch those men and their faction. They are not too friendly to 'renegades' who want to change things here in the capital. The schism scares too many people in power. Fear causes men to do stupid things."

"Thank you for your warning, sir. I'll be watchful."

"Share that warning with those you know in the House of Representatives who share your mind."

Mac walked back to the Stones' with much more on his mind than when he left.

THE FOLLOWING MONDAY, Laurel awoke earlier than usual. Something had changed, but she couldn't decide what it was. The fire had burned low over night, as it usually did, but outside the warmth of the tall bed, the room was much colder than she'd expected. She immediately rose and pulled her wool shawl around her. She found the main room frigid. She went to the back porch for firewood and realized that overnight the pleasant winter disappeared and left bitter cold in its place. Three inches of water in the bucket sitting on the porch had frozen solid overnight. Laurel returned to build a fire to warm the cabin before the children got up. She didn't want them to have to dress in a cold house.

At first, she wasn't too concerned. After all, it was January. She assumed Mac reached Little Rock over the weekend because the legislature was schedule to reconvene that morning. She returned to her Monday routine, preparing breakfast and sorting laundry for the day's wash. Yet when she went outside to start a fire under her black wash kettle, the temperature had fallen even more. As she was about to return to the cabin, she saw her father-in-law ride into the yard.

"Gracious, Laurel, whatever are you doing outside on this miserable day?"

"Thinking about starting the washing, but I decided to wait. It's too cold. I'm sure it'll be warmer if I wait a day or two. Come on in, and I'll make you some hot coffee."

"That'd be welcome. I'm going to put Tartan in the barn in out of this bitter wind."

They sat at the table. The kids ate their oatmeal and hot biscuits while her father-in-law drank coffee. "Laurel, this change in the weather is strange. Does it happen like this here every winter?"

"Well, Arkansas weather changes often, but this drastic fall in temperature is not usual."

"I wanted to come over and check on y'all when I realized we may be in for a winter storm. Where is Mac's herd pastured right now?"

"The herd? Well, they are in the south pasture. Do you think we should move them?"

"It may be hard to feed them if we should get a big snow that didn't melt off for a few days. Cold as it is, snow won't melt."

"Do you think we are in for a snow, Pa?

"I don't know Arkansas weather, but at home in Maryland, a huge change like this one would put me on alert. We need to move the livestock into the corral by the barn, just to be on the safe side."

"We'll do whatever you think is best."

"Well, kids, let's get our chores done. Cold as it is outside, we'll have to work fast and take breaks to warm ourselves when we get too chilled.

Andy, you and Cathy go fill the wood boxes on both porches. When that's done come warm yourselves. Then come back and stack firewood on the front porch up to the window sills."

"Yes, Granddaddy. We'll get our coats and scarves."

"Good lass, Cathy. Roy, go saddle your horse and let's move that herd from the south pasture. I'll feel better when I can watch over them."

"Yes, sir...John will be here in about an hour. Shouldn't take us no time to get 'em up here. We're used to moving 'em for better forage."

"I'll help you boys. Laurel, would you mind if I come over here to stay for a few days until we see what the weather will do?"

"You know you're always welcome here, Pa."

"After we get the cattle moved, I'll go back to the widow's and bring my animals over here."

"I'll be glad to have your company. The house seems pretty empty since Mac left last week. Bring any extra quilts and blankets you have, in case we need them."

The day was busy. Everyone came to the cabin often to warm themselves.

"Goodness, Mama. I don't think it ever got this cold in Tennessee. My fingers are plum blue!"

"Here, let me see." Laurel rubbed the cold hands of the six-year-old. "Goodness, Andy, your hands are very cold. Here let's sit by the fire a while and warm them. What about your toes? Are they blue too?"

"Ain't looked, but I got me two pairs of socks, so they don't feel too cold."

"Let's take off your boots and see." Andy pushed off his boots and striped off the two layers of socks. Thankfully, his feet were dry and warm. Regardless, Laurel decided the younger children had worked enough for one day. "You and Cathy stay inside where it's warm the rest of the day. I can't let you get frostbite. We may not be able to get to the doctor."

At noon, John, Roy and her father-in-law came to the cabin. They had rounded up and moved all twenty-two head of beef Mac had brought from Missouri. The three of them were chilled to the bone.

Laurel took their heavy coats and scarves and told them to sit next to the fire. She served up hot soup and bread as they warmed themselves.

"Laurel, the temperature is still falling. This time yesterday, we were out in shirt sleeves, and today our heaviest coats can't warm us enough in this bitter wind." It's coming straight out of the north. We may be in for a few days of real misery if things don't change."

"We'll do what we have to. When you and the boys get warm, go get your livestock and anything you need to stay the duration. We'll do better together."

To his relief, his daughter-in-law wanted him to stay. By nightfall, the family was back inside together, ready to deal with what would come. The cold continued and the bitter North winds blew hard through the night, but luckily, at least for a time, it was dry. Snow didn't come. Neither did the sleet nor freezing rain that had led to the ice storm of '57, a storm so frightening and deadly.

The following three days were copies of that horribly cold Monday. Roy and Thomas MacLayne did the outdoor chores as they had to be done, but John did not come to work. The cold was too dangerous for long trips across the county. The extreme weather confined the members of the Shiloh community to their homes.

Laurel decided to start daily lessons with Cathy and Andy. School was the perfect way to occupy them while they were shut in all day. Cathy loved the idea because she enjoyed school and had become a very good student. Andy didn't find the idea so appealing.

"Come over to the table, you two, and let's get our lesson done."

"Mama, I don't want to have school at home. I don't like them books and slates and all that stuff. Let Cathy play school with you. I'll set here by the fire and whittle."

"Andy, Mama don't play school. She's a real teacher...a good one."

"Andy, you were in school before Christmas with Miss Elizabeth. Didn't you do lessons with her?" Laurel laid her hand on his head.

"Not when I could help it. I learned to write my name, and I can copy letters, but I ain't no good at book learning. I don't need no more schooling."

"I am afraid your papa would disagree with you, Andy. He sets a high value on learning. You know he went to the college at Annapolis where they train officers for the navy." Thomas took on his grandfatherly role.

Andy's mouth dropped and his eyes grew the size of a small plum. "He did? He ain't in the navy."

"True, but he is proud of his education. It's allowed him to serve as a legislator in our state government. You don't want him disappointed that his son refused to learn to read, write, and figure, do you?"

"No, Granddaddy, but Mama, I ain't no good at it. I tried to read once, and it was too blame hard. All them kids at school laughed."

"That's not a problem at home. We'll start again. I can teach you to read, and when your papa comes home, you can read to him. He'll be so proud of you for learning."

"I'll try, but I don't know if I'm smart enough."

"You are very bright, Andy, and when school starts back in the spring, you'll be caught up. The kids won't have anything to laugh about."

Andy shrugged his shoulders, knowing he could not win the argument, but a frown showed on his face...not a smile.

"Andrew," Thomas spoke in a stern voice to his six-year-old grandson.

"Yes, sir."

"Your name is Andy MacLayne. All MacLaynes value reading, ciphering, and writing. You are a smart boy. If you work hard with your mama, you'll learn to love these things too. Do you understand me, boy?"

"You think I'm smart, Granddaddy?"

"I know you are. The only thing I wonder is whether you'll work hard enough to learn."

"Oh, yes, sir. You think I'm smart? I'll work so hard. If you want me to learn, I can. I want my papa to be proud of me." Andy rushed to the table and sat next to Cathy. "Hey, Cathy, my granddaddy thinks I'm smart, did you hear him say that?"

"Shhhh. It's time to listen to Mama teach us."

"Okay, Mama. I want to learn everything Papa wants me to know." Laurel smiled at the conquest.

Snow began to fall on the third day. The flakes were small and dense because of the brutal cold. When Thomas or Laurel had to go outside, they felt the sting of the grainy snow driven by the gale force winds. Because the snow was so dense, it didn't cover the ground quickly. The grainy snow was a blessing. It didn't stick to the tree limbs or branches. The cold produced snow so hard, almost crystalline, that it didn't cause the damage of a full-blown ice storm.

However, the snow continued to fall. The next day temperatures rose a few degrees, and as the temperature rose slightly, the snow gradually turned to big, fluffy flakes. Then the snow covered the area around Crowley's Ridge with a blanket of pristine white. When Thomas went out to feed the livestock and milk the cows, he had to break the way through snow six inches deep. The cattle in the corral had huddled on the south side of the barn to shelter from the harsh wind. He realized if an ice storm came, there would be no place to shelter the herd. The barn was packed full with three saddle horses, a pair of draft horses, two jacks and three milk cows. Mac had not built any kind of lean-to or shed to shelter his herd. Thomas knew that he and Roy would spend the day wrangling the herd so they would move enough to warm their bodies. Lord willing, the snow would be gone in a few days. As the day wore on, the temperatures did rise a bit, and the harsh north wind calmed. Compared to the previous three days, the weather seemed almost balmy, but no water dripped from the icicles hanging around the porch.

In the afternoon, the kids, including Roy, came to ask Laurel if they could go out to play in the snow. Laurel shook her head and laughed. "You've been out in that cold, wet mess several times today. Haven't you had enough?"

"That was work. We want to go out and play. We'll make snow angels and have a snowball war. It'll be so fun!"

"If you want to go, Cathy, I guess it'd be all right, but don't stay out until you get chilled."

Andy walked over and took her hand. "You come too. Come out and play with us." She looked down at the small image of her husband. He wanted her to come out and play with him. How long had it been since she'd played in the snow? Half her life? No, much more.

"Oh, yes, Mama! Please come out and play with us." Cathy took her other hand, and they pulled her toward the front door.

"All right, but we'll only stay a short while. Let me get a coat. Cathy, get Roy's and Andy's scarves and yours." For the next hour, the four ran through the new snow, pelting each other with snowballs. After their war, they rolled three large balls of snow to build a six-foot-tall snowman. They stood him next to a tall fir at the edge of the yard. "Kids, we need to go in. Frostbite is very painful, and I am very cold."

"Oh, please, Mama. We haven't made snow angels yet. Let's make them right here next to the snowman. Let's make one for each of us, and another one for Papa. It'll be our snow family."

"We'll have to make one for grandaddy, too."

"Okay, but let's hurry. We need to get in out of the cold. It's lesson time anyway." In turn, each of them stretched out in the fresh snow and waved their arms back and forth while they spread their legs in and out. Their erratic movement created four beautiful angels in the snow, and then Roy made two more. The six angels lay next to each other in the snowdrift. Laurel and the children laughed and clapped their almost frozen hands. Such a sight their snow angel family made next to their fine tall snowman.

"Come on, now. Let's go in and get warm! Now." They broke a new path to the cabin, just because they could. In high spirits, they entered the cabin and rushed to the fireplace. No sooner than they closed the door than Thomas MacLayne came in behind them.

"Beautiful afternoon. Warmer and the sun is trying to shine...good sign." Thomas beat his arms around his chest to warm them.

"Pa, where have you been?"

"Rousing the herd. They are doing a good job of breaking up the snow in the corral. If things hold, we'll see some ground by this time tomorrow."

"That'd be a welcome sight."

"You're all wet, Daughter. What happened to you?"

"I only went back to my youth is all. We've been playing in the snow.

Come look!" Laurel led her father-in-law to the window. "See our snow family? Mac and you are next to our tall snowman, and there we are, four more angels."

"Very impressive, but I'd say get into some dry clothes before you all get sick. I'm not much of a nurse." Again, everyone laughed. Even this cold winter day had been an almost perfect family day. Only Mac was not home to enjoy it.

# CHAPTER TWENTY-FOUR

*And thou shalt take no gift: for the gift blindeth the wise, and perverteth the words of the righteous.*
*Exodus 23: 8*

Following the call to order in the house, the first few days were busy ones. Speaker Oates, who was ill during the Christmas recess, asked for quick action. While he pushed the legislators to finish the work of the twelfth Legislative Assembly, he stressed the importance of working with integrity and wisdom for the good of the people. Debate on the bills from the fall session began in earnest, and in short measure, loyalty lines formed. Mac felt the tension build even before the end of the first week. Some things, like support for a railroad and money for swamp abatement, passed without rancor and in record time. However, when a discussion arose as to who and where to build these improvements across the state, debate became heated.

Before the end of the second week, Mac found himself in the middle of a dispute caused by the apportionment bill he'd sponsored earlier. The recommendation was four-fold. Land speculators found guilty of defrauding settlers would face jail terms. Next, they must repay all funds taken from the victims and pay fines to cover costs. Finally, their licenses to do business in the state would be permanently rescinded. Mac couldn't imagine anyone would question the committee's decision. When the bill was read, such an uproar came from the floor of the state house, Oates was forced to ask the bailiff to help him regain order.

"Will the chairman come before the body and explain this recommendation before the debate begins?" Speaker Oates requested. The chairman was absent, so Mac stood to take his place as he was the recorder for the committee. He'd been the one who had actually pushed the bill through on those last days before adjournment.

"Mr. Speaker and members of the House, the Committee on Apportionments debated the provisions of this bill for several days. In many parts of our state, mine being one, this is one of three issues the people asked us to consider. Far too many honest homesteaders are being robbed of all hope they'll ever own land. Dishonest land agents are selling deeds to land they have no right to sell. We want the victims compensated and the dishonest men stopped from plying their illegal scams on others. This bill will do those things. We urge approval of this bill."

"Mr. MacLayne, what about the honest bankers who sell these properties in error?" A representative asked.

"The law describes legal land transfer. There is no reason for anyone to sell land they can't prove they own. We do a fair job in this state of keeping land records, even if we fall short in some other ways," Mac replied.

"Anyone can lose a deed," another planter spoke up.

"The counties have tax records and also keep files of deeds and wills."

"The penalty is too harsh," A representative for the central area yelled. Speaker Oates banged his gavel.

"Sir, a prison term is a far cry from having a family's entire future stolen from them to enrich some charlatan." Mac turned and looked across the body he'd addressed. His voice was calm and professional, but the glower on his face was more than adamant.

"Where is all this illegal land stealing going on anyway? I ain't heard about it happening in my region," another opponent spoke.

"Where might that be?" The delegate lived in the delta.

Speaker Oates called for a response from the body. "How many representatives here are concerned about this issue before the house? Stand up." When the legislators rose, nearly half supported Mac and the committee's recommendation. By observation, Mac realized the highland part of the state was most impacted. The delta seemed unconcerned.

Mac spoke, "I believe this bill is important, and we need to vote on it. Also, after seeing the division on this question, the body may consider an investigation as to why this seems to be a problem only in the highlands. Some of our richest land is in the delta. You'd assume the land dealers would have no difficulty selling that land."

The assembly broke into an uproar again. Men yelled back and forth across the room. Name calling, threats, and insults increased. A desk or two was knocked over. "Order…bring this room to order." Oates slammed his gavel on the table several times. "Bailiff, bring this room to order. Go bring the police if need be."

The noise gradually subsided, and the legislators returned to their seats.

"Mr. MacLayne, do you have anything to add?"

"Only this. The bill was cleared for a vote. I say let's vote. If enough people don't like the bill, let them vote it out." Mac returned to his seat.

"So be it. We will adjourn for dinner. At 1:30, this house will vote on the apportionment bill concerning illegal land sales." The gavel fell again.

Mac walked over to his colleague Quinton Mason. "Did you ever think our bill would cause this much conflict?"

"Yes. I knew it would because some people are making a lot of money in these land deals. The people behind the land agents are the ones getting rich. Be careful, Mac. You're new at this game."

Mac went to the cloakroom and picked up his coat and hat and started for the Stones' for a noon meal. He approached the corner of the street near his boardinghouse when two familiar men stopped him.

"Hey, MacLayne. We'd like a word with you. Do you have a minute?"

He turned and saw two fellow legislators, one he'd met the previous week at the Gazette. He knew the other to be from the southcentral region of the state, although he couldn't remember his name. "Yes, gentlemen. I'll speak with y'all. What can I do for you?"

"The debate got pretty heated this mornin', didn't it?"

"I'm afraid it did. Truthfully, I'm surprised. The bill is fair and honest. I'd think anyone in the state can see it would benefit all parts of Arkansas to get rid of these parasites."

The legislator Mac barely knew clinched his fist, and his face was almost purple.

"Why you smug know-it-all.... I'll..." He raised his fist to strike Mac.

"Hold it, Raymond. Let's talk this out." The second man stepped between Mac and his colleague. "Look, MacLayne. If you remember the other day at the newspaper office, I told you there were a few bills that had to be voted down before they get to the Senate. This is one of those bills."

"Then, you had better go back and vote against it."

"You seem to have some influence in this group, although I can't figure why? You've got no connection with the Family. You sure don't seem to have any money. I think if you go back and recommend a slight change, we can come to an agreement."

"What change?"

"Let's ask to drop the prison sentence. Any land agent found guilty of fraud will have to the repay the price he took for the land. We also need to ask the house to lower the fine to... oh say, ten percent of the price. Let's call it a relocation fee. If we rescind the license to a year, that would be adequate punishment to rescind the licenses for ... oh let's say a year."

"That will make the bill all but useless. I see no benefit in changing anything. Let it stand on its own merit."

"You don't see the whole picture, man. Would two thousand dollars help you see any clearer? Might make life a little easier back on that homestead in Greene County."

"Glasses don't cost that much. Good day." Mac turned to walk the last half block.

The angry man yelled, "You fool. I'm sure you don't need glasses, but what about that little harlot you married over in Hawthorn? She still got her glasses? Or that boy who looks a lot like you, but not a darn thing like your wife? Can he see good?"

Mac turned back toward the men. "Is this some kind of threat? What can all this mean to you?"

"Remember. Some bills don't need to go to the Senate."

Mac stood and looked as they hurried back toward the chamber. He was no longer hungry.

Mac returned to the afternoon session only to find the proceedings to be as hostile and dissentious as those in the morning. When the assembly recessed for the night well after dark, he rushed out. He wanted no part of another confrontation like the one he'd encountered at noon. Besides, he was ravenous, having given up his mid-day meal. After inhaling what Mrs. Stone set aside for his supper, Mac retired to his small room, slumped in a chair, and sat brooding for some time. *Laurel, my dearest, how I want you here tonight. I need your kind spirit and an understanding ear. Why did I not demand you come back with me?*

Then he laughed, long and hard. Just the thought of demanding Laurel do anything brought his humor back. He would write to her tomorrow. He could put the long, difficult day in better perspective after a night's rest.

He wrote the next morning.

*My darlin' wife,*

*Before I go to the House chamber this morning, I had to "talk" to you a while. I am so in need of a good person to share this session with me. I could use a voice of sanity to help me through the nonsense that goes on down here. Can you believe that yesterday we spent more than two hours debating the question of whether we should supply locks and keys for the desks in the Chamber? Two hours! Such a waste of time.*

*Please forgive my grumbling. We did some good work. We passed some new laws to help finance schools. Every county is to have a common school with curriculum adequate to train teachers. We also have worked out some mail schedules to improve mail delivery by using the stage routes where they exist.*

*But then we passed some not so good ones too. The house supported the law to expel all free black people from the state before January 1860.*

*Enough, I just wanted to feel I could share with you. I miss you more than I can tell you. I want to wrap this business up and come home to Shiloh. And Laurel, my dearest life mate, take care that all is well. Ask my pa to remain with you at the homestead until I come home. I fear the workload is too much for you alone. Stay close to home. You know how strange the Arkansas winters can be. It is my prayer to find all of you safe and well when I there. I love you.*

*Until I can hold you again,*

*Patrick*

The letter to his father much briefer and far more serious.

*Dear Pa,*

*Please, safeguard my family at home. Things are tense here. I have reason to think people may be back there, watching. I can't explain now, but talk to Matthew and ask him to help you. Be aware of strangers. I'll write more later.*

*Your son,*

*Patrick*

~

THOMAS'S PREDICTION had been wrong. That night well after midnight, snow began to fall again, and when the MacLaynes woke the next morning, another three inches of snow had fallen. Nine inches or more covered the area, and the snow continued to fall until well past noon. Thomas's creased brow showed his concern. Roy and he had been able to keep the herd up and moving, but now snow was more than knee deep on them. Getting them up to move around would be difficult, and if they lay down in the snow and refused to move about, they could freeze to death if the temperature bottomed out again.

"You look worried, Pa. Are you well?"

"This is the strangest weather, Laurel. I thought sure the snow would be gone in a day or so, but now we've got more than ever. Arkansas is not part of the plains or the Ohio Valley where they get blizzards from November to March. I'm concerned whether the herd can survive more of this. We hadn't planned to shelter them this winter. We could've built a shed, but whoever thought?"

"I'm sure they'll be fine. You've been rousing them several times a day."

"But now the smaller ones can hardly walk. The snow is more than a foot deep in some of the drifts."

"We could put the smaller ones in the barn."

"No room. Let me think..."

After breakfast, Thomas asked Roy to bundle up. They left the cabin to go to the corral. Laurel sat Andy and Cathy at the table to begin their lessons for the day. They'd been busy for less than fifteen minutes when Thomas returned, asking Laurel to forgo the school work for the day. He wanted everyone to help him create a shelter for the herd.

"You see, Laurel, this lean-to is a good storage area for wood and such, but if we move some of the wood to the porches and take what's left and stack it on the north and east sides, we can make a shed for the cattle. I don't know if they'll be room for all twenty, but it will shelter most of them. The barn will block the wind from the west, and the south end will be open. The wood won't stay dry if we use it to build the walls, but we'll have time to move it to the porch when we use up what we've got there."

"Sounds like a good plan, Pa, but are we going to a lot of work unnecessarily?"

"I don't think so, Laurel. Look at that bank of dark clouds. Those are snow clouds. I'm afraid we'll get another round of the white stuff before we can get a shelter up for those animals. Let's get to work. Kids, carry wood to the porch. Fill the wood box again, up to the top and then stack a double row on the front porch, up to the window sills. Laurel, you can help if you want. The job will go faster once we have a good path to the porch."

"I'll try to clear a path for the kids."

"Roy, let's you and me start double stacking this wood as high up as we can make it. Two rows will be sturdier and less likely to fall over if the herd gets restless."

And the family worked together all morning to provide a shelter for Mac's herd, taking only short breaks at the hearth to warm cold hands and faces. Laurel prepared a hot filling dinner. After dinner, the five returned to the task. Cathy, Andy, and Laurel carried split logs, and Thomas and Roy continued to stack the firewood higher and higher within a couple of inches of the roofline of the lean-to. About 3:00, large wet snowflakes began to fall again. By that time, the family had about completed their task. Thomas stretched two ropes across the length of the lean-to where he could tether the animals. Andy and Cathy helped Roy lead the animals out of the snow into the makeshift shed, a dry, protective shelter where they could wait out the next round of the winter storm. Once the animals were tethered inside, Roy and Thomas made quick work of providing hay and water, enough for their evening feeding. Thomas moved the milk cows into the same stall to make room for the bulls Mac had brought from Missouri. They'd done all they could to safeguard his investment. A very tired troop made their way back into the MacLayne cabin. Already, the newest round of snow had filled the snow angels they'd made after the first snow, and the tall snowman had lost about three more inches as the snow continued to build up around him.

The third round of snow lasted just under 24 hours. When it stopped, the entire area around Crowley's Ridge had been covered with a foot to fifteen inches of snow. The snow had isolated the family for more than a week already, and the cold would insure their isolation for a good while longer. However, the MacLaynes were warm, well-fed, and safe in their sturdy cabin.

Further, Mac's herd was protected in their temporary shelter, thanks to Thomas' ingenuity.

Besides keeping up with outside chores, Laurel and Thomas found themselves creating things to keep the younger part of the family engaged. Being cooped up in the cabin for so many days brought on spats and short tempers easily. Laurel insisted the children do their schoolwork each morning. At times, Roy participated. Thomas took to his role as grandparent quite well, and he continued to tell the children of the MacLayne family history. Andy was especially attentive. Thomas retold in detail the story of his father, Patrick MacLayne, who had emigrated from Scotland and become a soldier in the war against England.

"My pa got his name from that Scotsman, didn't he, granddad?'

"Yes, Andy, he did. Patrick was my father's name so I named my son for him, just like your mother named you in honor of her father. That's pretty common in lots of families."

January came to an end before the sun melted enough snow to make travel safe. Before they could go anywhere, Laurel had used every activity and game she'd ever known as a girl in an attempt to occupy Andy and Cathy. She'd taught them the Hens and Fox game using her buttons from the button jar. Thomas taught Andy and Roy to make patterns with string. Andy became very frustrated because he couldn't get his Jacob's Ladder to work, but he delighted in beating his grandfather in a nightly checkers match. "Mama, when Papa gets home from the capital, I'm gonna let him win the first game, but after that, he'll have to watch out! He'll have a hard time taking a game from me."

"You've gotten pretty good at that game."

"Mama, when is Papa coming home? He's been gone forever," Cathy spoke up. Laurel thought the same thing. She kept herself occupied during the day, but at night when the house was quiet and Laurel lay in the four-poster alone, time lay heavily on her mind.

"Soon, darlin'. Very soon, I hope."

She knew soon was not the truth, but she smiled as she returned to her sewing. She was restless. If only there were a letter, but in the terrible weather, mail delivery would be delayed for weeks. She missed contact with Mac. She told herself he was well and busy in Little Rock, but if she only knew.

After they'd provided shelter for the herd, the workload at the homestead lessened considerably. Thomas and Roy would go out a couple of times a day to rouse the cattle and let them wander around the corral a while. They took care of all the outside chores, morning and evening. Laurel's workload was reduced to meals and indoor tasks; nevertheless, nevertheless, by mid-afternoon she found herself worn out. Some afternoons, she would drift off to sleep, sitting in her chair near the fire while reading or darning. Whenever that happened, Cathy would shush the boys and make them leave the room. A time or two, Cathy let her sleep into the late afternoon, and she prepared supper so Laurel could finish her nap.

One Saturday, Laurel sat down about 1:30 to read her Bible for a while, and within five minutes, she had fallen asleep. Cathy took a quilt, covered her mama, and tiptoed from the room. Mid-afternoon, Laurel awoke from her nap when her father-in-law came in the back door.

"Goodness me. What time is it? I hadn't planned on dozing off."

"Still early, daughter. Are you feeling all right, Laurel dear?"

"Yes, of course."

"You've taken to this afternoon nap all of a sudden. I don't recall you sleeping much in the daytime."

"It's a bad habit I got into while I was in Little Rock with Mac. I didn't have much to do...sort of like it's been here since we've been snowed in. Having to stay in all the time can get boring."

"I suppose it can–even when you're home. Good news, though. The temperature is up, and the ice is melting. I rode out on Tartan to let him stretch his legs. I think we can get the wagon over the road to Shiloh church tomorrow if you want to go."

"That'd be wonderful. I would love to get out and see Uncle Matthew and my family."

"May not be a lot of people out yet, but I'll bet your uncle holds service tomorrow."

"And do you think we can go into Greensboro next week to see if we have any mail? Surely by now, we'll hear from Mac."

A few days later, Laurel finally received two long-awaited letters from Mac. The same day she also received a letter from Elizabeth Wilson in Hawthorn Chapel. Laurel was so excited she could barely play hostess to her Uncle Matthew who'd brought the mail from Greensboro, but she did try.

She slipped the three letters in her apron pocket and asked her uncle in for hot coffee.

"No, Laurel Grace. I've got to ride out to the Taylor homestead. They didn't get to church on Sunday, and when I was in Greensboro this morning, John McCollough told me they'd sent for Dr. Gibson."

"Someone must be pretty sick to send for the doctor."

"No one seems to know what ails them, so I'll go over there to check on them. Y'all doing okay here, niece?"

"All's well. Mac's pa has been staying here since the snow. It's been nice having him here. I miss Mac, though. He's been gone six weeks already and who knows how much longer the legislature will meet. I'll be happy when the legislature adjourns, and Mac comes home."

"I know you miss him. Maybe you won't campaign so hard the next time. How are things going with Andy?"

"He's been good. At first, he didn't want to work on his lessons, but Pa helped me with that, too. Since he's learned he can do his lessons, Andy's taken to the schooling really well. He misses his papa, though. Mac made it a point to spend time with him every day. They'd read together or play checkers. Andy misses that attention, but he won't play with me or Cathy. He says it's a man's game."

"He took to Mac real fast."

"And Mac to him. There is no denying the link between them."

"Well, niece. I've got to be on my way. I just wanted to bring the mail. Your aunt Ellie told me you've been frettin' about Mac. Maybe those letters will help."

"Thank you for bringing them. We'll see you on Sunday." Laurel hurried to her chair and pulled the letters from her pocket. She ripped open the first one.

*My dearest wife,*

*I won't let an opportunity pass to send you my love and prayers that you are well. I'll make sure these letters get posted...I'll hand them to the postman myself.*

*This is my second night away from you. Already I miss my place next to you in our four-poster, but at least tonight, I have a bed and shelter in a little community called Elizabeth, a little community near the confluence of the Black and White Rivers. The local circuit rider lives here, and he and his wife offered me a roof, a bed, and a hot meal. Riding has been easier this way than crossing the sunken lands. It's been cold, but the weather has not been a problem, yet. The roads seem better cleared and better cared for than many we traveled when we came from Washington County in '57. I am making good time, and if the weather holds, I think I'll be in the capital by Friday afternoon. Although riding long hours is hard, I believe riding across country is the fastest and most direct route between Shiloh and Little Rock.*

*I hope the kids are keeping you company and that the workload is not too much. I should have asked my pa to come over and stay with y'all. I am forever thinking of your welfare when I can't do much about it. Kiss them for me and tell them I'm missing them all.*

*Wife, pray for this legislative session to go smoothly and quickly. I want to be home with my family more than I want to serve in the government. Who'd ever have thought I'd say that? You have bewitched me, Laurel.*

*For now, I am your Loving Husband,*

*Patrick*

Laurel skimmed the letter a second time. Whispering a silent prayer, she thanked God that Mac was safe. She wondered in what county the settlement of Elizabeth was. She'd never heard anyone speak of it. At least, Mac had found some good people there to help him on his way, and his travel conditions, at least at the start of his trip, were fair. *God be praised.*

Laurel opened the second letter from Elizabeth. Her friend had written in small script on both sides of a single piece of paper.

*Dear Laurel,*

*Thank the Lord! We've had some good news. Last week, Rachel's Pa got a letter from some Army colonel. The colonel told him that Gracie was one of the little ones rescued from the Mormons. He said she had been placed with a young Mormon couple, and she was well and was cared for by them. He didn't tell us when they'd bring those children home, but he did tell us they'd stay in touch. We are gonna get her back, I just know it.*

*The winter here has been very harsh. Since mid-November, we had snow on top of snow and two ice storms in the mountains. It's been as cold as any winter I can remember. Your pa's friend, John Latham, lost four head of cattle that froze to death back in late December. We're praying for an early spring.*

*The cold and wet has brought us a lot of sickness, too. Near every family has had someone down with the croup and more have influenza. Thankfully, it ain't spreading much. Seems we haven't been visiting or attending church much this winter 'because it's been so bad.*

*Brother Caldwell and Jane Ann send their love and told me they are praying for you. He also asked me to tell you the stone marker for your Pa is up and standing next to your Ma's. He had the stone mason to cut 'Mark Campbell, Husband of Leah and Father of Daniel, Samuel, and Laurel' and his dates into the stone. I'm going out to look at it as soon as the weather allows.*

*Well, I'm out of paper so I'll stop. I'm sending my love and wish the best to you and your family. Write soon.*

*Your friend,*

*Elizabeth*

"Well, Laurel, did you get some good news from your letters?"

"Yes and no, Pa. Are you about ready for some lunch?"

"When you get it ready, no hurry. How far had Mac gotten when he sent the letters?

"I've only read the first one, but he told me he was two days out and making good progress. He wrote he thought he'd reach Little Rock by mid-afternoon the first Friday after he left. That would be a very fast trip if he did get there by then. But goodness, how late these letters are. Both of them are more than a month old. Mac could be headed home from the legislature by now."

She replaced the letters in her pocket and began to prepare lunch. Routine claimed the rest of the afternoon. Cathy wanted Laurel to show her how to make a double purl stitch so she could add a pattern in the scarf she was knitting. Andy asked her to listen to him read from the book he'd gotten for Christmas. He seemed so proud he'd mastered the second story. Laurel could hardly ask him to wait until she read a letter from Mac. Her father-in-law decided to spend his time with the family, and he occupied Mac's armchair for most of the afternoon. Not knowing what the letter contained, she felt it would be rude to read it and not share its contents with the others who loved Mac, too.

Laurel decided to work off the nervous energy by cleaning the cabin. She swept the walnut plank floors. She dusted the furniture and cleaned the globes to all the lamps in the room. She decided she'd wash the inside of the windows, but as she dipped water into the small dishpan, all her energy drained from her body. She held onto the dry sink to keep herself from falling.

"Pa, I'm feeling a little light headed. Will you help me to my chair?" Thomas hurried to her side before she'd even finished her request. He took her by the waist and led her to the chair beside the fire.

"Laurel, I'm concerned about you. One second, you are working like a demon's chasing you and then you're pale and haven't the strength to hold yourself up. I believe we need to make a visit to see Dr. Gibson tomorrow."

"That's not necessary. I'm all right really. I'm just a little tired. I'll be up and back to myself after I rest a few minutes."

"Mama, do you want a blanket?"

"No, Cathy. Please just bring me that blue wool shawl on the peg. I'll cover myself with that."

Andy stood nearby with a furrow across his brow and eyes wide with alarm. "Granddad, Ma ain't bad sick, is she?"

"No, boy. I think she's just tired. Maybe a nap will help her feel like herself again. Laurel, I've got to take better care of you. I promised Mac I'd see to your welfare while he's gone. You nap a while, and we'll decide later whether we go to Greensboro tomorrow or not."

"Yes, Pa. I'd like to doze off for a few minutes." Laurel's few minute nap turned into more than two hours. Cathy began to prepare the evening meal while Thomas and Roy went out to tend the livestock.

"Goodness, Cathy. You shouldn't have let me sleep so long. I've got to get supper ready."

"Just sit and rest, Mama. I've got potatoes baking in the hearth oven, and a big pot of rabbit and gravy simmering on the spit. We'll have plenty to eat because Roy found two big swampers down by the creek. Lots of good meat on those big old rabbits. Can't you smell that fine gravy bubbling in the pot?"

Laurel did smell the rich gravy. Her first reaction was hunger. How fine that rabbit and gravy would taste at supper, but then within a few seconds the thought of her favorite meal turned to nausea. Laurel rushed to the dry sink and gagged two or three times in reaction to the smell.

"Mama, I'm gonna go get Granddad. Just sit here at the table. I'll be right back."

"No, Cathy. Wait. I'm feeling all right now."

"No. You are pale as a ghost." Cathy ran to the back porch and called out to Thomas MacLayne and her two brothers to come at once.

"Laurel, you aren't well. I thought as much. I'll go get Dr. Gibson now."

"No, Pa...I'm pretty sure he can't fix anything just yet. Babies take a while before they are ready to see a doctor. I'm pretty sure now that we'll have a new family member in the fall."

"Praise be, Laurel. I can't wait for Patrick to know."

"No news in a letter, promise. Surely Patrick will be home before spring. That legislature can't have too many more things to do."

"I will promise not to write, but this news will be hard to keep."

"Well, let's keep it. No word to anyone. I want to tell Mac myself."

"Can't I even tell Brother Matthew, Mama?"

"No, Andy. We will let it be our family secret until your papa gets home. Promise."

"Yes, ma'am. I'll try real hard to not let it slip out."

Laurel's hopes and suspicion had been confirmed. The Lord had given her another child. Her emotions ran high and were erratic all at the same time. Mixed together, she felt joy, relief, fear, and longing. She wanted Patrick so much at that moment. The longing to have him wrap her in his arms was more than a feeling. She ached to be held.

Cathy and Andy both hugged her. "Mama, I'm so glad we're having another baby."

"Me too, Cathy. Will you excuse me?" She walked to her bedroom and closed the door. She pulled her shawl closer about her neck and shoulders as the fire had died out during the day. She could wait no longer to read the letter. She sat in her rocking chair and took Mac's second letter from her pocket.

*My dearest wife,*

*How did I think I could survive this long separation from you? I've only been away from you four days and every inch of me craves your presence. This morning as I rode across into White County, I tried to sing 'Annie Laurel' thinking it would bring me comfort, and instead I had to wipe tears from my eyes.*

*All I've thought about on this long hard day's ride are memories of us in our tall four-poster, your curls tousled around your precious face, and the feel of your warm tender kisses. Cursed duty! I want nothing except to be home with you.*

*Now that I've told you how miserable I am without you, some eighty-five miles from home, I'll try to tell you something about this trip I am making across the state. Tonight, I am in a little town called Searcy. Remember that night we stayed near the campground in Searcy County on our trip from Washington County? We met that wonderful old couple of sweethearts who had loved each other more than fifty years. They too began in a marriage of convenience. The town name brought all those memories back to me. All those hopes for a family, yet ridiculous fears that wouldn't let me love you then. What a fool I was...Sorry, I let my yearning for you pull me off task again.*

*This little settlement has a nice store and several cabins and even a clapboard building or two. I didn't notice a church here, but I did find a bed for the night in a widow's boarding house. She sets a good table, even had a berry pie for dessert. She can't make a decent cup of coffee though. There is no need for you to be jealous, wife. Mrs. Cox has to be at least eighty years old! Sweet, she is, but not a match for the spitfire of a mate I have in Shiloh.*

*Dearest Lord, how I love you, Laurel. I pray every day that the work of the legislature will be accomplished within a few days so I can return to you. Please tell Pa and the kids I send my regards and know, darlin', that my thoughts are with you every second of my waking day. I will write as soon as I reach Little Rock. God keep you until I can hold you again.*

*Your husband,*

*Patrick*

Laurel pressed the letter to her cheek where a tear dampened the paper. She placed the letter back into her pocket and went to the little washroom to splash cool water on her face to wash away the traces of her happy tears. Mac's declaration of love had renewed her energy, and she was ready to return to her family. She shared parts of Mac's letters with the family. Having his letters in her pocket brought calm and peace. The ache was gone for now.

## CHAPTER TWENTY-FIVE

*Therefore, I say unto thee, what things soever you desireth, when ye pray, believe that ye receiveth them and ye shall have them.*
*Mark 11:24*

January passed into February, and Mac was true to his word. He wrote letters several times a week, always filled with news of his daily work, followed by words of love and longing to be home. He told of the severe flooding along the major rivers: the Mississippi, the Arkansas and both the White and Black Rivers. Laurel could sense his anger and frustration when he told her of the failed levee systems across the state. Most of the work had been done with the federal money. Much was contracted out to supporters of the "Family," He learned so much about how state government worked since he'd begun his service. Too often the work was slipshod and inadequate to keep the massive flood waters at bay. All the rivers were above flood stage that year because of the heavy winter snowfalls. Nearly all the levees were obliterated by the winter floods. The Apportionment Committee found that some of the contracted levees had not been built at all. He told her of massive damage that occurred in Napoleon, and places they visited only a couple of months earlier were at the bottom of the Mississippi River. Thousands of dollars badly needed to improve the state's waterways had been wasted. Mac did not write of the threats that he received whenever he "voted the wrong way."

Day by day, Mac toiled on in his role as the legislator from Greene County, fighting for bills his county needed. He never shirked from a debate when called for, nor did he involve himself when he felt the topic outside his realm of interest. Few days passed that he was able to go back to the Stones' house without a headache from the strain and tension of work in the state house. Too many nights he went to bed without supper, too tired to eat. He prayed for the Twelfth Legislative Session to come to the end of its agenda. Two major bills stood between him and home. The bills would bring major conflict on both sides of the General Assembly. Both dealt with money. Mac stood on the "wrong side" of both issues.

The death of Speaker Oates in the middle of January lengthened the session by more than two weeks. The appointment of a temporary speaker and getting used to his ways of doing business added to the already difficult atmosphere. When the house took up the agenda again, the legislators' tempers were short. Courtesy was lost to efficiency in getting the work finished. Mac was not the only one who wanted to go home.

When the bill allowing widows to inherit their late husbands' property was read, a moan of dissension echoed that could be heard across the Arkansas River. Again, Mac was in the middle of the debate. This was one bill he'd pledged to support...a pledge he made to more than one Greene County widow. The debate raged for two days. The opposition used familiar arguments. They spoke of women's delicacy and their lack of financial understanding to discourage passage of the bill. Mac and the other members who supported the law put up a strong argument. They recounted stories of the impoverishment of widows who lost their homes and farms. All knew of numbers of plantation wives who were the business minds in their families. Nothing changed the minds of these men. The vote was not even close. Mac knew he had little hope of winning, but he had kept his word. He tried to change the law to be fairer to wives and families.

After the vote, another of the delta legislators stopped Mac on the steps of the Capital. "MacLayne, you better be glad that bill failed. You've been a thorn in my hide since the beginning of this session. Don't you get it? Things are like they are for a reason. Do you have any idea of what would happen in the delta if women started owning property?"

"I guess we'd have to start treating them like people instead of chattel. A fine woman in my county asked me to see if I could help change this law. She makes dresses for a living now. For twenty years, she and her husband homesteaded and made a fine living, but he died. His son by his first marriage inherited their land. He turned her out and sold the farm. He said, "She's not my mother so what obligation do I have to take care of her? He hadn't lived on the homestead in fifteen years. He didn't take care of his father his last four years when he was nearly bedfast. Now Mrs. Marcum has three children to raise on a dressmaker's pay. I'd say she's not the only one who suffers from this archaic law."

Mac walked away.

The last day of the week, the last and most dread issue came to the floor for debate. The collapse of the State Land Banks and Arkansas laws that forbade the state to build banks. This had crippled the economy. The financial committees faced the dilemma of helping large plantation owners when they fell into debt. However, small businesses and yeoman farmers were angered by the "Acts of Relief". The legislature could forgive massive debts if a representative made a good case. The money, of course, came from taxes.

Mac, by his role in the Apportionment Committee, once again found himself in the fight. He believed the Acts of Relief should be discontinued. He also knew the opposition would bring on their biggest fight to date. The clerk read the bill.

"Be it enacted, all Acts of Relief will be discontinued. Debts will no longer be forgiven by acts of the state legislature. Parties may request a loan to be used in repayment of debt. Loans will be repaid with interest to the state treasury."

At first, there was silence. Proponents then applauded briefly. Chaos erupted from the opposition. Yelling, scuffling, swearing, and other forms of mayhem made order impossible. One congressman hurled his inkpot toward the speaker. It shattered on the hearth of the blazing fireplace. The speaker adjourned the meeting until the next morning.

Mac barely made it out the door before he was stopped.

"MacLayne, you gotta stop this bill. Your committee drafted that outrage. What have you got against the planters of this state?"

"Griggs, I am not the chairman of that committee, but I won't deny I support the bill as it is written."

"I warned you, MacLayne. If that bill gets to the Senate and is passed, you'll rue the day you came to Little Rock."

"I am getting' pretty tired of your threats every day. I only have one vote. Go vote against me."

"You know you have more influence than one vote. You need to go get your friends on that committee to change that bill before it comes up for a vote."

"I am finished with my work. Tomorrow I am going to come to the house and vote for this bill. Then I am going home. I've done what I came here to do. Now let me be." Mac again began to walk to the Stone's house. He wanted to rest and then he planned to pack. He could almost feel Laurel in his arms.

Perhaps it was his brief daydream that allowed the other men to catch him off guard. One caught him from behind, and a second hit him squarely in the face. Mac fell to the ground and cut his brow on the cobblestone in the street. Blood ran into his eyes and down the side of his face.

"Get up, man. We warned you." Another man jerked Mac to his feet and hit him again. Mac shook his head to clear his senses. He pulled free and landed a fist in the stomach of the man nearest him.

Mac didn't recognize these men as members of the legislature.

He tripped a second man and kicked him in the ribs when he fell at his feet.

"Who are you? Who sent you after me?"

No answer came. The men again flailed away, at times landing blows and at other times missing entirely. The leader of the attackers spoke, "You got one chance to make this right. Get this bill off the floor. Ain't nothing you care about, we can't get to. You know what I'm saying?"

The men laid into Mac at the same time, but they didn't know their most recent threat was the wrong approach. Mac's demeanor changed. He jumped up and fought as a man deranged. He bloodied the face of the first man to the point he couldn't see. He wrenched the arm of the second man behind his back until he heard a bone crack. The attacker screamed, and his wails sent his companions running from the scene.

Mac's beating was more than obvious when he appeared for the vote the next day. His left eye was black and his lip swollen from several blows. He didn't wear his usual suit coat, which suffered a fatal thrashing. The cut above his eye had been stitched up by a local doctor. Strangely though, one young man with a splint and a sling sat behind a planter from the southeast part of the state.

After about an hour of debate, the bill came to the floor for a vote. The vote sending the bill to the senate passed by two votes. The supporters cheered—loud and strong. There was no assurance the bill would get passed the state Senate, but it was the first time it had reached this point. There was real hope this would put all the farmers in the state on the same playing field for the first time.

Mac bowed his head in a brief prayer. Now he wanted to leave Little Rock and go back to Greene County. The last item of business came as somewhat of a surprise. The joint committee on Enrollment put forth the bill to establish Craighead County. Like most of these bills, it passed in one fast vote.

The clerk announced the house had finished its business. The Speaker of the House pounded his gavel. "The twelfth session of the General Assembly of Arkansas is adjourned."

Representative Griggs caught Mac as he was leaving the steps. "Don't think you've won, MacLayne. You've made a big mistake. Lots of planters and big businessmen ain't gonna like what you did."

"Griggs, I wondered who was behind the opposition to the Apportionment Committee's report. Funny! I thought you were a more reasonable...and honest man. Just know, sir, I don't like threats any better today than I did yesterday. If you're anyway bright, you'll warn your friends to steer clear of my family. Anyway, I won't be here to be a snag in your plans anymore. I don't live in Greene County anymore."

~

ON THE SECOND Saturday in February, Thomas returned from Greensboro with mail. That day, he had gotten a letter for Laurel, but also one for himself as well. This one brought him no pleasure. His son had often written him a weekly report of his activities. With each letter came a plea to take care of his family. This letter was stark. Only a dire plea to care for his family. Thomas knew things in the capitol were not going well for Patrick.

"Daughter, I want you to know that I appreciate you more than I can tell you. You are a true blessing to this family."

"Thank you, Pa, but goodness. What brought all this on?"

"You did. I just got another letter from my son. Since he's been in Little Rock, he has written me every week. Do you know how often his mother and I longed for any word that he was alive and all right? Anne and I had to put his care in God's hands for seven years because we didn't know where he was or how he was."

"He told me some about those years, not much.

"I believe the only two good things that came out of those times. Patrick developed a hunger that brought him to the Lord. And thank the Lord, we got Andy."

"Patrick did tell me something about his need to go home and about the duel with Louis."

"Louis Rawlings was Patrick's best friend after Sean died in the war. When he killed Louis that day, I thought I'd lost my son, but he came to Arkansas and started a new life."

"Mac likes to quote Romans 8:28. He believes that the Lord used all things that happened to bring him back home."

"I believe it too, Laurel. You were the catalyst that brought Patrick, the man he was meant to be, back to us. God bless you, daughter. He loves you. You are his purpose and ambition. All he does, he does to make life good for you and make you proud of him. I'm forever indebted to you. You have brought my son back to me." Thomas kissed Laurel's cheek. "Thank you from his mother and me."

Laurel was overcome with the praise and affection from her father-in-law. Life would be so perfect if Mac were not so far away.

But the time continued to drag by. February was typical for Arkansas...very cold and very wet. Laurel and her family did what all homesteaders did that time of year, waited and planned for spring. Thomas was relieved when the weather warmed enough that he could move Mac's herd to another pasture. They had been cooped up near the barn and shed a long time since the winter snow storms, and forage was all but gone.

Early March, the temperatures took on the feeling of springtime. and Laurel began to plan her garden for the year. She asked Roy and John, who'd come back to work after the roads cleared, to begin the plowing and cleaning of her garden plot. She wanted to be busy to help the time pass. On March 3, Laurel received one last letter from Mac, dated Thursday, February 21, 1859. He had written one short paragraph.

*Laurel,*

*I am headed home today. The legislature adjourned at 1:00 this afternoon. I have so much to tell you about what happened here, but my want to have you in my arms is greater than my need to write you a long letter. I am leaving Little Rock within the hour. I am headed back to Shiloh.*

*God grant me speed,*

*Mac*

Laurel was beyond happy! The legislative session had been much longer than either she or Mac had expected. The thirty-one days between January 17 and February 21 had been an eternity for them both. How long had he been riding? Quickly she counted the days and realized Mac had been riding more than a week already. He should be home any day!

She bustled around the cabin, making sure everything would be perfect when Mac came through the front door. She wanted him to find his home exactly as it should be. She went to the root cellar to find fruit and vegetables to make the best homecoming meal possible. She'd make

Mac a fresh pone so he could have cornbread and buttermilk the first night home. She went to the bedroom and opened the bottom drawer of her mother's bureau. She found the tiny booties she'd crocheted and placed them in her pocket. She would have Mac's welcome home gift ready the minute he arrived.

Yet, night fell and Mac was not home. Though not too worried, Laurel went to bed disappointed. Perhaps she had expected Mac's trip north to be as fast as the trip to Little Rock in January. She hadn't accounted for flood-swollen waterways or washed-away levees. The trip Mac had made in six days to Little Rock could take much longer if he could not cross the rivers between Pulaski County and Greene County. When she lay down for the night, she slipped the booties under Mac's pillow for safekeeping. Her fatigue would not allow her to stay awake any longer. Besides, it was senseless as Mac could be days away from home.

Around midnight, Mac opened the door to the second pen. He'd removed his boots on the porch so as not to awaken his family. He didn't want a crowd. He only wanted Laurel in his arms. In the glow of the dying embers, he saw her asleep in the tall bed. Her tawny curls were in wild array, as he'd pictured them so often. He latched the door and walked quickly to her side. He moved a curl from her eyes and kissed her forehead.

"Laurel, I'm home." She awoke without any hint of startle. She'd been dreaming the very scene she awoke to. Mac pulled her into his arms and crushed her to him. "I'm not leaving you behind ever again."

"Thank God, you're home." Her prayers were cut short by his kisses. Their need for each other was greater than their need to talk. When their need was sated, Mac and Laurel fell into the best sleep either had since the last night they'd shared the tall bed. When they awoke the next morning, Mac sat up with his back to the tall carved headboard. He pulled Laurel back into his arms and draped the wedding ring quilt over their bare shoulders. The fire had burned out during the night.

"I should have gotten up and built a fire, but I couldn't stand being that far from you. It's at least four feet to that fireplace, and four feet is too great a distance for me to put between us."

"I am so glad you are here. I slept well for the first time in two months. But Mac, we need to get up and dressed. The kids and your pa are in the loft."

"Not yet. I want you here next to me for a while longer. Tell me how you've been since I've been away."

"Lonely. Family is wonderful, and they did help me fill my days, but Patrick, those forty nights were years too long. Thank God, you are back where you belong."

"Amen to that! I'm planning to stay here permanently."

"You say that now. When do we have to start campaigning again for the thirteenth legislative session?"

"Never again, wife. I voted myself right out of my seat in the State house."

"You did what? How did that happen?"

"Pretty easily actually. One of the many arguments this term was that counties are too large. The last week of the session two men, a senator named Jones and the representative from Poinsett County named Craighead, put a bill into play. They wanted to reduce the area of Greene and Poinsett Counties into more manageable sizes. When I considered all the pros and cons, I had to vote for the bill. Matthew warned me it could happen. He said I might have to choose between what was good for the people and what was good for me. Sure enough, it happened. Dear wife, we no longer live in Greene County. Our homestead, Greensboro, and the Shiloh community are now a part of Craighead County. I can't hold a seat for a county I don't live in. Thanks to Senate Bill 180, I am a homesteader again. Thank the Lord for his grace and mercy in bringing me home."

"Craighead County? Oh well, I don't care where we live as long as we're together. I'm more than happy to be the wife of farmer MacLayne. You never had to be a legislator to make me proud of you."

"Do you know how much you mean to me? I learned it really fast. I hadn't gotten out of the county before I wanted to rein Midnight around and come home."

"Your letters kept me going when I felt so alone. But you could have written one or two I might have shared with our family."

"Those letters were meant for you. I wrote Pa letters he could share with all of you."

"Well, they made the time bearable. I also kept myself occupied with teaching, reading, and crocheting. I managed to keep busy most of the time."

"Did you make me another scarf? The blue one you made surely helped on those cold long rides."

"No, not a scarf.... If you look under your pillow...." Mac quickly pushed back the pillow.

Mac looked at the tiny crocheted booties and then back into the eyes of his waiting wife. He hesitated before he spoke. "Laurel, are we having another child?"

"Yes, darlin'. Thank God, Patrick. We'll have our baby in the fall, late September or early October."

"Dear gracious Father in Heaven! Since I left the Rock, I've pushed Midnight and myself to get home. I was driven to get here, and I didn't know why. Now I know. My world is here. This home we've built together is the best dream I ever had. I've learned I need nothing beyond Shiloh." Mac moved into an urgent, yet tender embrace. "A call to be a good parent is as important as being a lawmaker, don't ya think?"

Laurel smiled. The Lord answered her prayer. She rubbed her hand against Mac's bearded cheek. "Or perhaps your true call is to make your wife the most content woman in the state."

"I'll give it a try for fifty years or so." A kiss sealed his promise. "Life is good, Laurel."

## OTHER TITLES BY PATRICIA CLARK BLAKE

At twenty-eight, Laurel Campbell has accepted her fate as the spinster of Hawthorn. She long ago gave up her dreams of love and a happy life, leaving her broken and inadequate—at least in her own mind.

The state of Arkansas is seven years younger than Laurel and a thriving destination for pioneers and homesteaders. State law forbids women from owning property—a fact Laurel's dying father understands all too well. To protect his daughter, Mark Campbell arranges a marriage of convenience to Patrick "Mac" MacLayne.

The situation doesn't sit well with Laurel, who's no man's chattel—not even a handsome and godly man like Mac. For Mac's part, a past heartbreak has left him leery of "falling in love" even with his new wife.

Together, the two begin the long and dangerous trek to Shiloh, Mac's distant homestead. The only thing Mac and Laurel have in common is faith, but is faith enough to build a new life together as husband and wife? Will love play no part in their relationship?

The first story in the Shiloh Saga, *In Search of Shiloh* celebrates the Arkansas pioneers' strength, loyalty, and devotion to both God and each other.

The Dream of Shiloh: An Arkansas Love Story is the second volume of The Shiloh Saga. The story opens as Mac and Laurel MacLayne begin to break virgin soil to build a homestead together. They have survived a perilous journey across northern Arkansas in the first volume of this saga, In Search of Shiloh. The MacLaynes look back and can hardly believe they survived the trip. The weather was cold and wet. Roads, where they even existed, were obliterated by spring rains more days than not. Shelter was often a make-shift tent under the bed of the small wagon that carried Laurel's family keepsakes. Those obstacles were small compared with the misunderstandings, arguments, and trampled feelings they caused each other, not in spite, but simply because they were strangers. Mac and Laurel had married after knowing each other only four days…a marriage of convenience to satisfy her dying father. They had pledged their lives together based on a common faith, a belief in a loving Father God, and a dream of Shiloh.

Shiloh is a dream so distant that the MacLaynes can hardly believe it's within reach. Mac made promises to Laurel's father that he has yet to keep. The tangible one is not impossible. He could erect a cabin and would with the help of his Shiloh church family, but that last promise to help Laurel understand she is a worthy person, valuable and esteemed by others, and more than that, by herself, seems more difficult every day. The fact that he won't not allow himself to love her doesn't help matters. Laurel will be his treasured friend and helpmate all his life, but he will never fall into that devastating trap of giving his heart to any woman again.

Laurel's demons place obstacles between her and Mac. The shadows of the past hinted at in her nightmares blighted her life since she was fourteen. Mac took away her title of 'Spinster of Hawthorn' but not her sense of inadequacy. Laurel lives with the belief that she is plain and dull, fit to be a helpmate but little more and that Mac married her for that purpose. Only a growing faith, a connection with a community at Shiloh, and a sense of purpose in her role as the subscription school teacher begin to diminish Laurel's sense of inadequacy so she learns she may become worthy ... not loved or adored as other women, but cherished, by her husband.

As the story progresses, we see community celebrations common in frontier life. The Shiloh church celebrates frequent dinners on the grounds and Sunday afternoon singings. Ladies of the community welcome their new teacher with a quilting bee. Laurel gets the opportunity to witness a town debating contest when Mac participates with a local citizen and wins a contest by declaring that a "nagging wife is better than a smoking chimney because she plants her husband's feet on the path to Heaven" as he has to pray for patience. The MacLaynes help raise a barn and go to a camp meeting, all a part of mid-nineteenth century life in northeast Arkansas.

Then Mac is called home to Maryland by his father. Mac's mother is dying. Laurel remains behind to finish the school term and to take care of their homestead. Mac's past is in Maryland. Perhaps his life was back there with his family. Laurel will live with the fear that Mac may not want to return to their arranged marriage as she has stepped across the boundary they had set. She declared her love for him. An encounter with the woman from his past and witnessing the precious love between his parents teach Mac a lesson he'd not understood in his youth. The love he'd been running from was what he wanted most in the world. The adolescent feelings he'd experienced before he'd gone to Arkansas led him to make fatally bad choices, but those feelings were not love. What he wanted waited for him at Shiloh...didn't she?

Made in the USA
Middletown, DE
07 November 2022